CRITICAL ACCLA

'Racy legal thrillers lift t   at the b

'Murphy paints a trenchant picture of establishment cover-up, and cannily subverts the clichés of the legal genre in his all-too-topical narrative' – *Financial Times*

'Peter Murphy's novel is an excellent read from start to finish and highly recommended' – *Historical Novel Review*

'An intelligent amalgam of spy story and legal drama' – *Times*

'A gripping, enjoyable and informative read'
– *Promoting Crime Fiction*

'The ability of an author to create living characters is always dependent on his knowledge of what they would do and say in any given circumstances – a talent that Peter Murphy possesses in abundance' – *Crime Review UK*

'Murphy's clever legal thriller revels in the chicanery of the English law courts of the period' – *Independent*

'The forensic process is examined in a light touch, good-humoured style, which will evoke a constant stream of smiles, and chuckles from nonlawyers and lawyers alike' – **Lord Judge, former Lord Chief Justice of England and Wales**

'A gripping page-turner. A compelling and disturbing tale of English law courts, lawyers, and their clients, told with the authenticity that only an insider like Murphy can deliver. The best read I've come across in a long time' – **David Ambrose**

'If anyone's looking for the next big courtroom drama… look no further. Murphy is your man' – *ICLR*

A STATUE FOR JACOB

PETER MURPHY

Oldcastle Books

First published in 2021
Oldcastle Books Ltd,
Harpenden, UK

noexit.co.uk
@noexitpress

ISBN
978-0-85730-417-9 (print)
978-0-85730-418-6 (epub)

2 4 6 8 10 9 7 5 3 1

Typeset in 11 on 14pt Minion Pro
by Avocet Typeset, Bideford, Devon, EX392BP
Printed in Great Britain by CPI Group (UK) Ltd, Croydon, CR0 4YY

In honour of Thelma Weasenforth Lunaas and her attorney, Jo Beth Kloecker of the Texas Bar, who on behalf of the de Haven family took on the might of the United States Department of Justice in an attempt to secure the long-overdue recognition of Jacob de Haven.

This debt was not contracted as the price of bread or wine or arms. It was the price of liberty.

Alexander Hamilton

'Eso no,' respondió el ventero, 'que no seré yo tan loco que me haga caballero andante: que bien veo que ahora no se usa lo que se usaba en aquel tiempo, cuando se dice que andaban por el mundo estos famosos caballeros.'

'Certainly not,' the innkeeper replied. 'I myself shall never be mad enough to become a knight-errant: because I well understand that nowadays it's not the thing to do; it's not as it was in those days, when, so people say, those famous knights went about throughout the world.'

Miguel de Cervantes Saavedra, *Don Quijote*
Primera Parte, Capítulo XXXII, *Part One, Chapter XXXII*

1

Kiah Harmon

'KIAH,' ARYA ASKED ME once, 'didn't your mother ever tell you what your name means in our language?'

I'd been seeing Arya regularly since the Week from Hell. I guess you could call our meetings counselling sessions, though Arya would never have called what she did counselling, and I wouldn't have cared what you called it, as long as I could sit back in that enormous soft leather armchair in her living room, inhale the ever-present aroma of her Neroli incense, and let her soft, hypnotic voice wash over me until the pain began to recede a little.

I have memories of that voice from as far back as I have memories of anything in my life, because Arya was my parents' closest friend and we were in and out of each other's houses all the time from my earliest years, and I had the sense, even as a small child, that my parents thought of Arya as a source of wisdom and hung on her every word. I remember wondering, when I became old enough to formulate such questions, what Arya actually *did*, whether she ever claimed a specific profession or vocation. She was older than my parents, and lived alone, having been widowed much earlier in her life. But when I asked my parents about it, they never answered directly, almost as if they were afraid that defining her, putting her in a box, giving her a label such as mystic, healer, counsellor, soothsayer, or astrologer, might somehow diminish her. I accepted this, and never felt the need to ask her myself. If she ever made use of any chart or instrument of divination, it was done out of my sight. For me, Arya was the voice, and it was Arya I needed after the Week.

I'd begun to drop in to see her after school and at weekends, without my parents, from the age of eleven or twelve. I don't remember whether she suggested it, or whether it was my idea, or whether it just happened; but it continued as and when we both had the time, throughout my schooldays, and later when I did my undergraduate degree at Georgetown University, and then went on to the law school. Neither can I remember in detail everything we talked about together. But I do remember that she showed endless patience in listening without interruption to whatever I wanted to say; I remember that never once did she judge me; and I remember that she always seemed to have some word, some idea, for me that brought order to some area of my life that had become chaotic and was about to spiral out of control. I can't say exactly, in fact I'm not sure I can even estimate how much influence she has had on my life, but she has been a constant wise presence, and I don't think there is any part of the woman I am that doesn't owe something to her.

Arya was the first person I told about my ambition to become a lawyer. My family, immigrants to the United States from India, had been doctors as far back as anyone could remember, until I defied the tradition. They had settled in Arlington, Virginia, and adopted the American surname 'Harmon' in place of their Indian surname of 'Hariya', believing that this would ease their integration into American society. That was two generations before me, and by the time I made my appearance as my parents' only child, there was nothing, except our obvious Indian physical attributes and a few small images of the Hindu deities in our house, to mark us out as in any way different from any other American family. My decidedly non-religious, non-traditional lifestyle didn't bother my parents. My departure from the doctor tradition, on the other hand, bothered them a lot. My undergraduate grades would have been good enough to get me into several leading medical schools. But Arya's comforting and encouraging words, both to me and to my parents, poured oil on the troubled waters. She also supported me after I had graduated from law school and been admitted to the Virginia Bar, when I opted for the freedom of my own office in Arlington, rather than a life of indentured servitude with one of the large national law firms that offered to take me on as an associate.

I'd been in practice for about five years when the Week from Hell hit me. I'd built up a respectable client list in the DC and Virginia Indian communities, and I was just beginning to attract some significant commercial litigation from the wider community. I was thinking about expansion. Then the Week struck.

On the Tuesday, my parents died together in their car on the Custis Memorial Parkway, when the driver of the speeding truck ahead of them misjudged a bend at the junction with Lee Highway at East Falls Church. The truck turned over and burst into flames, giving my father no time to react. On the Thursday, Jordan, my live-in boyfriend of three years, told me that he was leaving me to move in with his secretary, who, in contrast to me, was not the kind of selfish bitch who insisted on putting her career ambitions ahead of settling down to start a family with him. He had chosen that day to break this news to me, he explained, because with my parents dying it was going to be a time of change for me in any case, and so there was no point in delaying matters. Might as well get it all over with at once.

I closed the office for three months while, with Arya's help, I gradually crawled, inch by inch, out of the seemingly endless dark tunnel I had come to inhabit in my mind; until I clawed and scratched and dug my way through deep layers of primeval mud back to the surface; until I began to see daylight and the trees and the moon again; until I remembered how to breathe freely.

It was at some point during this darkest period of my life that she asked me whether my mother had told me what my name meant in our language. She had, I'm sure, but it had become buried in the deepest recesses of my memory.

'It means "new beginning",' Arya reminded me. 'It's your time for a new beginning now.'

I remember shaking my head. When you live in the kind of tunnel I lived in then, you can't accept that there is any good news, much less a new beginning. Such a thing doesn't exist, and even if it did, there is no oxygen to sustain it. To believe it then was impossible. So I filed it away for possible future reference. But I knew that Arya attached no importance to whether you believed something she said right away. She never said anything unless she knew it to be true, and if it was true, it would manifest itself at the right time, and then you would know it was true, and she would never say 'I told you so.'

2

'Do you handle debt collection cases?' she asked.

She hadn't made an appointment. She just walked off the street into my office. If she had come before the Week, when the office had a real bustle about it, she would have had to come back when I had time to see her. But this was about eight months after I reopened, and although I had some work, the bustle was missing. When I closed the office, I'd had to hand over my cases to other lawyers, and many clients had not returned.

She was two or three inches taller than me, a little over six feet, her hair and eyes dark brown. She was smartly, professionally dressed in a light grey suit with a white neck scarf, and grey heels, not too high, her make-up classy and restrained. She was pulling a large, flexible brown leather briefcase on wheels. Today, I would recognise her on sight as a van Eyck. It's the nose. There's no mistaking it. The van Eyck nose is high at the top, with a pronounced bony drop to the lower part, which descends slightly off-centre, to the right, as an observer sees it. I have seen that nose countless times since, on the faces of family members, and in their portraits, and in the photographs in their homes and on the faded pages of old newspapers. I would recognise it anywhere. But at the time, it barely registered. I was too busy taking in her clothes, and wishing guiltily that I had paid more attention to mine.

Before the Week I would have been dressed very much as she was, dressed as a lawyer in a dark suit and starched white shirt.

Every law professor and mentor I ever had insisted that success as a woman practicing law depended on it – and by the way, did I understand that the harshest critics of my sartorial standards would be, not men, but other women? But since the reopening, none of that seemed to matter to me. I did apply some basic make-up, and my clothes were well cared for, but they were clothes I felt comfortable in – coloured blouses and beige slacks, and there was still enough of India in me to prefer bare feet indoors, as we always had at home and at Arya's house. The shoes I'd abandoned near the door of my office were casual with almost no heel, not the court shoes I hated but had once felt obliged to wear. As I stood to walk around my desk to greet her, I realised that they were out of reach. If she noticed, she didn't seem to mind. She smiled.

'I am Samantha van Eyck, the actress,' she said. 'Please call me Sam. Everyone does.'

We shook hands.

'I'm Kiah Harmon.'

'Kiah. That's a pretty name.'

'Thank you. It's Indian.'

I waved her into a chair. She sat down and wheeled the briefcase into place beside her chair.

'So, you're an actress?' Arlene had shown Sam in without giving me any clue about what she wanted. Apparently, Arlene had decided not to give me the option of turning Sam away without even knowing why she needed help, or putting her off to another day, which had become my post-Week default setting when faced with a new client.

'I'm sorry. I'm sure I should recognise your name, but I haven't been out much lately. I can't remember when I last went to the theatre.'

It had been about eighteen months before, with Jordan.

She laughed. 'There's no reason at all why you should know my name. I'm a repertory actress. I've worked in the DC area, and out as far as Georgia and North Carolina, for the last five years since I graduated college, and that's about it so far. Multiple nominee for best actress in a role nobody notices very much. A steady diet of Arthur Miller and Tennessee Williams, and one movie.'

'Oh? Is it one I would have seen?'

'I hope not.'

We laughed together.

'In case you were wondering,' she said, 'I got your name from my cousin, Shelley Kinch. You handled a case for her, about two years ago, and she recommended you very highly.'

That was another effect the Week had. I had almost no memory for cases I had done before. Even my clients' names seemed unfamiliar. Mercifully, this one rang a distant bell.

'She worked for a private school in Bethesda teaching modern languages,' Sam added.

It came back to me. Thank god (even though I don't believe in him, or her, or them).

'Sure, I remember. They discriminated against her; they wanted to pay her far less than the men doing the same job. They settled out of court.'

'That's it. The money you got her helped her start her own school. She's doing great now, and she says you were so caring; you supported her emotionally as well as being her lawyer. You made a real difference for her.'

Did I? I was glad to hear that. Every boost to my confidence, however small, was welcome then, but the reference to emotional support surprised me. Had I been capable of that once? I wasn't sure it was still in my repertoire now.

'So, Sam, what can I do for you?'

Which was when she asked: 'Do you handle debt collection cases?'

I said I did.

3

'ASSUMING, OBVIOUSLY, THAT THE amount involved is large enough to be worth your while, and mine,' I added immediately.

As a young lawyer with your own office, you soon discover that there are any number of aggrieved people out there whose landlords have screwed them out of $300, by refusing to return part of their deposit or failing to pay for some repair to the common part of the building, and who think that retaining a lawyer and resorting to litigation would be an effective method of seeking redress. You get used to giving them more practical suggestions.

'There won't be any problem about that,' Sam assured me.

'OK. How much are we talking about?'

She reached down into the briefcase and took out a yellow pad, which, I could see, had some scribbled calculations on the top page. She took a moment or two to stare at it.

'Before I go into that,' she said, 'in fairness I think I should warn you that it's not your average collection case. It's going to take a lot of time, and a lot of work. And as far as your fees are concerned…'

'I assume it will be a contingency fee,' I said. 'That means I take a percentage if and when we recover the debt. If we don't recover, you don't owe me anything. I have a standard form of agreement. All lawyers do. I'll take you through it and explain how it works before I ask you to sign up. That's fine with me, as long as I know how much we're looking at.'

She nodded, and looked down at the yellow pad again.

'It's difficult to say precisely, and even if I could, the information would be out of date five minutes from now, not to mention hopelessly out of date some time in the future when we actually recover the debt. So let me put it like this: taking an apparently random period of 250 years since the debt accrued – which isn't really random, as I will explain – the debt would be a little more than 672 billion dollars.'

She looked up from the yellow pad.

'When I say "a little more than",' she added, 'I mean 672 billion plus several hundred thousand.'

Another thing you soon discover as a young lawyer with your own office is that there are a significant number of crazy people out there who have seriously deranged ideas about how others have wronged them; about the vast sums of money they think they are entitled to by way of damages; and about the availability of punitive measures – such as incarceration or serious violence – they should be allowed to visit on the perpetrators. But you can usually see them coming a mile away, and they almost never get as far as my office. Arlene gets rid of them without any help from me. When she arrived, Sam didn't strike me as playing in that league at all, and she must have made the same impression on Arlene. I found myself surprised, and a little disturbed, that she had got past both of us without raising any red flags. But seemingly, we had missed a live one, and I now had to figure out what to do about it. I settled on calling Arlene and asking her to have building security on standby, just in case. We had a code for such situations: I would ask her for the file in the Dangerfield case. But before I could make the call, Sam laughed again.

'Yes, I *do* know that's a lot of money,' she said. 'May I explain?'

I looked at her again. She didn't *look* crazy, and she wasn't acting crazy. I couldn't see an axe or a .357 Magnum sticking out of her briefcase. Apart from her saying that she wanted to recover a debt of a little more than $672 billion, there was no overt sign of craziness at all. Perhaps I could let it run a bit longer. I took my hand off the receiver, but kept it close.

'I think that would be a good idea, Sam,' I said. 'Why don't you start by telling me who you want to sue?'

'The United States government,' she replied.

'The government?' I asked. 'You want to sue the government for 672 billion dollars?'

'Yes. Is that a problem? You are allowed to sue the government, aren't you?'

'Yes, but –'

'We're not out to collect every last dime – even if that would be possible, which I'm sure it's not. It's not just about the money. We can settle for less.'

4

SHE DIDN'T *SOUND* CRAZY. I decided provisionally to treat her as a serious client who had come for help with a case one might reasonably pursue. Whether that would be the final verdict was another matter, but I would give her the benefit of the doubt for now. I smiled.

'Well, sure. Perhaps they would offer us a small state to go away. How about Rhode Island?'

She laughed. 'Sure, why not?'

'All right, Sam. But let's get serious, shall we? Tell me why the government owes you 672 billion dollars.'

She nodded. 'Not me, Kiah, my family.'

'OK. Your family.'

'How's your history?' she asked. 'Do you remember the story of the War of Independence?'

'I took some history classes in college,' I replied. 'I guess I remember the basic outline, but –'

'Does the name Valley Forge, Pennsylvania, ring a bell?'

'Sure. Wasn't that where George Washington took the army during the winter, that cold winter when they almost froze to death?'

'You got it. It was the winter of 1777–1778. They'd just got their asses kicked by the Brits in two battles. They were almost out of food, clothing, weapons – all the basic supplies. They didn't have much money, and very few people thought they had much chance of winning, so they didn't exactly have a great credit rating. The Brits had the real money. They could buy whatever supplies they needed. And if that wasn't enough, as you say, it was a very cold winter. Washington's army was freezing to death, in addition to starving to death. But somehow, by the spring they had turned things around. When they left Valley Forge they were fully supplied. They started winning, and before long they had the Brits on the run.'

I remembered that much. 'OK.'

'Money and supplies had started to arrive, just in time, round about February. I'm sure it came from lots of different places. They were desperate, and they were taking help from anyone who would give it. The French kept promising to help, and they did eventually, but by that time the army was already back on its feet. The question is: who bailed them out during the winter? According to our family tradition, an ancestor of mine called Jacob van Eyck was one of their biggest benefactors. They say he contributed gold and supplies to the tune of 450,000 dollars.'

I raised my eyebrows. Suddenly I was catching just a faint glimmer of where this story was going.

'450,000 in today's money?'

'No, 450,000 dollars value at the time, in 1778.'

I sat back in my chair.

'But Sam, that was a fortune. If that's true, Jacob must have been –'

'As rich as Croesus, yes. He was. He was a merchant and a landowner, and if not *the* richest, he was one of the richest men in Pennsylvania. As a matter of fact, he owned the land around Valley Forge, on the west bank of the Schuylkill, right next to Washington's encampment.'

'But how did he make that kind of money?'

She smiled. 'Good question. There are lots of family stories about that. The polite version is that he made his money by importing wine and other goodies from Europe. But that's what they all said at the time, wasn't it, if they didn't want to talk about... well, you know...?'

'You're talking about the slave trade?'

'I have no evidence of anything like that. But it wouldn't surprise me. It was the easiest way to make that kind of serious money then, wasn't it? And Jacob had definitely made some serious money.'

'But he must have been something of an idealist as well,' I pointed out, 'to give so much.'

She smiled again. 'Yes. I'm sure he was. But independence wasn't just an ideal to men like Jacob. It had its commercial side. Don't forget the Boston Tea Party, Kiah. For all the talk of liberty, independence also had a lot to do with not paying taxes to the King.'

'True,' I agreed.

'There's another thing, too. Jacob and George Washington were close friends and they were both high-ranking Freemasons. I'm not sure how much that had to do with it. It wasn't a simple picture. Maybe none of that mattered very much. Jacob may have just figured that if Washington lost to the Brits he was screwed as well, so he might as well take his chances with Washington.'

She shrugged.

'Anyway, that's the family tradition. But his contribution wasn't a *gift*, Kiah. It was a *loan*. The Continental Congress had authorised loans to be raised for the war effort, so anyone making a loan expected to be repaid after the war.'

'And you're assuming that Jacob went through the proper channels?'

'I can't see him putting up so much money without intending to get back as much of it as he could. Can you? He was a businessman above all, and he must have known that lending so much could wipe him out – as indeed it did.'

I thought for a moment or two. 'I've never heard about these loans before. How did they work? How did you get your money back?'

'The Congress set up loan offices, which issued certificates to anyone who made a loan. The loans were repayable after the war with interest at six per cent compound per year.'

'Six per cent compound? But that's…'

'That was the deal. After the war, you would present your loan certificate to the loan office, and they would pay you in cash.'

I shook my head. Suddenly, $672 billion was beginning to make a bit more sense. Compound interest at six per cent over 250 years wasn't the kind of thing you could even estimate in your head, let alone calculate. An internet compound interest calculator would work it out in a second or two, and I must admit I felt my fingers twitching to reach for my keyboard. But Sam had been there before me, and I kept my curiosity in check. Even if she wasn't exactly right, it would obviously be a lot of money – a whole lot of money.

'And let me guess. The family tradition is that Jacob was never repaid?'

'Not one cent, principal or interest. The government probably didn't have the money – literally: they didn't have enough gold to repay that kind of debt. The country was pretty much bankrupt after the war; the currency was next to worthless, and they couldn't just go out and borrow. They paid people who had loaned smaller amounts, but with the amount Jacob was owed, it would probably have been impossible. Unfortunately for Jacob, it ruined him. He died in poverty.'

'I take it you don't have Jacob's loan certificate tucked away in your briefcase?' I asked. 'If you did, I'm guessing somebody would have done something about this before now.'

She hesitated.

'No one seems to know where the loan certificate is. I guess we will have to find it.'

'Assuming there ever was one,' I said, 'and assuming it is still in existence.'

'Actually,' she said, 'I don't think we're looking for just one certificate. There must have been any number of deliveries to the army over a period of time, to the quartermaster or whoever, either of money or supplies of different kinds, mustn't there? It stands to reason. And if so, there would have been invoices for each delivery. There wouldn't have been one single certificate for a grand total. There would have been a whole file of loan certificates. Don't you think?'

'What I think,' I replied, 'is that I'm swimming in the dark. I don't know anything like enough about loan certificates, or about Jacob, or about what happened at Valley Forge. I would need to know a lot more than I do before I can give you any real advice about this.'

'But you will take the case, Kiah, won't you?'

It was said almost pleadingly. That was another thing you soon learned as a young lawyer with your own office. Clients don't always give as much thought as they should to why they want a particular lawyer, and whether the lawyer they want is the best person to handle a case. Lawyers aren't much help in that situation. No lawyer wants to turn away work. But sometimes the red flags are just too obvious to ignore, and there were red flags all over this one. I was a lawyer in solo practice with no back-up. I had no staff except for Arlene, and no money to fund lengthy, complex litigation; and I was being asked to make the government cough up a sum that would do more economic damage to the Treasury than the War of Independence. The government was not going to allow that to happen without instructing the Department of Justice to put up a certain amount of resistance, and the Department of Justice was not short of either funds or staff.

'I do have quite a few documents with me,' Sam was saying. 'It's stuff my branch of the family has collected over the years. My father was very interested in the loans. He would go to family reunions and collect whatever people would give him; press clippings, historical articles, and so on, and it does give you quite a good account of things. There were even a few times when the family tried to do something about it, by approaching their congressmen, and so on. Nothing ever came of it. But no one has ever sued the government. My father believed that was the only option left to us. Now, he's gone, and I...'

She stopped, but she didn't have to say any more. I understood the call of a dead parent all too well. So that's why she was here. It was for her father. My heart went out to her. She wasn't crazy: optimistic, perhaps; unrealistic, perhaps; but not crazy. But that didn't mean I could just jump into this with her. In fact, if she hadn't told me about her father, I would probably have said no right there and then. But she had told me about her father. She had no way of knowing, but she had pressed exactly the right button. I couldn't just turn her away —not like that, not so summarily. I needed time: time to reflect on the story she had told me, and time to reflect on my options. I was thinking that the best option might be to choose a law firm to refer her to – perhaps the firm of Don Quixote and Associates, whose knight-errant partners had the resources and the inclination to tilt at windmills, because that did seem to be the best description of what Sam was asking me to do. In any case, given time, I could reflect on the best way to help her.

'Would it be possible for you to leave those documents with me for a day or so?' I asked. 'I really don't feel I can advise you properly without knowing much more than I know now. They will be quite safe. Would that be OK?'

'Sure,' she replied. 'I'll just leave the briefcase with you.'

'Here's my card,' I said. 'Call me tomorrow afternoon. I'm not saying I'll have a final answer for you then, but I'll do my best.'

'Thank you,' she said.

She stood and made her way to the door. As she was leaving, a thought came to me. I called her back.

'Sam, what did you mean when you said it wasn't only about the money, and you could settle for less?'

She turned and looked me directly in the eye.

'Kiah, if our family tradition is true, Jacob van Eyck played a large part in making sure that the War of Independence didn't end in failure. He is an American hero who has never been recognised. The government will erect a statue to Jacob van Eyck in Philadelphia, and the President of the United States will unveil it.'

5

AFTER SHE HAD GONE, I wheeled the briefcase to my conference table and started to take out the documents she had brought. There were a lot of them. It was just as well the briefcase was on wheels; she couldn't have carried it very far. The documents were neatly organised in folders of various colours secured with rubber bands. She had written titles in matching coloured inks on the front covers. I arranged the folders into a number of piles, grabbed a pen and a yellow pad, and pulled myself up a chair. They were on my table now, and much as I tried to resist the feeling, it felt as though I had taken possession of them.

There were several large blue files containing newspaper cuttings and magazine articles. Some of them went back a long way. I didn't go through them all, but there were several from the 1950s, and one or two were even older. The headlines suggested that, from time to time, family members had raised the question of the loan with their congressmen in different parts of the country. I didn't try to read through everything, so what I am about to say might be a bit unfair. But while the politicians had made a few general comments about what a wonderful thing patriotism is, and what a good guy Jacob must have been, I couldn't see anything to suggest that any of them had done anything tangible to help the family. Disappointing, but not too hard to understand, I thought. The repayment amount would have been a bit smaller back then, but it would still have been an eye-watering number, and any representative who suggested on the record that the government should repay it would have every reason to fear that it would come back to haunt him if he ever ran for higher office, or even if he stood for re-election. It occurred to me that if I took the case, I might have a similar problem with some judges.

There were numerous slim grey files containing photographs, many of them apparently taken during family reunions. They were of no immediate interest. I would have to go over them with Sam to find out who these people were, and whether we needed to deal with them. Like any group of people, no doubt the van Eyck family had its movers and shakers, some who acted as if they were more important than others, and some who actually were more influential than others. It would be important to know who was who, and what they were likely to think of Sam's plan to sue the government.

Then there were various red and green files entitled 'Research'. One of the green files also had the letters 'LDS' on the cover. I smiled. Good for Sam. I knew exactly what I was going to find before I even opened it. Kate Banahan, my wills and trusts professor at Georgetown Law, had clued the whole class in to this. There was, she insisted, no finer way to trace the ancestry of anyone in America, as you sometimes have to in a contested will case. Of course, today you can go to your computer and find any number of online sites for tracing your ancestry, but the LDS Church was in the business long before there was any such concept as online.

They go back to the days when records were made using quill pens and ink, and it might take you days, or weeks, to travel to where a record was kept. They started the Family History Library in 1894, and over the years they built up a huge collection of genealogical records from all over the world – registers of births, marriages, and deaths culled from churches and offices and the pages of family bibles and anywhere else they could be found —with the aim of enabling anyone interested in doing so to put together their own family tree. They have their own religious reasons for doing this, of course, which I'm sure make perfect sense to them, but the good news for the rest of us is that they have been open to sharing this vast treasure trove of information with anyone who needs or wants it. Originally, the only way of doing research was to go to the LDS library in Salt Lake City yourself and track down the documents you needed using the traditional card index system. But gradually the library began to travel via local family history centres, and increased its use of microfilm and microfiche, and now, of course, you can go online. The LDS collection remains the biggest and the best.

Sam had started with the first thing I would need to be sure of: that she herself was in fact a descendant of Jacob van Eyck. That wouldn't have taken her long – it doesn't take the LDS site long to go back 200 years – and she had printed out all the paperwork. There was no doubt about it. He was her ancestor. And then she had moved on. She had wanted to find out what else the site could tell her about her family. She had printed out a thick stack of records. But I didn't try to look through them in detail because I was distracted by a handwritten note she had paper-clipped on top of them. The note was short and stark. I didn't know whether she understood the significance of what she had discovered, but with my legal training it hit me full in the face.

Jacob van Eyck died intestate and without any surviving spouse or children. His three children died in infancy and, therefore, predeceased him. His wife and his parents also predeceased him. But he was survived by his seven brothers, all of whom had children.

She had circled the number seven twice, which suggested that, even without legal training, she thought this might be important. She was right, I was sure of it. I was assuming that the law in Pennsylvania when Jacob died in 1812 would be the same as it is in Virginia today. That may sound like a big assumption, but the law of Pennsylvania and the law of Virginia both grew from the roots of the English law, and the law of succession moves slowly. It doesn't get a lot of public attention. No political careers are made by promoting reform of the law of wills or intestacy. So the law of succession evolves mainly by way of judicial interpretation and meanders through time, like a tranquil river feeling its way gently through a flat, peaceful landscape. Unlike some other areas of the law, the law of succession can remain essentially unchanged for centuries.

I would have to call in to the Georgetown Law Library to verify it, but I had no real doubt about what I would find. Jacob had left no will. In the absence of a surviving spouse or child, each of Jacob's seven (circled twice) brothers would have been entitled to inherit from him in equal shares under the law of intestate succession. As would, in succession, his brothers' children, and those children's children, and so on for more than two hundred years. All their descendants alive today would be potential plaintiffs in the action Sam wanted to bring against the government, and there would have to be thousands of them. This would have to be a class action, and if we ever called a meeting of the class we would have to rent somewhere like Yankee Stadium.

I suppose all that should have been obvious to me as soon as she explained the case to me. She couldn't be the only surviving descendant of Jacob van Eyck. But somehow, my mind had not wandered to the question of how many living members the family tree might have. If all of them were equally entitled to a share of anything we recovered, they would all be entitled to a say in how the case was conducted, and on what terms, if any, it could be settled. I had just unfurled another huge red flag. How long I remained in my reverie before Arlene interrupted me, I'm not sure.

'Hun, y'all need anything? 'Cause I'm outta here. I'm fixin' to take Bubba to get doctored.' Arlene is from Lubbock, Texas.

She is a single mother. Bubba is her ten-year-old son, and

apparently it is already written in the stars that he is destined to play wide receiver for Texas Tech. She moved from Lubbock about two years ago, after Larry, her then husband and Bubba's father, finally revealed to her from the bottom of his whisky glass that he had gambled away the last dollar they had between them, and that the matrimonial home was about to be repossessed to repay his debts. In addition, he added almost as an afterthought, he had lost his job. He had coached high school football, teaching ninth and tenth grade biblical studies as his contribution to the children's academic development. But now, school board and parents alike had concluded that the example he set to the young of the town was no longer satisfactory.

Somehow, via a complicated family connection, Arlene ended up in Arlington, and one day she ended up in my office begging for a job, as if her life depended on it, which in a sense it probably did. She had no prior experience of running a law office, and the references she brought from her local library and her vet's office, where she had worked previously, were no more than formally complimentary about her organisational skills. But there was something about her. I took a chance. I gave her the job, and I have never taken a better decision in the practice of law. Within two weeks, she had the office humming like a well-oiled machine. We never missed a date for a court hearing or to file a pleading; our paperwork was impeccable; the clients received their bills promptly and they paid them promptly.

There's something else, too. She joined me about two months before the Week. When the Week hit and I closed the office, I paid her what I could afford to tide her over, which wasn't enough, and released her, feeling sure I would never see her again. She owed me nothing. But on the morning I reopened she was there, waiting for me at the door at eight o'clock, and she has been with me every day since. And for that I will love her forever.

'No, thanks, Arlene, I'm good. Go. Is Bubba OK?'

'Oh, sure, hun. He'll be fine. He pulled something in his leg going up for a high pass in training last week. I just wanna be sure he ain't fixin' to do any real damage if he trains this week. His coach says it's just a little strain, nothing ice won't fix, but you know me and coaches. I never can quite trust them any more.'

I laughed. 'I know. Get out of here. I'll see you tomorrow.'

She looked down at the mass of paper on my table.

'What did Lily Langtry want? Are you gonna take it?'

'I don't know,' I replied. 'It's a debt collection.'

'A debt collection? That must be one helluva debt.'

'It is. I'll tell you about it tomorrow.'

'Will you tell me before you decide?'

'You know I will.'

'Well, all right, then. Don't stay here all night, y'all.'

That was the night the dreams started. To this day, I cannot begin to describe the vivid impression the dreams made on me, or explain the detailed recall I had of them when I awoke. They even surpass the horrifying reality of my nightmares after the Week, and they remain with me today.

6

It is night time, *very dark. I can't see the moon or stars. It is
bitterly and mercilessly cold, with thick snow on the ground and a
vicious, cutting wind from the north. I am standing at the foot of a
steep hill. The area is heavily wooded. At the top of the hill is a large
house. Lights are burning inside. Below me, on the lower ground, is
a military encampment. There are rows of tents stretching in every
direction. There are some fires burning, and some lanterns. I hear
the muted voices of the soldiers, occasionally the voice of a woman,
the neighing of a horse, the barking of a dog.*

*A man is walking slowly up the hill towards the house. He is
tall and thin, and wears a long grey great coat, black boots, and
a short three-cornered hat of the kind favoured by officers. He
seems troubled. I sense this not from his face, which I cannot see
in the shadows as he walks away from me, but from his posture
and gait, which are uncertain and slow. I follow him up the hill. He
approaches the house and pauses before the door. He waits for some
time, as if he has not yet decided whether or not he wishes to enter.
When he is ready, he knocks, boldly, three times. A servant opens
the door to admit him.*

*We pass into a large living room. The ceiling is low. Because
the man is so tall, he must take care not to come too close to the
corner beams with his head. The wood that forms the beams looks
thick and solid, and shines pleasantly in the warm glow of the log
fire in the fireplace on the far side of the room. The room is simply*

furnished, but everything – the chairs, the tables, the carefully arranged bookcases – looks tasteful, expensive.

A man is standing in front of the fireplace with his back to the fire, holding a pewter tankard. There is something about his demeanor which marks him out as the master of the house. The servant escorts the visitor to the fireplace. He has taken the visitor's hat and great coat, and now I can see that the visitor is wearing a rough-hewn brown jacket and breeches, which feels odd to me, because I am sure that he is a man of breeding.

'God save you, General Washington,' the master of the house says, taking the visitor's hand. There is something about the handshake. I can't quite pin it down. 'This is no night for any of God's servants to be abroad. You must take a cup of mulled wine.'

'God save you, Jacob, and all within your house, likewise. Do not trouble yourself, I beg you.'

'There is no question of trouble.'

He turns to the servant. 'Ezra, a cup of mulled wine for the General.'

Ezra ladles the wine from the pot where it is warming by the fire into a tankard, hands it to the General, bows, and leaves the two of them alone. Their manner is now more urgent.

'Are the supplies safely arrived?' Jacob asks.

'Aye, they passed safely through the enemy lines, God be praised. Thank you, my friend.'

'I am glad of it.'

'The men have food to eat and clothing and boots to keep them warm, and that could not be said when we first came to this place.'

Jacob shakes his head.

'When you first came to this place? When you first came to this place, a more pitiable sight could not be imagined. It was not to be wondered at that you had suffered defeats in the field. A man cannot fight if he cannot eat, and if he has no boots to march in or weapon to engage the enemy.'

The General takes Jacob's hand.

'Jacob, my friend, I have no words of thanks for your generosity which I have not spoken before. You have saved us from starvation and provided us with the means to fight. As soon as this snow melts I will make preparations, and once the weather turns mild we will move against the enemy. We will not let them drive us before them again, I promise you. We are strong, we know our terrain, and in the spring and summer we will prevail.'

'I rejoice to hear it, General, and I pray daily to God for your victory.'

The General releases the hand.

'Jacob, there is another matter to speak of. I know that you have used up your fortune to save us.'

Jacob smiles, nodding. *'Aye. That I have.'*

'You have given everything, and I must ensure that provision is made for you.'

'It is true that I have given everything, General, but if I may speak freely…?'

'Certainly.'

'How could I have done otherwise? These are no times for withholding. Our case is urgent. If we do not give everything now, we are surely lost. If God favours our cause and gives us the victory, He will recompense me. If not… well, if not, I daresay we shall all hang as traitors and I would as soon die a poor traitor as a rich one.'

They laugh together.

'Well said, indeed, Jacob. Nonetheless, while God will undoubtedly recompense you, our country owes you a debt on this earth, and I would not leave this place to fight before I have done all in my power to ensure that you are restored in your fortune as quickly as may be.'

'The Congress has made such provision as can be made to restore the fortunes of those who have given, General. I have certificates from them to acknowledge the debt, and the terms are favorable enough. I am content.'

The General shakes his head.

'It is not enough, Jacob. Who can say what our fortunes will be

once we have our freedom? It may be that we shall have freedom but little else besides, the war having taken everything from us.'

'In such a case, what is to be done?' Jacob asks.

'If I may speak plainly also,' the General replies, 'in such a case there is much to be done. But to do it, you must see clearly in what position you will find yourself. You must expect that the Congress will take such steps as they can to avoid or delay payment to their creditors.'

'General –'

'You must expect it, I say.'

Jacob seems visibly taken aback.

'I cannot believe they would act so dishonourably. They must feel gratitude towards those who have given, those who made the victory possible. They must –'

'It will not be for want of gratitude, Jacob. They are not dishonourable men. It will be out of necessity. The debt will exceed their assets, and even such assets as they have must be expended in large part for the welfare of the people and the safety of the country. So they will send their agents to the loan offices in every state to attend to the business, as they must. But when men come with their certificates to be paid, they will take possession of them. If the amount be small, I doubt not that it will be paid. But if it be so large that it cannot be paid, they may take the certificate without making payment, promising to do so on a future day. They cannot do otherwise.'

Jacob begins to speak, but stops abruptly.

'Jacob, I wish to counsel you, if you will allow?'

'By all means, General.'

'When you bring your certificates to the loan office, do not bring them all at one time. And when you bring them, bring with you also a letter addressed to the highest officer of state in our Treasury. This letter must state that I have invested such influence as I have in ensuring that you are to be repaid. I have staked my credit on it. I am your surety. On his receipt of this letter, every officer of state will

take note, and I shall importune every officer of our government on
your behalf. Insist on retaining your certificates until I or another
officer of state shall have answered the letter, and instructed the
loan office to pay you. Do you understand?'

    'I understand, General.'

    'Your fortune may depend on it.'

    'I understand.'

I wake up suddenly. I am freezing. I feel as though I have just
walked down the hill from the house wearing nothing except
the two-sizes-too-big sweatshirt I sleep in. At five o'clock, I am
sitting in my kitchen wearing two sweaters and thick white socks,
drinking piping hot soup, with the heater turned up to level six,
and still I am freezing.

7

A CLASS ACTION IS a special kind of lawsuit, which is brought when a large number of plaintiffs have the same cause of action against the same defendant, for example an insurance company or an industry such as asbestos or tobacco. The plaintiffs are all suing for the same thing, but they may live anywhere in the country, and it obviously wouldn't work for all of them to sue individually. For one thing, there would be no end to the litigation. It would take forever to dispose of all the claims. For another, there might be inconsistent judgments in different courts, some for the plaintiffs, some for the defendant, which would give rise to huge legal headaches and trigger a fresh round of litigation. To avoid all this, the cases are consolidated in one particular court, which means that the plaintiffs sue as a group, and negotiate and settle as a group.

Sensible as this is, it does pose some problems. The plaintiffs must appoint a lead plaintiff to pursue the litigation on behalf of everyone. Whoever sues first is in pole position to become lead plaintiff, but it doesn't always work out that way. The attorneys representing the lead plaintiff are going to be the ones making most of the money, because they are doing most of the work and taking most of the financial risks, so there can be some competition for the position. If the lead plaintiff's attorney is someone like me, or a small firm, they may actually welcome a bigger firm with more people and resources riding to the rescue, and they may have no problem giving up the lead and slip-streaming behind a firm that can match the defendant for muscle power. But not everyone feels that way, and there can be some ugly battles between law firms trying to take over the lead position, battles the court may have to resolve. And while that goes on, the defendant can sit back happily and watch while resources are squandered on in-fighting instead of pursuing the case. And even after that, the legacy of bad blood between the law firms may hamper efforts to negotiate and settle the case; and if the case goes to trial, there may be some big egos arguing about who should be lead trial counsel.

To my amazement, I find myself playing through these scenarios in my head and getting territorial about a case I haven't even accepted, imagining arguments to persuade the judge that I should continue as lead counsel and march the members of the van Eyck class on to a famous victory. The only realistic part of my fantasy is that Sam and I would be the first to sue. Not much doubt about that.

Getting the case up and running would be simple enough, and, for me, would be like having home field advantage. For cases like this, contractual claims against the federal government, you sue in the United States Claims Court, a court in Washington DC established by Congress specifically to deal with such disputes. I am very familiar with litigation in the Claims Court. I've had a good number of cases there on behalf of plaintiffs, and I have a good professional relationship with the judges. There isn't as much competition for that kind of work as there might be.

You would be amazed – or perhaps you wouldn't – at the number of law firms in and around DC that are squeamish about suing the federal government. So many of them either are, or would love to be connected politically, and are desperate to attract work from the movers and shakers in the capital. They think that if they get caught playing for the away team, it may hurt their prospects of greater intimacy with Washington's political élite somewhere down the road. I don't give a rat's ass about any of that. I have no interest in the political élite, and I have no problem with screwing money out of the federal government in a good cause. It doesn't bother me even one bit. I like the Claims Court. You can only sue in the Claims Court if your claim is for more than $10,000. That's one problem we won't have. So why not?

Arlene was about to tell me why not. We were sitting side by side at my conference table, and I had just outlined for her the case Sam had brought to us, and she was not looking too impressed.

'Lord have mercy, hun,' she began. 'Now, I know that you have been through some tough times. Believe me I do know that, and I understand that, hun. I surely do. But... have y'all lost y'all's everlovin' mind?'

Odd as it may sound, this was not said at all unkindly.

'I haven't said I want to take the case,' I pointed out.

'I mean, have you thought this through at all? I mean, do you see an army of secretaries and paralegals anywhere in this office? 'Cause I sure don't. It's you and me, darlin'. That's it. And do you know how much money it would take to get this show on the road? Do you see a spare million or two in y'all's bank accounts? 'Cause I sure don't.'

'I haven't said –'

'Sorry, hun, but this dog won't hunt.'

I took a deep breath.

'I haven't said I want to take the case.'

'You haven't said you *don't* want to.'

'I haven't talked to Sam since she left the paperwork with me. I asked her to call me today.'

She nodded. 'Well, all right then. But may I take it that when she calls, you *will* refer her on to someone else?'

'Like who?' I asked.

It was something I had been asking myself ever since I had bought myself the time to think it over. I couldn't just throw her out on the street without making some effort to make sure that she ended up with a lawyer who would do justice to her case. Well, in theory I could, but in my own mind I was well past that point with

Sam now. Whether or not I had any strict professional duty, I had taken on the burden of making sure she was OK. That didn't mean I had to take the case myself, but it did mean that I had to find the right lawyer or firm for her.

With most cases that came into the office, that wouldn't have been a problem. I had a network of lawyers I could refer cases to, and accept cases from, when needed. But with this case, none of the names I was coming up with seemed right. Even Don Quixote and Associates would think twice about this one. This wasn't just tilting at windmills; it was tilting at a whole wind farm – a class action-size wind farm. You could spend a lot of money on this case, and the chances of ever making a single cent would still be in the range of negligible to zero. Even if Jacob had been provided with loan certificates, even if those certificates still existed – and those were huge ifs – you would have to find them. Without them, you would have no chance at all. But where would you even start looking? I felt pretty sure that any law firm big enough to handle this case would laugh in my face for even suggesting it. Actually, I wouldn't mind that. I just didn't want them laughing in Sam's face.

Alternatively, I could, I suppose, just tell her that the whole idea of suing the government for whatever happened the best part of 250 years ago was crazy, and that she needed to forget about it and get on with her life doing Arthur Miller and Tennessee Williams. But I knew I wasn't going to do that, and I knew that she wouldn't take my advice even if I did.

'Well, hun, that's a good question,' Arlene was saying. 'I sure can't think of anyone we know who would touch it. And that, right there, is why y'all shouldn't touch this with a nine-foot pole. It'd be like taking a lame mule to the rodeo and calling it a quarter-horse. Now, you may get to the rodeo, but you ain't about to rope yourself a calf.'

I called Sam and told her I needed another day to look at the papers, and asked her to come to the office the following afternoon.

8

I AM IN AN office in a city. I think it is Philadelphia, but why I think that I'm not sure. It is a government office. The tired, dreary furnishings and untidy appearance of the place would never be tolerated in the office of a private entrepreneur who knew that his livelihood might depend on making his place of business attractive and welcoming to the public.

There is a counter, and behind the counter stands a young man who seems to be about thirty years of age, an official of some kind. His dress is drab and uncared for, his manner is one of boredom or indifference, and all in all he matches the appearance and atmosphere of the office exactly. In front of him on the counter are several documents, ink on parchment, in formal script, but because of I am too far away, I cannot read them.

In front of the counter stands an old man. His appearance has changed since I saw him in the house at the top of the hill, but I know it is Jacob. He has aged greatly; his body is thin, and I see that he is in pain and walks with the aid of a stick. Not only that, but there is a young woman with him who is giving him additional support for walking and standing. Her name is Isabel. How I know that, I cannot say. His clothing is worn, and he has no hat. He is in conversation with the young man, and their demeanor suggests that the conversation is not going well.

'And I repeat, sir,' the young man is saying, 'that there is no gold to pay such claims. If it were a matter of twenty dollars I would pay

you, but I have no authority to pay such sums as you claim, even if you were to bring me proof of them. The country is not yet recovered from the war.'

'The war? The war has been over these twenty years,' Jacob protests. 'I doubt you were more than twelve years old at its end.'

The young man seems briefly amused by this.

'You speak truly, sir. Yet our credit abroad is uncertain, and after the war the government caused such masses of currency to be printed that the value of our scrip is even today far less than that of a like amount of gold. There is much distress among the people, and we have as yet no guarantee of our security from our enemies.'

He pauses.

'I beg you to understand, sir, that I have this from my superiors, not of my own knowledge. I have no such authority or position that I am privy to such matters myself. But my superiors tell me that such gold as we have must be expended for the public good.'

'There would be no public good,' Jacob exclaims, 'except such as the King of England would allow us, unless I and others like me had saved the General and his army from ruin when he camped at Valley Forge. It was after that winter that the war began to turn in our favour.'

'Be that as it may, sir, you bring me no proof of the debt owed to you. The Congress stipulated that those who loaned their gold were to be issued certificates which stated the amount thereof, and on presentation of those certificates to this office, they should be recompensed with the interest allowed by the Congress.'

He points to the documents in front of him.

'When you last came to me, you asked that I make a diligent search of the office. I have done so. The documents I found, you see before me. Two certificates I have from gentlemen I believe to be your brothers, one for some twenty-five dollars and the other for some forty. These were presented to this office and the amounts were repaid to them.'

'I have told you of my proof, both on the last occasion I came here

and on this occasion,' Jacob replies in a loud voice. He is angry now. 'I was instructed by the General himself to retain my certificates until such time as he had ensured the repayment and to submit them with a letter indicating his interest in the matter.'

'Yet you say you have not retained them?'

He is getting bored and frustrated with this discussion, and wants only to get rid of Jacob in any way he can. Jacob is also frustrated.

'Sir,' Isabel reminds him quietly, 'you dealt with another officer when you yielded the certificates. You must explain to this gentleman why you did so.'

'I have explained…' Jacob replies.

'Yet you must do so again. Be patient, sir, I beg you.'

'Very well,' Jacob agrees. "You must understand, sir, that when I first came with my certificates I spoke with another officer, your senior in rank – you will forgive me, sir, I mean no offense by this.'

'I take none. When came you?'

He looks at Isabel.

'Fully fifteen years ago,' she replies.

'More, I think,' Jacob says. 'Before our Treasury removed from Philadelphia to the new District. Notwithstanding, I brought with the certificates a letter, as General Washington had instructed me, indicating his surety for me in this matter, which letter was to be placed before the highest officers of state for their consideration.'

'Then, that could not be done in this office.'

'So I was advised. The officer with whom I dealt proposed to take the certificates and the letter with him and to present the same to the high officials who must see them.'

'No doubt that was done?'

'I have no intelligence whether it be done or not. I know only that I am not repaid. I have returned to this place to inquire many times, and am met with the same response, that the officer now in charge has no information, and must make inquiries in the Treasury. Then, when I return again, it appears that no one in the Treasury has intelligence of it. The certificates and my letter are nowhere to *be found, as if they are vanished into the air, spirited away by some malicious hobgoblin.'*

The officer shakes his head.

'I know not what I may do, sir.' A thought occurs to him. 'Did this officer, with whom you dealt, offer you no receipt for the documents you gave him?'

Jacob hangs his head, and does not reply for some time.

'I thought not to inquire for one,' he admits. 'It was foolish of me, perhaps. But I believed I was dealing with men of honour, who would deal with me honourably, just as the General had. I would believe it of them still, but I must tell you that my confidence has waned, and I no longer know whether I believe it.'

'I will report the matter to my superiors, sir. I can do no more.'

'I had the word of the General himself. He would have pursued my cause. He undertook to do so.'

'President Washington is deceased these ten years and more, sir.'

'Notwithstanding. I had his word.'

'I can do no more, sir.'

MY CLOCK RADIO IS telling me what the weather will be in the DC area for today. It is time to get up. I make coffee. I call Arlene, and tell her I will be late in this morning. I call Arya, and ask whether I can come to see her and talk. Of course I can, she says, without asking any questions of me.

As I am getting ready to leave my apartment, it suddenly occurs to me that it has been more than twenty-four hours since I last thought about Jordan.

9

ARYA SITS ME DOWN in my favourite chair with her Neroli incense and a cup of herbal tea. She says little at first, but carefully looks me up and down, and eventually pulls up a low stool so that she can sit at my feet. I know what's about to happen. It's another of those things I have a word for in my mind – reflexology – but it's a word I have never actually applied to Arya, because like everything else she does, it is just part of who she is, one of the labels I will never stick on her. I brace myself as she picks up my feet and holds them in her lap, because I know what's coming. Part of it will feel like a good strong massage – which of course I love – and part of it, when she finds a sensitive point and deliberately digs into it with those powerful fingers of hers, will hurt like hell. But I have been through it before, I have never protested, and I always feel better for it afterwards. Not always at the time, but always afterwards.

As she probes my feet and they start to get twitchy, I tell her about Sam, and about Jacob van Eyck, and about loan certificates, and about class actions, and about the money and time they consume. She has reached a point on the sole just beneath my big toe, and goes in as deep as she can. I almost scream. I grab the arms of the chair as tightly as I can.

'It's OK, Kiah,' she purrs. 'Breathe. Nice and slow.'

It's all I can do to breathe at all, let alone nice and slow.

'My, you *are* tense this morning,' she says. 'Come on. Breathe. Stay with me. Breathe.'

She goes in again. It's still very painful, but not quite so much this time. My breathing does actually begin to develop a bit of a rhythm.

To take my mind off the pain, I start to tell her about the dreams. She was listening before, but I feel an increased attentiveness now. After a third prod, noticeably less painful, she reverts to a massage of both feet while I am trying to describe where my mind has been going the last two nights. Suddenly, something releases in my shoulders and I somehow feel lighter. I quickly lift and lower my shoulders several times, and find that I am breathing more deeply.

'Do you want to take her case?' she asks.

'I don't see how I can. Arlene said it all yesterday. It would cost a fortune to take it all the way to trial, the government would fight us every step of the way, and the chances of recovering anything would be almost non-existent. To say nothing of the fact that I would have to neglect my other clients to devote the kind of time this case would demand. I don't know what to do except to refer it out, but I don't even know what kind of a law firm would take it.'

Her hands came to rest for a moment.

'Kiah, I didn't ask whether it is *practicable* for you to take it. I asked whether you *want* to take it.'

'If I could? If money and resources were no problem? Then would I want it?'

'That's what I'm asking.'

I closed my eyes. It wasn't a simple question. I felt as though I were being invited to step into quicksand. I was still on solid ground for now, but that could change in a flash if I just decided to jump. I was watching the solid ground disappear, and part of me wanted it back. There was a part of me that wished I could go into the office this morning and find that all the documents had magically disappeared from my conference table; that Sam and Jacob van Eyck were just as much a dream as the house on the hill and the office with the young official. But there was also a part of me that, for reasons I did not understand, wanted to be a part of this, and there was something about the dreams that was pulling me in.

There was something else, too, which Arlene didn't know when she gave me her obviously sage and sensible advice the previous afternoon. It was true that the practice was just starting up again, and that our bank balance and cash flow weren't in the most healthy of states. But I did have some money. It was money I desperately wished I didn't have, but I had it, and that was how it was. My parents had done well in the practice of medicine over many years, as had their parents before them. They had money, and they had an expensive house in East Falls Church they had bought for their retirement. I was an only child, I was their sole executor, and I inherited everything except for a generous cash bequest to Arya and a few smaller ones to relatives. It was a simple enough probate, and I had already wound up and distributed the estate except for the sale of the house. It didn't mean that I could afford to be reckless, but it did mean that I was not entirely at the mercy of my practice for my living. There were a few chances I could afford to take. I felt Arya reading my mind.

'What do you think the dreams mean?' she asked.

'I don't know.'

Wrong answer. You don't tell Arya that dreams may mean nothing, that they may be no more than the imaginings of an over-active mind while the body is trying to rest. She will just listen politely and ask you again. Besides, dreams – or nightmares, anyway – had been an ongoing topic of conversation between us since the Week. Since then, nightmares had been a constant in my life: I regularly suffered with disturbing dreams about my parents and about Jordan, and even though their meaning seemed obvious to me, Arya would encourage me to look deeper, to go into the detail of the dreams, what things were emphasised – especially about Jordan. Then she would ask me what I had learned from them. Other than the obvious lesson that men couldn't be trusted – which, for some reason, always made her laugh – I usually couldn't come up with much. But I did actually begin to understand that there were certain recurring features of my nightmares, and once I brought those into consciousness, they began to subside, not going away altogether, but reducing in intensity and losing their power to some extent. I had even regained some ability to turn over and go back to sleep. Once the crying and shaking stopped.

'I don't know,' is another thing you don't tell Arya when discussing dreams.

'Yes, you do.' Stock reply, delivered with assurance and without hesitation.

'I suppose there's a part of my mind that's already involved with the case, which is speaking to me. It can't be anything conscious.'

'No. Your conscious mind is too busy worrying about the law, and the technical aspects of it all, and how on earth you would ever manage a case of that size, and who you could offload it to, and all the rest of it. Which is fine. That's the conscious mind's job. So your subconscious mind has to feed you information, and dreams are one way of doing that.'

I nodded. 'OK. That makes sense.'

'Good. So what information is your subconscious mind giving you?'

I thought for some time.

'That it is real to me; that it is something I want to do. I never dream about cases, Arya, never. This is something I apparently care about. It seems crazy...'

'Why should it be crazy?'

'I only heard about Jacob van Eyck a couple of days ago. I know almost nothing about him, or about the case Sam thinks she has. I haven't had time to digest all this, much less form a burning desire to take up her cause.'

'You know what I'm going to say about time, don't you?'

I laughed. 'Of course I do. Time is an illusion, the greatest illusion of all; which is why in our language we use the same word to mean both "yesterday" and "tomorrow".'

She laughed too. 'Yes. You've been to India. Look, you're standing at a bus stop in Shimla, waiting for a bus that should have arrived twenty minutes ago. You ask someone when the bus will come. What does she say?'

'She says the bus will come in one hour.'

'And what does she mean by that?'

'The bus will come any time between now and never. The one hour is just to be polite; she doesn't want to discourage you. Besides, if it never comes, life goes on, you die and you are reborn, and the great wheel of Lord Shiva continues to turn, so what does it matter if the bus never comes?'

'Exactly. You may have known about this case all your life, or before your life began.'

I would never have this conversation with anyone other than Arya, or if I did, I would discount it instantly. But with Arya, I just absorb it.

'All right. Let's say I want it. That still leaves us with the problems.'

'Yes, but problems look different when you know you want something, don't they? They are hurdles to be overcome instead of excuses for running away from it.'

She looked at me.

'And you do have some resources.'

I bristled. 'Arya, I can't use my parents' money for this.'

'Why on earth not?'

I didn't really have an answer for that.

'It wouldn't be right.'

'Oh?'

'It's money they worked hard for all their lives. They left it to me so that I could… well, I don't know… improve my life.'

She squeezed my feet.

'And doing something you want isn't improving your life?'

I smiled.

'Kiah, listen to me. I have known you ever since you were born, and I knew your parents for much longer. And I know two things. One, you won't squander your money. You're a hard-headed girl, and you're not going to just let it all go. You'll use it responsibly, not let it use you. Two, your parents gave you that money so that you could live well. And there is no better way to live well than to do what you love.'

'So you're saying I should do it?'

'I'm not saying anything. The only thing that matters is what you say.'

She walked me to the door.

'Besides,' she said, 'I don't think it's true that you have no other resources. Actually, I expect you will have more than enough.'

'Not from Sam,' I said. 'She's a repertory actress, and she hasn't mentioned any family money.'

'No. But didn't you say there must be many members of the family who are entitled to claim?'

I nodded.

'How many? Do you know?'

'I haven't tried to work it out, but there must be thousands.'

'Well, there you are. Surely, there will be many of them who want to help? If they hope to benefit from the case, it's not unreasonable that they contribute something, is it?'

'No, it's not,' I agreed.

'And here's another thing,' Arya said. 'Bearing in mind that we are in America, how many of those thousands are likely to be attorneys?'

10

I FOUND MYSELF TRYING to make my entrance as casual as possible in the hope that Arlene wouldn't notice me. She was busy thumbing through a client's file, trying to find something, so it looked promising; my timing seemed good. I set the latte I had bought her as a subconscious peace-offering on her desk, wished her a cheerful good morning and breezed into my office, clutching mine. For a few moments, as I took my seat behind my desk and fired up my computer, I actually thought I had got away with it. It was all so silly.

Even if I had got away with it, how long would that last? I would have to deal with Arlene in a matter of minutes. I don't know what I thought I was achieving by sneaking into my own office like an indoor cat that's been out chasing mice all night when he shouldn't have been. But there has always been a part of me that believes that I can solve any problem, regardless of how long I have been puzzling over it, if I can just have a little more time. One more hour, one more coffee, one more night's sleep is bound to bring about enlightenment. It's a fallacy, of course. An hour, or a coffee, or a night's sleep later, the problem is still the same, and I solve it exactly as I always knew I would. But still I cling to the illusion.

Arlene opened the door and stood tall in the frame.

'Miss Kiah, I swear you are as ornery as a rattler stuck in a storm drain. You're fixin' to take Lily Langtry's case, ain't you?'

I looked over to the conference table. The papers had not miraculously disappeared overnight. They remained in place on my table. And Arya was still playing in my head. It was a moment I had waited for and dreaded and rehearsed in my mind a hundred times during my drive from Arya's house to the office, and now it had arrived. My heart was beating quickly, and I felt slightly faint, almost detached from my body.

'Yes,' I heard myself reply. 'Yes, I am.'

Speaking the words aloud had an immediate effect on me. While they were trapped inside me, they had produced only anxiety and indecision. But now that they were out there in the ether, their power was released. I was jolted back into my body to find that there were butterflies in my stomach, but now, it wasn't just anxiety. It felt scary, yes. Had I really said that? Was this really what I was going to do? But at the same time it felt exhilarating. For a few moments, I felt as I sometimes had before the Week: confident, in control, light-hearted, optimistic, feelings I'd thought the Week had robbed me of forever. I calmed down after a few seconds, as the immediate rush subsided. The feelings lessened, but to my delight they did not leave me altogether. It was so good to have them back, to rediscover that part of myself again, that I cried. I couldn't help it.

Arlene watched me, and I had the sense that she was ditching the lecture she had planned to deliver about the behaviour of rattlers stuck in storm drains. I realised then that I had tried to avoid her because I had been afraid of losing her, afraid that this would be a bridge too far after the ravages of the Week and the reopening of the office. But that wasn't Arlene. I should have known that by then. She had had her say; I had decided; and whether she agreed with my decision or not, she was going to stay and help to keep her crazy boss afloat for as long as she could. She allowed me time to recover, waited for the tears to stop.

'We're gonna need some help,' she said eventually.

I took a deep breath. 'I know.'

'I'll need someone in the office.'

'I'll get you someone. I promise.'

'And you're gonna need someone to run around for you, talking to people, finding documents, digging dirt. Y'all are gonna be way too busy acting like a lawyer to do that kind of shit y'all's self.'

I nodded. She was right. I would need legal support at some stage. I had no doubt about that. I'd originally thought I would have to hire an associate. That would have been a major expense, and I was baulking at the idea. But Arya had pointed out the obvious solution. Among the dispersed branches of the van Eyck family, there would have to be a good number of attorneys. Some wouldn't be able to help: those who worked in government or a big law firm; those who had retired or had some arcane specialty like international trade. But there had to be some who would be willing and able to help me if I needed some legal research done, or some document drafted. Even two or three would do if I could depend on them.

But that wouldn't be enough. Someone would need to work with Sam: interviewing family members; following up leads; building up a picture about what we knew, and didn't know, about Jacob's loans; finding out what evidence we had, or could hope to have. Because without evidence, there was no lawsuit. There was no way I was going to have time to do all that myself, and in any case it didn't need a lawyer. A paralegal, perhaps, or...

'What about Powalski?' Arlene asked.

'Powalski?'

'Sure. He has other work, so you wouldn't have to hire him. You could do a deal with him for so many hours a month.'

'Do you think he would do it?'

'Hun, he'd jump at it like a stallion jumping into a corral full of mares.'

It was a great idea. Powalski was a private investigator I'd used almost as long as I'd been in practice. He had come highly recommended by a lawyer I knew well and trusted. He was discreet and reliable, and he got things done without charging an arm and a leg for fees and expenses. I'm sure he has a first name. In fact, I'm sure he told me what it was one day, but I can't remember and no one ever calls him anything except Powalski.

When he got to know me better and we adjourned to a wine bar one evening on the eve of some national holiday and we were swapping life stories, he confided to me that his earlier career history had been with the CIA. It was something he wouldn't talk about in detail, and I had the impression that it wasn't just a matter of the usual professional discretion. It seemed to me that he was very glad to have left that world behind him. But we were likely to make enemies in high places with this case, and some insight into the darker side of Washington would serve us well at some point down the road. Powalski would know how to talk to the kind of people we would need to talk to without rubbing them up the wrong way, and that was going to be important.

'Arlene,' I said, 'I think you may just have come up with the perfect solution. Way to go, girl.'

She smiled modestly.

'Aw, shucks, hun. Even a blind squirrel stumbles over an acorn now and then.'

11

'SO: WE ARE GOING to have to decide what our immediate priorities are,' I said.

I was sitting at the conference table with Sam and Arlene. Arlene was with us because she needed to know everything I knew, and everything I was planning. This was going to be a team effort or nothing, and there could be no secrets. Sam had been delighted, jumping up and down, when I told her I was going to take the case. That was understandable, and I didn't want to cut her off. It was going to be important for her to maintain her enthusiasm over the long haul, because this was going to be a long haul. But we also needed to have a serious conversation now, in which I explained to her the realities of conducting a case on this scale when we still didn't have any actual evidence. Painstakingly, I took her through the mechanics of litigation in the Claims Court, and the basics of class actions. I probably took far too long about it, but Sam needed to know what she was about to embark on.

'First, we need to find out what evidence there is out there. We need to find out what the family knows. The impression I get from reading the documents you left with me is that there are different family members, all with different information, who are not talking to each other. It's like a giant jigsaw puzzle and no one has all the pieces. We need to find those pieces and put them together.'

'I figured as much,' Sam said. 'That's why I came to see you now. The family has get-togethers from time to time in different areas, but every four years there is a major national reunion, and we are due for one six weeks from now in New Orleans. You can expect people from all over the country. It would be a great opportunity.'

'What goes on at these reunions?' I asked.

'It's mainly a social gathering. One evening they have a sit-down dinner; another night they may have a cocktail party with finger food. But sometimes they will have a business meeting to discuss something of interest, and my dad always said that was when the subject of the loans would come up, if it ever did. But they could never agree to do anything. The rest of the time, they break up into small groups and catch up with family news, go sight-seeing, generally have a good time.'

'If they're doing stuff like having a major reunion,' Arlene suggested, 'they must have a membership list of some kind.'

'There's a small, hard-core group of family members who are the real cheerleaders and they are the ones who always seem to take the lead organising these things.'

'Can I get names and email addresses?'

Sam nodded and made a note for herself. 'Sure. I think I know where to go for that.'

'We need to be there in New Orleans,' I said. 'We need to be on the agenda. We need to contact the cheerleaders and make sure they call a general meeting, so we can let them know what we are doing, and start building our database of potential plaintiffs.'

'Not to mention letting them know we'll be expecting a contribution towards expenses from every last one of them,' Arlene said.

'Not to mention that.'

'We'll need a website,' Arlene continued, 'a website where they can download a form to register as a plaintiff, and pay their contributions. I can fix that for y'all if I can get Bert, down the hall, to help me some.'

Sam and I looked at her questioningly.

'He works for the CPA two doors down, and he seems to know

all about that kind of shit, and I think he has the hots for me. If I smile the right way at him, he'll come running. Leave it with me.'

'Go for it,' I said. 'OK. The next priority is the search for the Holy Grail. If we don't get our hands on at least one loan certificate with the name of Jacob van Eyck on it, the case is going nowhere.'

'How do we do that?' Sam asked.

'I'm not sure yet. I need to research it. I need to know a lot more about loan certificates and loan offices than I do now. But even that's not going to be enough. There will be some places we can't go. I'm pretty sure that at some point, we are going to need the government's help in tracking them down.'

Arlene laughed. 'Hun, I don't think the government is going to be exactly falling all over themselves to help us with that. I reckon they'll be running the other way faster than a turkey on Thanksgiving.'

I smiled. 'They won't want to. But the government is going to be a party to this lawsuit, and we are entitled to ask the court to make the government look for evidence and tell us what they have. The only problem is that we have to give the court some idea of what we are looking for, and some idea of where we expect the government to look.'

'I can help with that,' Sam volunteered. 'I've already done quite a bit of reading about the Continental Congress and the loans, and I'm happy to hit the library again if you can give me some direction.'

'Good,' I replied. I paused. 'I think this means we are going to have to file suit quickly, within the next week or two. We definitely need to have it done before the reunion.'

'Whoa, hold your horses there, Tex,' Arlene said. 'Ain't that a bit like letting the bull out of the gate before the bell rings? I mean, shouldn't we have just a teeny-weeny bit of evidence before we ask the government to hand over 672 billion dollars and change?'

'It's not ideal,' I agreed. 'I would prefer to wait until we have done as much evidence-gathering as we can. That's the general rule. But that's not going to work in this case. We need to put in a discovery request as soon as possible, and we can't do that until we file suit. Plus, we need to let the family cheerleaders see that we are serious about this, and give them something to sign up to. Just talking about filing a lawsuit isn't going to make them sit in the hotel for a business meeting instead of exploring New Orleans and getting started on the mint juleps. We need to show them we already have the show on the road.'

On the way home I called in to Georgetown Law on the off-chance, and found Kate Banahan, my wills and trusts professor, in her office. My timing was good. She had just got out of class, and she was happy to see me. It was a few years since I had been in her class, but we had got on well then; she had given me an A, and we had run into each other at receptions at the law school since. We drank coffee from the machine in the faculty common room. I told her all about the forthcoming lawsuit to be entitled *Samantha van Eyck (individually and on behalf of all those similarly situated) v United States.*' Her eyes lit up as she listened. Kate is of Irish extraction, and she has that Irish combination of jet black hair and bright blue eyes. There is the odd fleck of grey in the hair now that she is in her early fifties, but the eyes still sparkle. She was a trial lawyer before she settled on academia for the long term, and she still remembers the thrill of the chase.

'Kiah, this is amazing,' she said excitedly. 'This would make legal history. Does anyone know yet?'

'No. I'd like to keep it under wraps until we file.'

'My lips are sealed.'

She demonstrated with her finger. I hesitated.

'Kate, the reason I came to see you is that I am going to need some help in the office, and I wondered whether...'

She laughed. 'You wondered whether I could steer the odd student your way?'

'We can pay them for some time if they can fit it in between classes, and I think it would be interesting for them.'

'I can do better than that,' she said.

'Oh?'

'I will offer my wills and trusts class some course credit if they do four half-days during the semester and write me a report about it. Any further time is up to you to arrange with the student.'

I took her hand.

'Kate, that is fantastic,' I said. 'Thank you. Can you do that, really?'

'Sure. Why not? Professors often give partial credit for outside work if it's relevant to the class. It's something they can take to the bank before they take my exam. Most of them will jump at the chance. Besides, when would they ever get the chance to work on something like this? This is a one-off.'

'How many do you have in your class?'

'Thirty-five. About the same as in your day. It doesn't change much. It's pretty much the same every semester.'

She walked me to the elevator.

'You know, Kiah, I am as sure as I can be that you're right about the intestacy law in Pennsylvania back then. But I'd be glad to look at it for you and give you a call if you like.'

'Thank you,' I said. 'That would be great.'

She grinned. 'No problem. OK, I have a hidden agenda. Don't you think you may need an expert witness on the law of intestacy somewhere down the road?'

'I'm sure we will,' I replied, shaking her hand, 'and you are hereby retained.'

12

Dave Petrosian

I CAN SAY WITHOUT any hesitation that the day the file landed on my desk was the most interesting day of my career. All right, that's not saying much. Representing the federal government in the United States Claims Court doesn't usually get the blood pumping. It's a steady diet of government contracts, pension disputes, and insurance coverage claims. Not the kind of stuff most people get excited about, certainly not the kind of stuff novels and movies are made of. But it's a steady job. When I come into the office in the mornings I see my name on a small plaque perched on the front of my desk, and I am content: United States Department of Justice, Civil Division, David R. Petrosian, Senior Litigation Attorney. I think of Maria, and I think of little Raul and Cindy, and I am content.

I guess there is part of me that would like to be out there in the private sector, with some huge law firm, drawing down a junior partner's salary, or even a senior associate's salary for that matter. But you know what? I know some of those people. They were my classmates in law school. They are lawyers I have been pitted against in the courtroom. I see them from time to time, and they talk a big game about being close to the centre, about being able to feel the power, about playing in the major leagues. I know some of them earn more in a month than I earn in a year. But I also see them swallowing their ulcer medication in the corner of the court cafeteria when they think no one is watching them. I look in their eyes and see the exhaustion. I listen to them talk, and I hear the premature cynicism, the tales of carnage and devastation in their personal lives, and any trace of envy I might have felt disappears.

I'll be honest. It's not like the big law firms were beating a path to my door to hire me when I graduated law school. That doesn't happen to you when you are working and have to study part-time, when the high grades don't come easy, and when you give any time you have left to your wife and children instead of writing articles for law review or participating in moot court competitions.

I went to law school late. When I graduated from college in Minnesota, I'd already met Maria and fallen desperately in love. In our senior years we both had part-time jobs waiting tables in a burger joint in downtown Minneapolis to help fund our tuition, and we fell for each other in a heartbeat. I'd always found that dark Latin look irresistible and in any case I wasn't trying very hard to resist. It was a magic time. But then, life intervened. Towards the end of the year she became pregnant. It wasn't what we had planned, but, as much in love as we were, neither was it unwelcome. So, very happily, we did what we had to. We got married. I took a job as an insurance claims adjuster, while Maria looked after Raul. Two years later, Cindy came along. It turned out that I had a flair for claims adjusting. I was promoted rapidly, and we were doing pretty well financially. But there was no spare money for either of us to think about going back to school full-time.

I had harboured thoughts about law school in my junior and senior years of college. I'm not sure why, really. I have no family connections in the law. I'm from a blue-collar family of Armenian immigrants, and while my family encouraged my education right through school and college and were always reminding me that it was the key to a better life, they didn't have many ideas about what exactly I should do after graduation. Law school was my idea, and I guess for some reason it seemed like the natural next step. But now, it seemed, I would have to put thoughts like that behind me, and embrace claims adjusting as my life's work. And so time went by.

Then one evening, after we had eaten dinner and put the children to bed, Maria sat me down with a glass of wine. Someone had told her about William Mitchell Law School in St Paul, a private law school which would allow me to study part-time. It would still be tough to find the tuition, but the children were six and four now, and she was comfortable making arrangements for them so that she could take a part-time job herself. I think she had a touch of cabin fever by then, and was itching to be out of the house. It made sense. My undergraduate grades were good and with a reasonable score on the Law School Admission Test, I could get in. It would be a hard grind at my age, but it was what I wanted to do, and delaying it could only make it harder. I took the plunge.

I had no clear idea what I was going to do once I was admitted to the bar. As I say, my age and part-time student status were not what the big boys were looking for. Opening my own office had few attractions. I needed the security of a reasonable salary. Then, one day in my final year of school, two attorneys from the Department of Justice appeared on campus to interview students who might be interested in a government career. Most of my classmates, if they were interested at all, were attracted to the Criminal Division with its promise of glamorous high-profile prosecutions. No one else took up the offer to talk about the Civil Division's work in the United States Claims Court. But it was a position the Department needed to fill urgently. I talked to one of the attorneys, Harry Welsh, for almost an hour. He asked me in detail about my experience in claims adjusting. For once, instead of being a drawback, my age and experience actually gave me an advantage, and I could hear the click as we talked. I was invited to Washington to interview formally the next month, and I was offered the job a week later. Maria was more than happy to move to Washington, and we were able to find a home we could afford, in a good school district in Bethesda. We were happy then, and we are happy now, and if the work is often routine, even boring, well, that's a sacrifice I am glad to make.

But that doesn't mean I wasn't very pleased when the file landed on my desk. It seemed like my reward for all those years of mind-numbing pensions and insurance cases.

13

WHEN I SAY THAT the case 'landed on my desk' I'm employing a figure of speech. It didn't so much land on my desk as get placed there with great care, and with an elaborate protocol. The morning began with a summons to drop whatever I was doing – not a problem, I'd only just arrived and I'd barely had the time to take the lid off my morning cappucino – and report to my former interviewer and now immediate supervisor, Harry Welsh, who is in charge of the Civil Division's litigation in the Claims Court. Harry is a good lawyer, a nice enough guy, and a decent manager. He leaves his attorneys alone to do their jobs unless something seems to be going wrong, and he doesn't usually try to micromanage cases once he has assigned them. But he can get stressed out sometimes, which is not good for his high blood pressure, and when he gets stressed out he starts trying to control everything, and when he realises he can't control everything he starts to panic. On this morning, he was already showing signs of nervousness. He was pacing up and down in his office when I put my head around the door.

'What's up?' I asked.

He pointed to a thin brown file on his conference table, and continued to pace.

'Read that,' he replied.

I sat down and opened the file. It contained a single document, and if Harry was watching, he must have seen my eyes open progressively wider as I read through it. It was a Complaint, a pleading used to start proceedings in the Claims Court. The case was entitled *Samantha van Eyck (individually and behalf of all those similarly situated) v United States*. The Complaint said that Samantha van Eyck was suing the United States to recover the principal sum and interest due on loans made to the government by an ancestor of hers called Jacob van Eyck during the War of Independence, in the winter of 1777–1778. The Continental Congress had authorised loans to be raised for the conduct of the war, and its agents were authorised to issue loan certificates as evidence of the amount of a loan and the identity of the lender. The loans were to be repaid with compound interest at the rate of six per cent per year – that got my attention – on presentation of the certificate to a government loan office. The United States had repaid nothing, as a result of which Jacob van Eyck had been ruined and had died in poverty. The causes of action against us were: breach of contract; and the unconstitutional taking of private property for public use without just compensation. The Complaint claimed repayment of the principal and interest, a declaration that the total sum was held by the government in trust for the heirs of Jacob van Eyck, costs, and attorney's fees. It concluded by reassuring the court that the sum satisfied its minimum jurisdictional requirement – in other words, the claim was for more than $10,000. No kidding.

I couldn't help it. I laughed out loud, and couldn't stop for a minute or so.

'I'm glad you find it humorous,' Harry said. He stopped pacing and sat down at his desk.

'This is for real?' I asked.

'Well, it's signed by an attorney, and that sure looks like the court clerk's stamp on it, so what do you think?'

The first time through, I had been so diverted by the content that I hadn't looked for the name of the attorney who had filed the suit. I looked now. Kiah Harmon?

'You know her, don't you?'

'Kiah? Sure. I've had several cases with her.'

'And…?'

'She's good news. She's a straight arrow, a good lawyer, a Georgetown grad. She's always been completely honest with me, and she's a nice lady.'

It was true. I breathed a sigh of relief whenever I saw I had Kiah as an opponent. It meant the case on the other side would be competently prepared, everything would be done ethically and by the book, we would have honest, realistic discussions to see if we could settle the case, and there would be no lawyers' games. You couldn't say that about many of the lawyers I had to deal with. Kiah and I had settled every case we had together except for one, in which we went to trial and she kicked my ass.

'So, we can assume it's for real, then, don't you think?'

'I guess so.'

Harry stood and started pacing again.

'Dave, this case may *seem* like a joke, and there will be a lot of people out there in the press and among the great American public, not to mention our superiors in this office, who will think it *is* a joke, and expect us to knock it on the head accordingly. But you and I know it doesn't quite work like that.'

'It's going to need careful handling,' I admitted, 'especially with Kiah on the other side.'

'Damn right. And you know what? It's the kind of case where, when we win, everyone will say, "well, sure, it was a joke; how could they not win?" But, if, God forbid, we were to lose… guess what they're going to be saying then?'

'That would not be good,' I agreed.

'Right. So you and I are going to handle this case together. Here's how it's going to work. You're my senior trial attorney. You're going to conduct the case on a day-to-day basis, file pleadings and motions, attend hearings – all the usual stuff. You and I are going to talk about this case every day without exception, at least once, and you are going to report to me everything that happens.'

'OK.'

'After you report to me, I am going to report to my boss Maggie Watts, who, as you know, is Assistant Attorney General in charge of the Civil Division. Maggie is going to report to the Attorney General; and the Attorney General is going to report to the President.'

'The President?' I exclaimed incredulously. 'The President is involved in this?'

'Dave,' Harry replied, 'Samantha van Eyck, whoever she may be, is trying to hijack some number of billions of dollars from the federal budget. How much exactly, I don't know. Have you ever done a compound interest calculation? Trust me, it's a large number. So, yes, the President is taking an interest.'

He resumed his seat.

'The resources of the office are at your disposal. Whatever and whoever you need – attorneys, paralegals – you come to me and ask and I will give them to you. I'm clearing out one of the storage rooms for you and putting in a couple of desks. All the case papers will be kept there under lock and key, and all work on the case will be done there. You and I will have keys, and I will issue keys to anyone else on a need-to-know basis.'

'A need-to-know basis?' I asked. 'Why all the cloak and dagger stuff? Everybody in the office will know what's going on.'

'I know that. But it's going to be all over the media from later today, and we don't want any leaks. What was it they used to say? Loose lips sink ships? What they don't know, they can't talk about. Oh, and while I'm on the subject, no one in this office talks to the media – no one, myself included. Maggie will control all communications, and she, or the Attorney himself, will handle press conferences. Understood?'

'Understood.'

'I want you to start on this right away. Whatever you're dealing with, drop it. I will reassign it as of this morning. By this afternoon, I need to give Maggie some kind of assessment, however general it may be.'

I shook my head.

'Harry, this isn't a routine insurance claim. There are going to be some legal questions, and God knows where we even begin with the facts of the case, and –'

'I know that, Dave. I'm not asking for the complete picture. I need to make some reassuring noises, that's all. I need to tell Maggie what areas we are exploring, what the basic issues are, what defenses we may have, and, most importantly, what steps we are planning on taking. Remember, whatever she reports higher up the chain is going to end up in the Oval Office. We have to make it look like we are doing something, taking action.'

'We *will* be taking action,' I tried to reassure him. 'For one thing, we have to respond to the Complaint, and tell the court how we answer all this. We can probably make a request for further details of the claim, buy some time if we need it. But… OK. Let me think about it, and I'll get back to you with a plan of action this afternoon.'

'Good.'

'I want Ellen Matthews to do legal research for me, and I want Pam as my paralegal.'

'Are you sure? Ellen is good, but she's just out of law school –'

'That's why I want her. She's exactly what this case needs. This is the moot court case from hell. It could have been written by a sadistic law professor. We need someone who still thinks the way they do in law school, and hasn't had her mind blunted by years of wading through the everyday realities of practice.'

For the first time, Harry allowed himself the suggestion of a smile.

'OK. You got it. Talk to me soon.'

14

I RETURNED TO MY office with the file, closed the door, sat down at my desk and swivelled my chair around so that I could look out of the window. I sat staring out at the city for some time.

Eventually, I turned my chair back around, read the Complaint again, and started an internet search for names. I started with Samantha van Eyck, and I learned that she was an actress. There were numerous photos of a good-looking young woman, several notices and play bills relating to productions in which she had appeared, and reviews of the same in provincial newspapers, all very favourable: 'one to watch'; 'up and coming'; 'deserves a chance to show off her range'; that kind of thing. I also found a bio giving her educational details; she was a graduate of the University of Virginia, majoring in theatre and performing arts, graduating cum laude; the bio also gave the name of her agent. I felt some sense of disappointment. What had I been expecting?

I suppose I was still clinging to some hope that this might be a joke, that she was a flake who couldn't be taken seriously. But there was nothing to suggest that the Samantha van Eyck I was reading about was a flake, or that she would have any reason to play a joke like this. In any case, she would never have talked Kiah Harmon into going along with it. If Kiah had even suspected that it was all some kind of hoax or publicity stunt, rather than a viable lawsuit, she would have shown Samantha van Eyck the door in a New York minute. There were some lawyers, attention-seekers or simply buffoons, who would file all kinds of ridiculous lawsuits without even thinking about the time and money they were wasting. I spent enough of my time getting their lawsuits dismissed to know that. But that wasn't Kiah Harmon.

Then I searched for Jacob van Eyck. There wasn't a lot. There was a Wikipedia entry that said little except that further information of a factual nature was needed to update the entry. That was something of an understatement. Beyond giving his dates of birth and death – 1730 and 1812 – there was almost nothing. The article noted that he was a Pennsylvania landowner and reputed friend of George Washington, and that he had sacrificed – interesting choice of word, I thought – all his worldly goods in the cause of the War of Independence, in return for which he had been spurned and ignored by an ungrateful nation. This had to be a contribution by some self-serving descendant who would be joining in the class action before long.

Other than that, there were a few old local newspaper articles. From time to time, it seemed, some family member or other would persuade a congressman to take some interest in the alleged loans, and naturally, the congressman concerned took advantage of the situation to create a photo op, allowing the local press to quote him on the subject of patriotism, self-sacrifice, and other American virtues, and how shameful the government's treatment of Jacob van Eyck was. It reads well, but you only have to be in Washington for five minutes to know that it is completely meaningless.

It is language crafted for the congressman by an experienced aide, and it is in code. It says to the powers that be: don't worry about it; I have to create a bit of a fuss to keep my constituent happy, but it's not going to come to anything. Once the photo op had come and gone, the congressman would return to Washington, assuring his constituent that he would do all in his power to right the wrong. If the constituent pressed, he would receive further assurances that the matter was in hand.

Eventually, either the constituent would give up, or he would be informed of the congressman's deep and most sincere regret that despite his best efforts, nothing could be done. There was one exception. In the mid-1960s a congressman from Georgia had actually proposed an amendment to the budget for the relief of the van Eyck family to the tune of $20,000. How he came up with that figure, which bore no resemblance to any figure mentioned by anyone else, heaven only knows. In any case, the amendment died in committee and was never resurrected.

In none of these sources did I find any reference to the actual existence or whereabouts of any loan certificate with the name of Jacob van Eyck on it. It was tempting to continue searching, but this afternoon I would have to give Harry a bit more than internet searches to put in the report that would eventually reach the Oval Office. There was research to be done and strategy formulated. As if by a sixth sense, Ellen made a timely entrance.

'Well, this is fun,' she said brightly.

She was clutching a copy of the Complaint, from which I deduced that Harry had already indoctrinated her about the protocol, and I'm sure it was quite a lecture. If so, it hadn't fazed her. Ellen Matthews was young and energetic and, as I had told Harry, exactly what I needed for this case. She had graduated high in her class from the University of Denver law school, and still thought enough like a student to get her head around problems like 200-year-old war loans. She looked young, too. She was dressed in the same austere dark suit all government lawyers wear, but somehow she looked too young for it. I couldn't quite work out why. Perhaps it was that she was still a bit full in the face, as if she hadn't outgrown it yet; or that her make-up was still experimental in some ways; or perhaps it was the way she moved with all her energy. But it still looked as though the suit should belong to an older sister.

'This is your idea of fun?' I asked, smiling. 'At your age? You need to get out more.'

She laughed. 'No, this is so off the wall; it's wild. It's the kind of problem law school professors give their students to drive them crazy, and make them wish they'd chosen psychology or anthropology instead of law.'

'My thought exactly. That's why I asked for you.'

'I guess I'll take that as a compliment. Harry said you know her attorney?'

'Yes. I know her quite well.'

'Well, good for her for taking the case. I don't think many lawyers would.'

'No, well, that's Kiah,' I said. 'And we're not going to underestimate her. She knows her stuff, and the one time I tried a case against her she handed me my head on a silver platter.'

She laughed again. 'I like this woman already. I can't wait to meet her.'

She took a seat in front of my desk.

'So, what can I do?'

'Well first,' I replied, 'I want you to look at the history of these war loans. I assume there must be quite a lot written about them. According to the Complaint, the Continental Congress laid down a procedure for issuing loan certificates and repaying the loans. So there must have been proceedings in Congress, reports from the loan commissioners, and so on. There have to be some records of what loans were made and how much was repaid. We are talking about a lot of money, and they must have been administering the loans long after the war ended.'

'There's a quicker way than tracking down the original records,' she suggested. 'Historians must have documented the work of the loan offices. It's an important part of the history of the war. The academics must have been all over it. There will be articles and books. That could save us a lot of time.'

'Good. Start there. But at some point we may need the original records. I am assuming that somewhere there is a collection of surviving loan certificates, paid or unpaid. We need to know where that collection is and how we can access it.'

'Presumably they would have been stored in the Department of the Treasury originally,' she suggested, 'but today they are probably in the National Archives, I would think.' She paused to write herself a note. 'But we can't assume anything. When did this guy van Eyck die?'

'In 1812,' I replied.

'Right. And what happened in 1814?'

I nodded. 'The Brits burned Washington.'

'Yes, including the Treasury, and we lost a lot of documents. Who knows what we still have from 1812? I'll check. What else?'

'That will keep you busy for now,' I said. 'I need you to check in with me every day and keep me up to date with where you are. I'm sure Harry told you that we will be reporting up the chain of command on a daily basis?'

'He did. We *are* reaching the dizzy heights, aren't we?'

'Yes,' I replied, 'and we'd better be ready for them. I'm going to make a start on the law, and try to figure out some kind of strategy for handling the case, starting with filing our initial paperwork. Any suggestions welcome.'

She looked at me for a moment with that bright law student look of hers.

'Well, only one thing has come to mind so far. It's so obvious, I almost hate to mention it.'

I stared back at her. I had a feeling I was about to feel stupid, but for the life of me, I couldn't make my mind click into the right gear. She hesitated.

'I'm not trying to be cute, Dave. I'm sure you and Harry have already talked about it.'

'Humour me,' I said.

'OK. If these loans were made, they were made well over 200 years ago, yes?'

'Yes.'

'What's the limitations period in the Claims Court?'
I sighed.
'Six years,' I replied helplessly.

15

Kiah Harmon

I HAVE TO BE honest, and I know it makes me sound like a terrible snob – or worse, a complete sceptic – but when Sam told me that the van Eyck family reunion was to be held in New Orleans, the first picture that came into my mind was a motel somewhere on the way to Lafayette. I couldn't have been more wrong. The venue turned out to be no less than the Intercontinental Hotel, from where the French Quarter was just a short stroll across Canal Street. The van Eyck family obviously did things in style.

Someone had negotiated group rates for the rooms, and the hotel had put a sizeable conference room at the family's disposal for a plenary business meeting on the first morning. As she had promised, Sam had been in contact with the group we were calling the cheerleaders, and had arranged for us to be on the agenda for the meeting. What our reception was likely to be she couldn't predict, but at least we would get a hearing. The cheerleaders knew that the lawsuit had been filed; the news had been spreading like a bush fire via emails and social media. There had already been a few calls and emails to the office from family members who couldn't attend the reunion but were interested in what we were doing. There was a definite buzz in the air. One or two local radio stations had picked it up, and Sam and I had fitted in a couple of quick phone interviews before we left Arlington.

Sam had arrived in New Orleans on the Thursday, two days before the start of the reunion, and I followed with Arlene and Powalski on the following afternoon. As Arlene had predicted, Powalski had jumped at the chance to work with us. Like me, he found the case irresistible, and I had the impression that being on the opposite side to the government also had its attractions for him. We had worked out a flexible agreement. He would work as and when needed, and would give me an estimate of the time he thought he would need for any particular assignment. Very generously, he had offered to donate his time in New Orleans during the reunion, to get things off to a good start.

Sam met us in the lobby within two minutes of our climbing out of the taxi we had taken from the airport. She helped us check in and took us up to our rooms. The family's block of rooms were on the eighth and ninth floors, but Sam had talked the hotel into giving us a suite with two bedrooms on the tenth floor for Arlene, me and herself. It worked out cheaper for us than having our own rooms and the suite also had a good-sized living room where we could work and organise the paperwork we had brought with us. Sam and I agreed to share one bedroom, which had twin beds, leaving the other with the queen-size for Arlene. Powalski had the room next door. As we unpacked, Sam told us that there was work to do that evening.

'The cheerleaders have an organising committee,' she explained. 'The committee is in charge of planning everything that goes on during the reunion, including the business meeting tomorrow morning. I had a cup of coffee with them this morning, to introduce myself. They would like to meet with you this evening.'

'We're already on the agenda for the meeting, aren't we?' I asked.

'Yes, we are. But the committee wants to hear about the lawsuit from the horse's mouth before tomorrow. It's probably just because they are the committee, and they want to feel important. But it could make a difference. If we can get them onside, I think it will make it a lot easier for us at the business meeting.'

'OK,' I said. 'I have no problem with that. Did you arrange a time?'

Sam reached into the large handbag she was carrying.

'Yes, six fifteen in the bar. I have copies of the program for you. The only event this evening is a welcoming cocktail reception at seven o'clock. After that, everybody goes their separate ways for dinner. So they are setting aside forty-five minutes for us before the reception.'

'That should be enough,' I said. 'What's happening the rest of the weekend?'

'The plenary business meeting is at ten o'clock tomorrow morning, Saturday. The afternoon is for people to get together in groups and catch up. Tomorrow evening, reception and sit-down dinner for everyone, seven for seven thirty. Sunday morning in groups, catching up again, then a closing lunch at noon, after which everyone goes back home.'

'Do we know how many folks are attending?' Arlene asked.

Sam fiddled in her handbag again.

'Eighty-two. I have a list with names and email addresses.'

Arlene smiled. 'Way to go, girl. That's a pretty good number, don't you think, y'all?'

I did. Of course, it was a small fraction of the number of potential plaintiffs, but these were the activists. If we could get them excited about the case, they would bring the others out of the woodwork. The list showed that they were widely spread across the country. We had fifteen states represented, including eight family members in the DC area, which was the first thing I looked for. Not a bad start at all.

'Powalski and I have to try to talk to as many of them as possible during their unsupervised play periods tomorrow afternoon and Sunday morning,' Arlene was saying. 'Any reason we couldn't just set up in the lobby?'

'I think that's the best way,' I replied. 'Everybody has to pass through the lobby. If you are hiding away in a room, they have to come and find you. In the lobby, *you* can find *them*.'

'We need to talk to them to give them more information?' Sam asked.

'That, and to get information *from* them,' Arlene said. 'Leastways, that's Powalski's job. Mine is to sign as many of them up as I can, and extort money from them. I'll have my laptop, so they can sign up to be plaintiffs right there and then. If they won't do it right away, there's a form they can download from the website, or they can get one from me and send it in the old-fashioned way, by mail. One way or the other, I'll get them.'

Sam laughed. 'I bet you will, too.'

'You can count on it, hun.'

'Who are the committee members?' I asked.

'We are meeting with three this evening,' Sam replied. 'I think there may be a couple of others, but they're not getting in until later tonight. There's Joe Kenney, retired stockbroker, now lives in West Palm Beach, Florida. He and my dad knew each other, so we should be OK with him. Then there's Jeff Carlsen. He's mid-thirties to forty-something, I would guess. He's from Salt Lake City, and guess what, Kiah, he's a lawyer.'

'No kidding. What kind of law?'

'I'm not sure, but he did say he was with a law firm there. And, last but not least, there is the legendary Aunt Meg.'

'Aunt Meg?' Arlene said. 'Sounds like someone I knew back in Lubbock, one of them gypsy fortune tellers.'

'No, Arlene. Quite the contrary. Aunt Meg is the most important person you are likely to meet this weekend. Her full name is Megan Sylvia van Eyck. She's lived her whole life in Montgomery County, Pennsylvania – the van Eyck family heartland – and she is what you might call the matriarch of the family. Nobody knows how old she really is. She admits to eighty-five. Most people think ninety-plus would be nearer the mark. But she's got all her wits about her, and she still gets around. She never misses one of these reunions. She knew my dad too.' She smiled. 'He had all kinds of stories about her. She never married, but she certainly seems to have led a colourful life.'

'She sounds like the kind of character who would have a lot of pull with the family,' I said.

'If we can get on the right side of Aunt Meg,' Sam replied, 'she will bring the family with her – at least, everyone who matters.'

16

FOR A FRIDAY EVENING the bar was not too crowded, and to my relief we were able to find a quiet enough corner with an unoccupied table and chairs. Sam and I were wearing demure dark cocktail dresses for the occasion. Arlene had chosen a dark blue two-piece suit. Powalski was immaculate in a conservative grey suit and blue tie. Altogether, I thought we made an impressive group. Sam introduced us to the three committee members. Joe Kenney, in a black leather jacket and open-necked shirt, gave her a quick kiss on both cheeks.

'I was sure sorry to hear about your dad, Sam,' he said. 'He was a good guy. Always had a good word for everybody. I always enjoyed meeting him.'

'Thank you, Joe,' Sam replied.

'I'm pleased to meet you,' Jeff Carlsen said to me, extending his hand. He had fair hair and blue eyes, and wore a casual beige suit with a tie with red and green stripes. 'I've been hearing all about you, and it's good to put a face to the name.'

'Pleased to meet you too,' I replied, taking his hand. 'Sam says you practice in Salt Lake?'

'Sure do. Insurance defense and general commercial litigation.' He grinned. 'Nothing as exciting as you folks in the DC area get up to.'

I laughed. 'It's not as exciting as it's cracked up to be.'

Sam took my hand and walked me over to Aunt Meg, who was

sitting in the corner chair. She was wearing a long black dress, her grey hair firmly pinned up in a bun. She wore no jewelry except for a small mourning brooch pinned high on her chest on the left side. I extended my hand. Aunt Meg did not respond immediately, and I had the impression that she was eyeing me rather suspiciously.

'So, you're the lawyer who wants to represent the family?' she said eventually, giving my hand the briefest of shakes.

'Yes, ma'am.'

She shook her head. 'You don't have to call me ma'am. Everybody calls me Aunt Meg. I've been around too long to stand on ceremony. Joe, get these folks some drinks.'

'Right away, Aunt Meg,' Joe replied, and disappeared in the direction of the bar. Powalski went with him.

Aunt Meg waved me into the seat next to her. Sam and Arlene sat on either side of us.

'Miss Harmon, there's no point in beating about the bush. Do you agree?'

'Absolutely.'

'Good. What I want to know is: do we have any hope of getting anything from this lawsuit of yours?'

'Well –'

'Let me tell you why I want to know. Lord knows, it's not to do with the money. The van Eyck family has been trying to get these loans repaid ever since Jacob died, and I think we've long since given up any hope of getting rich off of it. And it's not like we haven't tried. Most of these folks are too young to remember, but a few years back we were all trying to stir things up, writing letters to our congressmen and what have you. Much good it ever did us. Just got us all riled up, and for what? For nothing. They promised us the world as long as we would remember to vote for them again, come the election, but when it came right down to it, they didn't do a damn thing, and that's the truth.'

Joe and Powalski returned from the bar, and joined us at the table.

'The waiter will be right over,' Joe said.

'We were all brought up on the story of Jacob and his loans as children,' Aunt Meg continued, 'but when I went to school, and they taught us about the War of Independence, the teachers never mentioned Jacob. For the life of me, I couldn't understand why. I kept waiting for them to tell us about him, but they never did. When I finally asked my teacher why not, she had no idea what I was talking about. So then, I had to go home and ask my parents, and they explained that there was no actual proof of the story. And I was left feeling rather foolish, to tell you the truth.'

'It's kind of like finding out about Santa Claus,' Joe said, smiling. 'It's something every child has to go through. This is our family's version of Santa Claus.'

'It's a story about buried treasure,' Aunt Meg said. 'Of course, when you're a child you love stories about buried treasure. And even after you grow up there's part of you that believes the treasure is there and that you could find it, all those pieces of eight and priceless jewels, if you only had a map and knew where to dig. That's what this is, if you want my opinion. It's a story about buried treasure. It's about as real as Blackbeard's gold. You can dig for it all you want, but you're not going to find it.'

'You don't think Jacob made his loans, Aunt Meg?' Joe asked. Oddly, after what he had said, he sounded surprised.

'Who knows? Maybe he did, and maybe he didn't. I guess there must be something in the story, if they've been telling it ever since he passed. Maybe Jacob loaned George Washington thousands of dollars, or maybe he just took him for a good lunch. Who knows? I'm eighty-five, and I've never met anyone who thinks he can prove what happened, one way or the other. And without proof, the government isn't going to pay us a red cent. So all we do is get ourselves riled up for nothing. I think it might be better to let it go and stop driving ourselves crazy with it.'

'Aunt Meg,' I replied, 'let me be honest with you. I can't guarantee the result will be any different with this lawsuit than it was with the congressmen. But I can guarantee you that we will do something the congressmen never did, as far as I can see. We will try. A lawsuit is the one thing that's never been tried, and it's something the government can't ignore. They have to respond to it. If there is any proof out there, we will find it. If not, then... well, at least the family will know, and maybe then they can put it behind them, as you say, and not drive themselves crazy any more. At least we will put it to rest, one way or another.'

The waiter approached with our drinks on a huge tray. Red wine for Sam and me; gin and tonic with ice and lemon for Aunt Meg; a Corona for Arlene with a twist of lime in the neck of the bottle, and no glass; Bud Lights for Joe and Jeff, with glasses; Jack Daniels over ice for Powalski – I never saw him drink anything else. A huge carafe of water for all of us. We toasted Jacob; it was a family tradition, I was told.

'I hope you won't be offended if I ask you this, Miss Harmon,' Aunt Meg said. 'But how long have you been out of law school?'

'Five years, going on six,' I replied.

She nodded, and turned to Jeff.

'Mr Carlsen, I believe you have read the lawsuit that's been filed?'

'I have, Aunt Meg, yes.'

'What is your opinion?'

Jeff seemed taken aback to be asked so directly.

'Well, Aunt Meg, you have to understand that I'm no expert in that particular court. To my untutored eye, the pleading reads well, and it's a bold step. And as Kiah says, nothing like this has been tried before, and it will mean that the government has to give us an answer of some kind. I guess the only reservation I have is that, like you said, no one really knows what happened back then at Valley Forge, and unless we suddenly come up with some kind of proof that no one has been able to find during all those years, we could waste a lot of time and money and still be back where we were before.'

Aunt Meg turned back towards me.

'I agree,' I said. 'As I said before, there are no guarantees here, but I still think this will bring some closure, because at least the case will be properly investigated, and if there's nothing in it, then at least you will know. I have a feeling there is something in it, but we won't know until we do some digging.'

'Why would you feel that way?'

I thought about it for a moment. That was one question I couldn't answer entirely frankly. That would have involved me talking about Arya, and about my dreams, and I wasn't ready to do that.

'I'm not sure. Part of it is that when you have such a long, unbroken family tradition – in this case, going back more than two hundred years – there has to be something in it. Families have all kinds of stories, but you don't come across such a long consistent narrative very often. Even the courts accept family tradition. It can be used as evidence in some cases. So, I think it's worth a shot. As for the waste of time and money, that's mainly my problem. I won't receive a fee unless we prevail. I think it's worthwhile.'

I looked around the table at everyone in turn.

'I mean, just imagine if we *were* able to prove our case, and the government *had* to talk to us about commemorating Jacob. Just think about that; just imagine it for a moment. Wouldn't that be something?'

No one spoke for a while.

Joe smiled. 'It sure would.'

I turned back to Aunt Meg. 'I can understand your concern that I haven't been practicing law all that long, but...'

To my surprise, Aunt Meg actually laughed, and reached out a hand to touch my shoulder.

'Oh, no my dear, quite the reverse, I assure you. Only a young person could take on something like this. In later life, we all become far too cynical. If you'd said twenty years, I would have dismissed you as a speculator, if not a confidence trickster. No, if anyone can do this, it has to be someone who hasn't yet become disillusioned with the world; someone who still has her ideals intact; someone who doesn't shy away from trying something just because it seems impossible.'

17

I HAVE NO IDEA where I am. Outside, somewhere. There is a church and a graveyard. The place seems desolate, neglected, overgrown. A young woman is standing silently in the middle of the graveyard, looking down at the ground. She is dressed in black. She has her back to me, so I can't see her face, but I feel sure it is Isabel. The graveyard is enclosed by a grey stone wall, some four feet in height, I estimate, which once would have been covered by climbing plants. In one place on the wall, opposite to where I stand at the side of the church, a single branch is clinging to life, a single red rose, withered and dying, hanging forlornly down from it.

There is something odd about the graveyard, and I am trying to fathom what it is. As I turn to go, it comes to me. There are no headstones, nothing to tell me who may be buried here, when they were born and when they died, whether they had spouses or children, whether anyone left any epitaph for them. Nothing. There is something else, too. I am not in a city now, I feel sure. I am in the countryside. Yet I think I hear a sound, a roar of some kind, not loud but steady, and I have a sense of some tall structure behind me. I think perhaps an aqueduct with a great mass of water flowing along it, but I cannot turn my head to see.

With this, the dreams come to an end for now. But so, too, do the nightmares.

18

When I woke up, Sam was standing over with me with a cup of coffee. She was fully dressed.

'Time to rise and shine,' she said. 'I brought this for you. White, no sugar, yes?'

I sat up abruptly, rubbing my eyes.

'Yes, thanks. What time is it?'

'Relax,' she replied. 'It's just after seven thirty. You have plenty of time.'

'I'm sorry. I was sound asleep.'

'I know. You looked like you needed to be sound asleep for a while, so I didn't wake you. Arlene and I got up early because we had stuff to do, but there was no reason to disturb you.'

'What stuff?'

'We wanted to be sure we had enough copies of the Complaint and the forms for signing up as a plaintiff. We want to be able to hand them out as people are coming in. We are also handing out your card, and Powalski's, so they have no excuse for not knowing how to contact us.'

'OK,' I said, 'I'll jump in the shower and get moving.'

I began to sit up, but she pushed me very gently back down.

'Drink your coffee first. It's all under control. Just get yourself ready to wow the van Eyck family. That's your only job for today. Leave the rest to us.'

Arlene and Powalski had set up trestle tables at the entrance to the conference room, and were welcoming the family members as they arrived, and handing out the paperwork. Sam was also standing at the back of the room, introducing herself to the family members as they made their way to their seats. The committee had reserved places for Sam and me at the top table, which was perched on a low platform, with Joe Kenney and Jeff Carlsen. The two committee members who had got in late the previous night were also to sit at the top table: Susan van Eyck Poulson from Boulder, Colorado; and Edwin van Eyck from Los Angeles, another attorney – and in his case, a sole practitioner, a trial lawyer who did personal injury and fatal accident cases. It was pretty obvious that Jeff had already briefed them about our meeting the evening before, but they weren't giving away any clues about what they thought about it all.

It was while I was watching the family streaming in, with their coffees and bottles of water and guides to New Orleans in hand, that I knew how right I had been to file the lawsuit before coming to the reunion. I had knowingly given a hostage to fortune by filing before we had even begun to collect evidence, but, as I had hoped, I had their attention. We were going to be very close to one hundred per cent attendance, which I suspected might be a new record for a business meeting at a van Eyck family reunion. As I took my seat, I saw Aunt Meg sitting in the very centre of the front row, resplendent in a mauve blouse and long grey skirt.

When everyone was in place, and the waiters had refreshed the supplies of coffee and iced water at the back of the room, Joe Kenney rose to his feet. There was a microphone. It was a close call whether it was needed in a room of that size, but if it was a close call it was probably a good idea. I decided I would use it. It seems to be a rule that, when people who are not used to microphones are confronted with them, there is always an outbreak of feedback. Today was to be no exception. Joe got far too close to it, and then for some reason, tried to remove it from its stand. It was pretty loud and jarring, and Aunt Meg had a finger firmly in each ear.

But a waiter came and whispered in his ear, and calmed things down. After that, Joe stood back a bit and left the microphone alone, and all was well.

'Ladies and gentlemen, it is my pleasure to welcome you to the city of New Orleans for this reunion of the van Eyck family. I know you are all going to have a fine time, seeing people you probably haven't seen for quite a while, and catching up with the latest news. I've already seen a few people myself that I haven't seen in… must be five or six years at least. And I hope you will all feel that the program allows you enough time to talk and catch up, as well as giving you time enough to enjoy New Orleans. I am told – I can't verify this from personal experience – but I am told that there are a few acceptable restaurants and other places of entertainment in the city.'

He paused for a ripple of laughter.

'Laissez les bons temps rouler!' someone shouted from the back.

'Yes, indeed – whatever that may mean. Now, I want to keep this part of business meeting as short as possible, because as you all know, we have one particular item of business to deal with that's causing some excitement. But before we get to that, as we always do, I do need to share with you the names of those members of the family who have passed since we last met.'

This put a bit of a dampener on things for a few minutes, as Joe read out a litany of the departed, and invited a moment or two of silent reflection. The list included Sam's father, and she bowed her head as his name was read. I touched her briefly on the back of the hand. She looked up at me and smiled, quickly brushing away a tear. Mercifully, the moment or two of reflection did not last too long, and people sat up in their seats as Joe announced that he was now handing the meeting over to Sam.

Sam and I had both decided on business suits for today. Mine was the lawyer's traditional black. If I had harboured any doubt about that choice, it had evaporated when I met Aunt Meg the previous evening. Sam, however, had settled on a bright yellow suit with an orange scarf and shoes. She looked spectacular. But it was what happened next that stopped me in my tracks. I suppose I shouldn't have been surprised. She's an actress, and she was on stage now; she was in her element, and it looked effortless. But still, it was the closest thing to magic I had ever seen. The atmosphere in the room changed in an instant.

19

HOW SHE DID IT, what were the mechanics, if that's even the right word, I can't begin to say. For what seemed like a long time, she simply stood in place silently and I watched her hold her audience without saying a word, by the sheer force of her presence. She drew every eye in the house to her, mine included, and the room fell utterly silent. I know it's a cliché, but truly, you could have heard a pin drop. Even when she must have known that she had complete control of the room, she was in no hurry. She waited until she was ready, and when she was ready, she smiled and began to speak. They listened, spellbound. As did I.

'Good morning, everyone. My name is Samantha van Eyck, but I hope you will all call me Sam; everyone does. Most of you knew my dad, Gerry. Joe read out his name just now, because, sadly, he passed a few months ago. If you knew my dad, you know that he was a regular at these reunions. As far as I recall, he never missed one. He looked forward to them. He looked forward to them because it meant a lot to him to be a member of this family, and because he valued his friendship with you. He wanted to be here with us today. If he could have been here, he would; and he would have told you, more eloquently than I ever could, how much it means to him that we have begun the fight to have Jacob recognised as the hero he was.'

She paused.

'Like most of you, I was brought up on the story of Jacob van

Eyck and the loans he made to keep George Washington's army supplied long enough to defeat the British. I learned about Jacob from my dad before I could read or write, and I have never forgotten the story. My dad laid it on pretty thick. To hear the story from him, you would think Jacob saved the War of Independence from failure pretty much single-handedly, kind of like Superman swooping down to save the day. Well, OK, when I grew up, of course I figured out that it wasn't quite like that, that Jacob didn't rescue America all on his own. Apparently, there were a few other people involved, not to mention our French allies, so OK, maybe my dad gilded the lily just a little bit.'

She waited for a ripple of affectionate laughter to die away.

'But if he talked the story up, he talked it up out of love and pride. And he was right about one thing. Maybe Jacob's loans didn't win the war by themselves, but they played a big part in winning the war. They set Washington free to win.'

Applause.

'And in my dad's eyes, that made Jacob an American hero.'

More applause, louder and longer. She stopped and once again held the audience in silence for a while.

'The great heroes of that early time in our history – George Washington, Paul Revere and our founding fathers, they all have their memorials, don't they? If you go to Boston, Philadelphia, Washington, there they are for all to see. But you can travel the length and breadth of this country and, search wherever you will, you will find no monument to Jacob van Eyck; not a statue, not a portrait, not a plaque on a wall; nothing.

'My dad believed that wasn't right, and he wanted to put it right. Now, I know the family has made efforts in the past. Some of you here today have been involved in those efforts,' she looked down at Aunt Meg and held her gaze for a while, 'and I know you must be discouraged that those efforts didn't meet with more success. But what's important is that you tried. The fact that you tried must mean that you agree with my dad. You believe, as he did, that the government must do something to recognise Jacob's place in American history.'

Applause again.

'That's why I am here speaking to you today. I'm here because my dad asked me to continue the fight, and I'm asking you to join me in making one more effort. I'm not asking you to go back over the same ground. In the past, we relied on politicians. We tried that, and it didn't work. They ignored us. It's not the kind of thing politicians will go out on a limb for. So my dad believed that we needed to do something they can't ignore. I believe that too. If we can bring the government before a court, they can't ignore us any more. I'm not saying we're bound to win; I can't promise you that. But at least they can't ignore us. And at least, this way, when we look back and tell our children and grandchildren about Jacob, we can say we tried everything there was to try.'

She was silent again. Suddenly, I envied Sam for having no fear of silence; for her embrace of silence as a source of strength, not a sign of weakness. I saw myself in the courtroom: dreading silence; doing my best to talk non-stop; constantly filling the void with sound; experiencing the way the fear of silence stretches time, so that every second feels like a minute; desperate never to allow silence to descend as long as I had power to stop it. And I saw myself in conversations with Jordan when I had felt the same fear. Why? I had never asked myself that. What was I afraid of?

A man in the third row back, to my left, raised a hand. Sam smiled and pointed to him.

'I'm Ben Stevens from Atlanta, Georgia. Sam, when you talk about making the government do something for Jacob, it seems to me you're preaching to the choir. We all want to see that. But the problem is, we've been let down so often in the past, it's hard to believe it could be any different now. It seems the government doesn't give a damn. We need to know why you think it might be different this time. We're going to need to know a lot more about this lawsuit. How much chance do we have of winning?

How does it all work? And how much is it going to cost?'

There were many heads nodding in agreement, and murmurs of assent all through the room.

'I know, Ben. And for that, I'm going to hand over to the expert, someone who knows far more about it than I do, our attorney, Kiah Harmon.'

20

I WOULD HAVE LOVED to flirt with silence, to see if some of Sam's presence was still out there, hanging in the air, to see if I could harness it for myself. But this wasn't the moment to indulge myself. The stakes were too high. Unlike Sam, I had no right to speak to this audience. I wasn't a member of the family. I had no personal interest in what bound them together. I was here on sufferance, and that sufferance would wear thin unless I could justify my existence to them. I had to stick with what I knew for now.

'Let me cover the basics,' I began as soon as Sam had introduced me, 'and then I will answer any questions you have, for as long as I need to.

'First, why a lawsuit? As Sam said, it's the only way to make the government listen and make them at least address our concerns. Now that we've filed, they have to give us a written response, and if they're not prepared to agree to what we want, they have to explain why. In addition, the court can order the government to search their records for any evidence in their possession that proves that Jacob made the loans and was never repaid.

'So I have filed suit in the United States Claims Court in Washington DC, which is a court the government set up in the nineteenth century so that citizens could sue the government to recover money they are owed. I have filed the suit as a class action. All that means is that anyone who can prove that he or she is a descendant of Jacob van Eyck is entitled to join in the action as a plaintiff.'

I had expected to get through the basics before the inevitable interrogation began, but that wasn't the way it was to be. The interruptions began almost straight away. Sam shot me an anxious glance. But it was OK. I didn't mind interruptions at all. I might be afraid of silence, but questions and argument hold no terror for me. They are my bread and butter. I'd had enough experience of arguing before appellate courts to know that questions are a good sign. That's rather counter-intuitive, I admit. To most people it might not seem encouraging that the three judges begin bombarding you with questions as soon as you have told them your name and who you represent; that they tear up the neat plans you had laid so carefully to present your arguments in logical order; that they eat into your time to such an extent that you think you may never get to present your arguments at all before the clerk flashes the red light. But to me, that is a sign that the appeal is going well, and it has always made me relax in the courtroom.

As long as the judges are asking questions, you know they have read your written brief; you know they haven't made up their minds yet; and you know you are still in with a chance. Their questions give away what they are thinking; you can see the way their minds are going, what problems they see with your case; and you have a chance to answer them. It's not the judges who pepper you with questions that scare me; it's the judges who sit there without saying a word, who don't give you the first clue about what they are thinking, or even whether they are thinking at all. Those are the ones who scare me.

It was Ben Stevens again.

'Miss Harmon, what makes you think you can win this case?'

'Good question,' I replied. 'In all honesty, I don't know whether we can win or not. The only thing I know is that we can't win without evidence. That means that we have to find one or more loan certificates with Jacob van Eyck's name on them. We can ask for the court's help in ordering the government to produce what they have, but we are going to have to look for ourselves too.

'One reason we're here today is to find out everything the family knows about Jacob's loan certificates. Mr Powalski is going to be here this afternoon and tomorrow in the lobby, and I want everyone to talk to him. If you have some document or photograph at home that you could lend us; if you heard something from a grandfather or an uncle; even if it's some story you heard, and you're not even sure whether you believe it. Some detail that may seem unimportant may connect with a detail someone else has. So don't be afraid to come forward and tell us whatever you know. We need all the help we can get. That's the only way we can win.'

Terri Ayles from St Louis.

'I read in the newspaper that you're expecting to get some crazy amount – more than $600 billion dollars – from the government. I don't believe they even have that kind of money. How are you ever going to get them to pay that much?'

There was some laughter around the room. I joined in.

'I wish. No. Look, that's just a number you come up with if you do the compound interest calculation. There's no way the country could afford to pay that amount, and there's no way I'm going to ask them to. We're going to ask for a financial settlement, but I know Sam's main goal is to make the government do something to recognise Jacob. If we can lay our hands on some evidence, I am confident that they will talk to us, negotiate with us.'

'Who gets to decide how much we accept?' Terri asked.

'You do. Anyone who becomes a plaintiff has a say in what we accept. It's not up to me. I will advise you about what I think is reasonable, but you have the last word.'

'How do we get to be a plaintiff?'

'It's simple. You need to prove you are one of Jacob's descendants. You can do that online. Arlene will show you how. You need to do a search and send the results to our website, and we will register you as a plaintiff. You don't need to do a separate search for your children. If you are a descendant, so are they. Just make sure you list all your children on the website.'

'Arlene said there was a fee of fifty dollars to register?' Jack Simmons from Albuquerque asked.

'That's correct. Please understand that we will have significant expenses in investigating and following through with the case. The Department of Justice will represent the government and believe me, they are well-funded and efficient. They're not about to roll over. We need a war chest.

'What I can promise you is that we will not waste money. We are a lean machine. Apart from student interns, our entire team is here this weekend. I'm going to ask for help from any family members who are lawyers and are willing to help. But apart from that, if you ask me what kind of team we have to work on this, you're looking at us. If you're going to be part of this case, you're going to have to help us, and I can't promise you that fifty dollars will be enough. What I can promise you is that we will use it wisely, and I will also promise you that if I come to believe that the case is hopeless, I will advise you of that before we incur any further expenditure.'

'Mary Jane Perrins from Boston, Massachusetts. What's in this for you, Miss Harmon?'

I'd been expecting that one, of course. But when it eventually came, it was disquieting. It wasn't the question itself as much as the way it was asked, with more than a trace of suspicion, perhaps even hostility. The woman who asked it was a plain forty-something dressed in a Celtics T-shirt and blue jeans, all of it too tight, and she had sat through the entire meeting with her arms folded firmly across her chest. Mary Jane Perrins sounded like a woman with a chip on her shoulder. Why, I had no way of knowing, but there was no mistaking it.

'Like all lawyers,' I replied, 'I work for a fee. In a case like this, the only realistic way is a contingency fee agreement, which means that I will take a percentage of any recovery. I have a standard fee agreement, which is in the form approved by the courts in Virginia, where I practice. You can find it on my website. Sam has signed it, and I will need anyone who registers as a plaintiff to sign it also. Please be assured that the more I recover for you, the smaller percentage I will take. Everything will be above board and transparent, and I will answer any questions you have as we go along.'

There was some murmuring around the room as the family started to imagine what a percentage of $600 billion would look like. Sam and I exchanged glances. For a moment or two, the atmosphere had changed, and Mary Jane Perrins was smiling like a woman who had made her point. But she hadn't quite finished.

'Why can't we have our own lawyers?' she asked.

'Each one of you is entitled to consult your own attorney,' I replied, 'and if you feel you need to check out what I've been telling you, please feel free to get a second opinion. But bear in mind that attorneys cost money, which we could be spending on the case.'

'But why should *you* be handling the case?' Mary Jane wanted to know.

'Because Sam is the first plaintiff to file, and I am her attorney,' I replied as calmly as I could. 'Please understand that the court is not going to permit multiple lawsuits. That's the whole idea of a class action – that we don't have a series of cases about the same thing that drag on forever. I hope all of you can see that it would serve no good purpose at all to fight among ourselves. All that would do would make the government's job a lot easier.'

I was glad to see that most people in the audience were nodding in agreement, but I had the impression that Mary Jane was far from satisfied. Whether she would have spoken again, I don't know. But at that precise moment, I saw Aunt Meg stand, slowly and majestically, and make her way forward towards the top table. That simple action reduced the whole room to silence. Sam walked over to meet her, and helped her negotiate the steps up to the platform. From the steps, Aunt Meg found her own way to the microphone.

'You all know me,' she began, 'so I'm not going to waste my time introducing myself, and suchlike.'

There was some affectionate laughter.

'And you all know me well enough to know that when I have something to say, I get on and say it. And I have something to say now.'

She paused for effect, and it worked.

'I'm eighty-five years old, and nobody can prove different.'

More laughter.

'And for all those eighty-five years, I've been hearing about Jacob, and about the loans he made, and about how he saved the War of Independence, and about how the government doesn't give a damn about it. And I was one of those who turned to congressmen for help in the past, and got nowhere. And that's when I learned for myself that the government doesn't give a damn. And, you know what? I'm sick to death of it.

'I've been coming to these reunions since I was knee-high to a daisy, and all I've ever heard is talk, talk, talk, complain, complain, complain. "It's not fair. It's not right. Something should be done about it." And you know what? In all that time, I've learned that this family is pretty damn good at complaining.'

'You got that right, Aunt Meg,' a male voice from somewhere said.

'But we don't seem to be too good at doing something to help ourselves. What have we ever done, except ask a few politicians politely whether they could find time to help us, and then give up when they didn't follow through?'

'Not a damn thing,' the same male voice responded, even though I'm pretty sure Aunt Meg had intended her question to be rhetorical.

'That's right,' she continued. 'But today, we are being offered a chance to do something, and I think that we ought to be grateful to Sam and to Miss Harmon for starting this off, and for coming here to tell us about it and giving us all the chance to join in and help. There's no way to tell whether we can win this thing. But, win or lose, at least we may eventually learn the truth. There are only two ways this can go. Either we win, and America finally honours Jacob van Eyck as it should; or we lose, and we finally know that all the stories we heard are just so much hogwash, or at least no one can prove otherwise.'

She paused again.

'Actually,' she said, 'I think we win both ways. Even if we lose the case, at least we can stop obsessing about this, and we can stop boring each other to death with it every time we have a reunion. Maybe we can finally get a life.'

This produced some applause and cheers across the room, though not from Mary Jane Perrins.

'So,' Aunt Meg, concluded, 'what I want to say to this family this morning is: the time has come to either put up or shut up.'

More applause and cheers.

'I say thank you, Sam, and thank you, Miss Harmon, and now I'm going to put my money where my mouth is. I'm going to talk to Miss Arlene, and pay my fifty dollars and get myself signed up for this thing, and I hope you will all join me. And then, I'm going to talk to Mr Powalski until he can't stand to listen to me any more, and I'm going to tell him everything I know. And I hope you will all join me in doing that, too.'

21

AT THE END OF a long afternoon, we left the lobby together, rode the elevator to the tenth floor, and gathered in our suite, where we collapsed into chairs and on to the sofa. Sam and I kicked off our shoes in grateful unison. For some time, we were all silent, sipping the Cokes and coffees we had brought up with us.

'Well, I thought that went pretty well,' I ventured tentatively. I wasn't sure I entirely believed that. I had talked to so many people over the past few hours, trying so hard to sound positive to them all, that my head was spinning and my smile felt as though it was hard-wired in place on my face. I could easily have sat where I was without saying another word for the rest of the day. But we were all tired, and some encouragement was needed.

'Thanks to Aunt Meg,' Sam replied. 'Wasn't she great?'

'She's something,' Arlene said, 'that's for sure, and she sure did get them energised. But y'all did great, too. Ain't that right, Powalski?'

'Absolutely,' he replied. 'I heard some great comments about you both. They liked you, and they liked what you had to say. You walked them up to the gangplank, and Aunt Meg made sure they came on board.'

'Which is just where we need them,' Arlene said.

She swigged her Diet Coke. She had made a quick diversion to the bar as we were winding up in the lobby, and I wouldn't have put money on her drink being entirely unadulterated. But what the hell. She deserved it, and we were in New Orleans after all. And it was nice of her, and of Powalski, to say what they did, even if they felt as unsure as I did.

I smiled. 'OK, but what do we have to show for it? How many do we actually have on board?'

There was no immediate reply.

'Arlene?'

Arlene retrieved her briefcase, which she had thrown down beside her chair, reached into it, and extracted a file folder. She opened the folder and took her time thumbing through a pile of paper. Finally, her pencil moved up and down a list of some kind, indicating some mental arithmetic going on.

'Actually, we're doing pretty good. If my addition is right, I have forty-two signed up as plaintiffs, and a bunch more who say they will do it online, once they figure out how many children they have.'

We laughed, a bit too loudly, but it was good to release.

'They don't know how many children they have?' Sam asked.

'Well, that's what it sounded like. Maybe they meant they had to talk to their kids or grandkids first before they signed up. I'm sure some of them were bullshitting me, but I figure we'll get some more. And it's early days; don't forget that. We had people with us in the lobby most of the day, and the news is going to hit the street once the reunion's over and they all go home to spread the word.'

'I hope so,' Sam said. 'But I don't think Mary Jane Perrins from Boston, Massachusetts, will be signing up any time soon, do you?'

Arlene snorted. 'Jeez Louise, what a piece of work she is. I mean, I'm not exactly warm and fuzzy myself, but I'm telling you, you could freeze ice on that broad's ass. Lord have mercy. But don't lose any sleep over Mary Poppins, y'all. She's not the kind that's gonna make friends and influence people. I mean, would you want to spend time with that?'

'She could make trouble, though,' Powalski said, 'all on her lonesome, if she wants to. I don't think we've heard the last of her.'

'She will be complaining as long as anyone will listen to her,' I agreed. 'But there's nothing we can do about that for now. Did you learn anything from all those folks you talked to?'

'Yeah,' he replied. 'Matter of fact, I found out all about Jacob's loan certificates.'

Needless to say, we were all jumping out of our seats on hearing that, and Powalski had to raise a hand to indicate that he was speaking in an ironic vein. We collapsed back again.

'According to who you ask, the certificates: never existed; or did exist, but were lost by Jacob or by his family; or burned by the Brits in 1814; or were eaten by a dog; or were taken to France for safekeeping; or were taken to London for safekeeping; or were entrusted to someone in the family, and their descendants are hiding them away – there are several suspects around the country – or, well, you name it. There are almost as many stories as there are family members.'

It was as though the air had been sucked from the room. We were deflated, and the weariness descended again.

'I'm sorry to be the bearer of bad tidings,' he said, and I think he really meant it. Powalski was on board himself by now. It wasn't just another case for him, any more than it was for me. 'But actually, I think I may have picked up on something.'

'Go on,' I said encouragingly.

'Well, don't read too much into this, OK?'

'OK.'

'OK. Well, as many stories as I heard, there was one that I heard any number of times. The dog that ate the certificates I only heard once, but this one I must have heard fifteen or twenty times. It has some variations, but basically the story is that Jacob took some of the certificates to a loan office to try to collect his money.'

'That would have been the proper procedure,' I said.

'Right. But when he got there, he was told the government didn't have the money –'

'They didn't,' Sam confirmed.

'Right. So the story goes that the loan officers told him they needed to take the loan certificates to the Department of the Treasury, to verify them and arrange payment. Now, depending on when this happened, he could have done that himself. The Treasury was in Philadelphia until 1800, because that's where the seat of government was at that time; it didn't move to Washington until 1800. But in any case, the Treasury never did arrange payment, and those certificates haven't been seen since. One or two family members said they paid him something, a small sum to fob him off, but they never paid anything approaching what the certificates were worth, and after that, he had no evidence that he had ever loaned any money: end of story. But most of them said that after the first batch disappeared, Jacob gave the remaining certificates to someone he trusted to look after them in the event of this death, and as we know, he died in 1812.'

I suddenly felt cold, though it was rather too warm in the room. I stood and walked to the window and gazed down on to St. Charles Avenue for some time, my arms folded tightly across my chest, watching the cars drive slowly past the hotel. The story fifteen or twenty members of the family had told Powalski resonated with me. How could it not? I'd been there. I'd seen and heard part of it. But I couldn't tell anyone that, and it didn't bring us any nearer to solving the problem. I came back as Sam was in the middle of asking me something and I had to ask her to repeat it.

'Kiah, if that's true, the government may still have at least some of the certificates. It can't be hard to find out where they would have stored documents once the loan offices had been closed. They had to take them somewhere for safekeeping, and from there – well, they would have been moved around from time to time, but once we had the National Archives, that's where they would have wound up, wouldn't they?'

Before I could answer, Arlene stood, walked behind Sam and gently put her arms around her neck.

'I wish,' she said, 'but in your dreams, hun.'

'Why do you say that?' Sam asked. She sounded hurt.

'Hun, if you worked for the government and you had loan certificates that might cost the government billions one day, what would you do with them? I know what I'd do, and it sure as hell wouldn't be storing them in the National Archives, or anywhere else. I'd be feeding them straight into the shredder.'

Tears were forming in Sam's eyes.

'They didn't have shredders in those days,' she protested sullenly.

'Maybe not,' Arlene replied, not unkindly, 'but they had discovered the secret of fire, and they probably used it – assuming the Brits hadn't already done it for them.' She bent down and kissed Sam on the top of her head. 'Sorry, hun, but maybe we need to face the facts.'

I returned from the window.

'It's not necessarily that simple,' I said. 'For one thing, governments aren't always as well organised as that. Governments depend on civil servants, and civil servants tend to hoard things. They say the Nazis hoarded enough paper to convict them all several times over. Besides, no one would have thought in terms of billions of dollars back then. That's two hundred years later.'

'Maybe so, but it was still a pretty large sum,' Powalski said quietly. 'Arlene's right: it has to be possible that someone got rid of the certificates while they had the chance.'

'It is a possibility,' I agreed, 'and if we never find them, maybe we will conclude that they did. But for now, we are going to work on the assumption that at least some of them survived. If we can find even one, it might be almost as good as finding them all.'

'How do you figure that?' Arlene asked.

'If you don't have a document, or a copy of it,' I replied, 'the next best thing is evidence to prove that someone destroyed the document – especially if that someone had a lot to lose if the document were ever to be produced to a court. If we only find one surviving loan certificate, the obvious question is: what happened to the rest of them? And if the answer to that is that the government may have destroyed them, a sympathetic judge might go with us.'

'There's something else, too,' Powalski added. 'Even if the government got rid of the certificates they had, there are still the ones Jacob gave to his friend for safekeeping.'

'But how do we know who this friend was?' Arlene asked. 'Assuming it ever happened in the first place.'

'We don't, right now,' Powalski conceded. 'But Aunt Meg bent my ear for a good hour. She's one of the main proponents of the theory that Jacob didn't hand everything over to the government, and she says she has some evidence to back it up.'

I felt my heart race again.

'What evidence?'

'She wouldn't say. She said the lobby was too public. She will show it to us when the time is right.'

'When the time is right?' Arlene protested. 'What in the hell does she mean by that? How is this not the right time?'

'I think she means, not during the reunion,' Powalski replied. 'Aunt Meg strikes me as the cautious type, and with people like Mary Jane Perrins around, I can't say I blame her. I think she'll be as good as her word. I don't think she was bullshitting me.'

We were silent for some time.

'The hell with it,' Arlene said suddenly. 'Come on, y'all. There ain't no point sitting here moping about stuff we can't fix, leastwise not today. Let's get our asses out of here.'

'Where to?' Sam asked.

'Where to?' Arlene replied. 'Hun, it's Saturday night and we're in the city of N'Orleans, the Big Easy. It's time to party, girl.'

'Are you going to show us the town?' I asked.

'I surely am.'

'Are you going to lead us astray?' Sam asked. She had perked up again, and was smiling.

'I'm sure going to do my damndest, hun.'

'I didn't know you were an expert on New Orleans,' I smiled.

'Hun,' Arlene replied, 'if you live in Lubbock, Texas, you need a place to party, and it sure ain't gonna be any place in Texas, and it sure as hell ain't going to be Lubbock, Texas. No, ma'am. If you live in Lubbock, Texas, and it's time to play, you head for the airport and you get yourself on a flight to N'Orleans. So, yeah, I've spent some time in this town, and I reckon by now I know my way around. Y'all coming, or what?'

22

'Whoa, slow down, hun,' Arlene said. She placed a restraining hand on Sam's arm and lowered the hand in which she held the famous bulbous glass. 'That ain't no fruit juice you're drinking. Take it slow.'

'It *tastes* like fruit juice,' Sam protested. 'I'm not tasting any alcohol.'

'With the really lethal concoctions you never do, hun,' Arlene grinned. 'But trust me, the alcohol is there. You drink that too fast, and you're going to be sitting on some corner on Bourbon Street early tomorrow morning trying to remember your name.'

'Are you speaking from personal experience?' I asked.

'There are some things you don't ask a gal in New Orleans,' she replied, 'and that's one of them.'

The fresh air had felt good as we walked from the Intercontinental across Canal Street into the French Quarter. The walk and the air somehow blew away the exertions of the day. The Quarter was warming up for the evening, and there were a lot of people on the streets, but it was still only just after seven, early by New Orleans standards. Arlene had steered us straight to St Peter Street, and had managed to usher us into Pat O'Brien's before it got too crowded. At her insistence we ordered the legendary 'Hurricane' – except for Powalski, who stuck resolutely to his Jack Daniels over ice – and adjourned to the rear garden to enjoy the drink and the balmy air. We were beginning to relax now. The alcohol was indeed there, and as always after a hard day, it loosened us up. It felt good.

'The last time I was here in Pat O'Brien's,' Arlene said during a rare lull in the conversation, 'was just after I finally threw my useless, no-good, asshole of a husband out of the house. It was that very weekend. I left Bubba with my momma and flew out to New Orleans, determined to spend what little money he'd left me before the goddamn debt collectors could get their hands on it. And I'm here to tell you, I did a pretty good job of it.'

'What did your husband do that you had to throw him out?' Powalski asked. He and Sam hadn't heard the story. 'Was he running around on you?'

'Well, he was a hard dog to keep on the porch,' Arlene replied. 'He never could keep his pants zipped up for long. But it wasn't the screwing around that did us in. Truth to tell, I could have matched him screw for screw if I'd had a mind to, and I was past caring by then. What did us in was the betting and the drinking – the betting, mainly. The booze cost him his job, but it was the gambling that did the real damage. Even now I don't know much money went that way. He borrowed from the bank on our house until they wouldn't lend him any more, and after that he borrowed from the Texas Mafia.'

'The Texas Mafia?' Sam grinned.

'You bet your ass, hun. Oh, they might not be the Cosa Nostra. They might just be a couple of good old boys driving a pickup truck with Willie Nelson playing on the sound system and a dog in the back and a couple of shotguns on the gun rack. They ain't gonna leave no horse's head under your pillow. But you still don't want to mess with them. I got the hell out of Dodge as soon as I got back from N'Orleans, before they had time to find me. I took Bubba and headed for Virginia and that's where I'm fixin' to stay.'

'What happened to the asshole husband?' Powalski asked.

'Damned if I know, and damned if I give a tinker's cuss what happened to him. If they took a shotgun and blew his balls off, I would give them a high five.'

'You're not planning to reconcile then, I guess?' Powalski asked. We all laughed out loud, good and long.

'But I sure did spend some money in this town while I had the chance,' Arlene said, draining her Hurricane glass. 'I stayed at the Monteleone. I ate at Antoine's, Commander's Palace, the Court of the Two Sisters – every good restaurant I could fit into a long weekend, ending up with Monday brunch at Brennan's before I headed out to the airport.' She looked at her watch. 'Including Tujague's,' she said, 'where I took the liberty of booking us a table in about twenty minutes. We need to haul ass.'

'You booked us a table?' I asked.

'Well, sure. I booked as soon as I knew we were going to be here. It's Saturday night in N'Orleans, hun. You can't just walk into a restaurant without a reservation – leastways, not one y'all would want to eat in. Come one, drink up.'

'I could go for another of those Hurricanes,' Sam said, emptying her glass reluctantly.

'You really don't want to do that,' Arlene said authoritatively.

23

WE WALKED QUICKLY THROUGH the growing crowds down to Decatur Street, turning left towards the French Market, and arrived at Tujague's right on time. We were shown into the elegant panelled restaurant at the rear of the building, where a corner table awaited us.

'It's the second or third oldest restaurant in New Orleans,' Arlene announced proudly as the waiter seated us. 'I forget.'

The waiter smiled. 'Second, ma'am,' he said politely.

'Second,' Arlene repeated.

Powalski whispered conspiratorially with the waiter for some time, and within five minutes, as we were browsing through the menu and chatting, absinthe-style shots appeared for all of us, accompanied by two bottles of an excellent California chardonnay for dinner.

'I'm taking care of the drinks tonight,' he announced. 'Cheers.' He downed his shot in one, and we all followed suit. He signalled to the waiter, and a second shot arrived in seconds.

'You've been pretty quiet tonight, Powalski,' Arlene said. 'But you sure have the waiter following you like a faithful old hunting dog. Do you have some history in this town you haven't told us about?'

'There are some things you don't ask a guy in New Orleans,' he replied, 'and that's one of them.'

'OK. You got me there,' Arlene laughed.

'So, what do you recommend?' Sam asked.

'You ever had crawfish étoufée?' Arlene asked her.

'Never.'

'It's to die for. It's one of the great Creole or Cajun dishes – I'm never sure what the right word is.' She turned to Powalski and me. 'Y'all ever had the étoufée?'

'Never,' I replied.

'Years ago,' Powalski said.

'During the time we're not allowed to ask you about?' Sam asked.

'Exactly.'

'Well, I'm up for trying it now,' I said.

'Way to go, girl. And you might want to try the lobster bisque to start. And don't forget to leave room for the bread pudding with whisky sauce.'

'You may have to carry me out of here later,' I grinned.

'There'll be some big dude called 't-Jean who'll carry you all the way back to St Charles Avenue for five dollars, hun, trust me,' she said.

'You I trust,' I replied. 'I'm not sure about 't-Jean.'

We finished with a chicory coffee and a glass of Armagnac, by which time we had forgotten all about the trials and tribulations of the day; even Mary Jane Perrins of Boston, Massachusetts, had lost her menace. We had been talking one on one for some time, but then there was one of those silences that come about sometimes when several individual conversations happen to finish at the same moment, and in the silence Powalski spoke up.

'I was here several times during my training with the CIA,' he said. 'We used New Orleans for tradecraft games, street work. It's a good place to learn to follow people, or to lose them. The crowds are a huge challenge, and there are so many places, little side streets and alleyways you never notice when you're just walking around, to disappear into. It's perfect, especially at night in the

Quarter when there are so many people on the street. We used to spend hours following each other, and then, when we were off duty, we would go out on the town. I got to know the bars and restaurants pretty well.'

'Interesting,' Arlene said after a pause. 'But I think there's more.'

'So do I,' Sam said. 'Come on, Powalski. Out with it.'

He drained his Armagnac and raised a finger in the direction of the waiter, which was all it took to produce another.

'I met this woman,' he said simply.

'I knew it,' Arlene said.

'She was a lawyer, actually, had her own practice in the city doing family cases and such. She was really something. I met her here, as a matter of fact – not in the restaurant here, in the bar at the front, where we came in. I was waiting for a couple of colleagues; we were going to have dinner, and there she was, sitting at the bar. We got talking, and we exchanged phone numbers, and it went from there.'

'It went from there?' Arlene protested. 'What in the hell does that mean? You can tell us, Powalski. We're pretty broad-minded, ain't we, ladies? I reckon we've heard it all before.'

Sam and I nodded.

'Not much to tell,' Powalski said. 'We had an affair. It was very special. She was very special. But then my training came to an end, and I had to leave. The last sight I had of her was after our last drink together on Jackson Square on a misty autumn evening, watching her disappear into the mist as she left.'

We were silent for some time. I think it was the sense of inevitability about it that shook us.

'That was it?' I asked. 'You didn't try to keep in touch?'

He shook his head. 'When you work for the Company it's not exactly conducive to stable relationships. You can be moved anywhere at a moment's notice. I didn't see what I had to offer her. I did make inquiries after I left the CIA, some years later. By that time, she had married and moved to California.'

'Didn't that…?' Sam began. She didn't finish the question.

'It broke my heart,' he replied. 'I'm still not over it, and I don't know whether I ever will be.'

Sam's turn came. She'd had a series of boyfriends, none serious, which she attributed to her unpredictable life as an actress. She was torn. On the one hand, she loved her life and hated any thoughts of giving it up. On the other, there was something missing, and she was aware of the ticking of her biological clock. Life wasn't simple any more. There was one young man who was showing an interest, and she didn't know what to do. She was worrying about it.

Which left me. Of course, Arlene knew about the Week in outline, but the only person I had fully confided in about that horrific period in my life was Arya. Sitting in her house, with the tea and the incense and the foot rubs, I had eventually brought myself to tell her the whole dreadful business – the devastating loss of my parents; the eviscerating sense of betrayal, of worthlessness, when Jordan cast me aside as casually as a necktie he had lost his taste for; the nightmares and the nights I spent throwing up – all of which was then still my daily experience of living.

I had hated talking about it. It was like torturing myself all over again. At first it had made me feel weak, foolish, defeated. As time went on, and as Arya listened without judging, I gained confidence that talking about it was also helping me to move on – painfully slowly, it was true – but moving on, nonetheless. But it was never easy, and never once in all that time did it occur to me to open up to anyone else. It was far too personal and far too humiliating. Despite what Arya had told me time and time again, I could still convince myself with little effort that everything that had happened was somehow my own fault.

Now, without warning, on this evening, in this city and in this restaurant I didn't know at all, there was a silence that meant it was my turn to share – yet another kind of silence to scare me. But scary as it was, I felt I was among friends. Yes, our relationship was a professional one and a relatively new one, and yes, it would be the wine talking, to some extent – I was drunk enough and sober enough to know that. But I had embarked on something special with these friends. They had all opened up in their own way and it hadn't hurt them. Perhaps I could take a chance.

So I clutched my wine glass, took a long drink, and told my friends about the Week from Hell, about the nightmares, and about Arya. The only time I cried was when I talked about how much I missed my parents. That wound was still so raw, it was almost unbearable. As I talked about them, Sam took my hand and held it between hers, and kept it there until I had said all I wanted to say. Then, something wonderful happened. When I moved on to talk about Jordan, I cried no tears. I felt no urge to cry at all. Suddenly, Jordan was no more to me than a bad taste in my mouth which I spat out with every word; by the end, he was just another typically arrogant asshole of a corporate lawyer who'd had the staggeringly original idea of cheating on his partner by banging his secretary. Suddenly, Jordan was something that had happened to me in my past, something I had put behind me, something that no longer had any importance in my life whatsoever. When I announced this, there was a spontaneous burst of applause around the table.

The drink was catching up with me now. But I knew the difference between the drink and the demons that had followed me for the past year. And I knew that the demons, if not gone altogether, were in retreat. It was an exhilarating feeling. I felt free again.

'I know a couple of good old boys with shotguns,' Arlene suggested. 'I could give them a call if y'all want him taken care of.'

'I wouldn't want to waste their time,' I replied.

As we left Tujague's, each of my friends gave me a long hug, and Sam walked arm in arm with me all the way back to the Intercontinental.

24

Dave Petrosian

I'D ARRANGED TO MEET Kiah for lunch. For some reason I couldn't quite define, I'd wanted her to have my pleadings as soon as the ink was dry on them, and handing them to her in person somehow seemed the right thing to do. It wasn't the standard procedure, obviously. Civil procedure has moved on a bit since every piece of paper had to be delivered personally to the recipient. I could easily have sent the pleadings to her electronically, which nowadays is the usual way of communicating with opposing counsel. If I had been worrying about them being missed, lying overlooked and unopened in her inbox, I could have sent them over to her office by messenger, or I could simply have given her a call to make sure she checked her email. But I did none of those things. I arranged to meet her for lunch. Why? It was because these particular pleadings were so final, I convinced myself eventually. It was because they were about to bring the case of *Samantha van Eyck (individually and on behalf of all those similarly situated) v United States* to an abrupt end. So what? I got cases dismissed on some procedural ground or other, I got summary judgment against some plaintiff or other, on a regular basis. What made this case so special? What made it special, I admitted to myself eventually, was that I was going to miss it.

Once I got over the humiliation of having to be reminded by

my assistant trial attorney of something as basic as the statute of limitations, it didn't take me long to come up with a plan of action. But how in the hell had I forgotten to ask the first question you ask in any case on the defense side? How old is the cause of action? It's civil procedure 101.

There's a limitation period for any civil claim. For claims of this kind against the government the period is six years, which means that if the plaintiff doesn't file suit within six years of the claim accruing, the claim is barred. It's a sensible enough rule. As time goes by, witnesses die, or they forget what happened, documents are lost, and it gets progressively more difficult for a court to establish the truth. The longer the delay in bringing suit, the harder it is. So the law imposes a burden on plaintiffs not to let the grass grow. It's not a harsh burden: six years is more than enough in any normal case for a plaintiff to get her act together, hire a lawyer, and file a claim. If she didn't know the claim had accrued, the limitation period can be extended to run from the time when she did know. So there's little excuse for missing the deadline. All the same it happens pretty often, usually because of negligence either on the part of the plaintiff or on the part of her lawyer. When it happens in a case in which my office is defending, we ask the court to dismiss the case, and they do. It's a routine occurrence, and Samantha van Eyck was about to go the same way.

I think the reason I had to be reminded about the statute of limitations was that the debt went back such a long way. In most cases, everything has happened within the last decade or so, and the only question is whether the plaintiff should have known of the claim at some time within the last six years of that decade. You don't get cases where the cause of action goes back more than 200 years. But the same principle has to apply. The only thing different in Samantha van Eyck's case was that it certainly wasn't Samantha's fault, or Kiah Harmon's, that the deadline had been missed. It had passed many years before either of them had been born.

From my point of view, as simple as it was going to be to win this case, and as little credit as I deserved for my part in doing so, it was an unexpected boost in terms of career – not just for me, but for Harry and Ellen as well. News of our routing of the opposition, of our saving America from the spectre of having to fork out billions of dollars to repay a 200-year-old debt, would go directly to Assistant Attorney General Maggie Watts, from Maggie Watts to the Attorney General, and from the Attorney General to the President. The name of Dave Petrosian might even be whispered in the Oval Office. It would, no doubt, be forgotten in the same amount of time it took to whisper it, but the prospect was beguiling, nonetheless. It would be something to talk about over drinks and dinner for the rest of my life. For all that, I was going to miss the case.

As I said before, this was easily the most interesting case I had even been involved with. There was a certain romance in the idea of digging into the history of America at a time when its independence – its very nationhood – hung in the balance, when they could have been snuffed out like a candle if events had unfolded differently. It was interesting, challenging, and passionate. And even for someone like me, who slogged through law school part-time and took a very mundane view of legal practice, there was a feeling that this is why you go to law school, this is why you pay so much money, and why you subject yourself to so many tests to become a lawyer: not only because you can earn money at the end of it, but because maybe there will one day be a chance to be involved in something that becomes a part of history. And this case could have been it. I would never have said any of that to Harry, or even to Ellen, though I think Ellen would understand and I wouldn't be surprised if she feels the same way. I wouldn't say it because it's just too personal.

When I called her, Kiah told me she was going to New Orleans to meet members of the van Eyck family, so we had arranged to meet on the Monday, the day after she returned. We met at Benny's, a new casual diner not too far from my office, which was getting to be popular with local office workers. I set out in good time to make sure of a table where we could talk undisturbed. As one of his first customers I still had a little influence with Benny in such matters, though the more popular the place became, the faster that was going to disappear. On this Monday, my clout was still sufficient. As I walked, I was clutching the pleadings in a brown envelope under my arm. I suppose I hoped we might mourn the case together.

25

SHE ARRIVED ON TIME, and we shook hands before taking our seats opposite each other at our corner table. I hadn't seen Kiah for quite some time, and I'd heard that she'd had some kind of trouble that had made her close her office for a while, so I wasn't quite sure what to expect. But she looked really great. There was something different about her. She was dressed less formally, for one thing. Whenever I'd seen her in the past she had looked like your stereotypical female corporate lawyer: the dark suit, the starched white blouse, the heels and all the rest of it. That had all changed. She was still smartly dressed, but there were colours now: red, green and gold; a light jacket and grey slacks had replaced the suit, and the shoes were low and comfortable-looking. There was a confidence about her, an openness. She looked around her.

I perused the menu for a moment, although I knew it like the back of my hand. A board propped up by the door advertised daily specials of chili con carne and homemade lasagna.

'So, this is where you government boys have lunch these days?'

'Yeah. On our salary, it's all we can afford. We can't compete with you rich guys in the private sector.'

'Right. I still can't talk you into Indian food, then?'

'I'd love to, Kiah, but I can't do spicy any more. I took Maria out for Mexican last week and I was up half the night with heartburn. I must be getting too old.'

'We have some very nice mild Indian dishes, not spicy at

all. You really should try. How is Maria? How's the family?'

'They're great, thanks. Maria is doing some volunteer work with the library now the kids are older, and Raul and Cindy are both future soccer stars already.'

She laughed. 'That's great.'

'Yeah, you should see them. It makes me tired just watching them.'

'Soccer scholarships on the horizon, you think?'

'Scholarships? Hey, I'm way beyond that. I'm thinking they may go play for one of those big teams in Europe, you know, Real Madrid or Barcelona. Make some money for their old man.'

We laughed together.

'How is…?' I paused. I couldn't remember his name. I was embarrassed. She must have told me, because I remembered he was an attorney who did banking law or something of the kind for a mid-sized firm in the District, but for the life of me I couldn't remember.

'Jordan? Jordan is gone. Jordan is long gone.'

'Oh, I'm sorry, Kiah…'

'Don't be,' she replied, 'I'm not.' She paused for a moment, then smiled. 'Best thing that ever happened to me – well, almost.' She paused again. 'So… what's good here?'

We both examined the menu again until the moment passed.

'The soup and salad is always good, same with the baked potatoes. The burger is OK.'

We both settled for soup and salad with iced tea, and returned the menus to the waiter.

'So, I brought something for you.'

'Oh?'

I leaned down and picked up the envelope, which I had propped up against the leg of my chair. I handed it to her. I intended the gesture to be casual. I wanted to watch her as she took it, and as she opened it. I didn't want to ambush her. With other lawyers I might have relished the moment for its own sake, but I thought far too much of Kiah to want to embarrass her. I just wanted to see her reaction. I had overlooked the statute of limitations because the case went so far back in time, until Ellen had pointed it out to me as the first and most obvious line of defense. It seemed inconceivable that two of us could have been thrown off track by the same illusion. But could it be? Kiah was a veteran of the Claims Court; a lawyer of her calibre would surely never have filed suit without at least thinking about the limitation period. But if so, she must have worked out some strategy for getting around it, and I couldn't even imagine what it might be. The limitation period is technical and inflexible, and 200 years is a long time. I was curious about what, if anything, she had come up with.

'What's this?'

'Government's defence and motion to dismiss based on the statute of limitations.'

It was just the briefest of moments. She hesitated very slightly in the act of unsealing the envelope, but it was enough to tell me what I wanted to know. She had been blinded by the age of the case, just as I had. I felt certain of it. I knew what effect it must have had. She would have been feeling as if someone had just punched her right in the solar plexus. The room would have gone dark for a moment, and then her heart would have started racing. She recovered magnificently.

'Statute of limitations?'

'Yeah. You get six years in the Claims Court. You know that. By our calculations, you missed the deadline by more than 200 years.'

She leaned forward in her chair.

'Have you listed your motion for a hearing?'

I nodded. 'One week from today. I didn't see any reason to delay, but if you need an extension to respond, just let me know; I won't oppose it.'

She nodded. 'Who's our judge?'

'Tomorrow,' I replied.

I didn't mean I would tell her tomorrow. Our judge was to be the Honourable Thomas Oliver Morrow, one of the more senior judges of the court. Given his name, the nickname became almost inevitable, and the bar had bestowed it on him just after his appointment some fourteen years before. The allocation of judges is in theory random, though I have always suspected that the clerk occasionally assigns a case on the basis of a feeling about what kind of judge the case needs. I wasn't sure whether that had happened here or not. I started with the assumption that none of the judges would be too enthusiastic about being asked to order the government to pay out however many billions of dollars Kiah was claiming. On the other hand, there would be those who would relish a brush with history, as I did.

I found it difficult to predict Tomorrow's reaction to it. He is a good, thoughtful lawyer, and more than capable of rising above the mundane world of insurance claims and government contracts that occupy most of his working week. But as to which way he would go in our case if presented with an arguable question, I felt far less sure. Tomorrow had been a Marine legal officer earlier in life. In one way that might be good for the government. He would be mindful of the need to protect the federal budget from any damage that might impact military spending. Harry and Ellen both thought that was the way he would go, for that reason alone. I wasn't entirely persuaded. As a former military officer, he might also have some sympathy with the idea that an unsung hero who had saved America's earliest army deserved proper recognition. And that was an idea Kiah might be very well equipped to sell him.

She nodded again, but made no comment. She smiled.

'I'm disappointed in you, Dave,' she said. 'The statute of limitations? Are you really going to get technical on me just because of 200 years?'

I returned the smile.

'Yeah, sorry about that. Government work. You know how it is. We have to tick all the boxes.'

I couldn't leave it at that.

'Kiah, to tell you truth, I'm really sorry to have to do this. I'm going to miss this case.'

'You seem very confident that Tomorrow will grant your motion to dismiss.'

'He has no choice. In the Claims Court, failure to file in time takes away the court's jurisdiction. You know that as well as I do. What else can he do?'

She was giving nothing away. She waited for some time.

'So, Dave, tell me: why will you miss the case?'

I laughed out loud.

'Kiah, are you kidding me? Do you know what I usually do all day?'

'Of course I do.'

'Then you'll understand. This is the most interesting file ever to cross my desk in all my years of practicing law. I actually look forward to getting up in the mornings. The entire office is jealous of me. They all want in on this. Hell, we practically have to keep the file locked up in case somebody steals it.'

'Well, in that case, why don't you forget about the statute of limitations? Fight me on the merits. Dive into history with me. Have some fun.'

'You know what? I really wish I could.' I meant it. 'But unfortunately, I have people higher up in the office, not to mention the Attorney General, not to mention the President, who seem to think that getting rid of this as quickly as possible is the way to go.'

We were silent, awkwardly, for a minute or so.

'Kiah, can I ask you something?'

'Of course.'

'You don't have to answer, but I'm curious. What do your people want out of this? Assume you had a fairy godmother who could wave her magic wand and find you a way around the statute of limitations. I don't think that's possible, but just suppose for a moment. What is it you want? I assume you realise that there's no way the government could pay even a fraction of what you're asking for?'

'We're open to reasonable offers. Perhaps a small state no one would miss? How about Rhode Island?'

We laughed together again.

'Hey, why not? Tell you what, I'll speak to the President about it and get back to you. What else?'

'Dave, the van Eyck family aren't crazy people. They're not vindictive. They're as patriotic as you or me or the next family. They don't want to bankrupt the country. They just want Jacob to be recognised for the hero he is. He deserves his place in history.'

'So…?'

'So the government will erect a statue to Jacob van Eyck in Philadelphia,' she replied, 'and the President of the United States will unveil it.'

I must have stared at her for a long time. I could have said nothing, I suppose, but that wasn't the way I felt. Her words had had an effect on me.

'You know what, Kiah, if the facts are as you say in your Complaint – if Jacob van Eyck really did what you say he did – I wouldn't have any problem with that. I truly wouldn't. But there are some people above me who probably don't share that view. So first, you're going to have to find a way to beat the statute of limitations, and I don't see any way you can do that.'

'I have a call in to my fairy godmother,' she smiled.

'Tell her I said good luck,' I replied.

26

Kiah Harmon

THEY SAY THAT AS you are about to die, your whole life flashes before your eyes. I don't know about that, but I can tell you that when someone casually points out exactly how you have screwed something up beyond belief, there's a moment when a complete and detailed sequence of past events and decisions enters your mind, and forces you to see how you screwed up with absolute clarity in the time light takes to cross a synapse in your brain. In fact, you have a sense that this has somehow happened even before whoever is doing this to you even opens their mouth. It's as if you have a premonition of it, or as if, on some level, you have always known it. You also see, instantaneously and with complete clarity, just how terrible a catastrophe it is. And then your heart stops and your vision blurs for a moment or two, and you aren't sure you want to eat your lunch any more.

So even before Dave spelled it out for me, I immediately knew that I had forgotten about the statute of limitations. I also knew exactly why I had made a mistake I would never have made in any other case. Jacob's loans had been made in the winter of 1777–1778. But it wouldn't have been clear until much later that the new government had no intention of repaying him; he may not even have finally realised the truth until he was about to die in poverty in 1812. From that point, there could hardly be any doubt that his claim had accrued. But in 1812, there was no court in which to sue the government. In fact, in 1812 the very concept of suing the government would have made no sense at all. The rule of English law, on which our law was based, was that the King could do no wrong. However often the King taxed you unjustly, however much he dispossessed you of your land or chattels without due process of law, however much he locked you up without trial, there was no court to sue him in. You had to find a different remedy, such as bribing some minister or favourite close to the King, or if that didn't work, starting a revolution or a civil war. If that didn't work, your best bet was to abjure the realm: pronto.

Our Founding Fathers were determined to end the King's influence in America, but that didn't mean they were going to throw the baby out with the bath water. They were way too shrewd for that. If the King had a good idea working for him, they were quite happy to appropriate it, and the King could do no wrong was a really good idea – if you were the King. Now obviously, our thinking had to change over the years. We had become a republican, democratic nation, and in due course the Constitution and the Bill of Rights were bound to replace the tyranny of monarchical rule in the public psyche. But it couldn't happen overnight. You can't just expect a people to discard centuries of ingrained historical memory with a wave of the hand. There has to be a lengthy period of adjustment in their social and political discourse. But eventually, the view that governments should be accountable to the people was bound to supersede the view that the King could do whatever he wanted with impunity. So in 1855, Congress created the Claims Court, and for the first time, in certain limited kinds of case, the 'King' was made subject to the judgment of a court.

But that was the best part of a century after Jacob had made his loans. That's what had blindsided me. I had made the unarticulated assumption that his claims had to be judged as at the time they had accrued, and if there was no court to sue in then, how could there be a statute of limitations? It was meaningless. So what if

Congress passed a statute of limitations to regulate access to the Claims Court? How could that be allowed to prejudice Jacob, when he, or his heirs, couldn't possibly have filed suit within six years of his claim becoming due? How could his entitlement be removed retrospectively? If his claim was barred long before he had any way to pursue it, how could that be just or fair? What would have happened to the rule of law if that were allowed? And naively, I must have assumed that in a world where fairness held sway, there was no need to worry about the statute of limitations. And in a world in which fairness held sway I would have been right.

But now, I saw belatedly that there were two ways of looking at it. The second way of looking at it was that when Jacob's debt became due, there was no way to enforce it. Eventually a procedure was provided to enforce debts against the government, but it came too late to help Jacob. When Congress created the Claims Court, they didn't abandon the 'King can do no wrong' principle. They simply created a limited exception to it. You could sue the government, but only in the government's court, on the government's terms and subject to the government's rules. One of those rules might be that you could sue only in certain kinds of case; another might be that you couldn't sue in any case if you didn't file within six years of your claim becoming due. What was wrong with that? I knew before I even opened the envelope what Dave's motion to dismiss was going to say to the court. What I didn't know, or even have the first clue about, was what argument I could make against it that might have a snowball's chance in hell of persuading Judge Morrow to keep the case alive.

Arya, to whom I ran for comfort as soon as I could escape from lunch, saw immediately why the government's position was unfair. I had called into the office and told Arlene I wasn't feeling well, which was true, and that it must have been caused by something I had eaten at Benny's, which wasn't. She told me to go home and get some rest, get myself 'doctored' if I had to, and not to worry about coming into the office until the next day. She assured me that there was nothing going on that wouldn't wait until then, although I thought I detected a slight hesitancy in her voice as she said it. I felt a momentary anxiety, but in the state I was in, it could have just been my imagination. Either way, I was in no fit condition to be in the office.

I settled back in the armchair, inhaling the Neroli incense as if it were pure oxygen, and clasped the arms of the chair, anticipating the wonderful pain to come as Arya took hold of my feet and her fingers began their gentle probing. But there was to be no pain today. Perhaps because of what her fingers reported back to her, she changed tack and gave me a gentle, unhurried massage with a touch of oil. Gradually I relaxed back into the chair and closed my eyes. For the first time since leaving Benny's my body began to unwind a little. I explained to Arya what a fool I'd been, and how my career was over, and how I should have become a doctor, and how I'd failed to see what any first-semester law student would have seen ten seconds after Sam had told her the story, and why I was a complete failure who should be locked away for her own protection and that of the public. Eventually I started whining about how unfair the van Eyck family's situation was.

'So,' Arya asked, 'if the government's right, Jacob was out of luck before they even set up a court for him to sue them in?'

'That's the way it seems,' I said.

'So looking on the bright side, they can't blame you for missing the deadline, can they?'

'They can blame me for wasting Sam's time, and the time of all those people in New Orleans, by starting a case which has no hope of succeeding. I could have prevented that.'

Arya was silent for some time, her hands continuing to work their magic.

'Let me ask you something, Kiah,' she said, 'because I have a certain image of Sam in my mind based on what you've told me about her, and somehow I don't see her blaming you for any of this. Tell me: if you had foreseen this and you had told Sam before you started the case, how do you think she would have reacted to it? Would she have folded and said, "OK, well, let's not bother, then?" Or would she have said, "OK, let them hide behind their statute of limitations; let them show the world how cheap and unprincipled they are; let them show the world they don't give a damn about recognising an American hero?" What do you think she would have said?'

I smiled.

'She would have said, "Full speed ahead and damn the torpedoes."'

'That's what I would have expected of her, too.'

'But the torpedoes would have got us anyway.'

'Well,' she said, 'let's think about that for a moment. Let's think about what you might say to the judge about it. First, how is it fair that Jacob is owed a lot of money by the government, and he has never had the chance to sue for it? It's not that he allowed the deadline to pass. He never even had the right. How is that fair?'

'It's not,' I replied.

'Well then…?'

I sighed. 'Arya, one of the first things they teach you in law school is that there is no rule that the world has to be fair. You can't get up in court and say to a judge, "But, Your Honour, that's not fair." It's not a legal objection, and you can't sue someone for being unfair.'

Her hands stopped for a moment as she weighed up what I had said.

'How odd,' she replied. 'You know, that does surprise me. I'm not a lawyer, of course, and maybe I'm just being naïve, but I would like to think that's the first thing a judge would want to know: is what I'm being asked to do fair or not?'

Her hands resumed their work, and I was beginning to feel drowsy.

'The problem is,' I replied, 'how do you measure fairness? It's not an objective standard, is it? People can legitimately disagree about whether something's fair or not; what seems fair to one person may seem unfair to another. The courts need a more consistent standard to judge by.'

I must have been struggling to sit up to make my point, because Arya was pushing me back down into the chair, holding my shoulder ever so gently.

'No, don't fight it. Lean back. Go on. Lean back. Let yourself relax… Good girl.'

Gratefully, I surrendered to the chair, and closed my eyes again. This time they were heavy, and I didn't try to open them again.

'You may be right, Kiah,' she said quietly, after some time. 'But there are some cases where the fairness is all one way, and it's plain for everyone to see. You think that's true of Jacob's case, and it is.'

I was drifting away by now.

'And because that's true, I believe your judge is going to want to help you if he can,' she said. 'So perhaps your job is to show him how to do that in terms of the law; to present him with a legal way to allow him to be fair.'

When I came to, it was after nine o'clock in the evening. I was still in the armchair. Arya had covered me with a blanket and dimmed the lights. She was lying on her sofa, reading a book. I stretched, lifted myself slowly out of the chair, and looked around for my shoes, making as if to go home. Arya shook her head. She put her book down, took me into the kitchen and fed me soup and toast, and then put me to bed in her spare room. I went out again like a light.

27

I awoke the next morning just after five. Arya was still in bed. I went in quietly, and kissed her goodbye. She squeezed my hand and told me she loved me, then went back to sleep. I made my way home to get changed. I still felt shattered and I wasn't relishing the thought of the next round of embarrassment that was bound to come that morning, but the immediate trauma of my lunch with Dave had vanished, and my brain had started to work again. I still couldn't come up with a single argument to present to Judge Morrow as a legal way to be fair, but I wanted to get a head start on some research, if for no other reason, to reassure Sam – and myself – that I was on the case.

I started with a history of the Claims Court I had bought to provide myself with some background once I started to build up a substantial practice in the court and was submitting written briefs on a regular basis. It was surprisingly informative. The first thing I discovered was that the Act of Congress that created the court in February 1855 didn't include any statute of limitations. But neither did it give the court very much power. Its jurisdiction was limited to contractual claims against the government, and while it could examine cases brought before it and make findings, the court had no power to issue final judgments. Congress clung on to the right to grant or refuse relief when it received the court's findings. Eighty years on from independence the 'King' was still keeping a tight grip on the reins. In fairness, it didn't take the government long to realise what a silly arrangement that was – a court that can't issue judgments doesn't deserve the name – and in 1861 President Lincoln called for the court to be given the power to issue its own judgments. Congress granted that power by the Act of March 1863. In 1887 there was another important change. The jurisdiction of the court was expanded considerably to give it jurisdiction, among other things, over claims based on the Constitution.

The first time there was any mention of a statute of limitations was in 1863. The Act of that year established the six-year period, and allowed plaintiffs whose claims had accrued more than six years before that a further three years to file. I couldn't resist an ironic smile. Dave was wrong. We weren't late by over 200 years. It wasn't much more than 150. But it got even better. Part of our claim was based on the Constitution, the taking of private property for public use without compensation, and we couldn't have sued for that until the 1887 Act came into effect. That Act also had a six-year limitation period. So Dave was even more wrong: the period in our case shouldn't have started to run until March 3, 1893. So we were only late by something approaching 130 years. My satisfaction at proving Dave wrong about all that was, obviously, short-lived. The statute of limitations doesn't care whether you're late by 200 years or twenty-four hours. When you're late, you're late. This wasn't how I was going to find Judge Morrow a legal way to be fair.

Sam had committed to helping Arlene in the office at least two days a week, and they came into my office together to find out how I was, just after eight thirty. There was no point in procrastination. I sat them both down with a cup of coffee and broke the news. I tried to say I was sorry, but Sam smothered me with a hug before I could complete the sentence. There was a stunned silence for a while.

'Lord have mercy,' Arlene said eventually. 'I can't believe we didn't think of that, y'all. I mean, that's like offensive pass interference. It blows the whole play, with a loss of down.'

'It blows the whole game,' I replied.

'I'm not ready to give up,' Sam said.

I smiled, thinking of Arya.

'There must be something we can do about this. It's just so unfair.'

There was that word again.

'I know,' I replied. 'What I need to do is to translate that into a legal argument Judge Morrow can hang his hat on. I'm not there yet, but I've made a start this morning. We have seven days – well, six now, actually – before the hearing, and I'm going to spend all that time trying to come up with something. It just has to be something arguable at this stage, something to get us past the automatic bar. I'm going to do my best, Sam, I promise. I'm with you. We're not giving up.'

The room went quiet again. I fiddled with my pen. Arlene was examining her nails, a recent manicure with a violent red polish. Sam was looking absently up at the ceiling. She suddenly came back to us and saw that Arlene and I were looking at her.

'I'm sorry. I was miles away. I was thinking about something.'

'What? All those family members in New Orleans?'

She shook her head. 'No. It was something from the research I did on the Continental Congress and the war loans before I came to you. I read something… but I just can't place it.'

'Go on,' I said encouragingly.

'No, it's gone. I'm going to have to hit the library again. There was something that might be helpful. I'll try to find it again.'

'All contributions gratefully received,' I said.

Arlene ran her hands through her hair.

'Hun, Lord knows, this has blown us away like a tumbleweed in a West Texas dust storm, and I really hate to bother y'all with anything else, but…'

'Go for it. You might as well,' I replied. 'I don't think I can feel any worse this morning.'

She grimaced. 'I really wouldn't be too sure about that, hun.'

I brought my hands up to cover my face.

'Oh, God. What? What?'

She pushed a letter across the table in my direction.

'You're being audited,' she said, 'by the IRS. For the last five years.'

'What?'

I scanned the letter and threw it angrily aside.

'Oh, for God's sake, is this some kind of joke?'

'I've called Reg,' she added. 'He's all set to go. He says not to worry, everything's in order, but it's going to be hell on wheels having those guys all over the office, turning everything upside down, for a week or more.'

Reg is my CPA. He's a bit nerdy, but I like that in a CPA. He's a brilliant accountant, and there's not much he doesn't know about income tax. All the same, this was the last thing I needed to hear. Having the IRS systematically going through five years of tax records in the small space we had, taking up my time and Arlene's, would virtually bring us to a standstill. *Bring us to a standstill.* I paused to meditate on that thought, and the light dawned. I glanced at Arlene, and saw that the same thought had long since gone through her mind.

'I've never been audited before,' I said. 'Now, I get audited for the past five years? A couple of weeks after I file a big lawsuit against the federal government? Is that a coincidence, or what?'

'I sure as hell don't think so,' Arlene replied, 'and neither does Powalski. Powalski thinks the IRS is running interference for the Department of Justice. But I'll make sure to put them off for at least a couple of weeks, 'cause if Jesus tarries and the creek don't rise, y'all are going to be in the fight of y'all's life six days from now. The IRS don't have a dog in that fight, and I ain't about to let them put a leash on ours. No, ma'am.'

I sat back in my chair and pondered for a while.

'You know what?' I said. 'Bad as this is, there's also something really strange about it. Don't you think?'

'Strange, how?' Arlene asked.

'Well, according to Dave Petrosian, Justice figures they'll have this all wrapped up next week when Judge Morrow grants their motion to dismiss. They don't think we have any answer to it, and they may be right. So why would they need to resort to this? Why now?'

'Perhaps somebody at Justice isn't quite as convinced as Petrosian that they're going to win?' Sam suggested.

'Maybe so,' I replied.

'They're messing with your mind, hun,' Arlene said. 'They want to take your mind off of next week. Or else it's a reminder of how much power they have. And if y'all do win next week, look out. This is just the beginning. I'm telling you, hun, it'll be Katy bar the door then.'

28

I CAN'T GIVE YOU a full account of how I spent the next few days. In many ways it was an endless meandering cycle of misery and depression. We weren't saying much around the office. There was a lot going on. Sam was there every morning working with Arlene, and ironically, plaintiffs were signing up and offering help on a daily basis, even though we had told everyone by email that the government's motion to dismiss was coming up, and weren't sure we would even have a case left to pursue in another week. Jeff Carlsen and Ed van Eyck had both called and offered any help they could give as attorneys, though neither had come up with an answer to the statute of limitations. Kate Banahan had been as good as her word, and a nice young man called Eric from her Wills and Trusts class was desperately trying to make himself useful, while driving Arlene crazy by giving the impression that he had never seen the inside of an office before. Worst of all, Reg was beavering away on my tax records in a corner of my office, so the audit was never far from my mind. A lot was going on, but most of it was going on in a subdued silence. In the afternoons, Sam went to the library, or so she said. I wasn't sure whether she really was going to the library, or whether she just couldn't stand being in the office any more. I wasn't sure how long I could stand it myself.

By the time I had unburdened myself to Sam and Arlene, and we had recovered a little from the blow, Tuesday was all but gone. On Wednesday morning, I decided to make a positive start. I opened a new file in the van Eyck folder on my laptop and boldly typed in the words, 'Plaintiff's Reply to Government's Motion to Dismiss based on Statute of Limitations'. For two hours or so I typed non-stop. I began with a statement of the facts, which was pretty much the same as Dave Petrosian's statement of the facts, except that I treated them as facts in contrast to Dave's insinuation that they belonged more appropriately in the fiction section. In the second section I traced the history of the Claims Court and its statute of limitations, at the end of which I triumphantly demolished Dave's assertion that we had missed the deadline by 200 years, and demonstrated conclusively that it was close to 130 years, tops. I began the third section with the words, 'It follows, therefore…' At which point I hit a brick wall and stopped in mid-sentence.

Reg had questions about my tax affairs that took up most of Wednesday afternoon. I pretended to be frustrated at the interruption, but in a strange way it was almost a relief to be made to remember what had been going on in my practice four or five years ago. Anything was better than sitting at my desk without the faintest idea of how the third section could progress beyond 'therefore'. On Thursday, I rummaged through a number of files and went back through briefs I had written, or the government had produced, dealing with the statute of limitations in cases long gone. I don't know what I was expecting to find: some chance observation, some statutory provision or court judgment I had overlooked – anything that might offer a glimmer of hope. I found nothing.

On Friday afternoon, just after lunch, I gave up. The third section still consisted of a single incomplete sentence, and there was no prospect of developing it further. The plaintiffs had no response to the government's motion to dismiss. The hearing was on Monday morning. Dave was right. Our claim was barred by the statute of limitations. It was unfair, but the law was the law, and that was the way it was. I drafted an email of apology to all the plaintiffs who had signed up, the van Eyck family in general, and anyone else I thought I might conceivably have offended. I would send it when I returned from court on Monday. I tried to write the van Eyck case off in my mind. It had been fun, but it was time to move on to the next case. It didn't work as far as my feelings about Sam were concerned. Sam was personal: I didn't know how what I was going to say to her, but whatever it was, I wasn't going to say it in an email.

29

SAM GOT BACK TO the office at about five thirty, carrying a bottle of scotch in a brown paper bag. I was on my own. I had sent Arlene and Reg home for the weekend, saying that I would see them after court on Monday. Eric had left early to go home to Syracuse to see his parents for a couple of days. Despite the piles of paper lying around wherever you looked, the place felt abandoned. I felt as if I had just climbed on board the *Marie Celeste*.

'Were you at the library?' I asked.

She nodded. 'I thought we'd have a wake,' she replied, taking the bottle from the bag and placing it on the conference table. She walked to our minute kitchenette and returned with two glasses and a jug of ice. She kicked her shoes off into the corner of the room, next to mine, and took a seat. 'What do you think?'

'Why not?' I agreed.

I sat opposite her. She poured two glasses and added some ice. We clicked the glasses together as a toast and downed them without the whisky touching the sides. She refilled the glasses instantly. This time, we contemplated the drinks with their warm, almost golden glow, and took just a sip. I tried to work out what I wanted to say to her.

'Sam,' I began, 'I don't know how to –'

'Stop,' she interrupted.

I stopped.

'Kiah, I know you feel bad, but I don't want you ever to say sorry. You have nothing to be sorry for. It turns out, apparently, that there was nothing we could have done from day one. The government screwed Jacob over and there is nothing we can do about it. We didn't know that, and you didn't know that, when we started. If we'd never filed suit, we would never have known. At least now, we can lay it to rest. I can go visit my dad's grave and tell him I did the best I could.'

Her words hit me hard. I started to cry, and didn't stop. I lost it. I felt as if my heart was about to break. She put down her glass, walked over to me, and hugged me. She held me as I cried for what seemed like a very long time. In the end, her hair was making it difficult to breathe. I gently moved her head, and searched in my purse for my handkerchief to wipe my eyes.

'That's when I knew I wanted to take the case,' I told her eventually, in between sniffs, 'when you told me about your dad. I suppose it was because my memory of losing my own parents was so fresh. It really touched me. I wanted to help you to keep the promise you made to your dad.'

'And you did,' she replied. She was kneeling by my side now, looking directly into my eyes. 'You did. I did everything I could, and that's all he could ever have asked of me. I could never have promised him more than that. And if I'd never met you, if you'd never agreed to help me, I could never have done it.'

I smiled. 'Some other lawyer would have –'

'No, Kiah, they wouldn't. There were no other lawyers willing to touch this. You couldn't think of a single one who would even consider it. Remember? It was you, and I will always be grateful.'

She stood and walked back to her seat. We drained our glasses and she poured more. We sat in silence for some time.

'What have you been getting up to at the library?' I asked. 'I kept meaning to ask you, but with all this other crap going on...'

'Oh, just wasting my time, probably,' she replied.

'Tell me anyway.'

She sat up in her chair.

'OK. Before I came to see you originally, I'd been spending time in the library, reading up on Alexander Hamilton. I'm not sure why, really, but he was the Secretary of the Treasury, so he was very involved with getting the economy running again after the war, trying to make sure the currency stayed stable and all the rest of it. So I guess I thought I might find something to explain why Jacob and others like him were never repaid. I never did find anything definite. But then, on Tuesday, when you told us about the statute of limitations, I remembered something he'd said. It was during a debate in the House of Representatives, and at the time, there was something about it that struck me, but I couldn't remember where I'd seen it. So this week, I tried to find it again, and eventually, this morning, I did.'

'What did he say?' I asked.

'Well, you have to understand what was going on. You remember, after the war, the country was pretty much bankrupt?'

'Sure.'

'Well, there were a lot of people who were pretty much bankrupt too, and they included people who had made loans for the war, who the government couldn't afford to pay back.'

'Like Jacob,' I pointed out.

'Yes, like Jacob. But these were poor people who couldn't wait for the economy to get back on track, or for the currency to stabilise. They needed to eat, and they didn't have any money.'

I nodded. 'So what did they do?' I asked.

'They made deals with speculators,' she replied.

'Speculators?'

'Yes. These were guys who did have money and who could afford to wait. So a speculator would make a deal with a guy who couldn't wait for the government to pay him back. The speculator would buy his loan certificate at a huge discount, maybe as low as twenty or twenty-five cents on the dollar. So the guy who sold the certificate would have money to eat, but the speculator would take over his claim against the government, which he could afford to hold on to until the government could afford to pay.'

'And he could watch it grow at the rate of six per cent compound every year until it was paid,' I added.

'Right. A hell of a deal for the speculator, but the poor guy who couldn't wait was losing a fortune.'

'OK,' I said. 'I see that. But where does Alexander Hamilton come in?'

'Well, the speculators were not exactly popular with the Congress,' she replied. 'Many congressmen thought they were leeches, bloodsuckers, taking unfair advantage of patriots who had contributed all they had to the war effort.'

I nodded. "That's a fair point."

'Yes,' she said, 'but being congressmen, they didn't feel they could just leave it at calling them names. They wanted to do something about it. They asked Hamilton to put a stop to it.'

'How would he do that?'

'By refusing to pay out on any certificate that had been bought for less than face value, and making sure the repayment went to the original lender. They raised the matter in the House of Representatives and they made Hamilton give them an answer.'

For some reason, I felt my hands and feet begin to tingle, and there were butterflies in my stomach.

'What answer did he give them?' I asked. I'm sure I must have sounded nervous. I certainly felt nervous.

'Hamilton said he sympathised, but there was nothing he could do. The government had to pay the speculators. They had no choice.'

'Why?' I breathed.

'It was something to do with the Constitution,' she replied. 'He said the government had to pay because it was guaranteed by the Constitution.'

I truly believe that my heart stopped in that moment. When I could breathe again, I asked her to repeat what she had said. She did.

30

'I MADE A COPY of it,' she said.

She reached down for her purse and took out several sheets of folded paper.

'It's from the report of the proceedings. God only knows how accurate any of this is,' she added. 'They didn't have recording devices then, and it sounds as though it was going on at quite a pace. But this is what they wrote down.'

She unfolded the sheets, and moved her chair next to mine, so that we could read together.

House of Representatives
The 9th Day of February, 1790
Debate on the Public Credit

THE SPEAKER: Order! I will have order, Gentlemen!

VARIOUS MEMBERS: We will not pay! No gold for the Leeches! etc. etc.

THE SPEAKER: Order, I say! If there is no order, I will suspend the sitting and clear the House. Order! You will come to order, Gentlemen. Mr Secretary, you may continue, if you please, but on your request, I will adjourn the debate.

THE SECRETARY OF THE TREASURY (MR HAMILTON): No, Mr Speaker. We have weighty matters to resolve. Let us

continue. Gentlemen, you have been provided with my
report on the public credit. If you have questions, I will
do my best to answer them. I ask only the courtesy that
you do so one at a time.

Laughter.

THE SPEAKER: *The Gentleman from South Carolina, Mr Butler,*
is recognised.

MR BUTLER: *Thank you, Mr Speaker. Mr Secretary, I understand*
from your report that you propose to pay in full every
loan certificate presented to the Treasury. I would be
interested to know how you propose to do so in the light
of our present circumstances.

Laughter, shouts.

THE SPEAKER: *Order!*

MR BUTLER: *I would further ask, sir, how you dare to pay those*
speculators who purchased loan certificates at a discount
from the poor after the war, and who now demand
payment on terms equal to those afforded to the original
lenders. They are leeches, sir, parasites. I say they shall
have nothing.

VARIOUS MEMBERS: *Hear, hear!*

MR HAMILTON: *The Honourable Gentleman has raised*
questions of the utmost importance.

VARIOUS MEMBERS: *He has indeed! Answer! etc. etc.*

MR HAMILTON: *If I am afforded the opportunity, I will answer*
to the best of my ability. As to how we shall pay, I confess
that I know not. We have too little gold to pay in full the
debts owed to every man who has presented his certificate
to the Treasury. But I have this faith: that these United

States will not forever be in penury. We will be strong, and as and when we can, we will pay our debt in full. As to the Honourable Gentleman's second question, I am of opinion that we must pay in full even those whom he has rightly described as leeches and parasites.

VARIOUS MEMBERS: *Never! He must resign! They shall have nothing!*

MR HAMILTON: *I will be heard…*

VARIOUS MEMBERS: *Resign, sir.*

THE SPEAKER: *Order! Enough! I will clear the House.*

MR HAMILTON: *No, Mr Speaker. I will account for myself. I will be heard, Gentlemen. I share the feelings of the House about these men. When Congress appealed for the means to fight against our enemies, many patriots gave their all. We all agree that these patriots must be repaid on presentation of their certificates. What, then, of those base men who bought certificates speculatively, thinking to live off the blood of the patriots? Gentlemen, this is no easy question.*

A MEMBER: *I find it to be easy enough, sir.*

MR HAMILTON: *Then, sir, you are mistaken. Firstly, I say this: I say that our hope of future credit requires that all be repaid in full. If it be seen abroad that we cannot, or will not, repay our debts, I doubt that any nation will long trade with us or furnish us with credit.*

But there is another consideration I esteem as far more important. The repayment of this debt is guaranteed by the Constitution of the United States. By this standard, we are allowed to make no distinction, since the Constitution applies to all alike.

*Gentlemen, this opinion gains further strength from
the nature of our debt. The faith of America has been
repeatedly pledged for it. This debt was not contracted
as the price of bread or wine or arms. It was the price of
liberty.*

We looked at each other.

'What do you think?' she asked.

I looked down at the page again, and felt tears welling up in my eyes.

'I think Alexander Hamilton wrote the third section of my brief,' I replied.

'I'm not getting it yet,' Sam said.

I walked over to my bookcase and took down a volume I should probably have read more often during my legal studies. It's surprising how the most basic principles can be overlooked amid the din of modern law practice with its endless deadlines, and procedural rules, and local rules, and all the other minutiae without which we apparently find it impossible now to resolve legal disputes. But with all the crap we've imposed on the laws designed to protect us, there are still some enduring anchors to keep us from floating away on a tide of technicality, if we will only allow ourselves to hold on fast to them.

'This is what Hamilton was talking about,' I said, opening the book at the page I knew I needed. 'It's the first paragraph of Article Six of the Constitution.'

I read it aloud.

'*All Debts contracted and Engagements entered into before the Adoption of this Constitution shall be as valid against the United States under this Constitution as under the Confederation.*'

Sam nodded.

'That's it. That's what he was saying. They actually guaranteed the debt – Jacob's debt – in the Constitution.'

'Exactly, and Hamilton knew, even before the Supreme Court

spelled it out, that the Constitution prevails over any contrary law. So there was no way to avoid it. There was no law they could enact to shut the speculators out. The government had to pay them, whether they wanted to or not.'

'Connect it up for me,' Sam said. 'How does that help us now?'

'The Constitution still prevails over any contrary law,' I replied. 'That hasn't changed since 1790. So what if we argue that the statute of limitations is a contrary law? They can't shut Jacob out any more than they could shut out the speculators.'

'The government can't use the statute to defeat a claim guaranteed by the Constitution,' she smiled.

'That has to be an argument. Congress can pass any statute of limitations it wants, but Jacob still has a valid claim, and on the face of it, Article Six of the Constitution says that the war debt is valid without any limitation of time. Any judge who throws this case out because of the statute of limitations is effectively repealing Article Six of the Constitution.' I smiled. 'Judge Morrow will have to think long and hard before he does that.'

She screamed and hugged me.

'Kiah, does this mean we're going to win on Monday?'

We held each other for several moments. My heart was racing. I desperately tried to focus on what we had discovered. I sensed that Sam had made a vital breakthrough, but I still needed to keep my feet on the ground. I still needed to work out exactly what it meant.

'Not quite so fast,' I said. 'We still have to think this through.'

'Think what through? If –'

'The debt is valid, yes, but that doesn't necessarily mean that the government has to provide a remedy for collecting it, and if they do, maybe they can still attach conditions to using the remedy.'

'Such as a statute of limitations?'

'Maybe.'

She sighed and shook her head.

'But how can they say the debt is valid, but then not give us a way to collect it? It doesn't make sense.'

I smiled.

'That's what they'll have to explain to the court. It's not a guarantee that we'll win, Sam, but the government's case just got a lot harder to argue.'

'We have a chance after all?'

'We have a definite chance, particularly when you consider what else Hamilton said about the war debt: he said it was the price of liberty. When you put it that way, any judge is going to think twice about dismissing without at least letting us try to prove our case.'

I hugged her again and kissed her on the cheek.

'You've kept us alive,' I replied. 'You did that, Sam. We're in with a shot.'

She laughed.

'So, now what?'

'Now,' I replied, 'I'm going home to get some sleep, and tomorrow I'm going to write a brief that will tell Dave Petrosian he has a fight on his hands.'

'What can I do?'

'You can go back to the library and get me copies of Hamilton's reports on the public credit – all of them, however many of them there are. Then you can go back over the proceedings in the House of Representatives at about the same time and see if you can find anything else of interest, anything at all, either before or after February 9.'

She nodded. She was beaming. So was I.

'You got it,' she said.

31

Dave Petrosian

I FOUND KIAH'S BRIEF lying on my desk when I arrived in the office at eight thirty on the Monday morning. It was in a brown envelope marked 'extremely urgent'. I'd had a good weekend. Well, why wouldn't I? I was looking forward to the week ahead and its promise of success. There's always a certain pleasurable anticipation when you're about to go to court on a motion you can't lose. Motions you can't lose only come along once in a while, and when they do, I've always thought of them as a reward for working so hard on the tricky ones that you have to argue, that could go either way. As I opened the envelope, I fully expected it to be a concession, an agreement to dismiss the lawsuit without the necessity for a court appearance. Kiah wasn't one to waste the court's time. She'd had a week to contemplate her mistake; she'd realised she didn't have a leg to stand on; and she would have no appetite for appearing in court just for the pleasure of listening to Judge Morrow dismiss her case on such an embarrassing ground. Obviously. I would have done the same in her position. That's how confident I was about what I would find in the brown envelope.

Instead, I found a forty-five page brief, exclusive of the table of contents and table of authorities, accompanied by a polite handwritten note from Kiah apologising for its lateness and offering me an unopposed adjournment for a week to allow the government time to respond. Once I recovered my composure I called in Harry and Ellen, and we scanned the brief quickly together with the aid of some very strong coffee. As we read, my pleasurable anticipation gave way to something approaching shock. Instead of a sensible concession that the case was untenable in the face of clear black-letter law, I was reading an indictment of the government (myself, presumably, included) for knavishly trying to nullify an article of the United States Constitution; and, equally knavishly, trying to deprive Samantha van Eyck and all those similarly situated of their constitutionally guaranteed right to recover a debt – a debt that represented the price of liberty – without even allowing them their day in court. What I had assumed to be an unanswerable motion to dismiss was being painted as a flagrant disregard for the Constitution and a blatant abuse of executive power, which no court should countenance. I wasn't the only one going hot and cold. I could see Harry's blood pressure rising. Only Ellen kept her cool. In fact, she giggled several times as she was reading, and she actually applauded one paragraph.

'This is brilliant,' she said as we reached the end. 'Absolutely brilliant.'

'I'm glad you find it amusing,' Harry muttered sourly.

'Credit where credit's due, Harry,' Ellen persisted. 'This is amazing stuff. It raises questions of pure constitutional law.'

'I think Harry's main concern is with the more immediate problem of what we do about it,' I suggested.

'Questions of pure constitutional law, my ass,' Harry protested. He glanced anxiously at his watch. 'It's bullshit. Not only that, it's outrageous. It's a calculated ambush. *Now* she leaves this for us to find? *Now*? This morning, at nine fifteen, when we're due in court at eleven? We should get our asses down to the courthouse and tell Tomorrow that he can't allow her to file this; tell him it's a contempt of court and he should decide the motion on our papers, in addition to imposing appropriate sanctions for her abusive conduct in dropping this shit on us without any notice. And in addition to that –'

'Harry, just calm down for a moment,' I said.

I turned to Ellen. Together, we lowered Harry back into his chair.

'Get him some more coffee.'

'I'm not sure coffee's the right thing,' she whispered.

'Get him some more coffee.'

'I don't need more coffee.'

'Yes, you do. Drink it.'

'We can't get rid of it that easily, Harry,' I said as he accepted the coffee with a show of reluctance. 'I served our motion last Monday, and I fixed the hearing for today, so I only gave her a week for any response. Obviously, I only did that because I didn't think there would be a response. I thought she would throw her hand in. But Tomorrow would have given her at least two weeks to respond if she'd asked him. I would have given her at least two weeks if she'd asked me. He's not going to stop her filing her brief, and he shouldn't.'

'In addition to which,' Ellen said, 'she's raised some serious issues. This isn't going to be as simple as we assumed. We need to take some time and think about how to respond.'

'You both told me we were home and dry,' Harry objected petulantly. Ellen might have been right – the coffee might have been a mistake. It had given him another shot of caffeine, and he was getting worked up, which wasn't good for him. Nonetheless, he had a justified complaint. We had pretty much told him that it was in the bag.

'Relying on what the two of you told me, I assured Maggie Watts that everything was under control, that it would all be over today. She passed that message up the line to –'

'Yes, I know, Harry,' I replied. 'But it's only a short delay. It's not the end of the world.'

'Oh, you think? What do I tell Maggie now? What do I tell her when she asks me what she tells the Attorney General, and what he tells –?'

'You tell her that the plaintiffs have filed a late brief, at the eleventh hour, without giving us any warning. We don't think it has any merit –'

'Don't we?' Ellen asked quietly.

'No, we don't. But it would be irresponsible of us not to ask for time to consider it fully and file a reply.'

'And even if we didn't ask for time,' Ellen added, 'there's no way Judge Morrow would rule on the motion today, not with a brief like that coming across his desk at the last moment. No judge is going to rule on issues like this without being fully briefed in writing by both sides.'

Harry looked suspiciously at Ellen and me in turn.

'I want a report on my desk by four o'clock this afternoon,' he said, pointing a finger as he left my office.

'Harry, take one of your pills,' Ellen called after him.

'Don't nag me,' he shouted from the corridor outside. 'Just get rid of this.'

'You heard the man,' I said.

She smiled. 'I guess I'll get started on it, then.'

'Ellen, do we actually think this has some merit?' I asked, just as she was leaving.

She turned back to face me.

'It has some merit, definitely,' she replied. 'It's a great piece of lawyering, any way you look at it. Well, we didn't see it coming, did we?'

'No, we didn't.'

'But that doesn't mean she's right, and it certainly doesn't mean we don't have a response to it.'

I nodded. 'I need a progress report not later than two o'clock.'

I called the court and got Judge Morrow's clerk, Maisie, to adjourn our motion for a week. She offered no resistance at all. Judge

Morrow was reading Kiah's brief as we spoke, and they had both been expecting our call. I called Kiah to tell her.

'I got your brief,' I said, 'and Judge Morrow has agreed to the adjournment.'

'I appreciate the call, Dave. Thank you.'

She paused.

'What did you think of it?'

'Very impressive,' I replied. 'We may throw our hand in. Is the offer to take Rhode Island still on the table?'

She laughed.

'I'll talk to Sam. But we still want the statue as well.'

'OK. I'll see you next Monday morning.' I had to ask. 'Kiah, that brief is more like the kind of thing you see in the Supreme Court. How the hell did you do that in a week?'

'I told you,' she replied. 'I had a call in to my fairy godmother.'

32

THE UNITED STATES CLAIMS Court sits in the Howard T Markey National Courts Building in Madison Place, NW, a pleasant and short enough walk from our offices. When Ellen and I arrived in Madison Place at ten o'clock, an hour before the scheduled hearing time, we expected to have it to ourselves. The Claims Court doesn't usually generate much publicity, and it's certainly not a venue for the kinds of sensational cases the press and the TV networks love to report – the stories of bloodshed, corruption, and betrayal. You expect that kind of thing at the various criminal courts in and around the District. You expect it down the road at the Supreme Court, where there's always some kind of national drama unfolding. But those of us who toil in this little-noticed corner of the legal vineyard don't have the kind of cases that attract the attention of prime time news programs, and we're not used to being besieged by hordes of journalists clamouring for sound bites. We are used to having our courthouse to ourselves, used to being free to enter and leave the building without being caught up in the glare of the media spotlight. We are used to conducting our unremarkable legal business in a suitably quiet and unremarkable legal backwater. But not today: today, the word was out. Madison Place was the place to be.

As television cameras from every part of the United States and beyond tracked our every move, we had to fight our way into the building through a veritable throng of reporters thrusting microphones into our faces, some demanding to know why the government was refusing justice to a true American patriot, others demanding to know whether we were going to save the United States from imminent bankruptcy. I saw copies of Kiah's brief, no doubt downloaded from the court's website, in some of their hands. There were members of the public too, with placards denouncing the government's meanness and lack of concern for justice on behalf of veterans generally and the heroes of the War of Independence particularly. If it hadn't been for Donald and Shirley, two calm, experienced court security guards I'd known, for years, who intervened on our behalf, I'm not sure we would have made it inside without some kind of incident. Donald is a quiet but large black man in his late forties, a former high school linebacker. Shirley is a fading blonde in her fifties who chews gum and she is only half Donald's size, if that, but if you had a choice between messing with her and messing with Donald, you would probably mess with Donald.

Only when we were inside the courtroom did I remember Harry's stricture about not talking to the press. Had I? Had I remained totally silent during the scrimmage? I didn't think I'd said anything stupid to anyone. I had a memory of telling some reporter who kept shouting at me and wouldn't leave me alone, that today wasn't such a big deal, that it was just a preliminary hearing on a point of law – which was true as far as it went, but didn't quite do justice to the day's proceedings. But I didn't think I'd given them anything worth quoting me on.

'What in the hell kind of case do you have today?' Donald asked breathlessly, once we were safely inside the building. 'Is America about to fall apart?'

'That depends on who you ask,' I replied.

'They don't pay us enough for this,' Shirley protested.

'They don't pay *me* enough for this,' I chimed in.

Donald smiled.

'Welcome to the NFL, Bubba,' he replied.

The memory of Harry's instructions about not talking to the press also made me wonder how he would have coped with it all. Not well, I suspected, and he would be sucking down his pills like candy by now. Fortunately, we had persuaded him to stay at the office. He had wanted to come with us, but I had told him that I didn't want to present Judge Morrow with the image of three of us ganging up on Kiah. If we outnumbered her too much, it might suggest that the government was using its superior resources to bully her. I needed Ellen, because she'd written our reply and was on top of the law, and that was already two against one. Besides, I added, it was important for Harry to be available at the office to coordinate things and distribute information once we knew which way Judge Morrow was going to go. I wasn't really sure what that meant, but he seemed to like it. Thank goodness. I had enough to deal with today without having to worry about keeping Harry calm.

The courtroom itself was almost as bad as the main entrance to the building. Some of the reporters had followed us in, and others were already in place in the press seats. The public gallery was also full. It turned out that every law clerk, intern, and law student in the building had abandoned whatever court they were assigned to in the interests of witnessing what might turn into a historic occasion. Well, of course. They couldn't keep this quiet at the courthouse any more than we could at the office. This was the most interesting case to come to the Claims Court in a long time – perhaps ever – and no one wanted to miss the show. What was even more intimidating was that the law clerks, interns and students had all come prepared with laptops and yellow pads. Notes would be taken for later discussion. The disquieting thought came to me that Kiah and I were about to conduct a very public class in constitutional law and civil procedure, and there was every chance that whatever we said would be dissected and judged at leisure, not only by Judge Morrow, but by an unforgiving body of legal academics and commentators – in addition to the news reporters who just thought it was a great story. So, no pressure then.

I glanced at Ellen, who was systematically unpacking her briefcase, and depositing copies of the briefs and legal authorities on our table. Her hair was slightly out of place, but she seemed composed enough after our ordeal, and even managed a smile when she saw that I was looking at her. I joined her at the table and began setting up my own notes. I poured both of us a large glass of water.

'Did you say –?'

'No,' she said, 'not a word. At least I don't think I did. You?'

I shook my head. 'Nothing worth reporting,' I replied.

'Nothing worth… what do you mean?'

'I mean, nothing… worth reporting.'

I was saved from further interrogation by the arrival of Kiah, flanked by a young woman I recognised from her press photographs as Samantha van Eyck, and an older woman with big hair and bright red lipstick, who I took to be Arlene. I'd never met Arlene but I'd spoken to her, and had been regaled with her choice pieces of Texas wisdom often enough when I'd had occasion to call Kiah's office. Kiah was smiling as she approached our table.

'Well, this is quite a turn-out, Dave,' she said, indicating the assembled ranks of law clerks, interns and law students. 'Are they all your associates? I had no idea you had so many of them hidden away at Justice. No wonder you guys can come up with those killer briefs.'

We shook hands.

'I thought they were the Kiah Harmon fan club,' I replied. 'This is Ellen Matthews, who actually does write our killer briefs.'

Kiah took her hand with a smile. 'I knew someone had to,' she said.

'I am in awe of you, Miss Harmon,' Ellen said, with complete sincerity. 'Truly. Your brief is wonderful.'

'You wrote a good reply too,' Kiah rejoined. 'This is my client, Sam van Eyck, and Arlene, who runs our office.'

Sam shook hands with both of us briefly and with the hint of a smile. She was professionally dressed in a two-piece grey suit, her hair and make-up perfect. Between her and Kiah, you couldn't have said which one of then was the lawyer unless you knew; you might actually have gone with Samantha. Arlene didn't offer to shake hands. She raised one arm in the air – some form of Texas greeting, I supposed – and then walked over to their table to begin arranging their papers.

'Any indication from Tomorrow about how he's going to conduct the hearing?' Kiah asked.

'Not that I know of,' I replied. 'But I haven't had a chance to look for Maisie. We just got here. We had to run the gauntlet outside, as I'm sure you did.'

She grinned. 'Did you have any comment for the *Six O'Clock News*?'

'Absolutely not. That would be way above my pay grade.'

'He means, he said nothing worth reporting,' Ellen replied with a smile.

'Did you say anything?' I asked.

'Not much. Just a few words, the usual kind of thing.'

'The usual kind of thing?'

She was turning to join Sam and Arlene at the plaintiff's table.

'Yes: the importance of rewarding patriotism; the decadence of a government that won't honour its most sacred obligations and has no regard for the price paid for its own liberty; the evils of putting the letter of the law above doing justice – you know, the usual kind of thing. You'll be able to hear it all when you get back to the office.'

She suddenly turned back and stood looking slightly down at us, the palms of both her hands on the edge of our table.

'Last chance, Dave. Rhode Island and the statue. What do you say? Do we have a deal?'

She pushed herself back up and walked away before I could reply.

'I love her,' Ellen said.

33

'THE UNITED STATES CLAIMS Court is now in session, the Honourable Thomas Oliver Morrow presiding.'

It was a well-rehearsed drill, perfected over fourteen years of sitting in the same courtroom. Judge Morrow timed his walk from the door to his seat to perfection, exactly coinciding with the duration of the bailiff's announcement. He's a good-looking man, tall and well-built, the hair grey now, but the military firmness still etched in his rugged face. Tomorrow has one of the best courtroom demeanors I've ever seen, firm when he needs to be firm, but unfailingly even-handed and courteous to everyone who comes into his courtroom. He has a laid-back manner on the bench, which can sometimes mask a quick, keen legal mind. Kiah and I both knew him too well by then to fall into that trap, but attorneys who weren't familiar with him sometimes underestimated him, to their cost.

'Please be seated,' he said.

Everyone did, except for Kiah, myself, and Maisie. The hubbub of conversation that had filled the courtroom before the judge's entry had subsided almost instantly on his arrival. The reporters were on the edge of their seats, ready now for the serious business of the day, and the army of law clerks, interns and students also had their laptops and pencils poised for action.

'Call the case of *Samantha van Eyck individually and on behalf of all those similarly situated, plaintiffs, versus United States, defendant,*' Maisie announced. 'Your Honour, the case is listed for the hearing of the defendant's motion to dismiss based on the statute of limitations. Counsel, please state your appearances for the record.'

'Good morning, Your Honour. Dave Petrosian and Ellen Matthews for the defendant, the United States.'

'Good morning, Your Honour, Kiah Harmon for the plaintiffs. In court with me is the lead plaintiff, Samantha van Eyck.'

'Welcome to you all,' the judge said, 'and welcome to everyone in court. I see we have quite a crowd today. I'm pleased to see so many unfamiliar faces. It's not often that the Claims Court commands such an audience, not often we have so many people interested in what we do here. It looks like we missed out on an opportunity: we could have sold tickets if we'd thought about it yesterday.'

There was some laughter from the press seats.

'But I'm glad that the court is finally getting a chance to show off the work it does, and I'm glad you're all here to see us in action. The only other thing I should probably say is to all you law clerks and interns I see out there from my colleagues' courtrooms and from the Court of Appeals for the Federal Circuit: I hope you all got your judges' permission to leave your stations and come to my court. I'm glad you've come, but I don't want to catch hell from the other judges, so if you haven't done it already, fire off an email now and at least let your judge know where you are.'

More laughter, this time from the law clerks and interns. But I was sure Tomorrow needn't have worried about that. I would have put money on the fact that every judge in the building had ordered his or her clerks and interns to invade Tomorrow's court and bring back a first-hand report of the proceedings to their chambers. The judges would have been here themselves if they weren't so busy with their own work. In fact, having seen the crowd, I was slightly surprised that the other judges hadn't called a recess for an hour or two so that they didn't have to miss the fun.

'Now, Mr Petrosian, this is your motion.'

'Yes, Your Honour. Before I begin, may I ask how much time the court will allow counsel for oral argument? Will it be the usual twenty minutes for each side?'

If there hadn't been so much going on before court began, I would have confirmed this with Maisie before we started. In most cases in the Claims Court, there's no reason to ask. Twenty minutes is the rule, and if the judge has read the papers and your brief – which in the Claims Court you can usually take for granted – that's about eighteen minutes longer than you need. If you want longer, you are supposed to ask for more time in your brief, though most of the judges aren't too strict unless they have an exceptionally busy day, and they don't call time on you for taking more than your twenty minutes unless you are repeating yourself or rambling on pointlessly. In her brief, Kiah had asked for an hour and a half, emphasising the unusual nature of the case, but I hadn't seen any ruling from the court. It wasn't the time I was concerned about; it was the implications of Judge Morrow's decision.

I was hoping that I wouldn't need more than twenty minutes. My pitch was that the statute of limitations was six years; the plaintiffs had missed the deadline by quite a margin; and whatever the Constitution said about the validity of the debt didn't alter the fact that the Claims Court had no jurisdiction to adjudicate on a 200-year-old claim. If the judge agreed with me, then whatever constitutional arguments Kiah had raised in her brief weren't really relevant, and we didn't need to get side-tracked into exploring them in detail. I didn't need twenty minutes to say that, and Ellen and I, while admiring Kiah's scholarship, had convinced ourselves that this was the right way to look at the case. So if Judge Morrow was happy with twenty minutes a side, I figured that he was provisionally leaning towards the government and Kiah was going to have an uphill struggle to change his mind. On the other hand, if he gave her an hour and a half, I figured that he might have been seduced by the constitutional arguments and was going to accept her invitation to hold a law school moot court on the subject of Article Six of the Constitution. The answer to my question was not the one I'd hoped to hear. In fact, it was worse than my worst-case scenario.

'You may have noticed, Mr Petrosian, that I have no other matters listed in my courtroom today.'

'Yes, Your Honour.' I had noticed, but I hadn't thought about it long enough to draw any conclusions. I was drawing them pretty fast now, but even if I hadn't, Tomorrow was going to enlighten me.

'That's because I have deliberately left my list for today empty except for this case. I think it would be highly undesirable to place time limits on argument in a case such as this, in which the court may have to decide questions of importance involving our Constitution, questions that may well come before a higher court one of these days. I've read the briefs filed by both sides, which are well-written and helpful, but I have a lot of questions, and I'm going to need counsel's help to answer them. So I've decided to devote as long as necessary to this motion. If we need to take all day, we'll take all day. I want both of you to say whatever you want to say. Don't worry about time. Focus on the case.'

I saw Ellen looking at me with raised eyebrows. I nodded, hoping to convey an air of confidence. I had my notes in front of me. I wasn't going to panic. There was no need to change our strategy just because the judge had some questions he needed answers to. Our position was that this was a simple procedural question, and that's how I would deal with it.

'Your Honour,' I began, 'assuming that Jacob van Eyck made the loans in question in the period 1777–1778, and further assuming that he was never repaid, the plaintiffs are out of time to bring an action in this court to recover the debt. The period of limitation is six years. Now we can argue, as Miss Harmon does in her brief, about whether they're out of time by 200 years or more, or as little as 130 or so years. It doesn't matter. The period is six years, and that period is long gone, and there is no constitutional issue in question here.'

Judge Morrow was shaking his head.

'But if Miss Harmon is right, and the Revolutionary War debt is guaranteed by the Constitution itself without any limitation of time, how is that consistent with a statute of limitations?'

'It's perfectly consistent, Your Honour. The fact that the debt itself continues to be valid doesn't mean that a plaintiff can sue in this court to recover it. This court has no jurisdiction over cases where the claim accrued more than six years before suit is filed.'

'Well, if the plaintiffs can't sue here – which is where Congress says you're supposed to sue the government for claims such as this – where can they sue?'

'I'm not sure they can sue anywhere, Your Honour. Frankly, that's not our concern. Our point is that they can't sue in this court, which is what they have chosen to do.'

'So they have no remedy if the government fails to repay the loan, even though the Constitution declares the debt to be valid without limitation of time? Is that what you're telling me?'

This wasn't how I'd wanted the argument to go. I would have preferred to stay away from the moral aspects of it. Whenever Ellen and I had played lawyer and judge in preparation for the argument, with Harry sitting there and interjecting comments from time to time, we had always agreed that this wasn't the way we wanted to portray it. It wasn't that we weren't right, legally speaking, but it wasn't the most attractive position for the government to take: the van Eycks had a perpetually valid debt, but no way to claim repayment. We had decided to offer Tomorrow the only other possibility that made sense, one which didn't come with a statute of limitations.

'It's open to the family to petition the Congress for the redress of grievances,' I replied. 'They can take it up with a member of Congress or a senator, and ask for legislative relief on behalf, not only of the van Eyck family, but any other families who may have similar claims.'

'According to Miss Harmon's brief, they've been doing that periodically for the best part of 200 years, and they've gotten nowhere.'

'We don't know how well it was presented to Congress on those earlier occasions, Your Honour. They may have failed simply because they didn't have an attorney such as Miss Harmon working with them in the past. If they were to try again today, with an attorney of her ability –'

I turned towards Kiah, who was giving me an 'oh, please, spare me' look. The judge interrupted me in mid-sentence.

'If they were to try again today, we all know what would happen, Mr Petrosian, don't we? They would be stalled and rebuffed. If they pressed hard enough, eventually it might find its way into some congressional committee, but there wouldn't be much an attorney, whether it's Miss Harmon or anyone else, could do to move it along. Even assuming it made it into committee, it would probably die there; and even if it didn't die there, it would then have to find its way into some piece of legislation that had enough bipartisan support to pass both the House and the Senate; and then, years later, assuming the President didn't veto it, maybe – just maybe – the family might be awarded a few dollars that wouldn't affect the budget too much.'

He paused.

'I'm not sure I would call that a remedy. Forgive me if I sound cynical, Mr Petrosian, but I've spent much of my life in public service, and I've been around that block a time or two myself.'

Tomorrow was playing to the gallery – something I'd never imagined was part of his repertoire – but he wasn't far off base. Legislatures the world over know exactly how to bury troublesome petitions for the redress of grievances, and ours is no exception. And I wasn't unsympathetic to the point he was making; I hadn't been unsympathetic when Kiah had made it to me. But that didn't mean we weren't right in law.

'Your Honour put it to me that the family has no remedy outside this court,' I replied. 'I'm only pointing out that there may be a remedy. But frankly, Your Honour, even if it there isn't, that doesn't mean that this court has jurisdiction when the statute has run by more than 200 years.'

Judge Morrow was shaking his head.

'So, the answer to my original question is "yes",' he said. 'You're saying that they have a valid debt but they don't have a court in which to sue for it. And because this court wasn't even in existence when the claim accrued, they never did have a court to sue in. It's not a great advertisement for American justice, is it, Mr Petrosian?'

The sensible answer to that, of course, was that it wasn't for me to say. Or, I could have pointed out that it's for Congress to make the law, and if Congress agreed with the judge, perhaps they could take a fresh look at it. Those would have been the sensible answers. Instead I said: 'No, Your Honour, I guess it's not.'

The moment the words had left my mouth, I knew as if by revelation that I would be hearing them again on the *Six O'Clock News*. But they seemed to mollify Tomorrow. He was silent, nodding, for some time.

'Well, you've made the government's position clear, Mr Petrosian. I think I'd better hear from Miss Harmon, and I'll come back to you if I have any more questions later.'

'Yes, Your Honour.'

I sat down. I realised for the first time that I was sweating. Ellen was grinning at me. She leaned over to whisper in my ear.

'A government lawyer caused a sensation today by admitting in court that the government's failure to provide a remedy –'

'Yes, thank you, Walter Cronkite,' I whispered back.

'But you were right,' she said.

34

'He has a point, Miss Harmon,' Judge Morrow began, 'doesn't he?'

'He has a point, Your Honour,' Kiah replied. 'Just not a good one.'

There was some laughter around the courtroom. Tomorrow smiled.

'That depends on what you mean by "good", doesn't it? Mr Petrosian concedes that the government's position is somewhat unattractive, but he says that's irrelevant if the law is on his side. Why is he wrong about that?'

'He's wrong because, if he's right, then Congress, by enacting a statute of limitations, has effectively repealed an article of our Constitution, the first paragraph of Article Six. Congress can't repeal an article of our Constitution; the President can't repeal an article of our Constitution; this court can't do it; and for that matter, even the Supreme Court can't do it. In fact, not even Mr Petrosian can repeal an article of our Constitution.'

This drew some loud laughter. I grinned. I deserved it after the cheesy *faux* compliment I'd paid her.

'Well, there's no arguing with that,' the judge countered, 'but why do you say they are repealing it?'

'Because if they're right, taking account of the statute of limitations, every claim under Article Six was forever barred as of March 3, 1893, at the latest.'

'Why is that a problem?'

'Because Article Six is not limited in time. It's an indefinite constitutional obligation, and Congress can't place a time limit on it retrospectively. Your Honour, maybe I should start with what the Founding Fathers were trying to do?'

'It seems clear enough what the Founding Fathers were trying to do,' Tomorrow replied. 'They were telling everyone how important the war debt was, because they wanted to create confidence that the government would honour its obligations.'

'Yes, Your Honour,' Kiah replied, 'but they were doing a lot more than that. They were trying to make sure that the debt was in fact repaid in full. That was something they couldn't control. They couldn't do it themselves. The country didn't have the money at that time. We were essentially bankrupt. The currency was almost worthless. They knew it would be a long time before America became strong enough economically to pay the debt, and they knew there would be a temptation for future politicians and bureaucrats to find excuses for not paying.'

She paused to glance in my direction.

'And how right they were.'

Further sniggers around the courtroom. I wasn't entirely sure I deserved that one.

'If we look at the language of the predecessor of Article Six, which was Article Twelve of the Articles of Confederation, adopted on March 1, 1781, they said this: "*All bills of credit emitted, monies borrowed and debts contracted by or under the authority of Congress, before the assembling of the United States, in pursuance of the present confederation, shall be deemed and considered as a charge against the United States, for the payment and satisfaction whereof the said United States and the public faith are hereby solemnly pledged.*"

'I invite Your Honour's attention particularly to the words, "The United States and the public faith are hereby solemnly pledged."

'Then we go to the first paragraph of Article Six of the Constitution, adopted on March 4, 1789, which is the provision we're concerned with: *"All Debts and Engagements entered into, before the Adoption of this Constitution, shall be as valid against the United States under this Constitution, as under the Confederation."* The magic words there, Your Honour, are, *"Under this Constitution"*.

'Your Honour, these provisions were discussed in great depth before they were adopted. There was a high level of agreement about the proposed constitutional provision. We've covered this in our brief, beginning at page twenty-two, so I needn't take Your Honour through it all. Among those who spoke and submitted drafts of the proposed provision were Mr Randolph of Virginia, Mr Paterson of New Jersey, and Mr Pinckney of South Carolina. The House appointed a committee of five members to prepare a final draft for approval.

'But, Your Honour, this is important – this is at page twenty-six of our brief. Some members, including Mr Ellsworth of Connecticut, thought that the provision was unnecessary. He said: "The United States heretofore entered into engagements by Congress, who were their agents. They will hereafter be bound to fulfill them by their new agents."

'But Alexander Hamilton reminded the delegates that, in his words, "Contracts between a sovereign nation and individuals" – he means its citizens – "are binding only on the conscience of the sovereign and have no pretensions to a compulsive force." In other words, he was worried that future politicians might be less scrupulous than Mr Ellsworth and himself.

'So, enshrining in the Constitution itself a duty – a duty, not a mere power – to repay the public debt was the only way in which to guarantee that the United States would one day meet its obligations.'

Kiah paused for several sips of water.

'Hamilton was very aware of the need to ensure that later governments didn't renege on their obligations. He couldn't foresee what economic and political pressures, what temptations to renege later governments might face, but he knew it was a real danger. In his second Report on the Public Credit, he wrote: "*It can hardly happen that all the branches, or parts of government can be infected at one time with a common passion, or disposition, so manifestly inimical to justice and the public good, as to prostrate the public credit, by revoking a pledge, given to the creditors.*" But in case they did, there was only one remedy. If you made the obligation part of the Constitution itself, you took it out of the hands of the government altogether, so even if all three branches of government were tempted to avoid responsibility, the debt remained valid and must be paid.'

Judge Morrow nodded.

'All right, Miss Harmon, assuming I'm with you so far, you've established a moral case for making the government pay. But where do you get your legal case?'

She smiled.

'Your Honour, that story starts with the blood-suckers.'

35

'THE BLOOD-SUCKERS WERE SPECULATORS who bought up loan certificates from people who couldn't afford to wait for the government to pay them back.'

'You dealt with that in your brief,' Judge Morrow observed. 'They would pay as little as twenty or twenty-five cents on the dollar. But the people they were dealing with had no choice. They needed the money to eat.'

'Exactly, Your Honour. And for the first time, the government was presented with the temptation to refuse payment for reasons of policy. The speculators were an easy target. They weren't about to win any popularity contests. It would have been a good political move. Mr Butler of South Carolina summed up the feelings in the House – page thirty, Your Honour – "*A positive statement that the engagement shall be fulfilled might compel payment, as well to those blood-suckers who have speculated on the distresses of others, as to those who have fought and bled for their country. A distinction should be made between those classes of people.*"'

'You have to have some sympathy with that,' the judge remarked.

'Yes, Your Honour. But Hamilton insisted that they couldn't make that distinction – page thirty-one – this is from his First Report: "*It would be repugnant to an express provision of the Constitution of the United States. This provision is that, 'all debts contracted and engagements entered into before the adoption of this Constitution shall be as valid against the United States under*

this Constitution as under the Confederation'; which amounts to
a constitutional ratification of the contracts representing the debt
in the state in which they existed under the Confederation. And,
resorting to that standard, there can be no doubt that the rights
of the assignees and the original holders must be regarded as
equal."

'Your Honour, if ever there were to be a good policy reason for
interfering with the duty to repay a valid war loan, the case of the
speculators would have been it. But Hamilton tells us exactly why
it couldn't be done.'

Judge Morrow thought for some time.

'So now, tell me, Miss Harmon: does Hamilton also explain
why the government can't rely on the statute of limitations when
it's sued over a debt that's more than 200 years old?'

There was some muted laughter, but Kiah wasn't fazed for a
moment.

'He does, Your Honour.'

'Really?'

'Yes. Not in so many words, obviously. When Hamilton was
writing his reports in the late 1780s, early 1790s, there was no
Claims Court, there was no statute of limitations. There was no
way to sue the government. The law then was the law we took from
England: the King can do no wrong. It was our government now,
not the King, but that didn't affect the principle.'

'Exactly,' the judge said. 'Eventually, our government accepted
that citizens should be allowed to sue it, and they even set up this
court in which to do it. But they also laid down some conditions
that had to be observed, including the statute of limitations. I take
it you're not opposed to statutes of limitation in principle?'

'No, of course not,' Kiah replied.

'They serve a useful function, don't they? They ensure that cases
can be tried before all the witnesses have died and all the evidence
has been destroyed or lost in the mists of time. Nothing wrong
with that, is there?'

'Nothing at all, Your Honour, although I have to say that I don't see how the statute would help in our case.'

'Why not?'

'Because by 1893 all the witnesses to the van Eyck loans were already dead, and there had already been every chance for documents to be lost or destroyed, not least because of what the British did to Washington in 1814. In fact, because we now have the National Archives, and we've done a good job preserving such documents as we do have, it's probably easier today to reconstruct what happened back then than at any earlier time. The government isn't prejudiced by the delay at all.'

Tomorrow smiled.

'Not a bad point. But…'

'But it doesn't get me past the law. No, Your Honour, I know that. So, here's the real point. First, the Constitution is the supreme law of the land. Do I need to address Your Honour on that? We have the authorities in our brief…'

'I tell you what, Miss Harmon, if I start to waver on that, I'll let you know.'

Laughter we could all join in freely.

'Thank you, Your Honour. Starting from there, any statutory provision enacted by Congress that contradicts a provision of the Constitution is void. May I take it that we agree on that also?'

'Any wavering there to be notified also,' Tomorrow grinned.

'Thank you, Your Honour. The effect of the statute of limitations in this case is that no one has been able to sue to recover a war loan since 1893. Yet Article Six makes the war debt valid without limitation of time. The statute clearly contradicts Article Six, and it is void to that extent.'

'To that extent?'

'Yes. We don't suggest that the statute can't be applied generally in the Claims Court. Quite the contrary. In fact, this may be the only kind of case where it can't apply. I can't think of any other contractual obligations still hanging on from the days of the

Confederation. So, we're not talking about opening Pandora's box here. The case Your Honour is dealing with today is probably the only case where the statute can't be applied.'

The judge exhaled audibly.

'But Mr Petrosian suggested the answer to that, didn't he? He says that the debt itself may well be valid, but at this late time, the family can't sue for it in this court. He says that the government allowed itself to be sued, many years after the Constitution was adopted, and when they did, they were entitled to lay down the conditions under which they would allow themselves to be sued. One of those conditions is the six-year time limit. What's wrong with that?'

'Your Honour himself pointed out what's wrong with that. If we can't sue in this court, we are left with petitioning the government for the redress of grievances, and I think Your Honour and I agree on how far we'd get with that. It's been tried before, and it failed.'

She paused for a few moments.

'Your Honour, if you would, imagine this with me back then? Imagine that Congress created the Claims Court, but then said, "You can't sue for a war loan if your ancestor was a speculator, if he wasn't the original lender."'

The judge nodded. 'That wouldn't fly.'

'No, it wouldn't. It wouldn't fly in 1790 when Hamilton rejected the idea, and it wouldn't fly today. The only question would be whether or not you have a loan certificate which the government is obliged to redeem. The government has allowed you to sue since Hamilton's day. They've given you a remedy. Perhaps they didn't have to, but they did it, and now they have to live with it and honour it. If the government creates a remedy, it has to be a remedy compatible with the Constitution. You can't put a time limit on claims under Article Six.'

36

'Anything else, Miss Harmon?'

Kiah paused for some seconds.

'Just this, Your Honour. In *Marbury v Madison* – the citation's in our brief – the Supreme Court said, *"It cannot be presumed that any clause in the Constitution is intended to be without effect; and therefore, such a construction is inadmissible, unless the words require it."* That's part of the principle that the Constitution is the supreme law of the land – and I don't remember Your Honour wavering on that yet.'

Brilliant. It was said respectfully, and Kiah had the judge, as well as the courtroom, laughing quietly with her.

'But if you go with Mr Petrosian here, you're treating the first paragraph of Article Six as without effect. And the first paragraph of Article Six has never even been interpreted judicially, not once since March 4, 1789. If you look at all the ink that's been spilled, all the annotations on the other articles of the Constitution, and the amendments including the Bill of Rights, that's a remarkable fact. We have volume after volume of pronouncements by the Supreme Court, and lower courts, on every other article and amendment, but not a word about Article Six. If you decide to say what it means in this case, what you say will be the first word on the subject; and if you go with Mr Petrosian on this, it will be the last word, because it will have been wiped – erased from history – without ever having been given effect.

'If you go with Mr Petrosian, what happens to the price of liberty? What happens to the "charge against the United States, for the payment and satisfaction whereof the said United States and the public faith are hereby solemnly pledged"? What does that even mean, *solemnly pledged*, if you go with Mr Petrosian?'

I saw the judge lift his head and look up.

'If I may, Your Honour,' Kiah said, 'I would like Alexander Hamilton to have the last word, rather than me. This is from his first Report on the Public Credit. It's in our brief:

While the observance of that good faith, which is the basis of public credit, is recommended by the strongest inducements of political expediency, it is enforced by considerations of still greater authority. There are arguments for it which rest on the immutable principles of moral obligation. And in proportion as the mind is disposed to contemplate, in the order of Providence, an intimate connection between public virtue and public happiness, will be its repugnancy to a violation of these principles. This reflection derives additional strength from the nature of the debt of the United States. It was the price of liberty. The faith of America has been repeatedly pledged for it, and with solemnities that give particular force to the obligation.

Unless Your Honour has any questions?

Judge Morrow stared at Kiah for some time, nodding almost imperceptibly. She stood quietly, without moving, returning his look. As I watched, I felt a new admiration for her. She was harnessing the silence and making it work for her. She was holding the courtroom in her spell by the sheer force of her presence. How was she doing that? It was extraordinary to watch. I had a lump in my throat. Eventually, it was Tomorrow who turned his eyes away. They turned to me.

'Thank you, Miss Harmon. Anything further, Mr Petrosian?'

I glanced at Ellen. She shook her head. She was right. We had made our position very clear. If Tomorrow wasn't with us now, repeating ourselves wasn't going to change his mind.

'No, Your Honour, thank you.'

I'm not sure what we were expecting to happen next. Judges will often rule on motions like this from the bench at the close of argument, but where there are difficult issues of law they prefer to take the matter under advisement and issue a written ruling later. What was Tomorrow going to do? It's another thing I would probably have asked Maisie about before we started if it hadn't all been so frenetic. Thinking about it, putting myself in the judge's position, I would have taken time to reflect on it and put my reasons in writing as clearly as I could, even if I'd already made my mind up which way I was going. For one thing, I would have assumed that I wouldn't be having the last word on this case. In all likelihood, whatever I did, this was going down the hall to another part of the building, to the Court of Appeals for the Federal Circuit, and from there perhaps even to the Supreme Court. With so many more senior judges poised to dissect and criticise my every word, making sure I was clear in my own mind before committing pen to paper would seem sensible. I sensed that the same thoughts were going through Tomorrow's mind, but I wasn't prepared for what came next.

'I'd like to see counsel in chambers,' he said. 'Just Mr Petrosian and Miss Harmon.'

He was off the bench before we could react.

37

As we walked through the outer office leading to the judge's chambers, Maisie asked us if we would like coffee. We both said we would love some. It had been a tense morning, and until we found out what was going on in Judge Morrow's mind, that wasn't going to change. A shot or two of caffeine sounded good. As she showed us into chambers, Maisie was grinning. Whether that was because she knew something we didn't, I obviously had no idea. But we would have to wait. She wasn't about to enlighten us.

Off the bench, Tomorrow was quite informal. He had thrown his robe on to a chair in the corner, and he was in his shirtsleeves.

'Come and sit down,' he said, waving us into the two armchairs in front of his desk. 'Is Maisie getting you some coffee?'

'She is, Judge, thanks,' I replied.

Tomorrow took his seat and picked up a pipe from the huge porcelain ashtray on his desk. It was a gesture all the lawyers who practiced in the Claims Court regularly associated with him. Tomorrow was a dedicated pipe smoker, and although he wasn't allowed to smoke in his chambers, he found it comforting to have the trappings all around him, so that he was ready to light up if they suddenly changed the law, or, I suppose, when he had the chance to go outside. So the leather tobacco pouch, the lighter, a pack of pipe cleaners, and the tool for reaming the pipe were always at hand. There were rumours that when he was working alone in the evenings, after the staff had gone home for the night, he indulged himself surreptitiously, and I knew from Maisie that there were mornings when she walked into chambers and had the distinct impression of a whiff of Sobranie Flake in the musty air. No one begrudged him the indulgence, and no one even for a moment entertained the thought of ratting him out to the Chief Judge. He was too well liked for that. He went through the motions of patting some tobacco down in the bowl before taking the pipe into the left corner of his mouth. He took one or two dry puffs, and removed it again.

'Well, you two have put me in a fine position, I must say,' he began.

Kiah and I exchanged glances.

'How so, Judge?' I asked.

'How so? What the hell am I going to do with this case? If I go with the government, I go down in history as the judge who wrote the obituary for an article of the Constitution that's never even been judicially interpreted. If I go with the plaintiffs –'

He paused as Maisie came in with coffee for the three of us, in good-sized mugs. She left us a small jug of milk, white sugar lumps, and packets of sweetener.

'Thanks, Maisie.' He waited for her to close the door behind her. 'If I go with the plaintiffs, I go down in history as the judge who paved the way for the government to pay out a king's ransom – well, bad analogy in the circumstances, but you get my point.'

I smiled.

'I understand, Judge,' I replied. 'But if you dismiss the case for lack of jurisdiction, the wider issues go away.'

'No, Dave, they don't go away; they go next door to the Court of Appeals, don't they, Kiah?'

It was Kiah's turn to smile. 'Yes, Judge, they sure do.'

Tomorrow nodded.

'That's what I assumed. Dave, if push comes to shove, obviously I'm eventually going to rule on your motion. I haven't decided which way I'm going to go yet, but if you make me, I'll rule one way or the other. That's my job, after all. But before I do, I thought I would at least ask if there's any way we can deal with this without making this case into the next *Marbury v Madison*.'

'Deal with it?' I asked.

'I'm asking whether the two of you have talked about possible ways of settling this case?'

Kiah and I looked at each other.

'They've offered to take Rhode Island, Judge,' I replied. 'The President's thinking about it.'

The judge laughed.

'Sounds good – just as long as he doesn't give them Connecticut. That's my state, and I'd have a problem with that.'

'Connecticut is off the table,' Kiah said.

'Good.' He paused and went through the motions with the pipe again. 'Kiah, I want to ask you a question. You don't have to answer, but if you do, let me have it straight.'

'Shoot, Judge.'

'What evidence do you have to support the family's claim?'

'Well…'

'Let me explain why I'm asking, and I'm also going to speak frankly. Whether or not you have evidence at this stage shouldn't make any difference to the statute of limitations, but in this case it does: because if you don't have any evidence, I'm not sure I want to go out on a limb with this, and going out on a limb is what you're asking me to do here. You're asking me to give the van Eyck family billions of dollars on a 200-year-old claim, and if I deny the government's motion, I'm giving you the green light, at least for now. So I don't think I'm out of order in asking what you've got.'

Kiah nodded and thought for some time.

'First, Judge – and I'm sure Dave will back me up on this – the family have made it clear that they're not trying to claim the whole compound interest calculation. They know that's not realistic.'

'I can confirm that,' I said, jumping in. 'Kiah told me that on day one.'

'But, having said that, we're looking at a significant number,' Kiah continued. 'We've already got over three hundred plaintiffs signed up, and we're looking at thousands before we're done. But what they want most is some recognition for Jacob van Eyck – a statue in a prominent location – and those things don't come cheap.'

'All right,' Tomorrow said. 'So, what have you got?'

I turned to face Kiah. I was just as curious about this as the judge. I would have asked her myself some time ago if I hadn't been so certain of winning my motion to dismiss the case. As long as I was on track for that, whatever evidence she had didn't matter. But if Tomorrow was even thinking about going with the plaintiffs, it suddenly became a huge issue. I took some encouragement from the fact that Kiah seemed momentarily tongue-tied; and I reasoned that if she had a smoking gun, we'd have heard about it by now.

'You have to understand, Judge,' she replied, 'gathering evidence in this case isn't a simple matter. We have thousands of family members scattered across the country, and even a handful abroad, and all of them have information. But it seems they haven't talked to each other very much, so now, it's a matter of trying to put all that information together.'

'In other words, they have no evidence,' I said. I spoke out of a sense of relief that she wasn't putting her finger on anything definite, but Judge Morrow held up a hand, telling me not to interrupt.

'What is it you're looking for?'

'Jacob's loan certificates. You've seen from our brief the system the Continental Congress put in place for the repayment of war loans. Every loan was documented. Every lender was given a certificate to redeem after the war. Our belief is that Jacob had a number of loan certificates, probably quite a large number. We deduce that from the amount of his loans, and the fact that the supplies he paid for would have been delivered to the army over a period of time. It would have been a significant accounting exercise, and we doubt it could all have been reduced to a single document. He would have been issued with any number of loan certificates.'

'Makes sense,' Tomorrow said, nodding. 'Where are they?'

"We believe that Jacob handed some of them in to a claim office in an effort to get them paid. But the office kept them, probably because of the amount involved, which couldn't be paid at the time. We believe that they would have been sent on to the Department of the Treasury, either to ask for approval to pay, or to file them away for a time when payment became possible. After that...'

'After that...?'

'After that, when he didn't get paid, he probably kept the remaining certificates somewhere in a safe place. We're looking for those. As for the ones that came to Washington, we don't know where they are, and we'll need the government's help in tracking them down.'

'Excuse me?' I laughed spontaneously.

'It's called discovery, Dave,' Kiah said. 'The United States is a party to this litigation, and you can be ordered to make disclosure of any documents in your possession, just like any other party. I was hoping you would agree to that voluntarily, but if I have to ask Judge Morrow to make an order, I will.'

'She's right, Dave,' the judge said, smiling.

I shook my head.

'Judge, obviously, we'll comply with any order you make. But where exactly are we supposed to look?'

'You could start with the Department of the Treasury,' Kiah suggested.

'Sure, but if we're looking for documents from that period, there's no way to tell where they might be, or even whether they still exist. Vast numbers were lost when the British destroyed the city in 1814. Any that survived would have been moved to some place of safety, but they probably didn't have a chance to catalogue them first.'

I paused, hopefully for effect.

'Plus, I haven't heard any actual evidence that Jacob van Eyck ever had any loan certificates, much less that he handed them in to a loan office, or that they found their way to Washington. It all seems to be based on the family's belief, which doesn't give us much to go on.'

'I'm not suggesting that the Treasury is the only place to look,' Kiah insisted, 'but it's a logical place to start. The Bureau of the Public Debt is where I would expect to find something like this. If that doesn't work, you ask yourselves: where would documents have been stored, assuming that they survived 1814? We know the answer to that. There may be a few of historical significance that ended up in the Library of Congress, but the kind of document we're looking for is likely to be in the National Archives.'

Tomorrow was sucking on his pipe again.

'Sounds like a plan to me,' he said.

By now, I was imagining the hours of work involved in a search like this, and the resources it would require. That led me on to imagining myself asking Harry for those resources – for a case I had promised him would be over today based on the statute of limitations at minimal public expense. The request for a massive trawl for documents was a conversation I would much prefer not to have, but I had the uncomfortable feeling that Kiah was talking Tomorrow into it. I felt myself being painted into a corner. Somehow, I had to try to turn this around.

'Judge, this is a pure fishing expedition,' I protested. 'You can't make an order for discovery without some concrete basis for thinking that there are relevant documents in the government's possession. So far, you've heard nothing but speculation. The family believes this, the family believes that; nothing of substance at all.

'Besides, the plaintiffs are just as capable of searching the National Archives as we are. It's open to the public, and everything there must be catalogued. It's their burden of proof to produce the evidence they need, and it's not right to use the tax payers' money to fund a search they should be making themselves.'

'The government knows what records it has,' Kiah replied, 'and where they are. We don't. We don't have access to the Department of the Treasury, and if we have to trawl through every piece of paper in the National Archives, it's going to take us another 200 years. I know there's a catalogue, but if the government stores sensitive papers, they're not going to be anywhere you can get to with a catalogue.'

She looked across at me.

'Besides, discovery isn't just about making a search; it's also about having a party certify to the court that the search has been made. You know that, Dave. The court needs to know – and the family needs to know – that everything possible has been done to find the loan certificates.'

I spread my arms out wide in frustration.

'We've been given no reason to believe that they even exist.'

Tomorrow replaced his pipe in the ashtray.

'That's no reason not to look,' he said decisively. 'Kiah, file your motion for discovery. I'll grant it, and I expect the government to get on with it. Dave, I'm not leaving you out. There's no reason why the government shouldn't file its own motion for discovery. You're entitled to know what the plaintiffs have. If there's any evidence in the possession of the family, that evidence needs to be disclosed too. Kiah, that's your job.'

'No problem, Judge,' she replied.

'All right,' the judge said. 'With that understanding, I'm going to adjourn the statute of limitations for six weeks.'

'Six weeks?' Kiah exclaimed excitedly. 'Judge, we can't get it done in six weeks. We're only just –'

'I can't let the grass grow on this, Kiah. I understand that you have a lot of people to talk to, but frankly, the family has had more than 200 years to get its act together. I'd be very surprised if six weeks doesn't give you both enough time. At least we should know how the land lies. If at that point, there's good reason to believe you're on to something, I will probably give you a little more time if you need it. But let's see how we stand then. I'll expect a written report from both of you telling me what you've done and what the results are, and then we'll have another hearing.'

He paused for some moments.

'But I need to make it clear what I'm thinking, Kiah. If there's some evidence to justify a trial, I will think about allowing the case to proceed. I'm not saying I will. I still have to think about the statute of limitations, but I will think about it. But if there's no evidence, and no prospect of any evidence, I'm not going to waste further public money on it. Understood?'

'Understood, Judge,' she replied.

'All right, then. Let's go back into court, and I'll formally adjourn the government's motion to a date to be fixed.'

We waited with the judge as he retrieved his robe and put it on, and called for Maisie to tell her we were ready.

'So, the family wants a statue?' he asked while we were waiting.

'In Philadelphia,' Kiah replied, 'to be unveiled by the President.'

He nodded, buttoning up his robe, and turned to me.

'That might not be a bad option if she comes up with some evidence,' he said.

I smiled. 'It would cost a lot of public money.'

'Compared with what you're about to spend on the case, it might end up being cheap at the price,' Tomorrow replied. 'And it would definitely beat giving them Rhode Island.'

Maisie stopped us on the way out.

'Kiah, does the name Mary Jane Perrins mean anything to you? From Boston, Mass?'

Kiah closed her eyes, suddenly seeming rather irritated.

'Unfortunately, yes.'

'It's just that the court has received a communication from Miss Perrins inquiring about what she has to do to represent a separate group of plaintiffs, or intervene in some way. I had the feeling she was feeling me out about whether she could take the lead. I told her she'd better get herself an attorney and take some advice. I'm sorry, Kiah. I thought I'd better give you a heads-up.'

'Thanks, Maisie. I'll deal with it.'

'Bad news?' I asked. I'm sure she noticed that I couldn't resist a grin.

'Lucifer wants to take over my case,' she replied, 'but I'm not about to let her. No big deal.'

38

FEELING SOMEWHAT BRUISED AND battered, Ellen and I made our way back to the office and crept along the corridors as quietly as we could. I just wanted the chance to grab some more coffee and get my head together before the inevitable confrontation. The odds weren't good. Harry would be lurking somewhere, waiting for us. We'd called in from court, of course, to make sure we informed him of the morning's developments before he heard about them on TV, which I was pretty sure he would have been monitoring. He didn't say very much, which meant that he was going to brood over it until we got back. I'd decided that I couldn't worry about it any more. Harry was just going to have to get used to the idea that we had a real case on our hands. There was nothing I could have done about what had happened this morning, and there was nothing Harry could have done about it. I just about had time to pour myself a cup of coffee and dispatch Ellen to find out what we needed to do to make a search of the Treasury Department and the National Archives.

'So, what happened at court today, Dave?'

He was standing in the door frame, leaning against it with his arms folded in front of him.

'We made our argument,' I replied. 'We're right, but the judge hasn't made up his mind that we're right yet, so he's adjourned it. We're still right, and I still think he will see that eventually.'

'Tomorrow is actually contemplating letting this case go

ahead?' he asked incredulously, making his way further into my office. 'This 200-year-old joke?'

'Unfortunately, it's not a joke – not any more. But as I said, ultimately I think he will come round to our point of view.'

'How did this happen?'

I took a deep breath and leaned back in my chair.

'Kiah made a very persuasive argument,' I replied. 'Not right, but very persuasive.'

'I'm trying to understand this,' Harry said. 'Is Tomorrow being seduced into thinking that this is some kind of major historic case, which must somehow be allowed to proceed despite the fact that a ten-year-old child could figure out that it's time-barred?'

'No, Harry,' I replied. 'Tomorrow is playing the odds.'

'What's that supposed to mean?'

'He had us in chambers for coffee after the argument. He wanted to tell us what was on his mind, and he was pretty up front about it. He sees himself as being caught between a rock and a hard place. He's worrying about his place in history.'

'His place in history?'

'Yes. If he throws the case out, is he going to be condemned as unpatriotic for taking away Jacob van Eyck's last chance to be recognised as a true American hero who played a vital role in winning the War of Independence? On the other hand, if he lets it go ahead, is he taking the risk of pouring a huge amount of public money down the drain chasing some family's pipe dream, and getting reamed out for that?'

Harry was pacing up and down in front of my desk.

'It doesn't have to be like that,' he insisted. 'We gave him a perfect, unanswerable way around it.'

'He just hasn't seen it yet,' I replied. 'He will. As I said, he's playing the odds. It's very likely that six weeks from now Kiah will have come up with nothing, in which case he can't possibly be criticised for dismissing the case. That's the way to bet.'

'But what if she does come up with something? For that matter, what if *we* come up with something?'

'Then he will have to decide how good the evidence is. It may still not be enough to justify letting the case go to trial. Even if it does go to trial, he can find against the plaintiffs on the evidence. There's no jury in the Claims Court, so it's his call. Even if he makes an award, he can control the amount, and if all else fails, he can expect the Court of Appeals or the Supreme Court to have the last word.'

I smiled.

'You have to understand where he's coming from, Harry. We're having kittens about representing the government with so much at stake. It's not surprising that Tomorrow is feeling the heat as the judge. He has to decide the outcome of a case worth God knows how many billions of dollars.'

Harry eventually came to rest.

'How in the hell are we going to search the Treasury Department and the National Archives?' he demanded. 'We only just have the staff to manage our normal case-load. I don't have the people for something like this.'

I nodded.

'You'll have to ask Maggie for some paralegals,' I replied, 'perhaps even an attorney or two.'

He threw his arms out wide.

'In the present economic climate? In a case I told her would be all over today?'

'We don't have a choice, Harry,' I pointed out. 'Tomorrow is going to make an order for discovery, and we have to comply with it. It's not as bad as it seems. We can –'

'But –'

'Hear me out, Harry, OK? I've already got Ellen started on finding out what a search like this is going to take. Once she's got a handle on that, we'll have a better idea of what resources we need. So you don't need to push Maggie right away.'

'But –'

'In addition, the discovery order Tomorrow is going to make won't be against the Justice Department. It will be against the United States. We're the lawyers for the United States, so we have to organise the government's response, but that doesn't mean we have to do it all ourselves. We're entitled to all the help we need from Treasury and the National Archives.'

'You mean, we can use their people?'

I'd been giving this problem some serious thought since having my initial panic attack in Tomorrow's chambers. I'd known as soon as Kiah raised the question of discovery that Harry would want to know how we could cope with something on this scale, and as I calmed down on the walk back to the office, the solution had begun to suggest itself.

'We almost have to. We only have six weeks. They know their way around their departments; we don't. Our people will have to coordinate the search, but we must use their people to carry it out, otherwise we'll never get it done by the deadline. Plus, it's easier and cheaper that way. It's been done before. If we run into resistance from Treasury or the Archives, you ask Maggie to get the Attorney General on the case. With what's at stake, he'll have the President's ear. I don't think we'll have a problem getting their cooperation.'

Harry nodded.

'All right. I have to talk to Maggie later anyway. I promised her a report on the hearing today. I'll bring it up then. I want you with me in case she has questions.'

'No problem.'

He walked to the door and opened it to leave.

'Harry, there's one more thing,' I called after him.

He turned back towards me.

'You're going to hear on the TV news that I expressed the view that the government's position was unattractive.'

'You talked to the press? Dave, I thought I'd made it clear –'

'No, I didn't talk to the press. It was during the argument.

Tomorrow asked me point blank, in so many words, whether it was an attractive advertisement for American Justice that the van Eyck family could never have sued the United States for a constitutionally guaranteed debt because their claim had accrued before the Claims Court had even been created. It's not, and I couldn't think of a way not to agree with him.'

To my surprise, instead of landing on me, Harry stood there for some time, hands on hips, nodding without any suggestion of dissent.

'A debt for which the United States and the public faith were solemnly pledged,' he said quietly. 'The price of liberty.'

'Yes.'

He turned again to leave.

'Don't worry about it,' he said. 'It's not our job to be attractive. That's not our department. It's our job to be right.'

39

Kiah Harmon

THE NEXT MORNING, I assembled the entire team to assess where
we stood and where we were headed. It felt like an important
moment. We had survived the first challenge and we were still
in the game, at least for now. There was no telling what Judge
Morrow was ultimately going to decide, but we had been given
time to gather evidence and get our case up and running, and if we
came up with some evidence, I felt sure that he would give us more
time. We just had to come up with *something*, and if we couldn't
do that in six weeks, the chances were that it couldn't be done at
all. The point was, we were alive, and a few days earlier I wouldn't
have put money on that outcome.

It wasn't a meeting we could have had productively the previous
afternoon. We were too busy congratulating ourselves to focus on
mundane questions such as what to do next, and anyway we felt
we deserved a little celebration. After we emerged from court, I
had run interference for Dave by giving an impromptu press
conference with Sam while he made good his escape. I'd seen him
running the gauntlet on the way into court, and he hadn't had a
great morning. I didn't want him to go through that again while he
was coming to terms with having a live case on his hands instead
of the slam-dunk order for dismissal he had been expecting. Sam
and I had no difficulty in attracting the attention of the assembled

reporters, and unlike Dave, we had no constraints about talking to them. After that, Arlene had ordered Sam and me to take a long lunch while she got up to speed back at the office. After lunch we weren't in the mood for serious work.

But now, there we were, the currently successful van Eyck team: Sam; me; Arlene; Powalski; and Jenny, our latest intern from Kate Banahan's Wills and Trusts class who, like her predecessor, was very bright, but unlike her predecessor, actually had some idea of how an office works and was providing Arlene with some real support. We commandeered Reg to take a few pictures to commemorate the occasion. After all, we had no guarantee that we would have such an optimistic occasion again. Reg had finished work on my tax affairs now. The auditors were due in the office early the following week. It was an unwelcome diversion, but at least Reg had assured me that my affairs were in order. He took some great shots of the team, seated around the table and smiling.

Arlene had prepared an agenda. She handed out copies.

'Y'all are the new superstars since yesterday,' she began. 'The phone's been ringing off the hook with media wanting interviews. They're all over me like white on rice. I feel like the chief ticket-seller the day before the rodeo. I need to know what y'all need me to tell them.'

'Local radio stations?' I asked. We'd already done a number of talk shows and interviews of that kind, so I assumed it was more of the same. After the scenes at court the day before, I should have known better, but it hadn't yet occurred to me that we were playing in another league now. It had occurred to Sam. With her background in theatre, she was more at ease with publicity than the rest of us, and this wasn't coming as a surprise to her.

'I don't think so,' she smiled.

'Hell no, hun,' Arlene said. 'We're talking the networks – CBS, NBC, you name it. PBS wants an "in-depth sit-down", whatever the hell that is. Then we've got the news channels, CNN and such, and that's before we get to the *Washington Post* and God only knows how many other newspapers and magazines. If y'all do everything they want, you're gonna need six weeks just for that; forget about working on the case.'

She brandished the stack of phone messages she had taken and emails she had printed out.

'I need to know what I'm supposed to tell these guys, y'all.'

Sam reached out a hand.

'May I?'

'Be my guest, hun.'

Sam looked through the messages. After a minute or two, she looked up.

'All right. What we need to understand here is that we're not interested in making our case to Middle America. We're not fighting an election. We're involved in a potentially highly political lawsuit that affects the federal government. But it can't hurt to make the best case we can to the Washington establishment, because it could all come down to politics in the end, regardless of what the judge decides.'

'That's not a great thought, hun,' Arlene said. 'Are y'all saying that the judge –?'

'No,' Sam replied. 'Judge Morrow's not going to be influenced by anything we say – or anything the government says – to the media, nor should he be. I'm talking about looking way ahead. I'm talking about what happens if we win: actually getting our hands on the money; actually getting funding allocated for a statue, assuming we get that far. The court may make an award in our favour, or it may not. That's going to depend on the law. But if they go with us, we then have to enforce the court's order, and my guess is, that's going to be about politics.'

'You're absolutely right,' Powalski said. 'In the end, down the road, we're going to have to deal with Washington.'

'I agree,' I said.

'And that means that we can't afford to waste our time or resources,' Sam said. 'We need to focus on the interviews that will reach our target audience, and forget the rest. Give them a press release, but that's it. There's nothing they can do for us anyway, except maybe help to get the word out about the case, but the family's doing that for us already. It's not a productive use of our time to run ourselves ragged trying to pander to every radio station that's desperate for an unusual story. And that's all it is to them, an unusual story. In a few days, a local cheerleader is going to be caught smoking dope in the high school gym, and they won't care about us any more. That's how it goes.'

'So, what *is* a productive use of our time?' I asked.

'PBS first,' Sam replied. 'That's huge. If I had to choose one, I'd trade all the rest for that one. Then CNN, then the *Washington Post*, the *New York Times* and the *LA Times*. Maybe the *Wall Street Journal*, but we would have to be careful there; their editorial policy isn't likely to be too favourable towards us. Then the networks if we have time, but only if they give us the national and international news segments. That's it. The rest get press releases.'

Jenny raised a nervous hand.

'Miss Harmon, I'd be glad to take a shot at writing a press release this afternoon. I've done some for student organisations at Georgetown.'

'Go for it,' I smiled.

Arlene nodded.

'All right, then. Y'all better clear your calendars, and tell me if you have any dates to avoid, 'cause I'm fixin' to start making calls once we're through here, and once I do, y'all are going to be busier than a nest of hornets in a maple syrup factory.'

'What's next?' I asked.

'Item two on the agenda,' Arlene replied. 'We're getting requests for you and Sam to do a road trip, maybe more than one.'

'A road trip?' Sam asked, smiling.

'I don't know what else to call it, hun. What we've got is eight or nine groups of family members in different parts of the country that want you to come down and talk to them.'

'What parts of the country?' I asked.

'And that's the point, right there,' Arlene replied. 'We got to the people from the major cities at the convention, so you know it's not them. What we're talking about here is the city of Sorryass, Wyoming – some small town in the back of beyond where the good folks don't see the need to drive anywhere outside the city limits, never mind fly to New Orleans for a family convention. I'm from Lubbock, Texas, y'all, and I know whereof I speak. I know Sorryass, Texas, and trust me, Sorryass, Wyoming, is no different. There's a Sorryass in every state in the Union, and when you've seen one, you've seen 'em all. Here's the list.'

I looked at it, and I immediately understood Arlene's reluctance. This would be a difficult road trip, criss-crossing the country, flying between towns with small airports or none, or driving vast stretches of Midwestern interstate – and with very little to show for it except to boost some local egos. It wouldn't be a productive use of time, unless…

Arlene read my mind.

'I'm not hearing,' she said, answering my unspoken question, 'that these good folk have any new information to give us about the loan documentation. They say it's about putting the word out about the case and signing up more plaintiffs. But, you know what, folks? Go get y'allselves a computer and learn the magic of email.'

'Maybe we should do one or two of these,' Sam ventured. She had been reading over my shoulder. 'I can see going to the Carolinas, and maybe Iowa, if they could turn it into more of a regional meeting. Kiah, I could take a couple of these on my own if you don't have the time.'

'No,' I replied decisively. 'Arlene's right. We have six weeks, and if we're not careful, we could spend all our time doing interviews and personal appearances. It's going to distract us from what we should be focusing on – and that's finding some documents to use as evidence.'

'Amen to that,' Powalski said. 'Look, I'm in touch with these people as soon as Arlene signs them up, and I'm asking them for anything they have. Let's just say that so far, there hasn't exactly been a stampede to come forward with useful material.'

He sounded frustrated, and I couldn't blame him. There were times when the needle in the haystack simile didn't really cut it.

'Which is why,' Arlene said, standing and putting a hand on Sam's shoulder, 'I think there's one y'all have to do.' She smiled. 'I kinda kept this one for last.'

We all crowded round to read the message. It was from Aunt Meg, and it was marked urgent. She wanted to show us something, she said, something no one else had seen. She wanted us to come to visit her in Montgomery County, Pennsylvania, as soon as we could.

'This has to be whatever she didn't want to talk to me about at the reunion,' Powalski suggested.

'You're right,' I said. 'We do this one. Let's give her a call and set it up.'

40

TWO DAYS LATER WE took an early morning flight to Philadelphia. It had been a strange few days all across the north-east of the country, with sudden violent storms, the temperature alternating between cool and oppressively warm and humid, as if the weather couldn't make up its mind whether it was still summer or whether fall had begun. The day we arrived was summer; it was already sticky when we touched down just after eight in the morning. Powalski rented us a car and we made the short drive along the Pennsylvania Turnpike towards King of Prussia, where Arlene had arranged for us to stay the night at the Radisson Valley Forge Hotel, a stone's throw from the national park. I think she chose the place partly because she wanted to take the park tour, but it was unlikely we would have time this trip. We dropped our things at the hotel and set out to see Aunt Meg.

Aunt Meg lived in Conshohocken, a community in Montgomery County, just off the interstate. Her house was a large, three-story, rickety-looking wooden structure, the whole of which was surrounded by an enveloping porch. At the front was a collection of porch furniture – chairs and a couple of tables, all apparently of different designs – and there were hooks in the ceiling for a hammock, though the hammock itself was nowhere to be seen. On approach the house looked dark even in broad daylight, though the dark brown paint was recent, there was a pleasant herbaceous border in front of the porch, and the generous area of land around the house, which included some old oaks, was well kept.

Aunt Meg answered the door with another woman, a friendly soul with a full face and deep brown eyes, in her forties, I guessed.

'Welcome to Montgomery County,' Aunt Meg said. 'Come on in.' She kissed Sam fondly on both cheeks, and shook hands with the rest of us.

'This is Alice, who comes in every day to make sure I'm still alive and not doing anything too stupid.'

'I do some cleaning and drive once in a while,' Alice smiled. 'Aunt Meg doesn't need much more than that, and I get told off if I fuss too much.'

'As if I would tell anyone off,' Aunt Meg grinned. 'She does fuss too much though, sometimes. Come on back to the dining room. We'll have enough room to sit in there. Would you like some coffee? You must have had an early start this morning.'

The idea of a cup of drinkable coffee sounded good to all of us. We'd grabbed a cup of a very indifferent brew and a plastic croissant at the coffee bar in the boarding area in the few minutes we had before our flight, and it hadn't helped.

'I'll make it,' Alice volunteered.

She left us alone with Aunt Meg. The dining room was formal, almost Victorian in its austerity. The dark wooden table could have accommodated twelve for dinner very comfortably; the matching chairs had high, straight backs, and hard padded seats in a dark mauve design. The carpet seemed to reflect the same colour. Two corner cabinets held collections of plates and glassware. The windows were covered by long off-white lace curtains, and the blades of two ceiling fans rotated in a leisurely sequence in the high ceiling above our heads. Aunt Meg fitted in with the room's décor, wearing a long black dress, with a small white scarf tucked in at the top. We sat in silence for a few moments.

'We came as soon as we could, Aunt Meg,' Sam began.

'Yes, I know, my dear. I also know that you don't have a great deal of time, so I don't plan on wasting any. But if you will allow me, I do have something to ask.'

'Of course. We're here all day. We're not going back to Arlington tonight.'

'Good, because before we get to what I have to show you, I'm going to ask you to indulge an old lady. I want to take you on a short drive. It's not far. There's something I want you all to see, something I think may make a difference.'

'I'm not sure we can all fit in our car,' Powalski observed.

'It's no problem. Alice will drive me and you can follow behind.'

Anxious as we were to see any evidence Aunt Meg might have, we could hardly say no, and in any case, it sounded intriguing. Alice arrived with our coffee and some delicious cinnamon-flavoured cookies of a kind I didn't remember ever tasting before.

'They're called "speculaas", ' she replied when I mentioned how good they were. 'They're from Holland; not the kind of thing you find locally. I have to go into Philadelphia. But they're worth it, aren't they?'

'She spoils me,' Aunt Meg said.

'So she should,' Sam replied.

I think we all felt better after that. We piled into our car and Powalski pulled effortlessly into the light traffic behind Alice's station wagon. She led us along Interstate 276, turning briefly on to State Highway 23, and finally taking an exit marked Fourth Street, which led us back under the Interstate's overpass. We turned again into River Road.

And we came to the church I had visited in my dream: the church where I had seen Isabel.

I knew it instantly. There were some differences. If there had ever been a high wall enclosing the graveyard, it had gone. There was a low rustic stone wall as we entered the graveyard, but beyond at the far side, without any obvious boundary, were houses. Of course the area would have been developed since Isabel's day. But the layout of the church and the graveyard was unmistakable to me. In my mind, at least, I had stood in this place before. And as I gazed at the setting of my dream, leaning a bit unsteadily against the car, I noticed something else. The roaring sound, which in my dream I hadn't been able to turn to identify, was there. In my dream I'd speculated that it might have come from an aqueduct carrying water. Now when I closed my eyes, the sound was the same sound I'd heard in my dream. But my roar of water moving along an aqueduct was the roar of the traffic on the interstate.

Aunt Meg had gathered everyone except me together on the other side of the street, where a gate led into the graveyard. I knew the gate. I had used it in my dream, and just beyond it was the spot where Isabel had stood. I was shaken. I was feeling hot and clammy. Aunt Meg was looking back across the street at me. Somehow, I managed to force my body up from the side of the car, and I made my way slowly towards them.

'You OK, Kiah?' Sam asked.

'Yes, I'm fine. Just got up a bit too early, not enough sleep.'

Aunt Meg was still looking at me.

'This is the Old Swedes church,' she explained. 'Leastways, that's what everyone has always called it. Its real name is Christ Church, and these days it's Episcopalian, but it goes back a ways. As the name suggests, this was a Swedish settlement originally, and it's always been called Swedeland or Swedesburg. Jacob would have been a man of about thirty when the church was originally built. It hasn't changed too much since then; the tower was added after his day, but other than that, we're looking at something Jacob himself saw many times. He would have worshipped here often. So did Washington, by the way, while the army was here. The river's just over there, and we wouldn't have had those houses then, so he may have come in by boat from his camp.'

'This is where so many of the old van Eycks are buried?' Sam asked.

'Yes. Let's go in, and you can see for yourselves.'

We didn't have to walk far. There was a large collection of gravestones and memorials, not exactly grand but certainly well made and well kept, that bore the names of van Eycks, from the late eighteenth century to the mid twentieth, and we didn't explore every inch of the graveyard, so no doubt there were others.

'But nothing for Jacob,' Aunt Meg said as we gathered around one large tomb. 'He's here somewhere. This is where they laid him. Everyone in the family agrees on that. But no grave stone.'

We looked around in silence for some time, as if trying to make some memorial of Jacob exist, to conjure one up from somewhere.

'Why?' Sam asked.

Aunt Meg shrugged. 'Maybe they didn't have the money, or maybe there was no record of exactly where they buried him. Who knows? But it's a shame, don't you think?'

And that was when I saw the other difference. In my dream, the whole graveyard had consisted of unmarked graves. I had seen no gravestones or memorials at all. But there were gravestones and memorials everywhere here. Just not for Jacob.

41

By the time we returned to the house, the warmth of the day was getting to us all. The afternoon was unsettled and humid, and the clouds were gathering overhead, promising an early evening thunder shower. Until it came to bring relief, the warmth would continue to be uncomfortable. We gathered in the dining room where the heavy lace curtains were either keeping the heat out, or keeping it in: there was no way to tell. The softly whirring ceiling fans did nothing except to move the warm air gently around the room. Alice brought a large jug of iced lemonade, which tasted wonderful, and Aunt Meg arranged us around the dining table. I noticed a heavy black file folder on the table. She waited for some time before beginning. She smiled.

'I'm afraid I must begin with a confession. I told you that I was eighty-five years old. That's what I tell everyone. But now it's time for me to 'fess up: that's not exactly accurate.'

Sam laughed.

'I'd heard various rumours within the family,' she replied. 'Anything between seventy and a hundred. My dad's bet was somewhere around ninety.'

'It's silly, really,' Aunt Meg said. 'I should probably tell everyone the truth, but I don't want everyone thinking I'm senile, and it's none of their business anyway.'

'Believe me, Aunt Meg,' Powalski said, 'there is not a chance that anyone will think of you as senile.'

'Thank you, Mr Powalski. But when you get to my age and your memory isn't what it was, you start to worry about things like that. I'm actually ninety-four. My birthday was last month.'

There were some intakes of breath around the table.

'I believed eighty-five every time you said it,' Powalski replied. 'I didn't doubt it for a minute.'

'Are you kidding? I would have believed sixty-five,' Sam smiled.

Aunt Meg gave her a brief smile in return.

'Well, that's very nice of you, my dear. But in fact, I am ninety-four, and that's one of the reasons I've invited you here now. I can't go on forever, and I'm determined that I'm not going to die without telling you what I'm about to tell you. I've put it off for as long as I can, because I wanted to make sure I passed it on to folks I can trust. But now the time has come. Kiah, push that file over to me, would you?'

I got up and moved the file so that it was directly in front of her.

'I want to show you a document,' she began. She opened the file and carefully extracted something wrapped in a beige cloth of some kind and tied at its center with red ribbon, fastened meticulously in a clean, tight bow. 'But first, if you'll indulge me, I want to give you something of a history lesson. I know it's rather presumptuous of me, but it's not the kind of history lesson they teach you in school.'

She did not unwrap the document immediately, but sat with her right hand resting gently on it.

'It's easy to think of Jacob's day as being very remote in time from today,' she said. 'That's why we worry so much about whether we can ever know what went on back then, about whether we can find documents from that time so long ago. But actually, Jacob's time isn't remote at all; it's very close. What if I told you that the document I'm going to show you was written in 1813, a year after Jacob's death; but that I was given this document by a woman who was given it by the woman who wrote it, a woman who was close to Jacob himself?'

I have to admit I was taken aback. I'm sure my jaw dropped, and looking around, I saw that everyone was having the same reaction. Sam was rather obviously trying to do the arithmetic in her head while doing her best not to let anyone see the tell-tale movements of her fingers. Powalski was smiling and frowning at the same time; if he was calculating, you couldn't tell. Arlene was staring at Aunt Meg, her eyebrows raised. My mind wasn't even letting me calculate yet. I hadn't got past the point of finding it hard to believe.

'Let me save you all the trouble,' Aunt Meg smiled. 'I was born in 1928. I was eighteen years old when I was given this document in 1946. It was given to me by a woman called Joan Harrison. Harrison was her married name. She was born Joan van Eyck, and she was descended from Jacob's brother Samuel. Joan was born in 1868, so she was seventy-eight in 1946 when she gave it to me. She died two years later. Joan was given the document in 1878, when she was only ten years old. She got it from a woman called Isabel Hardwick, who had known Jacob and had looked after him in his old age. Isabel was twenty-four in 1812 when Jacob died. She was born in 1788, so she was ninety when she gave the document to Joan. She died in 1880.'

Despite the oppressive warmth of the afternoon, I had suddenly got very cold. I wrapped my arms around me as tightly as I could, but I was shivering and sweating at the same time. I was also staring straight ahead, and I am sure the others had noticed. I hadn't fully recovered from the experience of standing in the graveyard in which I had stood in my dream. Now I was hearing that the woman I had seen there, and whose name I had somehow known to be Isabel, had existed, and had left us a document from the period. I was rubbing my arms, but I couldn't get warm again, and my mind seemed to have been numbed.

'Aunt Meg, that's amazing,' I heard Sam say. 'All that time, and yet it's connected by the lives of just three women.'

'One of whom is still very much alive,' Powalski added.

'It makes Jacob's time seem so close,' Sam said. 'You can almost reach out and touch it.'

'Yes,' Aunt Megan said. 'Time shrinks when you think of it in terms of the human life span, doesn't it? It makes us see history a little differently. It makes us see that it wasn't so long ago, and the people of those days weren't so different from us.'

I somehow recovered enough to force my mouth open.

'Did you say the woman who knew Jacob was called Isabel?' I asked.

Aunt Meg looked at me closely. I'm sure she must have noticed the goose bumps on my arms.

'Isabel Hardwick,' she replied.

She looked around the table at all of us in turn.

'This will probably make more sense once you know what's in the document, but you should know that Joan entrusted it to me on the express condition that I show it to no one until I was sure that it was the right person. She told me that Isabel had entrusted it to her on the same condition.'

'The right person?' Powalski asked.

'Yes. Isabel meant a person who was not only committed to seeking justice for Jacob, but also had the means to get that justice for him. If Joan didn't find the right person in her lifetime, she was to pass it on to the most reliable person she could find, with the same instructions: to keep it safe until the right person came along. Despite all our dealings with congressmen, Joan never had confidence that she had found the right person. So she passed it on to me. I guessed she judged that I would take good care of it.'

'She couldn't have made a better choice,' Sam said. 'But... Aunt Meg, that must mean that you and Joan are the only two people who have seen the document since Isabel wrote it.'

'Yes,' Aunt Meg replied. 'But now I'm making the decision Isabel and Joan never got to make. I'm passing it on to you, Sam, and I'm doing this because I believe you are the right person, and because with Kiah, Arlene, and Mr Powalski to help you, I believe that at last, you have a chance to do what Isabel intended us to do.'

There was a silence. Then Sam walked over to Aunt Meg, knelt by her side and put her head in Aunt Meg's lap. She was crying softly. Aunt Meg quietly stroked her hair and we all allowed some time to pass, listening to the fans as they continued to whir languidly through the humid air. Eventually, Aunt Meg looked across at me.

'Kiah, why don't you read it aloud for us, so we don't all have to crowd round trying to read over someone's shoulder?'

I slowly reached out and took the file, untied the red ribbon, and carefully pushed the beige cloth aside to reveal the document. It consisted of six pages of parchment, with a few yellowish-brown markings at the edges of the pages, but generally in remarkably good condition. The document was written in black ink. The handwriting was small, and to my mind in a feminine hand, neat enough, albeit scrawling and blotchy in places, indicating the use of a quill pen. It was easily legible. I took a few deep breaths, and to my relief, I felt the suggestion of warming blood beginning to move again through my body.

42

I, ISABEL HARDWICK, BEING the wife of James Hardwick of Upper Merion Township in the State of Pennsylvania, being of sufficient age and of sound mind, have taken up my pen at ten o'clock in the forenoon, on this third day of December in the Year of our Lord 1813, and desire thereby to record the matters following.

I was born Isabel Johnstone on the fourth day of June in the year 1788, in the early evening, less than an hour after the sun had set, to Ezra and Mary Johnstone of Upper Merion Township in the State of Pennsylvania. I was married to my husband in 1806. In that same year, after my marriage, my father came to me on behalf of his employer, Jacob van Eyck, who lived close by in Upper Merion Township. I was well acquainted with Mr van Eyck, as my father had served him as his bailiff on his lands along the Schuylkill River and elsewhere for many years, and I had been in his presence many times. My father explained that Mr van Eyck, being now of more advanced years, and having no wife or children left alive to minister to him, had need of a companion to assist him in carrying on his domestic and business tasks, in return for which he would make some small payment as his means permitted. My father explained, though I already well knew, as it was generally known, that Mr van Eyck's estate was much diminished by reason of his generous sustenance of General Washington's army while it was encamped hard against his lands during the bitterly cold winter before he proceeded victoriously against the enemy.

With the consent of my husband, I agreed to assist Mr van Eyck, to his benefit, as I was able to perform many household tasks on his behalf, and also to accompany him when he left home, as he was already somewhat frail, though less so than he was to become. My employment also brought me great benefits, not greatly on account of my wages, which as my father had foretold, were modest, but on account of his generosity in other ways. Mr van Eyck took it upon himself, with my consent, to school me. My parents had never done so, it not being the custom of our community generally to school girls, no purpose, according to the general opinion, being served thereby. But because of Mr van Eyck's generosity with his time, I was instructed in reading and writing, in arithmetic, in the positions, transits, and retrograde motions of the planets, in the keeping of accounts, and in many other matters of business. This instruction, which I have passed on to my own daughters, has benefitted them as much as myself, and enriched my life more than higher wages could ever have enriched it.

In the summer of the Year of our Lord 1810, Mr van Eyck, who had by now become very frail, desired of me that I should accompany him to Philadelphia, which, with the consent of my husband, I undertook to do. Mr van Eyck had by this time entrusted me with many confidences regarding his affairs. He had confided to me that the cause of his penury was indeed his most generous support for General Washington, which was evidenced by certain papers supplied to him by Congress, recording the amount of his benevolence and the terms on which he was to be repaid. He had been unsuccessful concerning the repayment due to him, no gold being available to repay such a large amount. Mr van Eyck further confided in me that some years earlier, I know not when – he was not specific on this score – in accordance with certain advice offered to him by General Washington, he had personally carried some sixteen such papers to the loan office in Philadelphia. He carried with them a letter asserting that General

Washington was much interested in his being recompensed and proposed to assist him with respect to the same, though whether the General had himself written the letter, or whether Mr van Eyck had written it, I no longer remember, nay, I doubt that Mr van Eyck was specific on that score. The official with whom he then dealt required him to deposit the papers and the letter with the office, assuring him that suitable inquiries would be made of the Treasury, and causing him to hope that payment would be forthcoming. However, he received no payment, neither were his papers or the letter ever returned to him, the loan officers later in place, upon his making further inquiry of the office, denying all knowledge thereof.

Now, Mr van Eyck, having written many letters to the Treasury in the intervening years, to no avail, and feeling that his time to redress his grievances was drawing short, proposed to return to the loan office to press his case. I asked whether it might not be to his advantage to secure the services of an attorney, but he determined to make the effort himself, whether by reason of his penury, or of his personal desire, I know not. It was a most arduous journey, since although it was not one of truly great distance he was not strong enough to travel in haste, and suffered great pain in his bones, and we were obliged to pass a night in an inn. The loan office was in operation yet, though other government business was now also conducted there, the business of the war loans being by that time no doubt largely concluded. Mr van Eyck was courteously received, but once again his intervention was in vain. Plain it was that whatever papers he had delivered to the office, years before, had been conveyed to Washington, but their whereabouts were no longer known. Mr van Eyck was greatly affected by this development, after which it appeared to me that he ceased to entertain any hope of being repaid.

Upon his return home, Mr van Eyck made of me a most confidential request, a matter on which I was to speak to no one. He entrusted me with the custody of two-and-twenty papers, and

*charged me to deliver them to his Brother, who had agreed to
take custody of them until such time as the Government should
agree to deal with them, in circumstances in which they would
assuredly be preserved and their provenance proved. I agreed to
perform the task he had asked of me, and delivered the said papers
to his Brother in Philadelphia at eleven o'clock in the forenoon
on the fourth day of September in the Year of our Lord 1810. No
acknowledgement of the delivery was provided or requested, Mr
Van Eyck having full confidence in the benevolence of his Brother
in this regard.*

*Now, Mr van Eyck being deceased, and believing that he
would have released me from the obligation of confidence I then
undertook, I have made this record, so that it may be known what
was done with respect to his papers, and so that in due course
his fortune may be restored to his heirs, if not to Mr van Eyck
himself, when the Treasury shall be able to do so. However, I will
keep this record in a secure place, and speak to no one about it
unless it clearly appears that some benefit will accrue thereby
to Mr van Eyck's heirs. In the event of my approaching death, if
no opportunity shall have arisen to put this record forward in
advantageous circumstances, I will entrust it to the custody of a
person in whom I have the greatest confidence, on whom I may
rely to ensure that the record is preserved and used when the time
shall most favourably present itself.*

I declare that this record is true and correct in all points.

Isabel Hardwick, née Johnstone
Dated this third day of December 1813

43

As I laid Isabel Hardwick's record back down on its beige cloth, no one spoke. Sam gently pushed herself up, kissed Aunt Meg on the cheek, and stood behind her chair with her hands resting on Aunt Meg's shoulders.

'Joan always assumed,' Aunt Meg said, 'as did I, that the brother Isabel was referring to was Jacob's oldest brother, Samuel. Not all the van Eyck brothers got on with each other particularly well. There was always some kind of family feud going on, and that hasn't changed too much even today – that's one reason the family has never been able to get its act together to get anything done. But Jacob and Samuel were always very close, and Joan was Samuel's great-granddaughter, or great-great, maybe, I forget, and Joan thought that was one reason why Isabel had chosen her to pass the document on to, and it made sense to me.'

Powalski leaned forward.

'Aunt Meg, we have the complete genealogy back at the office, so we can trace Samuel's branch of the family easily enough. Obviously, in the light of this document, that's where our focus should be. But time is short, and you know the family better than we ever will. It would really help to know whether you or Joan asked any questions based on what Isabel recorded, who you spoke to, and what they said.'

Aunt Meg nodded.

'Over the years, we both did. We spoke to Samuel's family when we saw them. Of course, you understand, we had to do it quietly, because we couldn't give away the existence of Isabel's document. So it was a question here, a question there, at reunions and funerals and suchlike. Joan was pretty convinced that none of Samuel's descendants had the twenty-two documents, and I'm sure she was right. If the family still had them, they would have surfaced by now. Joan thought that Samuel had either hidden them away for safekeeping, or taken them to the Treasury in Washington. Either way, she never did get any clue about where they might be now, and neither did I.'

Powalski looked at me.

'Kiah, maybe I need to do a road trip, or at least get on the phone, and speak to as many of Samuel's descendants as I can.'

'Maybe.'

I had warmed up some during the time I was reading the document, and my mind had begun to work again. Based on what Isabel had written, Powalski's suggestion was logical enough, but I wasn't convinced. If Joan and Aunt Meg had come up with nothing over so many years, and if there had been no trace of the twenty-two documents since Isabel had put pen to paper towards the end of 1813, it seemed unlikely to me that they were about to appear magically now, more than two hundred years later. Powalski and Sam were understandably excited by this extraordinarily close link to Jacob, a link which undeniably telescoped those two centuries into a time you could almost hold in your hand, but I didn't see how it was going to bring us any closer to finding some evidence in the month or so that remained to us. At the same time, I had a feeling that I was missing something, something that seemed tantalisingly close but that I couldn't quite put my finger on; it was lurking somewhere in my mind, but somehow just out of reach.

Arlene was shaking her head.

'The way I see it,' she said, 'every which way you look at this, the trail ends in Washington DC. That's what we heard at the reunion, and I think that's what we're hearing now, y'all. The paperwork ended up in Washington because that's where it needed to be if anyone was going to pay any attention to it. The problem is, the trail's gone cold. Maybe the Brits burned the papers, and maybe the government did, or maybe they mislaid them somewhere and forgot about them. But it happened 200 years ago, and I never saw a bloodhound that could follow a trail that went dead 200 years ago. Now that would be a dawg I could sell at the Texas State Fair and make me a dollar or two.'

'Well,' Aunt Meg said, 'Kiah, didn't you tell us that the judge ordered the government to make a search in Washington?'

I nodded. 'Yes. They were ordered to make a search of the Treasury and the National Archives and report back to Judge Morrow in six weeks, the same time our report is due. But we can't just sit back and rely on the government to do everything for us. They can tell us what they find in Washington, but if they come up with nothing, we have to be able to tell the judge that we've ruled out any other possibilities before we have any hope of persuading him to widen the search. So yes, Powalski, I want you to go back over Samuel's part of the genealogy, but we don't have time for a road trip. Get on the phone and see what information might still be out there.'

'Is that what it's coming down to,' Sam asked quietly, 'proving that we have a good reason for failing to find any evidence?'

'I'm not giving up yet,' I replied. 'But Arlene may be right. Put yourself in Samuel's position. He had to figure that he couldn't do anything with the loan certificates without confronting someone in the Treasury. He couldn't get it done in Pennsylvania. Jacob had tried that with the sixteen documents he took to the loan office, and those papers ended up in Washington. The only difference was, Jacob lost control of them. Isabel would have told Samuel about that, and I can't see him making the same mistake. He had to go to Washington. He had to wave Jacob's name in front of their faces in the Treasury, maybe wave George Washington's name in front of their faces, but he couldn't do any of that without going to

Washington and taking the paperwork with him. There had to be a record of that, and we need to find it.'

'Plus,' Arlene added, 'like Aunt Meg said, the family's been at this for two hundred years. If there was paper to be found in some attic in Sorryass, Iowa, someone would have found it by now.'

'Why don't I get a shot of this on my phone?' Powalski suggested, leaning over Isabel's document.

'Good idea,' I replied, 'and before we leave I want everyone to make a handwritten copy.'

'Why do you need us to do that?' Sam asked.

'It's just a precaution,' I replied. 'We're taking custody of it now, and we'll take good care of it, but I want to make sure I can prove its contents in court if something should happen to the original. The more of us that read and copy it, the better.'

We took a fond leave of Aunt Meg. She and Sam spoke quietly together for a long time before we parted, and there were tears on both sides. We all knew that it was coming down to the wire now. By the time we met again, we would know the fate of our lawsuit. Time was running out, and there would probably be no more clues, no magical interventions. Arlene took me aside as Aunt Meg and Sam were talking. I was feeling much better now, but there was still a coldness deep in the pit of my stomach. I had somehow had contact with these people, with these events, through my dreams, and I couldn't shake the feeling that there was something I was supposed to be seeing. But I wasn't seeing it.

'What's your take on Petrosian?' Arlene asked.

'Dave? He's OK. Why?'

'Is he straight, is what I'm asking? I mean, if he finds something in Washington, is he really going to turn it over to us? Call me crazy, hun, but if he does, it would have to be a hell of a temptation to feed it to the shredder while nobody's looking and tell us they didn't find anything.'

'I don't think Dave Petrosian would do that.'

'How sure are you of that?'

I shrugged. 'I think I know him pretty well, Arlene. I trust him.'

'How about the guys who arranged to have you audited? Do you trust them?'

I nodded. 'They may be another story. But Dave's lead trial counsel, and I don't think he would be party to destroying evidence.'

'Maybe they wouldn't tell him,' Arlene said.

I smiled. 'So you don't think the government's going to give us the helping hand we need?'

'Give us a helping hand? Sure. You want to know when that will happen?'

'When?'

'When Quinn the Eskimo gets here, hun; that's when. And until he shows, even with what we got today, it looks to me like we're just whistling Dixie.'

44

THE IRS AUDITORS WERE called Mike and Todd and were unfailingly polite, and as Reg sat by my side at my conference table, they congratulated me on keeping such good records and assured me that my affairs were in order. They just had a few questions, just to clear up one or two things that weren't one hundred per cent clear, nothing to worry about, just so that they could close the books. It was only our third day back from Pennsylvania, and I had better things to do than waste my time answering questions from them when my affairs had already been determined to be in order. I was in a mood to give them their marching orders. Fortunately, Reg kept me under control. It took an hour for us to explain to their satisfaction a number of expense receipts a ten-year-old could have told you were related exclusively to business matters, and for them to make careful notes of what we said. Eventually, they politely pronounced themselves to be satisfied, and left with a polite handshake. They left the office door open, and I heard Arlene wishing them well on the way out.

'Y'all make sure to say "hi" to your friends in the Department of Justice for us,' she said.

'The Department of Justice? I don't understand the reference there, ma'am,' Todd replied politely. 'We work for the IRS.'

'Get out of here,' Arlene said.

'Yes, ma'am. You have a good day, now.'

I heard the door slam behind them. I thanked Reg profusely,

and he left. At last, I could get on with something useful. I took a
deep breath, sat down at the table, and began to read through my
copy of Isabel's document. I still wasn't seeing whatever it was I
was supposed to see. Behind her careful narrative, or concealed in
it, there was something more and whatever it was, I somehow had
to see it and make use of it within four weeks and counting.

I'm not sure how long I had been absorbed in my reading before
I heard the voices outside. At first, I thought that Mike and Todd
must have returned with more questions. But it didn't sound like
Mike or Todd. I heard a male voice – and there was nothing polite
about it – and then I heard Arlene's voice raised in protest.

'You can't just barge in there,' she was saying.

'I'm not barging in. I need to talk to Kiah about a case, and it's
urgent,' the male voice was replying.

They were closer to the door of my office now, close enough
for me to recognise the voice, and recognise it I did. The
conversation continued. She was telling him I couldn't see him,
and he was saying that he had to see me. For a moment or two
I froze, as memories of the Week began to flood back into my
mind, memories I had thought I had put behind me. At first I felt
overwhelmed, but to my relief, my feelings were not the feelings
that had haunted me during the Week. There was no punch to
the gut, no nausea, and no tears. I was able to bring my thoughts
under control and stay in the moment. I wasn't about to cave in. I
raised myself out of my chair, and took a number of deep breaths
before the inevitable knock on the door came. Arlene opened the
door and looked in.

'I'm sorry, hun. He won't leave. Y'all want me to call security?'

I shook my head. 'No. Let him come in.'

'You sure?'

'Yes, I'm sure.'

Arlene nodded reluctantly.

'Well, all right then. But I'm right here if y'all need me, and if he causes any trouble I'll have security here in a New York minute.'

'I'm OK, Arlene.'

She let him in and closed the door behind him. As she closed the door, she made a brief but unambiguously rude sexual hand gesture in his direction behind his back. I couldn't resist a grin. He stood just inside the door for some seconds.

'That's some attack dog you have there, Kiah. I guess that means you don't have to bark yourself.'

It was said with the smarmy fake good humor I remembered all too well. It was false and shallow, and as cheap as his latest suit, the pinstripes too wide for his height, the sleeves a little too short – to make sure no one missed the massive gold cuff links – the hair slicked back with too much lotion. To my relief, I found that I was able to stand back and take it all in with a detached amusement. The only question going through my mind was: how had I ever wasted three years of my life on this man? I couldn't answer the question, but at least I could be grateful it hadn't been any longer.

'What do you want, Jordan?'

'I need to talk to you about a case. May I sit down?'

I waved him into a chair opposite me, and removed Isabel's document out of sight in among a pile of other papers.

'No, I won't have coffee; I just had some, but thanks for asking.'

'Jordan, I have a busy day. Either get to the point or leave.'

He nodded. 'Your wish is my command.'

He opened his briefcase and took out some papers, which he placed on the table.

'As of yesterday, my firm represents a lady by the name of Mary Jane Perrins and three other residents of Boston, Massachusetts, who intend to file in the Claims Court to become the lead plaintiffs in the van Eyck family litigation. This is a copy of their Complaint against the United States and their motion to take over the position of lead plaintiffs.'

I took the Complaint, which, to put it diplomatically, seemed to be closely modeled on the one I had filed on behalf of Sam, and turned to the last page. The pleading was signed on behalf of the law firm of Schumer Berthold & Morris, by Jordan K. Leslie Esq., counsel for Mary Jane Perrins and three others whose names registered vaguely from the reunion. I closed my eyes and held my head in my hands for some time.

'Jordan, is this your idea of a joke?' I asked, raising my head. It wasn't that an intervention by Mary Jane Perrins was entirely unexpected. Maisie had tipped us off that she had made inquiries of the court about what she had to do to worm her way into the case. But that she was represented by Jordan was unexpected, and unwelcome. Jordan knew that all too well, obviously. He had that self-satisfied grin on his face, the one he wore when he thought he'd done something clever, the one that had always made me want to punch him in the face.

'It's no joke, Kiah. You want to see my letter of retainer?'

'How did you come to contact Mary Jane Perrins?' I asked.

'I didn't contact her. That would come perilously close to ambulance-chasing in the circumstances. We don't chase ambulances. Mary Jane contacted the firm, and asked specifically that I represent her.'

While I was generally disinclined to give Jordan much credence, in this instance I believed him. There was no reason for him to lie about this. My mind wandered back to the conference room at the Intercontinental Hotel. I heard Mary Jane asking her loaded questions. My instinct had been right. For whatever reason, that woman didn't like me, and didn't like Sam. But not liking me was one thing. Doing her homework thoroughly enough to retain my ex-live-in boyfriend to go up against me was something else again. This woman had it in for me, and for Sam, in spades.

'I'm asking the judge to hold a hearing to decide on the lead plaintiff motion next week. I'm aware of the discovery orders, and so I know there isn't much time.'

I shook my head.

'For God's sake, Jordan,' I replied. 'If you know about the

discovery orders, you'll know that it's completely irresponsible to waste our time with this bullshit. We have less than four weeks to gather evidence, and I don't need to be spending that time on crap like this.'

'On the contrary, we believe it's vital that our firm should get involved immediately,' he said.

'Oh, really? And why would that be? Your firm knows nothing about the case. You don't have a prayer of getting up to speed with the facts in the next four weeks, let alone handling the discovery, and you're not prepared for the legal argument we have coming at the end of the discovery period. All you're doing is playing into the government's hands, pretty much guaranteeing that the plaintiffs will fall flat on their faces.'

'I disagree,' he replied. 'Our firm can throw resources at this, resources you just don't have. I know you're working with your attack dog and one part-time investigator. You're calling me irresponsible, but how irresponsible is that? I would be working on the case myself full-time, and I can have two associates and three paralegals assigned.'

'Including the bimbo?' I asked. I shouldn't have, I know, but he was pushing a lot of buttons, so I pushed one of his in retaliation.

'Kimberley is not a bimbo,' he raised his voice, pointing a finger. 'She's my wife and she's not a paralegal, she's a secretary, so...'

He stopped himself before he could give me any further satisfaction.

'Look, Kiah, either you're going to agree to us taking the case over, or we'll ask the judge to make an order.'

'Ask the judge whatever you want,' I replied. 'It's a free country. Do you need directions to find the Claims Court? It's not your usual hunting ground, is it? Do you have a copy of their rules of procedure?'

He gave a sigh of fake exasperation, another gesture I was all too familiar with.

'Fine. Take that attitude. It doesn't matter. This isn't just about who's better equipped to run the class action.'

'Well, what *is* it about?' I asked. 'I know Mary Jane Perrins hates my guts and my client's guts, for some reason neither of us understands, but that's not going to impress the judge. It's *all* about who should run the class action.'

'It's also about whether your client is fit to represent the van Eyck family in this litigation.'

'Fit? What the hell are you talking about?'

Jordan reached into his briefcase and pushed a small brown envelope across the table to me.

'My clients don't think it's appropriate for the family to be represented by a porn star.'

'What?'

Slowly, I opened the envelope. It contained a DVD with a gaudy cover, featuring three scantily clad and heavily made-up young women with very large teeth, wild hair, and a lot of lipstick. The movie was entitled *Revenge of the Zombie Cheerleaders*. I looked at him.

'What is this?' I asked.

'Ask your client,' he suggested. 'Or better still, watch it yourself. That's what we're asking the judge to do before the hearing.' He smiled. 'She gives quite a performance. Oscar material, if they give Oscars for stuff like this. I assume they have some kind of porn version of the Oscars, don't they?'

He closed his briefcase and stood, pushing back his chair.

'I know you have a busy day, so I'll get out of your hair. Oh, and I should warn you, there's been some interest in this from the *National Inquirer*. Your client may be getting a request for a comment.'

I shook my head.

'Well, now we really have reached rock bottom, Jordan, haven't we?' I replied quietly. 'You leaked this to the *National Inquirer*?'

'Leaked it? There was no need to leak anything. This material is publicly available online and in stores, if you know where to look. The *Inquirer* was quite capable of finding it without our help. It didn't take Woodward and Bernstein.'

After he had gone, I stood, hands on hips, looking at the closed door of my office. Arlene came in.

'What an asshole,' she said. 'Are you OK, hun? Aren't you glad you gave him the bum's rush?'

I nodded. 'Yes and yes.'

'Are you sure you're OK?'

'I'm fine. Where's Sam?'

'She's over at Powalski's office, helping with the phone calls.'

'Tell her I need to see her this afternoon.'

'OK.'

'And let's order in some beer and pizza when she's here.'

She raised her eyebrows quizzically.

'We havin' ourselves a party, hun? It's a bit early to be celebrating, ain't it? Or is it just because you're so glad to see the back of your ex?'

'We're going to watch a movie,' I replied.

She nodded. 'Well, all right, then. Do you want Powalski here?'

'No, and send Jenny home for the day.'

45

WHEN SAM SAW THE movie lying on the table, she collapsed into a chair with her head in her hands. I stood behind her and put my arms around her. Arlene ruffled her hair as she walked past the chair.

'It's OK, hun,' she whispered.

'I told you when we first met that I'd made one movie,' Sam said quietly. 'I didn't go into detail because it's not a part of my career I'm proud of. I didn't mean to...'

'Sam, this is bullshit,' I said as comfortingly as I could. 'It's pure harassment. Either that, or Jordan has no idea what goes on in the Claims Court. They're not interested in this kind of crap over there. If that's all he's got, there's no way Judge Morrow is going to let Mary Jane Perrins take over as lead plaintiff.'

'It's going to be embarrassing for the family,' Sam replied, 'especially if they've got the *Inquirer* on my case.'

'It's a tempest in a teacup,' I insisted. 'If I know Judge Morrow, and I think I do, he isn't going to give a damn about you making a movie. This case has nothing to do with what you do for a living. If anything, it's more likely to turn him against Mary Bitch Perrins than against you. Judge Morrow's only interested in one thing, and that's what's best for managing the case.'

She sighed. 'It's just that I keep imagining Aunt Meg finding out about all this,' she said quietly. 'Have you watched it?'

'No. I figured we would watch it together, you, me and Arlene.'

'Do we have to?'

'Yes. Judge Morrow is going to watch it, and we have to see what he sees.'

I turned to Arlene.

'Are the pizza and beer on the way?'

'Any minute now, y'all.'

Sam managed a smile.

'You've ordered pizza and beer?'

'Sure, hun,' Arlene replied. 'Kiah and I have ourselves a rule: we never watch porn without beer and pizza.'

We laughed. Sam gave a deep sigh.

'It's not that bad,' she said. 'There's no actual sex taking place, nothing hardcore. I would never have done that. I shouldn't have done this. I knew it was going to be trash. But it was before I had an agent, and I wasn't working that much, and the company was in town one day and called auditions, and they were offering decent money, so...'

She let her voice trail away.

'Sounds like some of the stuff I had to do when I was starting out in practice,' I said, and we laughed again.

Revenge of the Zombie Cheerleaders wasn't what you would call a classic. There wasn't much of a plot. What there was seemed to consist of an endless series of biting attacks by the Zombie Cheerleaders (all of whom were female) on the members of a college football team while they were either partying, trying to catch some sleep after a party, or taking a shower in their frat house. The dialogue, accordingly, was pretty unimaginative. So it wasn't surprising that the film didn't bring out the best in the cast, of whom Sam – second senior Zombie Cheerleader under her then stage name of Sam de Zola – was one. The acting was pretty lame. But hardcore porn it wasn't. As Sam had implied, it was the kind of low-budget soft porn you saw everywhere. Jordan must have known that. What was he thinking? He and I had watched more explicit stuff together on cable in the days when we were together and did such things.

As we began to watch, Sam seemed mortified, though I thought the cast were about the only people involved in the movie who didn't have much reason to be embarrassed. In particular, Sam hid her eyes whenever the camera caught her naked, which was pretty often and not always artistically, but I wished she would watch herself. She was beautiful, and she was achingly, disturbingly erotic. I'd never had a sexual reaction to the female body before that afternoon and haven't since, but I did then, and although I never wanted to take it any further, it was a surprisingly pleasing and comfortable experience. I daresay a lot of men had felt the same way over the years about one or other of the cheerleaders, since that was the overriding goal of the film, and much as it pained me to admit it, I had to concede that the director's creative efforts had not been entirely wasted.

As the beer and pizza kicked in, we began to see that the film had another quality. It was one of those movies that was so bad that it was actually funny. Arlene was the first to crack. One of the cheerleaders (not Sam) was biting the quarterback in the shower to the accompaniment of canned music, apparently intended to be dramatic. The quarterback seemed powerless to resist her, and he was losing a lot more blood than the degree of biting suggested he should have. Arlene began to giggle. I tried not to get sucked in, but it was hopeless. As the cheerleaders were plotting the attack on their next victim – it turned out that they supported a nearby rival college and intended to take out the entire home team before the big game the following Saturday – I couldn't stand it either. I gave in and giggled helplessly. Two scenes later, Sam became infected, and by the end of the movie we were laughing hysterically. It was the best therapy we could have had. By the time we searched for our shoes to go home, we felt rejuvenated. Sam had recovered her spirits and was back in the game.

If Mary Jane Perrins had concluded from this movie – assuming she had actually watched it – that Sam was a porn star, she must have led a pretty sheltered life; and if Jordan thought it would make a difference to an experienced Claims Court judge, I was pretty sure he was on the wrong track. Our strategy was set. We would ignore *Revenge of the Zombie Cheerleaders* and carry on as if nothing had happened. If the *Inquirer* called, we would make no comment, and the same applied to the media generally and to any members of the family. As far as we were concerned, the incident was closed.

Even better, this attempt to throw us off balance had given us a renewed energy. The bustle was back in the office for the first time since the Week, and it felt great.

46

I SPENT THE NEXT morning writing a brief, explaining to Judge Morrow as straightforwardly as I could why Mary Jane Perrins, and three other residents of Boston, Massachusetts, had failed to provide the court with any good reason why the class action would benefit from a change of lead plaintiff. Most of the brief was technical, but of course, I focused on the fact that we were facing a critical stage of the proceedings, for which the law firm of Schumer Berthold & Morris, and Jordan K. Leslie Esq. in particular, didn't have a prayer of being prepared in the limited time available. Their intervention served no purpose except to distract counsel (me) from completing the discovery process and getting ready to renew the argument about the statute of limitations. In addition, I pointed out that contrary to the patronising assumption made by the moving parties and their lawyer, I was not running the litigation with minimal support. I had the very able support of two attorneys within the family, Jeff Carlsen of Salt Lake City, and Edwin van Eyck of Los Angeles. This was true. Both had made themselves available, and both had been generous with their time. Ed had done a couple of pieces of legal research for me, and I had developed the habit of sending any documents I drafted to Jeff, who with his keen editor's eye and unerring feel for the use of language in a brief, had made some brilliant suggestions. My message to Judge Morrow, and to Jordan, was: we're doing fine, thank you; get out of our way and let us do our job.

I couldn't quite leave it there, of course. As the subject had been raised with some fanfare, I had to say something about the Zombie Cheerleaders. I felt myself resenting the time I had to spend fighting off this crude and gratuitous attack on Sam. By way of retribution, I ended the brief with a few rather colourful observations about the tenuous grip on reality, not to mention the impoverished sex lives the moving parties and their lawyer must have, if they thought either (1) that *Revenge of the Zombie Cheerleaders* was pornographic; or (2) that even if it was, it had any relevance to a class action in the Claims Court for the recovery of a Revolutionary War Loan. I emailed the finished product to Jeff, who, as I had expected, returned it with a number of sensibly diplomatic amendments to the final section. With Jeff's amendments the brief still made the point very clearly, and I gave it to Arlene to file as I left the office.

It was a relief to get it done, but I was feeling frustrated. I wanted very much to rationalise my frustration by telling myself that it was about having to spend almost the whole day on Mary Jane Perrins when there were so many more useful things I could have been doing. But in my heart of hearts I knew that Mary Jane Perrins wasn't the real problem. The real problem was that there *weren't* many more useful things I could have been doing. We were closing in on the discovery deadline, and we didn't seem to be getting anywhere. We had one lead, and one only, and Powalski and Sam were working it as hard as they could. But their many calls to members of Samuel's branch of the family had turned up nothing new, and I still wasn't seeing whatever it was I was supposed to be seeing. That was the real frustration.

Fortunately, the evening promised to be more rewarding. Arya had invited me for dinner.

Dinner with Arya, in addition to being a delicious feast of Indian delicacies, is a kind of ritual, a ritual I've known and loved for many years. Whatever I know about Indian cooking I learned either from my mother or from Arya, but most of it I learned from Arya. My mother was a wonderful cook, but learning from her was a bit like trying to break into Fort Knox. She seemed to guard her recipes and techniques as if our national security depended on it. She would let me watch while she cooked, she would answer direct questions, and she would sometimes even allow me to do something to help her if I made enough of a nuisance of myself and refused to go away, but I always felt like an intruder in her kitchen. I found her hand-written book of recipes after her death, and I've tried to recreate some of them. The dishes taste fine, but there's something missing, something I can't quite pin down. With Arya, it couldn't have been more different. Arya was not only happy to have me in her kitchen, she insisted on it – and not as a spectator. I may have been her guest, but I was also assigned a role as sous chef, and it wasn't optional. Within five minutes of my arrival I was in the kitchen, barefoot and decked out in a huge white apron, ready for action. As we began, she invited me to get us both a drink from the fridge. This, too, was part of the ritual. Arya didn't drink much alcohol, but she wasn't averse to a beer while she was cooking. The beer was Cobra, from India.

Arya's kitchen was a paradise of colourful sights, sounds, and smells. She was frying fresh garlic, onion, and ginger in large pans. Even though it would have been much easier to use a commercial cooking oil, she insisted on cooking with ghee, the traditional Indian blend of oil and butter. She sometimes found it in the Indian quarter but if not, Arya would make it herself from a family recipe. Making ghee is a tricky and time-consuming process with no guarantee of success – trust me on this, I've tried and failed miserably many times – but this didn't deter Arya at all. She also made her own chapattis from scratch. She had mastered the critical balance of flour and water, and one of my jobs was to cut the dough up, roll it out, and heat it in a dry heavy pan. I also ground the spices together for her, using a heavy ceramic pestle and mortar. Arya didn't like blenders: in her mind, the preparation of spices, like everything else in the kitchen, was best done by hand. Besides, using a blender would have deprived me of an extraordinary sensual experience. As I measured the spices into the mortar, their aromas began to fill the space around me. Mingling with the garlic, onion and ginger that wafted in my direction from the stove, depending on what dishes she was preparing, there might be the trenchant aromas of turmeric and red chili powder, the more refined scent of cumin and coriander, the mundane feel of cloves and black pepper, or sometimes the exotic and sumptuous visual and olfactory assault of saffron. It was an intoxicating blend. Her signature dish is a chicken Jalfrezi that is to die for. Jalfrezi is a dish from Pakistan, but Arya's recipe had been handed down to her from a time before there was a Pakistan, a time before Partition, a time in which Hindus and Muslims had lived in Punjab together, for the most part in peace.

Once I had ground the spices and sifted them into different containers for different dishes – she never cooked less than three – she added chicken, vegetables or shrimp to the frying pans and after a minute or two, the spices. Everything happened very quickly from that point on, and although we chatted away quite happily most of the time while she was cooking, I learned to be quiet during this critical stage. There are so many moving parts to the machine, it has always seemed almost impossible that all of them should stop at the right place at the same time. To this day, I don't really understand how Arya does that. My cooking is pretty respectable, I think, but the timing always gets me. I always seem to be waiting for some dish to be done while others are starting to get cold. But not Arya: for her, as if by magic, all the elements come together at exactly the right moment, and as often as she has tried to explain and talk me through the process, it's the one thing I haven't yet mastered. About which I'm perfectly content. I need to feel that there is still a little magic in the world.

As we ate, I told her about the re-appearance of Mary Jane Perrins and Jordan K. Leslie Esq., both of them, I told her, about as welcome as Banquo's ghost: except, she reminded me, because it was something I always tended to forget, that unlike Macbeth I had nothing to feel guilty about. Arya wasn't much interested in the technical aspects of Jordan's motion to replace Sam as lead plaintiff and me as lead counsel. Serious as that was, she assumed that I had the technical issues under control. But she was very interested in my reaction to being confronted by Jordan. As I related the encounter to her, she smiled and nodded, and as I concluded, she asked me how I felt about it.

'I feel really good,' I replied, truthfully. 'I have no regrets, and he has no hold over me any more. I've moved on.'

'Then I want you to remember this moment,' she said, 'and remember how different it is from other days you've spent with me when I asked you the same question.'

I smiled. 'I've come a long way, Arya, thanks to you.'

'You've come a long way thanks to *you*,' she replied.

Then, as the meal was ending and we became quieter, I told her about my visit to Pennsylvania, and about standing in real time in the churchyard at Swedeburg in which I had stood in dream time. I told her about the elevated section of highway that explained the roar I had heard in my dream and had attributed fancifully to an aqueduct, and about the young woman called Isabel I had seen there and in the loan office in Philadelphia, who had, as I had dreamed, been an assistant and confidante to Jacob van Eyck. I shared with her the news about the document Isabel had written and entrusted to Joan until the right person could be found, and about Aunt Meg receiving it from Joan and entrusting it to Sam as the right person. Lastly, I told her about the huge weight of responsibility I felt on my shoulders to see what Isabel was trying to tell me, and about my inability to see it.

I'm not sure how much of Isabel's account I quoted to her – by that time I had read it so often that I could have recited almost the whole document from memory – but I certainly gave her the gist of it. She listened in total silence to all of this. Then she took my hands and held them between hers.

'Do you have it with you?' she asked.

I nodded. I had taken my copy everywhere with me since returning from Merion Township.

'If I may,' she said, 'I'd be interested to see it. Why don't you make us some masala chai while I look at it?'

47

I WILLINGLY TOOK MYSELF off to the kitchen and boiled water in the electric kettle. I selected two large mugs, poured the sweet, spicy, aromatic masala chai into Arya's ceramic black-and-white teapot, added water, and waited for two minutes to allow the chai time to brew. When it was ready, I poured it and added milk. Masala chai is another detail from home and from Arya's house that has always stayed with me: the perfect end to any Indian meal, its gentle vapors calm the stomach and ease the last remains of the fiery peppers out of the sinuses. When I returned to the dining room, Arya was engrossed in my copy of Isabel Hardwick's document. She had pushed some dishes aside and laid the pages out together under the pewter chandelier above the table. I didn't interrupt. I left her chai a safe distance from her right hand and sat down opposite her to wait.

She didn't seem to move a muscle for two or three minutes. Then she looked up and took her mug of chai in both hands, almost as if she was using it to keep warm.

'Kiah, you copied this exactly as written, right?'

'Yes. We all made an exact copy – Sam, Arlene, Powalski and me.'

'But exactly as written?'

'Yes.'

'And the original is where?'

'Sam has it. Aunt Meg gave it to her. It's hers now.'

Arya nodded. 'Would it be all right if I hold on to your copy for a day or two?'

'No problem. Do you…?'

I suddenly stood and made my way around the table.

'Arya, I know that look. You've seen something, haven't you? What have you seen?'

She smiled. 'I'm not sure yet. Don't get excited. It may be nothing at all.'

'But –'

'There are one or two things about the way she writes that I find… interesting, and I'd like to follow them up.'

'You're seeing something, aren't you?'

She shrugged. 'Maybe, maybe not. Tell me, you've read this document how often? Quite a number of times by now, haven't you?'

'I've lost count of how many times.'

'Don't you think there's something curious about the way she writes certain things?'

I stared at the sheets of paper again, but nothing was jumping out at me. In all honesty, by then, I didn't expect it. I guess I'd read it too often, and was too familiar with it, and with the pressure I'd put myself under to come up with something, I'd stopped using my critical faculties. At times I felt stupid, and sometimes it seemed that the sheets of paper in front of me were mocking me. It was not a good frame of mind in which to stand back and take another hard look.

'You're going to have to show me,' I admitted.

'Sit down here, beside me,' she said. She pulled the sheets closer to us.

'Look at this. There are three events she writes about for which she gives us not only the date, but also the place and the time. The first is her own birth: "*I was born Isabel Johnstone on the fourth day of June in the year 1788, in the early evening, less than an hour after the sun had set, to Ezra and Mary Johnstone of*

Upper Merion Township in the State of Pennsylvania.'"

I nodded. 'OK.'

'Then there's the way she talks about her writing of the document itself: "*I, Isabel Hardwick, being the wife of James Hardwick of Upper Merion Township in the State of Pennsylvania, being of sufficient age and of sound mind, have taken up my pen at ten o'clock in the forenoon, on this third day of December in the Year of our Lord 1813, and desire thereby to record the matters following.*"'

She ran her finger over the pages until she found the place she wanted.

'Then, lastly, the occasion when she handed over the two-and-twenty papers to Jacob's Brother, capital B. Oh, and while I'm focusing on that: the capital B is in the original, right? You said you copied it exactly.'

'Yes,' I agreed. 'I remember that specifically.'

'The word is used twice and it's capitalised both times.'

'Yes.'

'All right. Good. So, this is what she says about it: "*I agreed to perform the task he had asked of me, and delivered the said papers to his Brother in Philadelphia at eleven o'clock in the forenoon on the fourth day of September in the Year of our Lord 1810.*"'

She paused.

'You don't think that's curious?' she asked, when I didn't respond immediately.

'Is it?'

'Kiah, she was making a record of important events, so you can understand her giving us the dates; and maybe the place was important in the case of delivering the two-and-twenty papers to the Brother, maybe it's important for us to know that she took them to him in Philadelphia. But why does it matter where she was when she wrote the document, or what time she took up her pen? Why does it matter where she was born, and at what time?'

I nodded. 'That's a good question.'

'I mean, look how careful she's been about it. She says she was born, "*in the early evening, less than an hour after the sun had set.*" That's the one time, of the three she tells us about, that she couldn't have known herself. How does she know? Someone told her, obviously. Well, all children ask their parents what time they were born, don't they? Today, we all have watches and phones and clocks. Some people had clocks back then too, but did Isabel's parents have one? We have to assume not, because if they had, her parents would have told her the time. If you didn't have a clock, you had to get as close as you could, and you did that by comparing notes about what else was going on when the child was born. So they told her, "in the early evening, less than an hour after the sun had set," and if you have an almanac it's easy enough to find out what time sunset was in Upper Merion Township on that day, and then you have a pretty accurate time; not exact, but close enough to work with.'

'OK. I get that,' I said. 'But it still doesn't explain why she wanted to share that with us. Why was it necessary?'

'Exactly,' Arya replied. 'That's the question.'

'Do you have any ideas?'

'One idea, and that's why I want to keep this for a while, to check it out.'

She wasn't showing any immediate sign of continuing.

'Aren't you going to tell me?'

'I guess…'

'Come on, Arya, you can't leave me in suspense like this,' I pleaded. 'You have to give me *some* clue.'

She laughed.

'Well, all right. I guess I shouldn't keep you in the dark. But Kiah, please, bear in mind: I could be way off base here; I may be seeing something that isn't there.'

'If you're seeing anything,' I replied, 'you're way ahead of me.'

'OK,' she said. 'I think Isabel may have left us a clue. Look what she said about Jacob schooling her.'

She found the passage with her finger.

"*Mr van Eyck took it upon himself, with my consent, to school me. My parents had never done so, it not being the custom of our community generally to school girls, no purpose, according to the general opinion, being served thereby—'''*

'Oh, yes,' I interrupted, 'I love that bit. Why would you want to teach the girls? Obviously, a complete waste of time. Arya, I had to read this aloud at Aunt Meg's house, and when I got to that part I pretty much choked on it.'

She laughed. 'I'm sure you did. But, you know, it was 1813, so... Anyway, she goes on: "*But because of Mr van Eyck's generosity with his time, I was instructed in reading and writing, in arithmetic, in the positions, transits, and retrograde motions of the planets, in the keeping of accounts, and in many other matters of business. This instruction, which I have passed on to my own daughters, has benefitted them as much as myself, and enriched my life more than higher wages could ever have enriched it.*" What strikes you about that?'

I shook my head. 'I don't know.'

'Kiah, if he was going to school her, you can understand him instructing her in reading and writing, the keeping of accounts and other matters of business. That wasn't just generosity on Jacob's part, was it? Those were things she would have to know if she was going to be any real help to him in his business affairs, or even his personal affairs. But...'

Suddenly, I saw it.

'The positions and movements of the planets,' I said.

'Yes. Why would he school her in that?'

I shook my head. 'It does seem strange. Perhaps because astronomy was something you learned if you wanted to be seen as well educated at that time?'

'Possibly,' she replied. 'But in her case, I don't think so. Jacob wasn't running a school, Kiah. He wasn't going to send Isabel on to the university. This wasn't an academic exercise. He was tutoring a young woman in the things he thought she needed to know. He was giving her what he saw as a very practical education.'

I looked at her blankly. She smiled.

'The only people who are obsessed with times of birth,' she continued, 'are astrologers. You need a precise time to construct an astrological chart for an event. You need date, time and place. I think that's why Isabel was so careful to give us the times. That's why she went into detail about her birth. With the other times, she could be precise because she recorded the time herself, but with her birth, all she could do was to give us the information she herself was given, and leave us to do the rest.'

'Wow,' I said, helplessly. It was something that wouldn't have occurred to me in a hundred years.

'I think Jacob van Eyck was an astrologer,' Arya continued, 'and I think he schooled Isabel in astrology. She was obviously a bright young woman, and wise, too – she tells us how much she valued what she learned and how she passed it on to her own daughters.'

'But when she says the positions and transits and so on of the planets, surely that sounds more like astronomy than astrology,' I objected.

'Until modern times there was no distinction,' Arya replied. 'That's the way it's always been in India with the Jyotish, our Vedic astrology. The great Indian and Greek mathematicians, the great Arabic and European cosmologists, didn't distinguish between the mathematical aspects of the science – plotting and predicting the movements of the planets – and its interpretive aspects – attaching meaning to the movements of the planets, for the purpose of forecasting or seeking information. Today, of course, in the West, astronomers see themselves as pure scientists and they look down on astrology as junk science, if not outright superstition. But not in India: astrology is still regarded as a science in India, and in America in Jacob's time, there would still have been many people who saw no contradiction between the two.'

She paused to finish her chai, and turned her head to look at me.

'So that's my working hypothesis.'

I stared down at the pages before me and held my head in my hands. Could Arya really conjure up some new insight from Isabel's words, the same words that had been lying dormant and barren in my mind because of their sheer familiarity? The idea was startling, and at the same time intoxicating. What if I could hold such a breakthrough in my hands? It would be a game-changer: a revelation that would finally rip away the shroud that always seemed to hang over that long-gone winter of 1777–1778; a decisive piece of the puzzle that might finally provide a solution to the mystery of what Jacob had done, and what had become of his loan certificates? What if I could hold in my hands a piece of evidence that would finally put us on the front foot in our uphill struggle against the Department of Justice? But at the same time, I also began to imagine myself trying to explain to Sam how I had suddenly broken the case wide open with information that clearly wasn't there on the face of the document, and for which there was as yet not a shred of physical evidence. Actually, I thought, Sam would probably take it in her stride, but I'd get some hard questions from Arlene and Powalski; not to mention that if I were to find something resembling admissible evidence, I would one day have to provide some account to Judge Morrow of how I had come by it. Arya, reading my mind as ever, interrupted my reverie.

'Come with me,' she said.

48

WE WALKED UPSTAIRS TOGETHER in silence, with the cool, delicious feel of pinewood under our bare feet. I had been upstairs many times in the past, when I spent the night, but only once or twice had I been taken into the study, and we had never lingered there. The study was Arya's sanctuary as well as her place of work, and it was the one room in the house she preferred to keep to herself. The walls were taken up with bookcases. Most of the books were old – not antique, but earlier twentieth-century Indian, with dark-coloured cloth binding starting to unravel. I had seen such books many times. The schools in India were full of them, and my parents had their own sizeable collection. I grew up reading books just like them. A magnificent bronze statue of Shiva, depicted as ever inside the endless wheel of life, death, and rebirth over which he presides, dominated the room from the far corner to my right. It seemed eerily familiar. I had grown up with Shiva watching over me day and night from the wall opposite my bed at home. There were also a number of representations of Ganesh, the elephant god, with whose wisdom and benevolence Arya very much identified. Two stood on her desk, rather incongruously standing guard over her state-of-the-art desktop. Others were almost hidden away in spaces on the bookshelves.

In other spaces were family pictures, and pictures of Arya with me and my parents. There was also a grainy black-and-white print of a group of important-looking Indian dignitaries – a group that I'm sure included a relative of Arya's, because her family was connected politically in those days – shown standing on the lawn outside the Viceroy's residence in Shimla with Lord Mountbatten, Jawaharlal Nehru, Muhammad Ali Jinnah, and the Mahatma, on the eve of Independence. I know that picture was poignant for her. Her family had supported Gandhi politically in his futile struggle against Partition, and the Jalfrezi she had mastered was her expression of a grief for the senseless death and displacement that followed, a grief that had never left her. The room was dimly lit by two small desk lamps, and a hint of her Neroli incense floated in the air.

She gestured me to join her behind her desk. She opened a drawer and took out a thick grey file folder. She put it down on the desk, and held her hand on top of it. After some seconds she opened it and took out the sheet of paper on top of the stack.

'Do you know what this is?' she asked.

I smiled. I knew exactly what it was. The square diagram was different to the wheel in which western charts are presented, but I had seen many examples of Indian astrological charts in books my parents kept at home. After their death I had donated most of them to our local temple, but some I had kept for sentimental reasons. Then I looked at the name on the chart, and at the date, time and place of birth.

'Your parents brought this to me when you were very young, perhaps eighteen months, not more than two years old,' she said. 'It was cast and hand-drawn by an astrologer in Shimla. He has signed his name at the bottom: Rajiv. Anyone can draw a chart, but it's an old tradition to commission a fine piece of penmanship for a new child. Rajiv has a wonderful hand, doesn't he? And his use of different coloured inks is so evocative.'

She laughed, holding it up to the light.

'I could never do work like this, not if I live to be 200. My handwriting is atrocious, always has been, and I can't draw a square with straight sides to save my life, even with a ruler.

When I was in school, my teachers shouted at me for years for being untidy, but it made no difference and eventually they gave up. I was always too concerned with the content to worry about appearances. So I'm never going to get a commission to prepare something like this. But I can interpret the information Rajiv has recorded so beautifully.'

I was still staring at my birth chart, full of symbols of which I had no understanding, but that Arya could read, symbols that came alive for her.

'I was also schooled in astrology myself when I was younger, Kiah. My parents were determined that my sister Shesi and I should each do our best to master one of the four Vedic pillars. Shesi's was the Ayurveda.'

'The medicine of India,' I said quietly.

'Yes, a sad irony in a way because Shesi was always so fragile, and died so very young, bless her.' She picked up a family picture from the shelf behind her desk. 'This is Shesi, aged eighteen. She was dead less than a year later.'

She looked at the picture for some time before replacing it on the shelf.

'But mine was the Jyotish, the astrology, and I studied for many years. So your parents brought this chart to me. They wanted to know all about you at eighteen months, or two years, or whatever you were.' She laughed. 'I told them, "It's impossible. She's a baby still. I can't tell you anything now. You should wait until she's older." But of course, they wouldn't listen. Parents never do. It was only because they cared so much about you.'

She put an arm around my shoulder.

'But later, Kiah, when you were older, I came back to this chart many times. Whenever you came to see me with a problem at school, in college, when you wanted to become a lawyer and your parents wanted you to be a doctor, when you decided to open your own practice, and then, of course, when...'

'When the Week from Hell happened...'

'Yes, during that terrible time too. I came back to this chart, Kiah. I updated it according to the transits at the time, and I used what insight I had to offer you whatever guidance I could.'

I looked at her. 'My chart gave you information about all those things?' I asked. 'All those times when you knew exactly what to do, when my life was falling apart, when I didn't know which direction to go, when it all seemed so hopeless…?'

'Of course, Kiah, because your birth chart is a picture of you. It's a snapshot of the cosmos at the time you were born.' She smiled. 'It's not the only thing, of course. Often I just listened to you and said to myself, "Yes, I remember being nineteen too. I remember what it was like to be a young woman starting out in the world." But the chart is the basis for what I know about you.'

'Amazing,' I said.

She shook her head. 'What's really amazing,' she said, 'is that I didn't figure out what you should do, which direction you should take. Not once. You did – every time. You always had the answer inside you. My only role was to hold up a mirror to enable you to see it more clearly.'

'I suppose I've always known that you were an astrologer,' I said after some time. 'I mean, I know my parents came to you for advice, and I saw charts at home, so in one way it's no surprise. But you never told me before, at least not in so many words.'

'There was no reason to,' she said. 'If you had asked, I would have told you, of course. But the technicalities of what I was doing weren't important for you then. Now that you may have to take the information I give you out into the world, I think I owe it to you to tell you specifically what I'm going to do about Isabel Hardwick, who I suspect of being a kindred spirit.' She laughed. 'How you explain that to people out there in the wider world – if you do explain it – I leave to you.'

I laughed too. 'Gee, thanks.'

She handed me Rajiv's chart.

'Kiah, I want you to have this now,' she said. 'Your parents brought your birth chart to me because they loved you and they wanted you to have a light to see your way forward. This is your chart. Keep it safe.'

She drew me into her arms, and we embraced for what seemed a long time. Not too long before, I would have been a mess. Brought face to face so abruptly again with my parents' love for me, I would have cried inconsolably on Arya's shoulder and wondered how I would ever make it without them. But I was calm now. I still missed them and their memory was very precious. There was still an immense emotional undertow. But I was at peace with their memory.

'Give me a day or two with Isabel,' she said, kissing me on the cheek as we slowly released each other. 'Let me see where she's pointing us, where the path leads.'

49

I'D TAKEN THE PRECAUTION of getting Sam to court early, before the bulk of the reporters and TV crews arrived. I didn't anticipate the kind of crowds we'd seen at the summary judgment hearing, but needless to say, Mary Jane Perrins had given a press conference before leaving Boston, and once she had raised the spectre of pornography there was no chance of escaping the paparazzi altogether. It was the kind of 'story' the tabloids thrived on. As I had no idea what Sam – or I – might blurt out when confronted by these heroes of the Fourth Estate, I thought it would be better to protect both of us from the onslaught, at least until the hearing had been concluded. At that point, we would at least know where we stood: whether we had weathered the second critical storm, or whether all the work we had done would be hijacked by lawyers who knew nothing about the case, and who would almost certainly go down in flames when the next summary judgment hearing was held in three weeks' time. In that case, whatever we said to the press might not matter that much.

Some reporters had already made their way up to court, and once again there was an influx of clerks and interns from other courts, as well as assorted lawyers and members of the public. The level of interest wasn't quite as high as it had been on the first occasion, but the case was still a draw for those who enjoyed the thrill of a good courtroom brawl. Sam and Arlene sat behind me and we settled down to wait.

Mary Jane Perrins arrived with Jordan seconds before the hearing was due to begin. I had no doubt that she had been regaling the assembled journalists outside court with yet another lurid account of Sam's movie career. She was dressed in a frumpy brown blouse and beige slacks, her hair short and hanging down loosely at the sides. She presented a striking contrast to Sam, who, as ever, was immaculate in her light grey business suit and moderate heels. All right, I'm biased, but I'm still right about that. There was no sign of the other three residents of Boston, Massachusetts, who were allegedly also trying to join as plaintiffs. Jordan said not a word to anyone as he edged his way past Dave Petrosian to sit next to me in counsel's row. While I was taking all this in, Judge Morrow was taking the bench and Maisie was asking counsel to state their appearances. All three of us stood at the same time, Jordan to my immediate right, and Dave to his, but I was determined to stick my oar in the water first, just to remind Jordan who was in charge.

'Good morning, Your Honour. Kiah Harmon for the lead plaintiff, Samantha van Eyck, who is with me in in court, and about 2,000 other plaintiffs who have so far joined in this class action.'

'Good morning, Miss Harmon,' Judge Morrow replied.

'Jordan K. Leslie, Your Honour, with the law firm of Schumer Berthold & Morris, representing Mary Jane Perrins and three other plaintiffs.' He actually sounded irritated that I had beaten him to it. 'Mrs Perrins is in court.'

'Good morning to you too,' Judge Morrow replied. 'I know it's not the practice to say good morning in all courts, Mr Leslie, but if you should visit us more often, you'll find out that in the Claims Court we like to start out with a pleasantry or two in the morning.'

Jordan flinched. 'Excuse me, Your Honour. I didn't know that. Good morning.'

Dave flashed me a grin.

'Good morning, Your Honour, Dave Petrosian and Ellen Matthews for the United States. Your Honour, the government doesn't have a horse in this race, but we stand ready to assist the court with legal submissions if required.'

That, of course, had to be the government's official position. The government can't officially get involved in arguments about who is going to represent plaintiffs. But unofficially, the government often has an opinion on that subject. It makes the government lawyer's life easier to have stability and competence on the other side, and a lawyer of Dave's ability and experience understands that very well. His short written response to Jordan's motion was on the face of it a model of detachment, but somehow managed to give the impression that the United States was more than satisfied with the status quo, and Maisie had dropped me a hint that Dave had been even less diplomatic behind the scenes. It was one of a growing number of things I was grateful to him for.

'Good morning, and thank you, Mr Petrosian,' the judge replied. 'Well, Mr Leslie, I believe this is your motion. You have the floor.'

Dave and I sat, leaving Jordan to face Tomorrow.

'Yes, Your Honour, thank you. Your Honour, it's our position that this important case needs the attention of a real law firm.'

'Excuse me?' I exclaimed involuntarily, rising to my feet. 'Your Honour, would you please instruct Mr Leslie to avoid making personal attacks on opposing counsel?'

Jordan actually snorted.

'Typical. Your Honour, it's been my experience that Miss Harmon takes everything personally. But this is not personal. It's –'

Tomorrow cut him off at the knees.

'Mr Leslie, when I mentioned the pleasantry of saying good morning to each other in court, I was not meaning to imply that saying good morning represents the full extent of the civility this court expects of counsel. Whatever your experience of other courts may be, when lawyers come to the Claims Court, we expect everyone to be civil to each other throughout the hearing.'

'I apologise, Your Honour.'

'And before you proceed any further, you should know that Miss Harmon has appeared regularly in this court for a number of years, and that the court has the highest opinion of her work, in this case as well as in many others.'

I looked up gratefully at Tomorrow and thought I saw the trace of a smile cross his face.

'Of course, Your Honour.'

'Good. Then, why don't we try this again? Take two...'

'Yes, Your Honour. It's our position that this important case requires the attention of a number of lawyers, backed up by paralegals, and therefore needs a law firm that has such resources available. The law firm of Schumer Berthold & Morris is such a firm. If we take over as lead plaintiffs we will have at least three attorneys working on the case, of whom I will be one. We will also have extensive support staff committed to the case.'

Jordan glanced in my direction rather tentatively.

'And, Your Honour, just so everyone's clear, this is not intended to be personal or uncivil in any way, but I think I'm right in saying that with the exception of one investigator, Miss Harmon's full team is present in court this morning: one attorney and one secretary. That's all she has.'

'Plus an intern,' I added.

'Plus an intern,' Jordan said. 'Fine. It's just not enough. Your Honour, this is a complex case, and one of great historical importance, and it needs a full, detailed investigation. My firm has the resources to do that, and we are prepared to take over immediately, so that no time has to be lost.'

Contemplating my reply to this advocacy for a 'real' law firm to take over, I couldn't help remembering that in the beginning, when I was thinking about whether to take the case, I'd been preoccupied with the question of resources myself. I would have been delighted if there had been some law firm out there – preferably not Jordan's firm, obviously – prepared to come in with me and throw resources at the case. I'd been expecting a massive, labor-intensive paper case of the kind more suitable to a big firm. But in fact, that wasn't the way it had worked out. True, there were a lot of plaintiffs now, but their details were on the computer and Arlene kept them updated regularly by email; they were no problem, even if many more joined. We had not been submerged in paper. Actually, the problem was not that we had too much paper, but that we didn't have enough. It had become clear to me some time ago that our original vision of a massive family-wide search for evidence was not what was needed. The family had been interrogating each other about documents for more than 200 years, and nothing had come of it. The family-wide search was too blunt a weapon. We needed a smaller, more focused search. The problem was that we didn't know where and how to make that search, but I was convinced that if we could find out, we would have more than enough resources to carry it out. Since reading Isabel Hardwick's declaration, and talking with Arya about it, I felt sure that this was a case that in the end would turn, not on many documents, but on a very few.

'According to her brief,' Judge Morrow was saying, 'Miss Harmon has local counsel to assist her in Los Angeles and Salt Lake City. Is that right, Miss Harmon?'

'It is, Your Honour,' I replied.

The judge nodded.

'All right, thank you, Mr Leslie, I've got your point. Miss Harmon, what do say about all this? Does this case need Mr Leslie's resources?'

'No, Your Honour, and I'm afraid Mr Leslie's argument betrays his lack of familiarity with the case. This isn't a huge document case, and it doesn't need some kind of huge investigation. The van Eyck family did all that many years ago, and that's not what this case is about. The documents we're looking for are few in number, and we're closing in on where to look for them.' I admit, I crossed the fingers of one hand behind my back as I said this. 'Once we have that information – and we expect to soon – we don't anticipate any problem in terms of shortage of manpower or womanpower. As Your Honour has pointed out, we have local counsel and in fact there are other attorneys within the van Eyck family we can approach if we need to. That's cheaper than getting Mr Leslie's firm involved, because the family lawyers don't charge the family any fees.'

'All right,' Judge Morrow replied. 'So you're telling me that you're confident that you can handle this case with what you've got?'

'Completely confident, Your Honour. In addition, I would draw Your Honour's attention to the fact that we only have a little less than three weeks left to complete initial discovery, as Your Honour ordered. At the conclusion of that time, Your Honour will rule on the government's motion for summary judgment. If you allow another law firm in now, they will need all of that time to get up to speed, we will have to help them as best we can, and you take away all the remaining time we have to look for documents.'

'Thank you, Miss Harmon. Incidentally, Mr Leslie, your motion refers to three other residents of Boston, Massachusetts, in addition to Mrs Perrins, but they don't seem to be present today.'

'That's correct, Your Honour,' Jordan replied. 'They weren't able to make the trip from Boston.'

'I see,' Judge Morrow said. 'Mr Leslie, do you intend to pursue the second ground of your motion?'

This, of course, was what the press was waiting for.

'I do, Your Honour,' Jordan replied.

50

'Your Honour, Mrs Perrins further submits that it is inappropriate for a woman who has appeared in the kind of motion picture in question to represent this old and greatly respected American family in this historic litigation.'

Jordan paused, understandably not quite sure how to address the detail with Judge Morrow. Tomorrow didn't respond, and I had the distinct impression that he had no intention of helping Jordan out, so Jordan started to thread his way delicately through the cloud of judicial silence.

'Obviously, we don't ask that the court view this motion picture in open court... (silence). I don't know whether the court has had the opportunity to view it privately in chambers... (silence). But it's our position that the court must do so in order to fully understand what we're dealing with here...'

Eventually, Tomorrow seemed to react. He reached across his desk and held up a DVD.

'This is what we're talking about, Mr Leslie, is it? *Revenge of the Zombie Cheerleaders?*'

There was a certain amount of chuckling and sniggering around the courtroom, including some from Dave and Ellen to my right, from which I deduced that they had felt it to be their duty, as the government's lawyers, to scrutinise the evidence, even if they didn't have a horse in the race.

'Yes, Your Honour.'

'Would you like to hear my opinion about it?'

I heard Jordan swallow hard.

'So, I take it that Your Honour has viewed it?'

'How else would I have formed an opinion about it, Mr Leslie?'

'Indeed, Your Honour, of course. And yes, both Mrs Perrins and I would be most anxious to hear Your Honour's opinion about it.'

For the first time, Mary Jane Perrins, who had been sitting motionless behind Jordan, with her hands clenched tightly on her lap and staring fixedly ahead somewhere into the distance, ventured a slight movement, a nod of the head. I sensed Sam tensing up behind me.

'Very well,' Judge Morrow said. 'Hear it you shall.'

He passed the DVD between his hands several times before replacing it on his desk, folding his hands, and leaning forward to address the courtroom.

'A very wise judge,' he began, 'once declared that he wasn't sure whether he could ever define hardcore pornography, but that he knew it when he saw it. That seems to me to sum it up perfectly. Pornography, like beauty, is in the eye of the beholder, and as the beholder I have to consider what I have beheld. In my own opinion, this movie has no claim to be considered a masterpiece. It's unlikely that *Revenge of the Zombie Cheerleaders* will challenge *Schindler's List* or the *Godfather* trilogy for a place in the pantheon of the classics of the art of cinematography. Nor did it offer Miss van Eyck much of a vehicle for her talents as an actress, which I'm sure are far greater than depicted in this film.'

Tomorrow paused for effect, looking around the courtroom.

'But in my judgment, it comes nowhere close to pornography. It's the kind of titillating stuff you can find anywhere these days, on cable, and even occasionally on the networks – or at least, that's what I'm told. Apparently, there's a market for it. I'm not sure why, or what the market is, but I guess there must be one since they spend so much money making such films. But the real point is this: this movie may not be a work of art, but I'm sure it's the kind of thing many young actors and actresses do when they're starting out on their careers. There's no reason for Miss van Eyck or the van Eyck family to be embarrassed by it, and it certainly gives Mrs Perrins no basis for questioning Miss van Eyck's competence and suitability to represent the family as lead plaintiff in this litigation. I find that suggestion to be far-fetched and insulting, and frankly, it is regrettable that the court's time has been wasted on it. Indeed, with all due respect to Mrs Perrins and the three absent residents of Boston, Massachusetts, the phrase "get a life" springs to mind. Accordingly, I reject that ground of the motion.'

The judge glanced down at his notes.

'As for Mr Leslie's first ground, I accept that Miss Harmon is more than able to handle this case as lead plaintiff. Her work, both in written motions and oral argument, has been of her usual high quality and she has access to help when she needs it. There is no need for the intervention of a bigger law firm, especially when such a firm would have a very limited time to get up to speed. I'm encouraged to hear that this case is coming down to few rather than many documents, and I hope that means that both sides will be ready for the next hearing in just less than three weeks from now. For the reasons I have given, the motion filed by Mrs Perrins and the three absent residents of Boston, Massachusetts to be substituted as lead plaintiffs is denied, as is the motion for Mr Leslie's law firm to be substituted in as lead counsel.'

From behind, I felt Sam's hand squeeze my shoulder. Judge Morrow departed the bench in his usual brisk manner, and Jordan was out of the courtroom almost as quickly, again without a word to anyone. Not so Mary Jane Perrins, who remained in her seat as if transfixed, apparently unaware that Jordan had gone. I turned to Sam and Arlene, and we had a quick hug, after which we said goodbye to Dave and Ellen, who seemed very satisfied with the outcome, and made our way towards the door of the courtroom. The press would be lying in wait for us outside the courthouse, but

I felt sure that Sam wasn't going to be too bothered by them now. Then, as we were closing in on the door, we felt a sudden rush of air, and Mary Jane Perrins appeared as if from nowhere, in front of us, blocking our exit.

'You brazen hussy,' she snarled at Sam.

For a moment, we were all too startled to respond. Arlene recovered first. Holding Sam back with her arm, she placed herself right in front of Mary Jane, almost in her face, and from where I stood, Arlene's several inches of extra height looked intimidating. Mary Jane took half a step backwards towards the door, but kept her arms folded defiantly across her chest.

'Jealousy is such a sad thing in a woman, Mary Jane, don't y'all think?' Arlene said after staring at her for several seconds.

'Jealousy?' Mary Jane retorted. 'What reason do I have to be jealous of *her*?'

Arlene laughed.

'Well, hun, they ain't never gonna put your sorry ass in a Zombie Cheerleader movie. You can bet the farm on that. Now, you could get the lead in a remake of *The Hunchback of Notre Dame*, I grant you that, but in a movie where you have to show off your feminine charms? I mean, give me a break, hun; it just ain't gonna happen, and I bet it's eating you up inside.'

Mary Jane seethed quietly for a while, and you could see it building.

'How dare you?' she exploded eventually. 'How dare you talk to me that way? You have no idea of my reputation in this family. I can –'

'I know exactly what your reputation is, hun,' Arlene continued, unperturbed. 'You know how I know? Because I talk to people on the phone all the time, and I hear all about your reputation. And what I hear is, that y'all take the prize for Best in Show in the Pain in the Ass category, and it's a long way down to second place.'

'I'm going to –'

'And don't even think about trying to put the frighteners on me,

Mary Jane. I've faced down the Texas mafia, hun, crazy guys with dogs and shotguns playing Willie Nelson on the sound system, so I sure as hell ain't gonna be shaking in my boots on account of the likes of you.'

'You –'

'So why don't you take the judge's advice and get y'allself a life?'

'You –'

'And you can start by picking up y'all's broomstick and flying y'all's sorry ass home to Boston, Massachusetts.'

Mary Jane stared at Arlene for some time then abruptly brought her hands up to her face, burst into tears, turned around and bolted through the door. We stood together silently for some time.

'Wow,' Sam whispered.

'Well, don't hold back, Arlene,' I said. 'Tell her what you really think.'

Arlene threw her hands up in the air.

'Well, I'm sorry, hun, but do we really have to take all this crap from her and not say a word? I've had it with that broad. The way she went after Sam with all that bullshit. She's way out of line, and it's about time someone told the gal some home truths. Besides, I wasn't lying, hun. That's exactly what they say about her. She could do Pain in the Ass for America in the Olympics.'

'Thank you, Arlene,' Sam said. 'If you hadn't held me back she might have got even more of a mouthful.'

Arlene laughed.

'From you, darlin'? Now, that I would like to see.'

'I can be direct when I have to,' Sam protested.

'I bet you can, hun,' Arlene smiled. 'I just beat you to it, is all.'

'Come on,' I said. 'Let's get out of here and face the music.'

We made our way down to the main entrance to the courthouse, where we found Jordan, standing by the security desk, looking somewhat bewildered. When he saw us, he walked right up to us.

'What did you say to my client?' he demanded of Arlene.

'Nothing she didn't need to hear,' she replied.

'She's stormed off in tears. I don't even know where she's going.'

'She'll get over it.'

'She says you called her a witch. What does that make me, a warlock?'

'You, hun?' Arlene replied. 'No, hun, and I think I speak for all those present when I say you ain't no warlock. Y'all are just a weapons-grade asshole.'

Outside, inevitably, Sam and I were cornered by a crowd of reporters and TV crews brandishing microphones and hand-held recorders. A female television anchor from the DC area led off with the question on everyone's mind.

'Miss van Eyck, how do you feel now about appearing in *Revenge of the Zombie Cheerleaders*?'

Sam smiled. She looked strong and confident.

'It's not the kind of thing I would do now. But I was younger then, I didn't have an agent to advise me, and I was just starting out. When you're just starting out, you can persuade yourself that having any kind of work is better than having none. You take a role like that because you persuade yourself that someone might notice you, some big-time movie director, perhaps, that you'll be the one in a million. Eventually, you grow up and realise that there's no big-time director waiting for you in the wings, and that maybe it wasn't such a smart career move after all. It's a rite of passage.'

'So, you would advise young actors not to follow your example?'

'Maybe. But I think it's the kind of lesson we all have to learn for ourselves, and everyone has to make their own decisions.'

'And you don't think it reflects badly on your wider family?'

'No. I agree with the judge on that point, and apart from Mrs Perrins and three other people who couldn't even be bothered to come to court, I'm not aware of any members of the family who feel in any way embarrassed by the movie.'

Which said it all, really. After about ten minutes, the questions petered out, the interviews ended, not with a bang but with a whimper, and we went back to the office. The great van Eyck porn scandal was pretty much done.

51

THE FOLLOWING AFTERNOON ARYA called and asked me to come to the house on the way home from work. She was coy about what, if anything, she had found. I tried to coax it out of her, but she wasn't having any of it, and she hung up as soon as she could. All the same, I felt pretty sure that she must have found something. If the whole thing had been a waste of time, she would have told me – wouldn't she? The conversation left me with a nervous feeling in the pit of my stomach, and I left the office as early as I decently could. Overall, I was feeling fairly optimistic. We were in high spirits after Judge Morrow's demolition job on Jordan. There had been no negative messages about the result of the hearing, and several very positive ones in support of Sam, including one from a doubtful-sounding director in Los Angeles, who hinted that he had a role that could make her a star. She referred him to her agent, which, she calculated, would probably be the last she would hear about it. But we had survived two jurisprudential near-death experiences, and we were happy about it. Now, we just needed a break on the evidence.

Arya had papers scattered all over the dining table. I recognised a number of them as astrological charts, but there were endless scribbled notes on several yellow pads. She also had several books and a calculator to hand. It all looked impressive enough, but there were no obvious screaming headlines. She sat me down next to her at the table.

'So, how did you get on with Isabel?' I asked, as lightly as I could.

She laughed. 'I got on very well indeed with her. I really like her, and I'm sure the two of you would have got on like a house on fire.'

'Oh?'

'No question. She's a bright girl, very spirited and very articulate, probably a bit too much for her own good sometimes in 1813. She speaks her mind, and I wouldn't be surprised if that gets her into trouble once in a while. In fact, I've changed my mind completely about what she had to say on the subject of the schooling of girls.'

I smiled. 'How so?'

'Well, originally, I thought she was playing it straight, giving us the 1813 party line about the schooling of girls. Didn't you?'

'Sure.'

'But not any more. Now, I think she had her tongue in her cheek, to say the least.'

'She was poking fun at the Neanderthal attitude to women in 1813?'

'I think we're looking at a piece of early nineteenth-century sarcasm. Complete waste of time schooling girls like me. Yeah, right.'

I had to laugh. I'd never seen that before, but the more I thought about it, I was sure Arya was right.

'I think Isabel had a sharp tongue in her mouth,' she said, 'but at the same time I think she was very loyal to Jacob.'

'As her employer?'

'As her teacher. I think she would have valued his teaching above whatever money he paid her. She valued her mind, and she had a very good mind. I would guess that she was a wonderful teacher, in her turn, for her daughters.'

'And you got all that from running her birth chart?'

'And a good deal more, but we won't go into that now. Interesting as Isabel is, her birth chart doesn't take us any further in tracking down your documents.'

I must have looked crestfallen.

'Don't be discouraged,' Arya said, shaking her head. 'I wouldn't have expected to get that from Isabel's chart. I studied Isabel because I wanted to get inside her head, because she gave us the detail on the two events, and I wanted to see what she saw. But anything of any practical use to us I'd expect to find in the other two charts.'

She reached across the table and pulled the two charts towards us.

'These are the charts for the two events she gave us: the occasion when she took the papers to the Brother in Philadelphia; and the occasion when she began to make her record of it all.'

'Do they have something to tell us?' I asked, getting excited again.

Arya was silent for some time.

'I think they might,' she replied. 'But, Kiah, you have to understand that this is a matter of interpretation, and interpretation can be wrong.'

'You seemed very clear about Isabel's chart,' I pointed out. 'You obviously got a lot of detail about her.'

'Yes. But birth charts are one thing. You're drawing conclusions about what someone is like, but your conclusions are quite general. They're accurate, but they're general. Event charts are quite different. With an event chart, you're asking the chart to yield up some hard facts. There are rules about reading an event chart, and there are facts to be found, but in the end it's a matter of interpretation, and as I said, we can always get interpretations wrong. It's like weather forecasting in a way. You look at the weather patterns, and your experience tells you it's going to be fine all day, but you still get the odd thunder shower after you've left your umbrella at home.'

I smiled. 'What kind of weather do you predict in this case?'

She sighed and looked at the charts for several seconds.

'I started,' she said, 'not with the charts, but with the clue in the document itself. You remember I asked you about the capital B at the beginning of "Brother" and I asked you if you were sure you'd copied the document exactly as written?'

'I remember.'

'I just thought that was odd. It's not as if she uses capitals for all family words, is it? She uses "wife", "husband", "father" and she doesn't capitalise any of them. But with "Brother" she uses the capital B twice. With such an old document you could write it off as random – such things as spelling and punctuation were pretty fluid back then, and writers were often inconsistent in how they wrote. The writing can often look careless to readers today. But not this girl. I'm sure of that, now that I've got inside her chart. This girl would take grammar and spelling seriously. Well, you've seen the original, I haven't, but I bet it's neat and well organised, and I bet she's consistent with her spelling and punctuation.'

'Absolutely right,' I replied.

'Which means that she used the capital B for a reason: she was trying to tell us something.'

'And you have an idea what it is?'

'I have an interpretation. I keep saying this, I know, but it's important that you understand. It's an interpretation.' She paused. 'But it's an interpretation that follows from both charts. When you get the same interpretation from two charts dealing with events some distance from each other in time and place, it supports the case that you're on to something. It doesn't prove anything; we're not talking about proof in relation to what we're doing now. But the interpretation works with her careful use of the capital B, and that gives me a certain confidence.'

She pulled the chart for the delivery of the documents to Philadelphia up close between us.

'An astrological chart is composed of these twelve squares, which we call "houses". Each house has associations with different aspects of life: work, family, relationships, health, and so on. But each house can represent a number of different things; that's why it's always a question of interpretation. We're interested in learning more about the delivery of documents to Jacob's "Brother" in Philadelphia, so I went to the house that represents, among other things, Jacob's brothers. He had seven of them if I recall correctly?'

'That's right.'

'And guess what? There's nothing going on in that house at all.'

I stared at her blankly. 'What do you mean?'

'There's a total lack of energy there, no planets in the house, nothing transiting in any interesting way, totally quiet.'

'What does that tell you?' I asked.

'That we're not dealing with the seven brothers,' she replied.

'But –'

'On the other hand, there is a house in both charts with a lot of energy. That house deals with... it's not easy to express this, but things that Jacob was attached to outside his usual business, some kind of cause he believed in or society he belonged to. Sometimes men refer to each other as "Brother" in that context, don't they? For example, if he'd been a military man, you might look at the army, they might be his brothers in arms –'

But for the first time ever, I was ahead of her.

'The Freemasons,' I said. Even as the words left my mouth, I asked myself how I could have missed it. In fairness, we were new to the case. The family had missed it for more than 200 years. But you could hardly blame them. The seven brothers had been a very effective decoy.

'The Freemasons call each other "Brother",' I added.

Arya was smiling and nodding.

'Of course, and they would use the capital B, wouldn't they, because it's a title? Isabel would have known that, and she would have known that writing it that way would give us a clue.'

'Jacob was a high-ranking Mason. It makes perfect sense that he would trust his "Brother" with something important to him.'

'So there you go,' Arya said. 'Now all you have to do is identify the "Brother" he trusted so much.'

I called everyone together early the next morning. As quickly as I could, and glossing over the exact chain of reasoning that had led me – or rather Arya and me – to my conclusion, I explained that I now believed that our best chance of finding some of Jacob's loan certificates lay not with his biological family, but with his masonic family; that the search the van Eyck family had been pursuing, spasmodically but over a very long period of time, had been misdirected; and that we now had less than three weeks in which to redirect the search successfully. There was a long silence, rather than the barrage of questions I had been expecting. Some of that was no doubt due to the veil I had drawn over Arya and the astrological aspects of the breakthrough. I had drawn that veil, not because I felt any personal embarrassment about it – I'm still Indian enough at heart that it didn't feel all that strange to me – but because I was acutely aware that time was closing in on us, and I didn't want any doubts or questions about the new direction I was advocating. If I was wrong, I was wrong, and we probably wouldn't survive our third near-death experience. But I had to go with my instincts. If anyone asked, I would tell them the whole truth, and I would tell them the whole truth in any case once the case was over, one way or the other. But if I was right, I wasn't even sure whether we had enough time left for a new search, and every minute was precious. I needed everyone onside.

'All because of the capital B,' Powalski commented. 'I didn't even see that.'

'Me neither,' Sam added. 'And you know what? This explains something else I thought was really strange.'

'What's that?' I asked.

'That Isabel didn't tell us which one of Jacob's brothers she gave the papers to. Of course, if it was someone outside the family, it would have been too much of a risk after what had happened at the loan office, once the documents Jacob gave the loan officer disappeared. This "Brother" would be someone prominent in public life with contacts in Washington, and she must have thought that anyone in public life would be a target, that someone from the Treasury might nobble him and get him to give up whatever papers she gave him. With the family, that wouldn't have been a concern. She would have named the brother.'

I nodded. 'You're right,' I agreed. 'Frustrating as it is, because a name would really be useful right now.'

'You can say that again,' Powalski said.

'So, where do we go from here, y'all?' Arlene asked. 'Seems to me, we've just opened a whole new can of worms here.'

'We have,' I replied, 'and that means that we have to be really disciplined, and use our time to the best advantage. This is what I want you all to do. Make some notes.'

Everyone was poised, pen in hand.

'Jenny, I want you to find the website for the Grand Masonic Lodge of Pennsylvania. They probably have membership lists going back to the dawn of time, and we need lists for each year between 1778 and 1813. Powalski, if they don't have those lists on the website, I want you to fly to Philadelphia, get yourself inside the lodge and talk to the Grand Master, or the highest official you can find who will talk to you. The Masons are very historically minded. Those lists exist somewhere.'

'Got it,' Powalski said.

'Once we have those lists, Sam, you and I need to go back to see Aunt Meg. We have to figure out who on the list might have been a particularly close friend of Jacob's. My guess would be a family living in or close to the Merion Township area, but it could also be a business connection. Aunt Meg should be able to put us on the right track.'

'Right,' Sam replied.

'Then, we make a list of suspects. Arlene, Powalski, we will then need you to make use of the LDS site, and produce a family tree for each of the suspects. We have to start calling their descendants to see what information they have. This is the kind of story that might well get passed down through the generations in a family. There will be someone, somewhere, who knows about it.'

Powalski was shaking his head.

'I'm not so sure about that, Kiah. Freemasons are pretty obsessive about keeping each other's confidences, and it seems to me that Isabel would probably have sworn him to secrecy. He may not have confided in his family.'

'Possibly,' I conceded. 'But if she swore him to secrecy, I would have expected her to tell us that. Remember, she was trying to give us clues. Plus, we have to remember that she expected him to go to Washington to plead Jacob's cause, and once he did that, it would be difficult to keep anything quiet for long. So you may be right, and if you are, we're probably screwed, but we have to find out who this "Brother" was, and who his descendants are.'

They were nodding around the table.

'In any case,' I added. 'We have nowhere else left to go. This is the ballgame.'

52

Dave Petrosian

I HAVE TO HAND it to Harry. It may have taken him some time to
come to terms with the hard truth that Judge Morrow was going
to keep us in a case we had expected to walk out of on summary
judgment. But once that reality finally sank in, he rose to the
occasion magnificently. He arranged a conference the following
day with Maggie Watts, Ellen and myself, featuring a cameo by
the Attorney General, who attended for just long enough to allow
Maggie to sell him on the idea that we urgently needed some more
resources. As a gesture of good faith, Maggie pulled three of our
own attorneys off other cases – not a popular move with their
colleagues who had to take them over for a while, but Maggie can
be very persuasive when she wants to be. Her diplomacy worked
with the Attorney General too. Within twenty-four hours, we
had two attorneys and four paralegals seconded to us from our
Criminal Division, and a promise of more if we needed more.
With the staff we already had assigned to the case, the search we
had to make suddenly seemed feasible.

We had already decided that there were only three places that
made sense to look in. The Library of Congress was one. It was a
very unlikely source. There were relatively few documents housed
there, they were carefully selected, and they were of far greater
historical importance than run-of-the-mill Revolutionary War

loan certificates. But it was worth a quick look. The other two were far more serious candidates: the National Archives and the Treasury. In theory, whatever historic records Treasury had in storage ought to have been transferred to the National Archives many years ago, but historic Treasury records had a chaotic history, and no one knew for sure how many they had and where all of them had got to. Many were destroyed when the British burned Washington in 1814. Those that survived were mainly documents hastily whisked away to more secure locations when panic set in as the British approached, but there had been no systematic effort to retrieve them for some time after hostilities ceased, and their fate in many cases was unknown. The documents we were looking for, assuming that they still existed or had ever existed, might have been delivered to the Treasury either before or after 1814, but either way, the effort to identify and protect documents in the aftermath of the British attack had been so hit-and-miss that nothing could be ruled out. The National Archives seemed the mostly likely location, but we couldn't ignore the Treasury. We couldn't go back to Judge Morrow with assumptions we hadn't at least questioned. We had to look wherever it made sense to look.

Harry put me in charge of the Treasury search, and took charge at the National Archives himself. We divided our resources equally. It was the only way to start. We had no idea which search would be more difficult or take more time, so we had to be flexible and plan on moving staff around as needed. I had Ellen and our originally assigned paralegal, Pam Westlake, as the backbone of my team. Harry had the other litigators from our department. So on paper, we had two good teams in place, with an equal chance of coming up with the goods – if there were any goods to come up with. But there was one assumption we'd made that didn't quite play out on the ground: namely, our expectation of full cooperation from the institutions whose buildings we were searching. In theory, the searches had been coordinated at the highest level, and there was no reason why cooperation should have been an issue. But that wasn't how it worked in practice.

Looking back, perhaps we were just being naïve, but we were taken by surprise, and it was our team that bore the brunt of it. Harry and his crew were given a warmer reception at the Archives than we were at Treasury. The National Archives exists to enable people to search for documents. That's their whole purpose. They're set up for it, and they see themselves as performing an important public service. So the idea of a few government lawyers asking questions and rummaging around didn't faze them at all. It was a bit different at Treasury.

At Treasury, they definitely don't see themselves as a repository of documents, or as providing a service to those looking for documents, a sentiment made all too clear to us when we arrived. On the first day we were delayed and harassed as much as possible short of physically manhandling us. No office had been reserved for us, and there was even a delay of half a day in getting us our identity badges and fobs, without which we couldn't move very far inside the building. It was only when I confronted a high-level officer, and hinted that I was about to report their attitude to the Attorney General personally, that doors started to open. By that time, we had wasted almost two days.

It took another day before we were trusted with a plan of the building, and provided with the services of a minder to act as our guide to the likely places to search. His name was Roberto, and although he started working with us cheerfully enough, ostensibly helping us to navigate our way around Treasury's labyrinthine building, it was fairly clear where his loyalties lay. He was monitoring our every move, spying on us, and reporting on our activities to some nameless person on high. Understandably, the team were getting anxious, and I couldn't reassure them. I whined about the situation to Harry, but I had the impression that he wasn't very impressed by my suggestion of resistance, and in fairness, I probably wasn't very convincing; the whole thing seemed unreal, even to me. After all, Justice and Treasury are both agencies of the federal government, and we were on the same side in the litigation, so what was the problem?

Over the next three weeks, we developed a pattern. We would meet in our office at the Treasury (barely furnished, and with no amenities except an in-house phone) at nine o'clock. Roberto would take the team members to the rooms we had decided to search that day, and then he would run between them like a rabbit on speed, apparently to make sure they didn't try to extract any documents without his knowing about it. I would wait in the office to deal with any questions or problems, of which there were many. Three weeks may seem like a long time to search a building, but Treasury is a huge structure and even excluding the public areas and the many staff offices, we had identified a large number of rooms to be searched. Many held a dense population of documents. I'd given Ellen and Pam something of a roving brief, and in some cases, it became clear to them early on that a particular room wasn't likely to yield anything of interest to us. The protocol in such cases was that they would report their observations to me, I would take a look for myself, and if we agreed, we would tick that room off our list and move on to the next. But most of the rooms could not be dismissed so lightly, and a painstaking search of each filing cabinet and bookcase was the only way forward.

The Wednesday of the fourth week began like any other day. Although we were running slightly behind, and there was a worry about our schedule, I was convinced that we would conclude our work before we had to return to court – there wouldn't be much time to spare, but we would make it. But at about four o'clock that afternoon, the game changed.

I was day-dreaming, as I did most days by then, about the prospect of getting out of our bleak office and heading home, when the internal phone rang.

'Dave,' Ellen said, 'I need you here. Now.'

She hung up before I could even ask why. That wasn't like Ellen. Even her tone of voice was different, one I'd never heard before. She sounded genuinely alarmed. 'Here' was a room called 484B, at the end of a long, dimly lit corridor accessed by a rickety old staircase at the northwest corner of the building. She and Pam had started on the room on Monday, and it was a real headache. It was a large space with a high ceiling, warm and humid, covered in dust and cobwebs, fitted with an old-fashioned, very heavy lock, and generally giving the impression of having been sealed up when the British left and forgotten about ever since. There was paper everywhere, apparently thrown at random on to the creaking wooden bookcases and into the ancient wooden filing cabinets that occupied almost every inch of the room. Not surprisingly, much of the paper was in a very poor condition, mildewed and discoloured. There was no sign of even the most rudimentary card index system, and in fact, no evidence at all that any systematic filing had ever taken place. On the Monday, Ellen and Pam had been forced to take breaks every twenty minutes or so outside in the corridor, where mercifully there was an open vent in the ceiling, just so that they could take a breath of relatively fresh air and stop sneezing. On Tuesday, they had brought scarves to cover their noses and mouths as they worked.

I made my way to 484B as quickly as I could. Ellen closed and locked the door.

'We don't have much time,' she said, breathlessly. 'Take a look at these.'

She had cleared and dusted off the top of one of the filing cabinets to give herself some working space. On it lay four documents which looked very old. They were written in black ink on parchment, the surface yellowed with age and dirt, but in a neat hand and still legible. Three were immediately familiar from their appearance. In our research, online and otherwise, we had come across many examples of Revolutionary War loan certificates. Harry's crew had actually unearthed three or four at the National Archives with the name van Eyck on them, but they turned out to have been issued, not to Jacob, but to two of his brothers, who had apparently been repaid the small amounts in question with interest. So I knew at once what I was looking at, and following Ellen's finger, hovering above the document, I immediately saw the name of the government's creditor: Jacob van Eyck. Not only that, but the amounts were substantial. In total, they added up to more than $15,000 – nowhere close to what the family was claiming, of course, but still a substantial sum in 1778, and a very substantial sum if it were to be repaid at six per cent annual compound interest since then. Kiah's face flashed through my mind, and I admit I found myself smiling as I imagined her seeing them for the first time.

The fourth document was even more interesting. It was a fragment of a letter. The document had been roughly torn about halfway down, and the bottom half was missing. It bore a date in April 1811 and was addressed to the Secretary of the Treasury. The writer advised the Secretary that under cover of this letter he was sending sixteen papers concerned with war loans on behalf of his friend and Brother, capitalised but not named, and implored the Secretary to intervene personally to ensure that the considerable sums of money loaned were repaid speedily to the advantage of his friend and his family who had been plunged into penury. That was it: apparently all that survived of the letter. There was no name or address given for the writer, perhaps because he had written it on the missing fragment, or perhaps because he was well enough known to the Secretary that it was unnecessary. No indication was given of the total amount of money involved. Presumably that detail had been lost along with the bottom half of the letter and the other thirteen loan certificates, unless they were somewhere in room 484B, a possibility that certainly couldn't be discounted.

'Dave, we don't have much time,' Ellen repeated, interrupting my reverie.

'What do you mean?'

'Roberto is stalking me, breathing down my neck as usual,' she replied. 'He was here in the room when I found them and pulled them out of that filing cabinet over there in the corner. I knew what I'd found as soon as I laid eyes on them. I tried to act cool, pretend that it was no big deal, but he insisted on looking at them over my shoulder, and I couldn't really stop him.'

'Where's Pam?' I asked.

'On a break, unfortunately. She wasn't here when I found them.' She hesitated. 'Dave, I've been trying not to worry too much about Roberto, but I think we may have a real problem.'

'What kind of problem?'

'He told me that if anything like this came to light, his orders were to make sure that the documents stayed where they were until someone higher up could look at them, which means that he knew what to look for.'

'Someone higher up? Did he say who?'

'No. But you know what they're like here. I tried to explain to him that it's our search, and we're allowed to take possession of anything relevant we find. But he wasn't interested. He said I would have to tell that to the higher-ups. That's when he walked out, and I called you.'

She looked at me very directly.

'Dave, I need to speak my mind on this.'

'Sure. Go ahead.'

'I have a terrible feeling that if the higher-ups, whoever the hell they are, get their hands on these documents, we may never see them again. Am I being paranoid?'

I looked down at the documents again, and reflected on the way we had been treated during the whole search process, and on the brooding presence of Roberto.

'No,' I replied. 'I don't think you're being in any way paranoid.'

'What are we going to do?' she asked. 'Do you want to call Harry, or maybe try to contact the Attorney?'

I thought for a moment and shook my head.

'No,' I replied. 'If you're right, which I think you are, there's no time for that.'

I looked around the room.

'Do we have anything I can wrap these in?' I asked.

'There are a few old file folders lying on the floor in the corners,' Ellen replied.

I shook my head. 'No, I don't want anything that looks like a Treasury item. I need something innocuous that no one will question if they see me walking down the corridor with it.'

Ellen put her hands on her hips and looked around. Suddenly, she reached down to the floor, where she had left her briefcase, and took out her copy of the *Washington Post*.

'What about this?'

'Perfect,' I replied. 'Hold it in place for me.'

Gingerly, I opened the *Post* at its centrefold and laid it on top of the filing cabinet where Ellen had made her work space. She held it down flat while I took each of the four documents in turn, and placed them carefully, one on top of the other, on the right-hand page. I flattened and straightened them as much as I could without using force, then gently closed the left-hand page. Ellen nodded approvingly.

'That will work,' she said. 'What are you going to do?'

'I'm going to get them out of here,' I replied.

'What? How? How will you do that?'

'I'm working on it.'

'But where will you take them?'

'It's better that you don't know. If they ask, tell them I took the documents and I didn't tell you where I was going.'

'They're not going to believe me,' she objected.

'Yes, they will. They'll assume I've taken them back to the office.'

'Is that what you're going to do?'

'I'm working on it.'

'You don't know where you're going to take them?"

'Ellen, I'm working on it. I'll think of something, OK? Tell them the truth: that I took possession of the documents because Justice has an obligation to comply with the court's discovery order. We're obliged to secure the documents ourselves and not allow any third party to interfere with them. These guys aren't lawyers, they're not going to argue with you.'

'Dave, they're not fools, and these are Treasury documents.'

'No, Ellen, they're not: not any more, not until this case is over. Right now they're government documents and we're taking custody of them as the government's lawyers. Look, you can blame it all on me if you want. Say you told me to wait; you told me the higher-ups wanted to see them before I took them but I wouldn't listen; I overruled you.'

'I'm not sure that's going to help.'

I shrugged. 'What are they going to do, lock you in the basement and hold you to ransom?'

'You want my honest opinion?' she asked. 'I wouldn't put it past these assholes.'

I held her gently by the shoulders.

'Ellen, the moment I'm clear of the building, I'll call Harry and ask him to get the Attorney involved, I promise. And if that doesn't work I'll go to Judge Morrow and…'

'What?' she asked, as I stopped in mid-sentence.

'Nothing,' I replied. 'I just got an idea, that's all. Unlock the door, and don't say a word to anyone for at least ten minutes, preferably fifteen. I need to put the documents in my briefcase, which is in the office, and I need time to find a way out of the building without anyone noticing.'

'Fifteen minutes?' she said. 'Dave, they've already been gone a while. They'll be here any second. How am I going to hold them off for fifteen minutes?'

'Don't be here when they come,' I suggested.

'Where would I go?'

'I don't know. Lock yourself in the ladies' room, sneak into the cafeteria for a coffee, whatever it takes.'

'Can't I just come with you?' she asked plaintively.

'Better not,' I replied. 'That would look like we're trying to pull a fast one.'

'As opposed to what?'

'As opposed to doing the right thing – taking possession of relevant documents we've discovered in the building. Just act like everything is normal.'

'Oh, right, yeah.'

'I'm serious,' I said. 'What would you normally do when you take documents from a third party in the course of discovery?'

'Give them a receipt?' she suggested with a shrug.

'Exactly. So give them a receipt, and don't wait to be asked – offer them one. That way, they'll see we're playing by the rules.'

'By the rules. Right,' she replied as I hurried though the door.

53

As I'D SAID TO Ellen, my mention of Judge Morrow had given me an idea, and the more I thought about it, it was the only one that made sense. If the Treasury higher-ups were really determined to get their hands on the documents to make sure they never saw the light of a courtroom, there was no point in taking them back to the office. With the necessary authority they could walk into Justice any time they wanted to, and I wasn't sure that even the Attorney's influence would be enough to stop them. Treasury had a lot of clout in the higher echelons of the government. There would certainly be nothing that Maggie or Harry could do to slow them down, and it was absolutely certain that there was nothing I could do.

But invading a court was another matter. I was pretty sure that even Treasury would baulk at that, and even if they didn't, the documents would be safe by the time they figured out where I'd taken them. It bothered me slightly that we had no actual evidence that anyone at Treasury had any evil intent towards the evidence. It was possible that we had simply been spooked by their suspicious, over-protective attitude – not that I think anyone could have blamed us for that. But my gut was telling me that something more sinister was afoot, and Ellen's gut obviously had the same impression. The stakes were high, and I didn't want to take the risk. These documents were not going to disappear on my watch. Besides, I reassured myself, what I was doing was absolutely legal;

in fact, I was doing the right thing. I didn't answer to Treasury;
I worked for Justice, and it was my duty to secure the evidence
Ellen had unearthed. I was doing just what the court had ordered
us to do. My plan was even proper procedurally. Any party could
deposit documents with the court if there was a need to preserve
them. So what could possibly go wrong? I let the thought go. This
was no time for navel-gazing. I had to focus. I'd asked Ellen to
avoid the higher-ups for fifteen minutes. I couldn't reasonably ask
more of her. I had to move quickly.

I ran back to the office, deposited the four documents, still
wrapped in the *Washington Post*, in my briefcase, and hurriedly
camouflaged them using a couple of yellow pads and the remains
of the wrapping from my lunchtime sandwich. I took a deep
breath and reviewed the situation. Problem: how to get myself out
of the Treasury building without anyone noticing, assuming, as I
felt I had to, that security had been told to keep a look out for me
and detain me on sight. Solution…?

The obvious way was to use the public entrance on 15th Street,
which would be busy at this time of the afternoon. There would
be security guards in place, and there wouldn't be enough people
leaving the building to give me cover if the guards were actively
scanning the area for me, but it might be the best shot. I was
rapidly regretting not having studied my plan of the building in
more detail. I had been concentrating so hard on deciding what
rooms to search, and in what order, that I hadn't really taken in
the location of the various entrances. I'd always come and gone by
the 15th Street entrance, and it had never occurred to me to come
in or go out any other way. To make matters worse, I realised that
I'd given my plan to Ellen, and I didn't have time to trek back to
484B to retrieve it now.

I thought feverishly. The north and south wings boasted the
elegant formal entrances to the building. There were gates, but I
wasn't sure whether they were in continual use, and even if they
were, there would be security staff there, and they would be bound

to take a greater interest in me than if I were just part of a crowd leaving the building on 15th Street. The quiet west wing was an unknown quantity. I knew there were exits there. They led into East Executive Avenue, just across the street from the White House, and the tree-lined wall was usually quiet, but there would still be…

And that's when it occurred to me: it wasn't a question of where I exited the building; it was a question of when. I had to forget about my assumption. There would be security guards everywhere, and if the higher-ups had already sounded the alarm, it was already too late; there was nothing I could do. On the other hand, why would they have put out an APB so quickly? Until they'd spoken to Ellen they had no real reason to panic, and certainly no reason to do something as dramatic as having me, a senior government lawyer, detained. On the other hand, these people seemed to have an unhealthy dose of paranoia, and if Roberto had alarmed them, there was no telling what they might do. But I couldn't control that. The odds were that I had a window, at least for a short time, and the only thing that made sense was to play the odds. It was a matter of getting out now. The direction I took was less significant, but it seemed best to head for my usual exit into 15th Street, where at least there would be a crowd. I glanced at my watch. If Ellen had bought me the fifteen minutes I'd asked her for, I had just over five of them left.

I raced to the elevator, and joined a large number of staff and visitors making their way out. I mingled with them as much as I could and walked in their midst, head down, briskly but without running, to the exit. I was nearly there, when one of the female guards I recognised looked up at me as I was passing her desk. We'd wished each other good morning or evening a number of times. She seemed to focus her gaze on me, and I could feel my heart beating faster. The briefcase suddenly felt very heavy. For a second or two we stared at each other. Then she smiled, gave me a nod, and wished me a good evening. I wished her the same, pushed my way through the door, and found myself outside, gratefully inhaling a deep breath of fresh 15th Street air.

A cab was passing. I hailed it, and asked the driver to take me to the Claims Court.

54

As I entered the anteroom of Judge Morrow's chambers, Maisie was tidying up her desk, returning some papers to a file. I breathed a sigh of relief to find her still in chambers. I'd got myself to the courthouse as quickly as I could, but it was late enough for court staff to be leaving for the day, and I didn't have a plan B. Her purse and coat were on the chair in front of her desk, and she was moving briskly, giving every impression of being on her way out and of being pretty happy about it. She glanced at her watch and raised her eyebrows in surprise.

'Dave? What brings you here at such a late hour? Don't you have a home to go to? You didn't have anything in our list today, did you?'

'No,' I replied. 'Maisie, I need to see Judge Morrow. It's urgent. Is he still in chambers?'

She looked doubtful. 'He is. But I'm pretty sure he's anxious to get out of here.' She dropped her voice and added confidentially, 'It's his poker night with his friends from the Service, and he's probably dying to light up his pipe. But let me go ask him.'

She paused at the door. 'This is really urgent, Dave, right?'

'It's really urgent,' I assured her.

She nodded, knocked and went in. A few seconds later, her head appeared round the door.

'The judge says come on in.'

Judge Morrow was picking at the tobacco in his pipe with his reaming tool.

'You just caught me,' he said. 'Another five minutes and I'd have been gone. What's up? Do you want Maisie to stay, or can she go?'

Maisie was hovering hopefully by the door.

'I'd like her to stay for a few minutes, Judge.'

The judge nodded and replaced the pipe in his ashtray.

'All right. Come and have a seat. You too, Maisie. Now, what's this about? I'm sure I don't need to remind you that, if it's about a case, you're going to need a damn good reason to be here talking to me without opposing counsel being present.'

I nodded. 'I understand, Judge. I believe I have a good reason for seeing you, and everything I'm about to tell you I will be telling Kiah the first chance I get. If I'd had the chance I would have told her already, but everything happened a bit too fast for that this afternoon.'

'Kiah?' the judge asked. 'Is this about the Revolutionary War case, the van Eyck case?'

'Yes, Judge, it is.'

He took the pipe back from the ashtray and twirled it between his fingers.

'Don't tell me that damned Perrins woman is causing trouble again. I've heard about all I need to hear from her.'

I had to smile. 'No, Judge, not as far as I know.'

'I'm relieved to hear that.'

I opened my briefcase and took out the *Washington Post*.

'No, this is about the discovery order you made.'

'Relating to those loan certificates Kiah's trying to locate?'

'Yes. We've been searching for the past couple of weeks in two particular locations, the National Archives and the Treasury. I've been overseeing the search in the Treasury with Ellen Matthews, and this afternoon Ellen stumbled across these.'

I placed the newspaper flat on Tomorrow's desk, and opened it at the centrefold with the documents the right way up in his direction.

'I'd appreciate it if you would read these over, Judge. Best to be gentle with them, though. They're old, obviously, and they've been stored in damp conditions for God knows how long, so they're not in great shape.'

Judge Morrow leaned forward across his desk, and stared at the top document, which was the partial letter from the unknown writer to the Secretary of the Treasury. He seemed to hold his breath for a moment or two, and although he had his hands stretched out towards the document, he seemed reluctant to pick it up. He leaned over and read it without touching it.

'Well, I'll be damned,' he said very quietly. 'Dave, is this thing for real?'

'I'm sure it is, Judge,' I replied. 'We'll have to let an expert take a look down the line, of course, but there's no reason to think it's not genuine, given the circumstances in which we found it.'

Maisie was approaching the judge's desk slowly, as if asking whether she was allowed to see it too. I smiled and nodded, and she made her way behind the desk to stand by Morrow's side.

'Look at that,' she breathed. 'I mean, isn't it just beautiful?'

I smiled again. She was right. It suddenly dawned on me. I'd been so focused on what the document meant in terms of the case, and on protecting it just because of its value as evidence, that I hadn't even thought to look at it as something beautiful in its own right. But it was; it truly was. Almost every document you see today is typed using a piece of computer software and printed out on cheap paper. Even if it's signed, there's nothing unusual, let alone unique about it, nothing to tell us anything about the man or woman who created it. But this... this was a work of art, a living literary fossil, a letter a man had written in 1811, a letter he had written on parchment in an elegant hand to address a high official of state in aid of his friend. And we were close enough that we could have been reading it over his shoulder. It *was* beautiful, and for a moment I remembered how I had felt when Kiah and I had first talked about the case, the sense of being involved with a piece of history, something above and beyond the morass of everyday litigation, something that might make you proud to be a lawyer. I suddenly felt angry, and at the same time, sad at the thought of the mindless violence some higher-up might have used to destroy it without even seeing it for what it was. The judge was looking at me. I brought myself back down to earth.

'That's not all,' I said. I picked up the letter, and spread out the three loan certificates for them to see. 'Ellen found these also.'

The judge gave a low whistle.

'Well, that sure puts the case in a different light,' he observed. 'No sign of the other thirteen certificates whoever wrote the letter was referring to?'

'Not yet,' I replied.

The judge sat back down, and Maisie moved tactfully back to her seat by the door. He played with his pipe for some time, adding tobacco, tamping it down with his thumb, toying with his lighter.

'I suppose,' he said eventually, 'the question I have to ask is why you and I are talking about these documents, instead of you and Kiah talking about them?'

I swallowed hard.

'I'm here because the court is a place of safety,' I replied, 'and I can't think of anywhere else these documents would be safe.'

Judge Morrow stared at me.

'You're going to have to explain that to me,' he said.

So, for about ten minutes I regaled Tomorrow with the hostility we had experienced at Treasury, the constant sense of being stalked and followed, Roberto's reaction to Ellen's discovery of the evidence, his thinly veiled threat of action by the higher-ups, and finally, my smuggling the documents out of the building during a period of fifteen minutes bought for me by Ellen, whom I had abandoned in the building. The judge listened without interrupting, pipe in mouth, as if enjoying the wafting smoke of Sobranie Flake in his imagination.

'Do you or Ellen have any evidence that these people intend

to do harm to these documents?' he asked, some time after I'd finished, 'apart from what you've already told me?'

'No, Judge,' I admitted.

He nodded. 'So it's just professional instinct?'

'Yes. But I'm as sure as I can be that Ellen and I wouldn't have been allowed to leave the building with these documents.'

He shook his head. 'It would take some nerve, for some official at Treasury to take them from you after you'd seen them and taken possession of them. If you and Ellen were ever to testify as to their content, that would be just as much evidence as if a court saw the originals, and it would reflect very badly on the government if they suddenly went missing.'

'I'm not sure they're thinking that rationally,' I replied. 'It's as if they were determined from day one that we weren't going to find anything.'

'Of course, it's Treasury that has the biggest headache on account of this case,' the judge said. He paused. 'Well, I guess I have to err on the side of caution here. I'm not entirely sure that your fears for these documents are well-founded, but I sure as hell don't want to be proved wrong about it somewhere down the road, so I guess I'm going to go with your instinct, yours and Ellen's. What do you want me to do?'

'I'm here to comply with the court's order for discovery,' I replied. 'Under normal circumstances, I would make copies for Kiah and the court, I would keep the originals until trial, and that would take care of it. But I can't do that here. I'm concerned for the safety of these originals, and I believe it's appropriate for me to deposit them with the court for safekeeping.'

He nodded. 'It's certainly appropriate. But I'm concerned about a couple of things. First, what makes you think they're secure here? Second, I have no experience – I'm not sure whether Maisie does, but I sure don't – of looking after valuable ancient documents, and in the circumstances, I'm not sure you want me asking around for advice.'

'No, Judge. I can get you some advice about keeping the documents. I'll do that tomorrow. But don't worry too much about that. As long as they're reasonably warm and dry, they're way better off here than where we found them, believe me.'

'What about security?'

'I don't know,' I admitted. 'I guess that, if these people are really determined to find them, there's only so much we can do. They will probably figure out where they are eventually. What I do know is that we couldn't keep them safe at Justice, and they have to be safer here than in any government office. And they've now been seen and read by a judge, so even if anything were to happen to them, I'd feel good about the steps we've taken to comply with your order.'

The judge nodded.

'OK, I see that. All the same, it would seem prudent to make a few copies while we can. Maisie, would you mind? How many do you think we need? At least one for me, one for you, and one for Kiah, and maybe a few for luck, to keep in different places?'

'Judge,' Maisie objected, 'I'm no expert, but I'm not sure you can just run something like this through a photocopier. I'd do them one at a time, of course, but these documents are very fragile, and I'd be worried about the heat damaging the ink, or even the parchment.'

'I can get advice on that tomorrow too,' I said. 'But I have to take the risk now, at least to the extent of making one for the court, one for Kiah, and a couple for my office.'

She still didn't look happy about it.

'Maisie, if the first one seems to do any damage, we'll stop, I promise, but I believe it's really important to try.'

'You want me to take a court copy home with me?' the judge asked.

'Or put it somewhere safe away from home,' I suggested. 'That's what I'm going to do with one of my copies. The other I'm going to give to the Attorney General.'

'And we'll keep the originals wrapped up and under lock and key,' the judge said.

Apparently, having survived fire, neglect, and attempts on its life for more than two hundred years, the parchment was not going to be fazed by a modern contraption like a photocopier. The originals may have had the odd slight brown stain added, hardly noticeable, but they yielded good copies. I left with four in my briefcase.

55

BY THE TIME I made it back to the office it was somewhere between six thirty and seven o'clock. I felt exhausted, but at the same time the adrenalin was pumping, and I was wired. Ellen and Harry were waiting for me in my office. I'd been expecting them. I was sure they wanted to hear what had happened to the documents, Harry particularly. It was the kind of situation that would set his blood pressure soaring until I put his mind at rest.

'We were wondering when we might have the pleasure of your company,' Harry began, needlessly checking his watch. 'We thought you might have gone home.' He was pacing up and down, arms folded across his chest.

'No, Harry,' I replied, 'I hadn't thought about going home yet. I wanted to make sure I talked to you first.'

I walked over to Ellen, who was lying on my sofa, shoes off, looking white and shaken. I sat on the arm of the sofa by her feet and squeezed her toes for a moment or two.

'You don't look so great. Are you OK?'

'I'm OK now,' she replied.

'Those Treasury assholes gave her the third degree,' Harry said.

'What?'

'They seem to have an exaggerated sense of their own importance over there.'

'What happened, Ellen?' I asked.

'I went to the ladies', as you suggested, and I stayed there for at least ten minutes, until I assumed you were clear of the building. Then I went back to 484B. I was hoping Pam would be back by then, but it turns out that Angie and Sally needed her for something on the other side of the building and she'd gone to work with them for the rest of the afternoon. So I was alone when they came. There were two of them, guys in suits, plus Roberto, of course. They wanted to know where the documents were. I told them you'd taken them, and I didn't know where you'd gone. They weren't too happy about that. Actually, they got very aggressive.'

I looked at Harry. 'If they laid a hand on you…'

'No, they didn't lay a hand on me. I explained the rules of discovery, and offered them a receipt, just like you said. That didn't seem to impress them. They started shouting and screaming about the theft of Treasury documents, and did I realise that was a felony, and did I know how long I would get for that, and how they would go the bar ethics committee and have me disbarred, and God only knows what else. And all the time, Roberto was standing there, smirking.'

'How did it end?' I asked.

'Eventually, I called their bluff. I asked them whether I was under arrest. They said no. So I wrote out a receipt for the documents and left…' Her voice trailed away and there were tears in her eyes. 'I was shaking like a leaf when I walked past them. They had me so scared, Dave, I actually had visions of them taking me and making me disappear. I know that's stupid, but…'

'It's not stupid at all,' I replied. I turned to Harry. 'We have to do something about these people.'

He nodded. 'I'm sorry, Dave. I feel I owe you an apology. You told me what was going on, and I was too preoccupied at the Archives to listen.'

I held up a hand. 'No apology needed. I almost didn't believe it myself until today. The whole thing is so bizarre.'

'Well, I've arranged to see the Attorney with Maggie tomorrow morning. I'm calling off the search for tomorrow, to give him time to contact the Secretary of the Treasury and lay down the law before we go back. And, Ellen, I'll transfer you to the National Archives search and send one of the criminal guys over to Treasury.'

Ellen sat up. 'Thank you, Harry, but that's not necessary. I'm not going to let these assholes stop me doing my job.'

'Harry,' I said, 'I understand why you want to call off the search for a day, but what worries me is that you're giving them time to make their own search of that room, and if there are any more documents there in the same series, I wouldn't give much for their chances.'

'I'm pretty sure the Attorney will send a clear message to the Secretary about keeping Treasury's hands off our search,' he replied. 'But if you're worried about it, I'll ask Criminal Division to send an FBI agent over there to keep an eye on things.'

'That would be good. Actually, what about sending an agent in right now, to keep a lookout overnight?'

'Consider it done. And now, if it's not too much trouble, would you mind telling me what in God's name you've done with the documents?'

I smiled. 'They're safe. I took them to Judge Morrow and deposited them with the court for safekeeping.' I stood, retrieved my briefcase and emptied it on to my table. 'The judge has read the documents, as has Maisie, and she made some copies. We should make more copies from these before we leave tonight.'

Harry stopped pacing, picked up the copies and read them, shaking his head. Ellen padded over to join him at the table.

'Wow,' Harry said. 'We have a whole new ballgame, don't we?'

I nodded. 'We sure do, and we can't rule out finding more documents in the same series.'

'So what's the plan now?'

'I'm going to get a copy to Kiah first thing tomorrow morning, and then we'll carry on searching.'

Harry was silent, nodding, for some time.

'Good move,' he said eventually, 'taking them to the court. Good thinking.'

56

THEY MADE THEIR ENTRANCE just as Ellen was bringing the new copies from the copy room. We were all ready to go home for some much needed food and rest. But we had left it a few minutes too late and there they were, wearing their stereotypical ill-fitting grey suits, ties tied in tight untidy knots, hanging down slightly, and short-cropped hair. They held up badges, far too quickly to allow us to see what they were. Ellen seemed to hold her breath. She walked very quickly over to the sofa, and I stepped in front of her.

'Agents Johnson and Farmer, Treasury Internal Investigations Unit,' Johnson, the older of the two announced. 'Which of you is Mr Welsh?'

'I'm Harry Welsh.'

'Mr Welsh, I'm sure you know why we're here.'

'Not being a mind-reader,' Harry replied, 'I have no idea why you're here. But I'm sure you'll enlighten us.'

I looked at him in fascination. Something had suddenly changed. Harry was… different. The pacing had stopped the moment they walked in, and he was standing motionless with his arms at his sides. He had an expression on his face I'd never seen on him before – one of anger and determination – and his voice was ice-cold.

'We're here because two of your attorneys removed some documents from the Treasury building today without authorisation.

We're here to retrieve the documents and return them to proper custody.'

Harry looked at Johnson for several seconds.

'Could I see those badges again?'

Reluctantly the two men produced them and held them up in front of Harry's face.

'Treasury Internal Investigations Unit,' Harry said. 'I'm not familiar with that. Are you guys law enforcement officers?'

They hesitated.

'We are authorised to make investigations on behalf of the Treasury,' Johnson replied.

'I'll take that as a "no",' Harry said.

'We are authorised to make investigations.'

'*Internal* investigations,' Harry pointed out. 'You're a bit far from home, aren't you? A bit too far along the street? Treasury is a few blocks back the way you came.'

'We're here to recover Treasury documents,' Johnson insisted, 'documents that were removed from the Treasury building. That is an internal matter.'

'The documents in question were removed after they were found during an authorised search,' Harry replied, 'and your people were given a receipt for them. My staff followed the proper procedure.'

'That's not the point, sir,' Farmer interjected. 'Those documents are in the custody of the Treasury, and they need to stay in the custody of the Treasury.'

'Actually, Agent Farmer,' Harry replied, 'they're not "Treasury documents". In fact, there's no such thing as a "Treasury document". The Treasury is a department of the United States government, and any documents in its custody are government documents.'

'Be that as it may, Mr Welsh,' Johnson said. 'Our instructions are to recover the documents, and I would appreciate it if you would hand them over to us now.'

Harry took a deep breath.

'I'm going to explain this to you once,' he replied, 'and once only. The United States is a defendant in litigation brought by a number of individuals in the United States Claims Court. The Justice Department represents the United States in that litigation; we are the government's lawyers. We were ordered by the court to engage in discovery, which in this case means searching government records to find certain documents. If we find any relevant documents, we are obliged to retain them pending the trial of the action, and to provide the court and the plaintiffs with copies. That's exactly what my attorneys did, and they acted exactly as they should have.'

'But –'

'Treasury is entitled to a receipt for the documents, which Miss Matthews provided to your people, but that's all you're entitled to. However, just to show there are no hard feelings, I will throw in a copy of the documents. Ellen...'

Ellen stretched out an arm and gave Harry a copy of each document, which he passed on to Johnson.

'But that's it,' Harry concluded. 'The original documents stay in the custody of Justice until the litigation is concluded. If there's anything I've said that you haven't understood, I suggest you speak to one of the lawyers in your department. They'll explain it all you.'

'So, you're refusing to hand over the originals?' Johnson asked.

'Exactly,' Harry replied with the ghost of a smile. 'And since I have you here, let me make one or two other things clear to you. I'm meeting with the Attorney General tomorrow morning, and he will be talking with your Secretary to ensure that our search of the Treasury building continues without further interference. I'm sure the message will be passed down to you and your colleagues later tomorrow. But just in case, be aware of this. I'm going to have FBI agents in the building to protect my attorneys and paralegals from now on, and if there is any further harassment of them, those responsible will be arrested and charged with obstruction of justice. Now, my staff and I have had a long day and we're ready to go home, so I'll thank you to leave.'

Johnson was shaking his head.

'I want to know where the documents are. I think we'll just take a look around before we go.'

He advanced in the direction of my briefcase. In a flash, Harry was standing in front of him, blocking his path.

'If you are law enforcement officers, and if you have a warrant to search these offices,' he replied, 'show me the warrant. Otherwise, either you get the hell out of my building now, or I'll call my Criminal Division and have them send over a couple of real agents to show you out.'

They left.

Ellen and I looked at Harry in admiration.

'What?' he asked.

'No, nothing,' I said. 'Just that you were great.'

'You made my day,' Ellen added.

'What?' Harry asked. 'You don't think I can be tough when I need to be?'

'We never doubted it,' I replied.

'Not once,' Ellen added.

57

By the time I got in to the office the following morning it was far later than I had planned. When I arrived home the previous evening, I'd never been so desperate to crawl into bed, but I couldn't do that until I'd had supper with Maria and the children, who naturally wanted to know why I was so late home, and were enthralled by the story I had to tell. I was still also pretty wired, and it was after midnight when I finally crashed. The office, it seemed, was even more enthralled.

There was a real buzz of excitement in the air. Rumours had spread – via security, in all likelihood, as they were the source of most of the gossip running around the building – about the events of the night before. Everyone was talking about Harry, Ellen and myself as if we were a reincarnation of the Three Musketeers, who had valiantly crossed swords with the Treasury villains, and delivered Justice from a terrible fate against all the odds. I'd also received some sarcastic but good-natured emails from colleagues, some asking me whether I would now be applying to join the Criminal Division, or the CIA, or better still, opening my own private detective agency; one informing me that my new nickname in the office was to be Sam Spade.

The laughter the emails brought me was a real tonic. In fact, the whole morning felt good after the trauma of the previous day, and I'm embarrassed to admit that I played my transient fame as a musketeer for all it was worth. I was pleased to see that Ellen was also basking in the sunshine. As we were leaving the office the previous evening, I'd insisted on putting her in a cab to go home, over her half-hearted protests – her bicycle was her preferred mode of transport and she rode almost every day, come rain or shine. But I wouldn't have been happy with her on the roads; she was exhausted. She didn't fight me too hard, and now she looked as if a good night's rest had done her a power of good. She was back on top and acting like her usual self again.

The first item on my agenda was to talk to Kiah, but just as I was about to place the call, my phone rang.

'Dave,' Maisie said after wishing me a good morning, 'Judge Morrow asked me to bring you up to date on something that happened here at the courthouse late last night.'

I suddenly felt a shiver going up my spine.

'Late last night?' I asked.

'Yes. It all worked out OK, but it was somewhat disturbing. Our night security guard reported that two men in suits, who identified themselves as federal agents, tried to gain access to the building. They produced badges and suchlike, and were acting like they were entitled to be admitted.'

'What did they say exactly?' I asked.

'They told the guard they were here to collect some papers that had been delivered to the court by mistake earlier in the day. Fortunately, the guard kept his head and did the right thing. He called our night emergency number for back-up and told the so-called agents what he was doing, at which point they left.'

'And they didn't try to force their way in?'

'No, I guess they knew better than that. Dave, Judge Morrow said to ask you whether this might have something to do with the papers you brought us yesterday. No one at the court knows about that except us, but the Chief Judge has been asking whether anyone can explain the incident. Is there any reason why we can't tell him?'

'No,' I replied, 'no reason at all. Apparently, it's not exactly a secret any more. And yes, I would say that this incident is definitely related to the documents I brought yesterday. We had something similar happen at our offices.'

'I'll tell him,' Maisie said. She sounded relieved. 'The judge would like to get a federal marshal assigned to look after things in his chambers at night until this case ends and the documents are gone, and he thinks that will be a lot easier with the Chief's support.'

'If it helps,' I replied, 'tell him I think that would be a very good idea.'

I hung up feeling disturbed, and my first thought was to tell Harry, until I realised that he would still be in his meeting with the Attorney General. Instead, I called Kiah as planned. When she answered the phone, Arlene was abrupt with me, but that wasn't exactly unusual, so I thought nothing of it, and had no inkling that anything was wrong until she put me on to Kiah.

'What do you want, Dave?' she asked when I greeted her. 'Do you want me to describe the mess to you?' She sounded incredibly angry.

'Kiah, what's up?' I asked. 'What are you talking about?'

'Or perhaps you want to come and see for yourself?'

She hung up. I left immediately, drove as fast as I dared, and was at her office just over half an hour later. The awfulness of the scene hit me immediately. Arlene and Samantha van Eyck were sitting together at Arlene's desk looking gutted. Kiah was standing just outside her office, leaning on the doorframe. The door was open. I saw a man walking slowly around inside, picking his way carefully through piles of debris. The place had been ransacked. Files, papers, books, pens, scissors, staplers, and every other piece of office equipment you could think of, were lying in heaps on the floor. They were heavily stained with large quantities of what looked like black ink. Every piece of furniture had been overturned and destroyed. The computers and printer had been smashed to pieces, perhaps with a large hammer, certainly a very heavy blunt object. The walls had been stained with huge blotches of the same ink, or whatever it was, that had been poured on top of the piles of debris. Someone had deliberately trashed the office, or someone had been looking for something. As I continued to stare, I began to put two and two together, and it was getting depressingly close to four. My heart sank. Kiah turned towards me. Her face was ashen. She was shaking.

'Kiah, I'm so sorry…' I began. I didn't know what else to say.

'Y'all damn well should be,' Arlene answered. 'Y'all should be ashamed. It was y'all's people did this.'

'They're not my people,' I replied quietly.

Kiah turned towards me, walked the short distance and touched my hand.

'No, they're not,' she said. 'I know that. 'But do you know whose people they are?'

I looked down to the floor and breathed out heavily.

'Are you sure it couldn't have been kids, just messing around, causing as much damage as they could?'

I was snatching at straws, of course. She took a step towards the office door.

'Powalski,' she called out. 'Got a minute?'

A tall man dressed in a navy blue suit and light blue tie made his way carefully to the door. I put him at late thirties to mid-forties, difficult to say, good-looking in a rugged kind of way, but with a reserved air about him, as if he felt no need to speak without being asked – or perhaps his mind was still on whatever he had been doing in the office.

'I don't think you guys have met,' Kiah said. 'Our investigator, Powalski. And this is Dave Petrosian, who's handling the case at Justice.'

We shook hands briefly.

'Powalsaki, please tell Dave why this isn't a bunch of kids messing around,' Kiah said.

'This building is alarmed at night,' Powalski began. 'There's no guard, but the alarm goes right into the nearest police precinct and into a private security company. One or the other would be here in ten minutes or less, and all you have to do to set the alarm off is open any door or window. Whoever did this had a device that neutralised the alarm before it could even react. I don't know how much you know about electronic code-breakers, Mr Petrosian, but the speed and precision of the device they had was top of the range. Typically, when you find this kind of equipment, it indicates government involvement. I know this because of some work I did for the government during an earlier time in my career. It's conceivable that we could be dealing with a very well-funded organised crime syndicate, a drug cartel or the like, but Kiah's never been involved with cases like that, whereas she's very involved with a case against the government.'

He took three small items from the side pocket of his jacket.

'These put it beyond doubt. I found them while I was examining the phones. You'll notice that the phones and the fax machine are the only items left untouched. This is why.'

He held out his hand to let me see.

'Listening devices?' I asked.

'Japanese, also state of the art, planted during the visit. This is something else I used to do when I worked for the government. But the devices were an afterthought. If all they wanted was to bug the office, they could have come and gone without leaving a trace. They were looking for something. The vandalism was meant to cover that up, throw us off the trail. Whether they found anything of interest, we don't know. Kiah doesn't know of anything they couldn't have found out through the court filings or the press, but then again, we don't know what they were looking for.'

'I do,' I said.

Logically, it didn't make sense. There was no way I would have given custody of the originals to Kiah, but these were the same people who thought that the Department of the Treasury was entitled to withhold its papers from other departments of the government, and saw themselves as the Treasury's enforcers. Logic might not have come into it. They'd tried to infiltrate our building and the Claims Court, but they'd been denied by security. Here was a building they could just walk into. In their book, it must have seemed worth a try.

'You know what they were looking for?' Kiah asked.

I smiled. 'I know this has been a terrible day so far,' I said, 'but I think I might be able to brighten it up for you a little.'

'I'm ready for that,' Kiah whispered. She was close to tears.

I had brought her copies of the documents with me. I opened my briefcase while Arlene cleared a space on her desk, and laid the documents out for them, side by side.

'We found these yesterday in the Treasury building,' I said. 'I think this is what they were hoping to find – well, the originals anyway.'

I stepped back and watched as the four of them crowded around and read, silently at first, and then with gasps. Samantha took a step backwards, a hand over her mouth. She started to cry. Kiah was breathing rapidly.

'Are these for real?' she asked eventually.

'We're sure they are,' I replied. 'You can see the originals any time you want. I've deposited them with the court – frankly, because we were afraid of something like this happening at our offices.'

'That would suggest that you have suspects in mind,' Powalski said.

I nodded. 'There's a fake-cop outfit inside Treasury, calls itself the Internal Investigations Unit. They've been making our lives a misery ever since we began our search. Ellen and I didn't trust them. They didn't want to us to take the documents away, and in the end I had to smuggle them out of the building. We're convinced that they were after the originals to do them some harm, and sure enough, they showed up at our offices last night demanding that we hand the documents back. When that didn't work they tried to force their way into the courthouse, but fortunately the security guard saw them off.'

'Thank you, Mr Petrosian,' Samantha said. 'Thank you for bringing these to us.'

I smiled. 'You're welcome.'

Kiah reached into her purse and took out some pieces of paper torn from a yellow pad.

'In return,' she said, 'I'd like to show you this. We found it in Pennsylvania. You can see the original, of course.'

I began to read. It was a statement by someone called Isabel Hardwick, written in 1813, which rambled a bit and took some time to get to the point. But the point, once she got to it, was remarkable, especially given the documents we had found the previous day. According to Isabel Hardwick, Jacob van Eyck had entrusted her with twenty-two documents to take to his Brother, not named, in Philadelphia in 1810. The clear inference was that these documents were loan certificates, and that his Brother was to play some role in making sure that Jacob was repaid, presumably by delivering them to the Treasury in Washington. The value of the loans was not stated, but the significance of her statement was unmistakable. Isabel said she delivered twenty-two such documents to the Brother, while the anonymous writer said that he only delivered sixteen to the Treasury. But even with that discrepancy, there was a massive circumstantial case for believing that the anonymous letter-writer and the Brother were one and the same person. Kiah now held a huge piece of the puzzle in her hands.

But she also had a disaster on her hands. She could easily spend the rest of her discovery time reconstructing her office and nothing more. I looked up. I knew instantly that she had reached the same conclusion I had. I decided what I was going to say next in an instant.

'Kiah, do you have any idea who this guy, the Brother, might have been?'

'Not yet. We're working on the theory that he was a Freemason, possibly someone who lived not too far away from the van Eyck family. Jacob was a Mason, so the use of the word "Brother" seems significant. We're searching for the Grand Lodge of Pennsylvania membership records of the time .'

I took a deep breath.

'I'll call the FBI's Philadelphia field office this afternoon,' I volunteered. 'It might take you guys days to get that information. They'll get it in a day and fax it to me, and I'll send it over to you. What then? You'll pick out likely candidates and try to find out who their descendants are?'

'Exactly.'

'Send me the names when you have them,' I offered. 'I'll have the FBI run their addresses and phone numbers for you.'

Kiah took my hand.

'Dave, I don't know what to say. This is really above and beyond the call of duty. Why?'

I looked back into the office, and stretched out my hand in the direction of the devastation.

'This,' I said. 'I didn't become a lawyer for this.'

58

IN THE CIVIL DIVISION of Justice we don't have much to do with crime, at least in the conventional sense of investigating and prosecuting criminals, but you run into FBI special agents all the time in the building, and most of us have our friends and acquaintances. Mine is Marty Resnik. I'd met Marty at a drinks party in the Criminal Division to welcome the new Deputy Attorney General three or four years before, and we'd hit it off immediately. We'd discovered that we came from much the same kind of social background. He had fought his way through to a degree, as I had, without much in the way of financial support, and he had married his college sweetheart, as I had. We've met for a beer every so often ever since. Marty has a great, self-deprecating sense of humor, and a very sharp mind. He's easy to talk to, and you never have to tell him something twice. And he's always ready to help if he can, even if it's with something a little outside the usual scope of his duties. When I called him and told him what I needed to help Kiah, and why I needed it, he didn't hesitate. He told me he would get on the phone to Philadelphia right away.

That was all I had time to do when I arrived back at the office before being summoned into the Presence. Word had spread far and wide about what was going on inside Treasury, and the Attorney General was asking what the hell was going on over there, and why no one was listening to him. It was a fair question, and he had invited the van Eyck legal team – Maggie,

Harry, Ellen and myself – to his office to explain it to him. At my level, visits to the office, with its elegant furnishings, were something of a rarity and always somewhat intimidating; it looked and felt every bit the centre of power it was. We told him as much as we knew, which wasn't much. We knew there was a so-called Internal Investigation Unit which seemed to have an unhealthy interest in the search we were making, but as to who was behind it and what their motives were, we couldn't even begin to speculate. Whoever they were, if they thought that they were protecting the government by trying to suppress evidence, they were naïve and badly mistaken. The Attorney already knew about their attempt to frighten us into returning the documents, and about their late-night caper at the Claims Court, but no one had yet heard about what I'd seen at Kiah's office. There hadn't been time for me to tell them. When I described the scene in detail, there was a shocked silence in the office. The Attorney General, Henry Shilling – tall, African American, early sixties, with distinguished features and a massive head of silver hair – was a constitutional law professor at Yale, respected both as a renowned scholar and a true gentleman, and there was no mistaking the pained look that crossed his face.

'Mr Petrosian, is there any evidence that it was these people from Treasury that broke into Miss Harmon's office?' he asked quietly, after some time.

'No, sir,' I replied. 'But her investigator, Powalski, is a former CIA man. He says the kind of equipment they had, including the bugging devices, has "government" written all over it. And that's before you consider how much of a coincidence it is that it happened last night when we know these Treasury people were roaming all over town trying to find the documents.'

'Maybe so,' the Attorney said. 'But I can't go to the President with nothing more than Mr Powalski's unsubstantiated opinion, even if he's right. You're going to have to give me something more than that.'

Maggie raised an eyebrow.

'To the President, sir?'

'Well, yes, to the President. If this is coming from another department of government, there's something rotten in the State of Denmark, as Shakespeare might say. Something's gotten way out of line; it's going to hurt the government in this litigation and it could hurt the government in a wider sense. The consequences could be very serious, and the President needs to know about it. The problem is, I don't know what to tell him.'

Dave,' Maggie asked, 'has Miss Harmon called in the police?'

'I'm sure she has. I understand her wanting to let Powalski take a look first, but she would need a police report for insurance purposes, if nothing else.'

Maggie looked at the Attorney.

'Sir, I would advise that you ask the Director of the FBI to take over the investigation from the local police, and send a couple of agents over to Miss Harmon's office as soon as he can before they start dismantling the crime scene.'

Shilling nodded. 'I agree. Let's call Miss Harmon now and ask her not to disturb anything until the Bureau can get their forensic people in to take a look.'

Maggie got to her feet and headed for the door. 'Give me five minutes, sir.'

'All set, sir,' she said, as she returned. 'The police hadn't got round to it yet – apparently they had a busy night – so the Bureau will talk to the Chief and call his people off. The Bureau will deal with it from this point on. If there's some governmental involvement here, they'll find it.'

'Is Miss Harmon happy with that?'

'Very much so, sir.'

'Good,' the Attorney replied. 'Now, would someone please tell me where we're going with this case?'

'Sir?' Maggie asked.

'If I recall rightly,' Shilling said, 'I received a memorandum just after this case was filed, assuring me that it was covered by the statute of limitations, and that it would be gone in a week or two. Now I'm hearing that, not only has the case not gone away, but we've discovered some documents that give the plaintiffs reason to believe they might hit us for quite a large sum of money. That's something else that will get the President's attention, and before I have to explain myself to him, I'd like to know where we stand.'

'Harry has a better handle on the detail than I do,' Maggie said sweetly.

Harry looked at me. 'I'll ask Dave to feel free to butt in, too,' he said.

'I don't care who butts in,' Shilling said, 'as long as someone tells me what's going on.'

'The judge hasn't ruled on the statute of limitations yet, sir,' Harry began. 'That hearing's coming up in a couple of weeks. It's our belief that we have a solid legal case, and that Judge Morrow will go with us, and that even if he doesn't go with us, the Court of Appeals or the Supreme Court will.'

'If our case is as solid as you say,' the Attorney asked, 'why hasn't the judge ruled already? What's taking him so long?'

Harry looked at me.

'We think he's just being careful,' I replied.

'Careful? In what sense, careful?'

'Well, sir, this is a high-profile case, there are potentially some constitutional issues, and potentially, it's worth a lot of money.'

'Constitutional issues? I thought you said we had a solid case?'

'We do, sir. But the plaintiffs have raised some arguments around an article of the Constitution. We don't believe these arguments have merit, but the judge has to consider them, and you can't blame him for being careful. Whichever way he decides, this case is going further, and it could well end up in the Supreme Court. He's caught in the spotlight.'

The Attorney nodded.

'OK. But how do you square that with the judge making a

discovery order? What does it matter what evidence there may be if the case is time-barred? He's putting the cart before the horse, isn't he? If the case is barred, there's no point in discovery. It sounds to me like the judge doesn't find our case quite as solid as you do.'

'That's something we didn't understand at the time either, sir,' Harry said. 'On the face of it, it doesn't make sense to allow discovery with our motion for summary judgment pending.'

'That's what I'm saying.'

'Yes, sir, and we agree. It's our view that the judge wants to get a feel for whether the case has any merit. It's not logical, but we think he will be more inclined to throw it out himself if the plaintiffs have no evidence. It's a high-profile case, and he would be finding against a potential American hero who's never been recognised, so if there's nothing to the claim, it makes it easier. On the other hand, if the case seems to have some merit, he might think about letting it go to trial and leaving it to the Court of Appeals to sort out the law.'

'And to take the fallout for doing down an American hero?'

'Exactly, sir. We can't see any other reason why he would go the way he has.'

The Attorney took a deep breath and released it sharply.

'All right. Now I want to know what our exposure is if we happen to lose on this solid question of law. If the case goes to trial and we lose, what are we looking at?'

Harry and I looked at Ellen. She had developed a range of theories about our potential exposure after studying the loan certificates.

'Well, sir,' she said, 'when the case began, the plaintiffs alleged that Jacob van Eyck had loaned the government about 450,000 dollars, value at the time, in 1778, which at six per cent compound over almost 250 years would produce an astronomical total, somewhere in the region of 670 billion dollars.'

'Lord have mercy,' Shilling whispered.

'Yes, sir. But the state of the evidence doesn't support that. The evidence available now suggests that Jacob entrusted twenty-two loan certificates to a friend, and the friend delivered sixteen of those certificates to the Treasury with a request for repayment. We don't know why he only delivered sixteen, and we don't know the total amount in question. We only have three of them, and the total for those three comes to about 15,000 dollars, which with interest comes to a mere twenty-two billion dollars or so.'

'Oh, well I guess that's OK, then,' Shilling commented.

'Yes, sir, but I'm afraid that's not the whole story.'

'I can't wait.'

'I believe Miss Harmon will argue that she has a case for repayment either of sixteen or twenty-two certificates.'

'How would she argue that, for heaven's sake, if she doesn't even have them?'

'She will argue that there's a strong circumstantial case for the existence of those certificates, and for the fact that they were properly presented to the Treasury at some point for repayment. There's a clear link between Jacob and his friend who wrote the letter we have. What she doesn't know is the total value of all sixteen or twenty-two loan certificates. I'd expect her to argue that the Court should assume an average amount per certificate based on the ones we do have. That average is about 5,000 dollars.'

'That's a pretty dicey assumption, Ellen,' Harry objected.

'Maybe. We could argue for a much lower assumption. The reality is, we have no idea what the judge would do. But if she succeeded in that argument, sixteen with interest would run to about 119 billion dollars; and twenty-two would run to 164 billion dollars, give or take.'

'I don't think the judge would go with that,' Harry said. 'It's too speculative.'

'Maybe, and there is some basis for challenging those calculations,' she added. 'The plaintiffs seem to have made certain assumptions I'm not sure are valid: for example, that the interest would be credited annually, and that the six per cent compound rate continues to apply right up to the present time. In fact, Congress placed some limits on the recoverable amount subsequently, which would reduce the recovery considerably. I'm looking into that now, but it's complicated and I don't have a complete analysis yet.'

She paused for effect.

'But any way you look at it, it's going to be a large number – a very large number.'

'She has another problem, too,' Harry said. 'She has to prove that the government didn't repay Jacob van Eyck.'

'That won't be a problem,' I intervened. 'The interest would have been far less then, obviously, but he would still have been owed a large amount by the standards of those days, and if the government had repaid that kind of money, we would have a record of it.'

'It's their burden of proof,' Harry insisted.

I shook my head. 'Judge Morrow won't see it that way. Besides, Kiah can prove that Jacob van Eyck went from being a very rich man to being a very poor man in a very short space of time, just when Washington's army was being resupplied at Valley Forge. That's too much of a coincidence. Any judge is likely to find that if Jacob did make these loans, we never repaid him.'

'Tell me about Kiah Harmon,' Henry Shilling said.

'She's a good lawyer,' I replied, 'and as straight as they come.'

'What does she want out of this?'

'She wants some money for the family, obviously. We've never talked numbers. But she did make it clear early on that they're not interested in trying to recover the compound interest calculations. They know they can't do that. They want a reasonable settlement, and their main point is that they want the government to put up a statue in honour of Jacob van Eyck.'

'A statue?'

'Yes, sir.'

'Where?'

'In Philadelphia, sir.'

He thought for a few moments.

'OK. I guess I can see where she's coming from with that.'

'Yes, sir.' I paused. 'Do you want me to…?'

'No,' Shilling replied, 'at least, not yet. Let's give our solid legal case a run first and see what happens. If the judge is with us on that, all well and good. But if he's not, then I may have to talk to the President about playing safe. Has anyone looked into what putting up such a statue might cost?'

We all looked at each other.

'No, sir,' Harry said.

'Well, you may want to give it some thought,' Henry Shilling suggested.

59

Kiah Harmon

I DON'T KNOW HOW I would have got through the days after the break-in without Arlene. I can't describe the sense of violation, the sense of having been targeted in such a personal way, the shock I felt at seeing my whole professional life so maliciously shredded as if it counted for nothing. It was my personal life too that they'd destroyed with such rage. I'd lost framed pictures of my parents, my college and law school certificates, and other pieces I was attached to. I felt as if I'd been assaulted and dumped naked at the side of some country road with nothing left to me and nowhere to turn. I vomited constantly for three straight days, and I couldn't stop shaking.

Mercifully, Arlene had been with me when we made the discovery. Seeing my reaction, she sat me down with the blanket she kept in the office wrapped around me, and sent Jenny out, as soon as she arrived, for lots of coffee and hot soup. It was Arlene who quietly arranged for Powalski to make a thorough inspection of the premises before we called in the police, or even told the building management what had happened. If she hadn't taken that decision, we would never have found the listening devices. She took me home during the afternoon and made sure that I was comfortable before she left, and she made sure that I called Arya and arranged to see her, and she told me time and time again that I could call her 24/7, and that I would be hearing from her if I didn't call to let her know I was OK.

Powalski called it as a government job almost immediately. Of course, it wasn't until Dave Petrosian showed up that we knew that the government might have had a concrete reason for ransacking the office. Powalski called it before we had any inkling of that, and he was right. Until Dave arrived I'd assumed that this was an escalation – a serious escalation – of the harassment policy that had begun with the IRS audit. That thought alone was alarming enough. Even Powalski, with his experience of what the government was capable of, was unnerved. It felt as though we were being warned off with a vengeance. When Dave arrived, at least this latest blow began to make some kind of sense, and of course the copies of the loan certificates and the letter he had found at the Treasury were wonderful to see. But the trauma remained, and would remain, at least until we found some way of restoring order and our ability to function as a law office.

That took days of work by Arlene and Jenny. They first had to arrange for the debris to be hauled away and for the office to be deep-cleaned. Then they had to go out and purchase new computers, and rent furniture, and buy God knows how many coffee mugs and all the other day-to-day stuff you take for granted in an office, until we had the leisure, and the insurance money, to buy what we wanted. They also had to do whatever they could to reinstate the files that had been strewn all over the office. Thankfully, although many documents bore ink stains, almost all of them were recoverable, and Arlene had meticulously backed up our computers in the Cloud and on a series of memory sticks. But throughout this time, I remained at home.

After three days I'd been desperate to get back to work. I was going crazy, doing nothing useful at home, my only diversion being to drive myself to Arya's and back each day; and we were losing time. But Arlene was firm. There was nothing I could do to help in the process of restoring the office, and she didn't want me upsetting myself needlessly and getting in the way. The office was coming along, and the important thing was for me to be able to hit the ground running once it was fit for purpose again. She was right, of course. I would have fretted the whole time. But by the time I made it back to the office and we ready to work again, we had a week and a half left before we had to go back before Judge Morrow. Dave had called and said that if we needed more time, he would support us, but even with that support, we couldn't go back to the judge without showing him what use we'd made of the time we'd already had.

On my first day back, I found a fax from Dave, forwarding one from an FBI agent called Marty Resnik. At Dave's request, Agent Resnik had been in touch with the FBI field office in Philadelphia, and they in turn had been in touch with the Grand Lodge of Pennsylvania, the headquarters of the Freemasons in the State. Jenny had already been all over their website. It had an impressive historical section, which provided us with some interesting detail of early members, including a certain Benjamin Franklin; but interesting as that was, it didn't give us a lot to go on in discovering the identity of Jacob's Brother. The fax was far more detailed. There wasn't an annual membership list, but there were several lists for the period we were interested in, and in particular one compiled in 1811. The Lodge had also been able to supply details of where many of the members of that time lived, at least in general terms. I have no idea how long it would have taken Powalski to get his hands on that same information. Knowing Powalski, I would have backed him to come up with it eventually, but the FBI could open doors far more quickly than he could.

I called Dave to thank him, and to apologise for what I'd said to him on the day we discovered the break-in. I hadn't meant it. I was just venting. I knew that Dave would never be party to anything like that, and I felt terrible about it. He said he understood, and that it was already forgotten.

I gathered the whole team around our rented conference table and we went over every name on the list. In the end, we concluded that the two most likely candidates were men from what looked like well-established families whose family seats were within easy striking distance of Upper Merion Township: Peter Hoare and Abe Best. This was educated guesswork, of course, and no more. Jacob van Eyck could just as easily have had close friends in Philadelphia, or even farther afield, but we knew that he had grown frail during his declining years, and there was something to be said for the conjecture that he might have concentrated on friends closer to home. Before the break-in, the plan had been to return to Pennsylvania to take Aunt Meg through the list; to keep in touch with the office as the descendants of likely candidates were put through the LDS family tree procedure; and to see if we could work it out on the ground. There wasn't time for that now. I placed a call to Alice and asked if Aunt Meg would be prepared to talk to us over the phone.

Two hours later, I put her on speakerphone, and we spoke with her for over an hour. Many of the names rang a bell with her. But the one that resonated most was that of Abe Best. The Bests and the van Eycks had been on good terms for many years, she said, in the old days. She had an idea that Jacob and Abe Best had been partners in some business ventures together. She wasn't aware of any Bests living in the Merion Township area currently, or for some long time before. But the Bests had also been known for their masonic connections.

We decided to go with Abe Best. As soon as we'd said goodbye to Aunt Meg, Jenny went to work on the LDS site. An hour later, we had a printout of Abe's family tree, from which we saw that one of his descendants was a woman called Cathy Wallace, thirty-two years old, apparently single. We had to start somewhere. I called Dave, and within an hour, Agent Resnik had got us a phone number and an address in DC, where Cathy Wallace worked as an economic forecaster for a think tank.

60

CATHY AGREED TO MEET Sam and myself during her lunch hour the next day. We took her to a coffee shop near her office where we ordered soup and toasted sandwiches. She was a friendly, cheerful woman dressed in a colourful sweater and jeans. The think tank she worked for leaned towards the liberal, and apparently a dress code wasn't one of their priorities. She seemed genuinely pleased to see us. She didn't even ask how we'd tracked her down.

'Did you grow up in Pennsylvania?' I asked as we were taking our seats.

'No. I don't think there have been Bests in Pennsylvania for the best part of a hundred years now – not my branch of the family, anyhow. Unlike the van Eycks we were a pretty small clan, and we just drifted away over the years. I grew up right here in the DC area, and apart from four years of college at Northwestern, I've always lived here.'

'But you know the story about the van Eycks?'

'Sure. I heard all about Jacob from my parents, and now I've been following the case in the news, of course.'

'That must be interesting for you, given your background with the family history,' I said.

'Not only that,' she replied. 'It's interesting from a professional point of view.'

'Oh?'

'Kiah, I'm an economic forecaster. Want to hear my forecast for the economy if the government has to pay out an unfunded 670 billion dollars?'

It was said with a straight face and there was an awkward moment, just as the sandwiches arrived. Sam and I caught each other's looks.

'Cathy, we've tried to make it clear,' I began wearily. I'd lost count of the number of times I'd had to explain the family's position and I was getting tired of it. 'We're not out to collect the compound interest calculation. We're –'

She laughed and waved me away, a quick drop of the hand from sandwich to table.

'I know, I know. You don't have to explain. I'm just kidding. I get it, and I'm on your side, believe me. If you guys can prove that Jacob van Eyck loaned all that money, of course his family should get something back. I know you're not out to bankrupt the government.'

'It's really important to me that you understand that,' Sam said.

'I do. Look, everyone in our family would support the van Eycks over this.'

Gratefully, we all took another bite of our sandwiches.

'What got me all riled up,' Cathy continued, 'is how that stupid woman Mary Jane whatever-her-name-is went after Sam about that movie. I couldn't believe her.' She touched Sam's hand. 'I'm sorry you had to go through all that you-know-what, and I thought you handled it really well.'

'Thanks,' Sam replied.

'So, not that I'm not enjoying our lunch, but what brings you to see me? On the phone you said there might be some information I could give you. I don't know what it could be, but if I can help, fire away.'

I put what was left of my sandwich down.

'Cathy, from what we understand, your family – the Bests – and the van Eycks were close at one time. You understand, we're going back to the period just after the War of Independence, very late eighteenth century to early nineteenth?'

'Yes, absolutely. That's what I was always told. Grandfather Abe and Jacob van Eyck were good friends.'

'And they were both Freemasons?'

She laughed out loud. 'Is the Pope Catholic? All the men in my family are Masons going back to the dawn of time. It's a family obsession. They were back in Grandfather Abe's day and it's the same today. My two brothers are Masons. They live in California. And all the men talk non-stop about Grandfather Abe. You know why, of course?'

She was looking at Sam. Sam smiled.

'I'm not sure I do. Why?'

'Because, if you were a Mason in Pennsylvania in Grandfather Abe's day, that meant that you knew George Washington, or Benjamin Franklin, or both. That's why the family talks about Grandfather Abe so much. He's our family link to Washington, our one claim to fame. No one actually knows whether he ever met George Washington, but if he was a Mason, the argument goes, he must have – even though Washington moved away after the war and became Grand Master in Virginia, so who really knows? But why spoil a good story?'

I nodded. 'We understand that the Bests lived in Merion Township at that time, even though, as you say, the family moved on eventually?'

'Yes. That was our home during the war, for sure. It's a sore point, as a matter of fact. We had to retreat into Merion Township. We had some other properties, a bit farther out into the countryside beyond Valley Forge, but the British took them over and used them to store munitions. They appropriated them and made the family move out. Eventually, General Washington took the property back for us, but I heard it was a real mess, the way they left it, and of course they never paid a red cent by way of compensation.'

'Did you ever hear any talk about Grandfather Abe being in

any way involved in helping Jacob van Eyck to try to get his loans repaid? This would be during the time the family was living in Merion Township.'

She stared out of the window and thought for some time.

'No. Not that I recall. Helping him in what way?'

I saw Sam shake her head at me. I also had the feeling this was going nowhere. If so, we couldn't afford to waste any more time. We needed to get back to the office and move on to the next most likely Best family contact. As a parting shot, I decided to ask her point blank.

'Cathy, we have evidence that Jacob entrusted someone – we don't know who yet – with a number of documents in connection with the loan, and that whoever it was took those documents to the Treasury to try to make them pay Jacob what he was due. This would be in 1811, or thereabouts. Does that ring any kind of bell at all? Did you ever hear anything about that?'

'No,' she replied.

'Do you remember talk about anyone inheriting any of Grandfather Abe's papers after his death, or do you know anyone in your family who could have any documents from his day?'

To my surprise, she laughed.

'You're not from a masonic family, are you?'

'No, I'm not,' I admitted.

'If you were, you would know that you don't inherit masonic documents. The regalia and books, maybe sometimes, even though strictly you're not supposed to. But documents? Not if they have any real masonic significance. Not if they had to do with help you were giving to a fellow Mason.'

'So, what would happen to documents of that kind?' Sam asked.

'You would have a storage box at the Lodge,' Cathy replied. 'You'd leave them there, for as long as you needed to.'

I felt my heart start to beat a bit faster.

'Cathy, do you know whether Grandfather Abe had a box?' I asked.

'I don't know for sure,' she replied, 'but it's a pretty safe bet that he would have. It's an open secret. All the men in my family talked about their storage boxes, and I don't know of any reason why Grandfather Abe would have been any different.'

'Even if he did,' Sam said quietly, 'I'm sure his heirs would have cleared it out after his death.'

Cathy shook her head.

'No. That's not how it would work. They may have checked the box for family papers, a will, for example, but I doubt they would clear it out,' she replied, 'certainly not if it contained masonic materials. For one thing, that would require the consent of the Grand Master. Today, it wouldn't be a problem, but in Abe's day they liked to keep their masonic papers in-house, and the Grand Master's word was law.'

She paused for a moment or two.

'In any case, if the family had discovered any documents about the van Eyck loans, someone would have said something. Our family would have had no interest in keeping them, and any Mason would want to help his Brother. They wouldn't have kept quiet about it. They would have told Jacob's family and handed over the documents to them.'

'Cathy,' I asked, 'am I understanding you correctly? Are you saying that if Grandfather Abe had papers like that stashed away at the Lodge, it's possible that they're still there?'

'That's what I'd expect,' she replied simply. 'The building they have today isn't the original Lodge, obviously. I mean, the original was in a tavern that no longer even exists.'

'That's right, I said. 'The Lodge now is the Masonic Temple, which is late nineteenth century.'

'Right. What I'm saying is, I'm not sure how many times they've moved, and every time they move there's a risk that something might get lost. But yes, unless someone realised that the documents might be needed for something like your case, they might be left to lie there pretty much for ever.'

She smiled at each of us in turn.

'So, that's where I'd look if I were you.'

'They won't let us inside to look,' I said. 'I'm pretty sure of that.'

She nodded. 'No. You'd need a family member. Someone would have to bring proof of identity.'

'Cathy,' Sam began, 'we don't have much time. Would you…?'

She smiled again.

'Sam, if you can make arrangements with the Lodge, I'll come with you, with my passport in hand.'

61

BY THE END OF the week, with the help of one more phone call from Agent Resnik, who had somehow ingratiated himself with the Lodge during his inquiries, we had managed to secure an appointment with the personal assistant to the Grand Master of Pennsylvania. I felt badly that Cathy had to take a day off work, though it was a Friday, and it didn't seem to bother her at all. In fact, she seemed quite enthusiastic, in some ways even more than Sam and me. I don't think Sam or I had any illusions left by then. There was every chance that the search for Abe Best's storage box would be a wild goose chase: another story of groping around in the dark and coming up with nothing; the story we had inherited from those who had gone before us; the consistent story of the quest for the van Eyck loan certificates for more than two hundred years. All the same, we were almost out of time now, and we had been given a lead; we had to follow it. If nothing else, I tried desperately to persuade myself, what was true of Abe Best must be true of any other Mason of his period. Perhaps there were others who had stored papers at the Lodge, and perhaps there was information to be had there.

The Philadelphia Masonic Temple at One North Broad Street, just across from the City Hall, is a justly famous piece of late nineteenth-century grandiosity. If you didn't know what it was, you might think it to be a civic building, some local dignitary's personal folly, or even a splendid old hotel. The most promising aspect of it from our point of view was that, although it is a building in everyday masonic use, the Temple is also a magnificent museum and repository of masonic documents and artifacts. The Pennsylvania Lodge claims to be the third oldest in the world and traces its roots back to the Grand Lodge in London, long before the War of Independence. Virginia and one or two other lodges dispute that claim, but there's no doubt that the Pennsylvania Lodge goes back to at least 1730 – the year of Jacob's birth – and perhaps even further. They have a remarkable collection of antiquities to back up their pedigree. And that may have played some part in the way we were received. We had taken an early flight, and were at the Temple by eleven o'clock.

John Macey, personal assistant to the Grand Master, dressed very formally in a dark suit, a black bow tie, and white gloves, made us welcome and settled us in his office with cups of coffee. Cathy was ready to brandish her passport, but John didn't seem particularly interested in seeing it.

'Agent Resnik filled me in to some extent on what you're looking for,' he said. 'I know all about the case you're bringing on behalf of Brother Jacob van Eyck's family, of course. Do I understand correctly? You believe that there may be documents here at the Temple that back up your claim in some way?'

'That's correct,' I replied. 'We believe that one of Jacob's Brethren took charge of some important documents of his, not long before his death, and delivered at least some of them to the Treasury in Washington. It's important to us to discover who that person was. We haven't been able to trace him as yet, but we are sure that he would have been a fellow member of the Pennsylvania Lodge.'

John nodded. 'I'm sure you're right about that. Brother van Eyck's first instinct with something as important as that would be to trust a Brother, and, of course, the Best family would be a natural choice. They were a very prominent masonic family, and they were near neighbours of the van Eycks at the time, weren't they? There must have been a lot of contact between Abe and Jacob.'

I was impressed. John had been doing his homework.

'That's why Cathy is with us,' I replied. I opened my briefcase and handed him a document. 'This is a printout from the LDS ancestry site, proving her descent from Abe Best. She's brought evidence of identification with her.'

Once more, John didn't seem too concerned about it. He glanced at the family tree.

'I'm quite sure you wouldn't have brought an impersonator with you, Miss Harmon,' he smiled. 'Besides, despite the rumours you may have heard to the contrary, these days we Masons try not to be too secretive; we try to be open with information that may be useful to those with sympathetic causes.'

'Such as those seeking justice for a Brother?' Sam asked.

He smiled again. 'Of course. But I won't pretend that we're not interested in the outcome of your case for our own reasons. It wouldn't do us any harm to have yet another important American figure in our masonic history. The Grand Master is very well aware of that. Our heritage is very important to us, and if Brother van Eyck is indeed a true American hero, it would be a significant feather in our cap.'

I nodded. 'In that case, would you be prepared to tell us whether Abe Best had a storage box in the Lodge, or whether you may be in possession of any documents of his?'

John stood.

'I can do better than that,' he replied. 'Come with me.'

We left his office and took a narrow, winding set of stairs down two floors. It led into a corridor linking a number of anonymous-looking rooms identified only by numbers on the doors. About halfway along the corridor, John stopped and opened a door to our left with a large key. The room contained several filing cabinets and what looked like large boxes, some made of wood, others, apparently more recent, metallic. The door was heavy and fitted tightly into its aperture. The room felt cold. As the door slammed behind us, I looked around and saw that the room was air-conditioned. Not only that, panels on the wall suggested that the inside temperature was being carefully monitored and kept within a narrow range. We were in a controlled environment, designed specifically to store fragile documents and artifacts under constant conditions to prevent deterioration.

'Many members of the Lodge have had storage boxes over the years, obviously,' he said. 'It's standard practice. The boxes in use today are in another part of the building. They don't require any particular storage conditions, and Brothers can access them whenever they wish. It's just like having a safe deposit box in a bank.'

He indicated the stacks of wooden boxes.

'But these older ones require careful storage. What you see here are what we have left of the older deposits. Most of the very old ones were probably claimed and taken away by a Brother's family after his death. Many were simply lost over the course of time. This building was completed in 1873, but before that the Lodge had been accommodated in various places, beginning with the Tun Tavern. Along the way, boxes may have been taken out and never returned, or just gone missing.'

'It's still quite a collection,' Sam observed.

'Yes, and the good news is that a few years ago the Grand Master decided that the Lodge should be free to make use of anything stored here – items that haven't been claimed, or even looked at by anyone, for fifty years or more.'

'Free to make use of them?' Sam asked.

'For the purposes of our archives. We're in the process of cataloging them, making an inventory, and anything of real historical interest may find its way into our historical exhibit. We've already added quite a few items that were stored down here. The result is that we've opened all of our archives, not only to our own researchers, but to anyone who has a legitimate interest in seeing them.'

He smiled.

'That's why I haven't troubled you for your passport, Miss Wallace. The fact that this inquiry is being made on behalf of the van Eyck lawsuit is more than enough to get you in through the door. As long as the Grand Master is satisfied that it's a legitimate inquiry, there's no problem, and we're more than satisfied in the present case.'

Sam and I exchanged glances.

'And is there…?' Her voice trailed away.

John gestured us to follow him to the far corner of the room to our right.

'After I spoke to Agent Resnik yesterday, I came down here and looked through the indexes. I found this.'

He indicated a large wooden box, obviously very old, placed on top of a stack of similar boxes. It had a three-digit number faintly scratched on the top left-hand corner.

'According to our records, this would have been Abe Best's box. We're not absolutely sure of that. Any original labelling is long gone. But it was found with other boxes known to date from the same period, and there is some evidence to link the box number you see there with Brother Best. So, we will have to see, won't we?'

Sam and I looked at each other again.

'You haven't opened it?' she asked.

'No. The box is locked, so my guess is that our researchers haven't gotten around to it yet, and I don't remember seeing any reference to Abe Best documents in any of our exhibits.' He smiled. 'I confess that I was on the point of opening it yesterday; it was quite a temptation. But then I thought, as you were coming and as there's a family connection, I would leave it to you.'

He picked up a long metal tool that had been lying on the floor alongside the stack of boxes.

'This will open pretty much any old lock you're liable to come across.'

He handed the tool to Cathy.

'Would you like to do the honours, Miss Wallace?'

62

CATHY GLANCED AT SAM and me. We smiled encouragingly.

'Go for it,' Sam said.

There was a metallic keyhole in the front of the box. It looked rusted and worn, and when Cathy gingerly inserted the tool, nothing seemed to happen. John was prepared for that. He sprang forward clutching a can of WD40.

'Take it back out for a moment.' He gave the lock two good sprays of the oil. 'Try it again.'

This time the lock yielded as easily it would have done when the box was new, more than two hundred years ago.

'Works every time,' John observed happily.

Cathy gently lifted the lid, and the stood back as a wave of dust rose into the air. She waved it away from her face with her hand.

'Wow, I don't think anyone's been in here for a while,' she said.

'Let's put it up here,' John suggested. He picked the box up and carried it carefully to a large table by the window at the rear of the room. 'There's something in here. I'm going to put this protective sheet down on the table, and we can put the contents on display.'

Having laid down a thin white plastic sheet, John stepped back to allow Sam and me to approach. I looked down into the box, and saw a number of pieces of parchment.

'We have something,' I said.

As gently as I could, I reached into the box and felt my way along the sides down to the bottom.

'It feels like we have six or seven pieces,' I reported. 'They look very fragile. There are some small fragments broken off, and I'm seeing a light brown colouration.'

'The colour may change once we get them into the light,' John advised us. 'It could go either way. They may look different in the light, or they may discolour slightly when we expose them to it. Either way, it shouldn't hurt them. Parchment is tougher than people think.'

I lifted the pieces of parchment slowly, one by one, on to the protective sheet, and Sam arranged them to lie next to each other in a sequence. When the last piece was in place I closed the box and lifted it down to the floor. I turned back to Sam, who was standing over the documents. She looked as though she didn't know whether to laugh or cry, and seemed to be attempting both at once. I turned back to look at the documents we had found, and almost at once I found myself feeling exactly the same way.

Six of the documents were loan certificates, the creditor named as Jacob van Eyck, and the total of the certified loans was in the region of $42,000. Six here plus sixteen delivered to the Treasury would equal the twenty-two entrusted to Abe Best by Isabel Hardwick. In the blink of an eye, the evidence of the chain of circumstances had become overwhelming. We had proved the identity of the mysterious Brother: it had to be Abe Best. The seventh document was the icing on the cake. It was a handwritten note, signed by Abe himself and dated June 1811 – or least that's what it purported to be: we would have to compare the handwriting with the writing on the document Dave and Ellen had found, and we might need to call in an expert handwriting examiner. But I felt sure of the conclusion that would ultimately be reached. We were way beyond the realm of coincidence now.

June 1811

I am lately returned from the Capital, and beg by these presents to record that while in that city I delivered to the Secretary of the Treasury sixteen documents, being certificates bearing witness to loans made by my friend and Brother Jacob van Eyck for the support of the army in the late war. These were sixteen of twenty-two such documents entrusted to me on Brother Jacob's behalf by a young woman, his servant and confidante, in September last. I undertook to impress upon the Secretary, Mr Gallatin, who is well known to me, and I believe, well disposed towards me, the necessity that my said Brother should be recompensed what is due to him with all possible haste, he having fallen into ruin in the service of our Republic as a consequence, not of enemy action, but of his own benevolence and patriotism. I therefore urged Mr Gallatin to direct that such funds as the Government can spare for the purpose should be devoted to Brother van Eyck's relief. Monies being as yet in short supply, it seemed to me politick not to advance all the certificates in my possession at the same time, but to retain six of them, which may be presented at a later time, when those presented have been honoured and when further funds shall be available.

(Signed) Bro. Abe Best, Philadelphia Grand Lodge

John and Cathy had crept forward to look too. I felt Sam take my hand and squeeze.

'That's amazing,' Cathy whispered.

'I take it this is what you'd hoped to find?' John asked.

'Yes,' I replied, testing my voice as I went. 'Actually, it's better than we could ever have hoped.'

'I'm pleased to hear that. How can we help further?'

'You've done so much already,' I replied. I took a deep breath. 'But John, we need to take these documents with us so that copies can be made and so that they can be kept in readiness for the trial.'

John raised his eyebrows. You could see the reluctance. Showing documents to visitors as evidence of a new openness on the part of the Freemasons was one thing. Letting those documents out of the Lodge was another.

'I promise you that they will be safe, and that they will be returned to the Lodge as soon as they are no longer needed.'

'I'm not sure about that,' he replied. 'I would have to ask the Grand Master...'

'If it helps,' I added, 'you can tell the Grand Master that when we bring them back, we will also bring you some further documents of Brother Best's to add to your collection.'

'More of the same? Like these?'

'Yes. Together, they should add up to a unique exhibition of Revolutionary War loan documents. I don't believe any other institution will have anything to match it. The reason I can't bring them until the trial is over is that the court needs them as evidence. But after that, they're yours, and in the meanwhile they will be in good hands, I promise you.'

He was nodding. I was watching the indecision.

'In addition, the Lodge would be making a decisive contribution to Brother van Eyck being recognised finally for the hero he was. In fact, from now on, this Lodge may always be associated with the successful outcome of the war. I can't think of a better addition to your historical heritage than that. Can you?'

I watched him take the last step. This was potentially the biggest historic coup in the history of the Lodge, and it was happening on his watch.

'I'll need a receipt,' he said decisively.

63

THERE WAS A REAL sense of *déja vu* about it all: the throng of
reporters outside court; the crowded courtroom; the army of
reporters, law clerks, and law students; and this time, even two
other judges of the Claims Court, who had decided to delay the
start of proceedings in their own courtrooms to witness what, one
way or the other, might be a moment of legal history. Inevitably,
it had taken us time to fight our way into the courthouse, fending
off reporters demanding that we predict the unpredictable for
viewers who would know the actual result before they heard the
prediction. When we arrived in court, the room was overflowing
with bodies and it was already getting hot and stuffy. To add to all
that, Sam and I had been on edge all morning. I hadn't slept well
and I was pretty sure Sam hadn't either, and when we approached
Dave and Ellen to shake hands, I was conscious that we weren't
disguising it very well. Our nerves must have been all too obvious.

'I owe you one, Dave,' I said, and I meant it, 'especially for Agent
Resnik. I owe you both a drink some time.'

'I'm going to hold you to it,' Dave smiled. But then I saw that
his smile, too, was nervous. Well, of course. This was a big case for
everyone involved, the Justice Department as well as the plaintiffs.

For the judge, too. I'd been meditating on how to handle the
hearing ever since we'd returned from Philadelphia. Should I
press the argument again, or rely on what I'd said last time? Judge
Morrow wasn't the kind of judge who needed to be told anything

more than once, and if you tried, it usually tended to irritate him. He had the arguments in his head, and we had made use of the discovery orders he had made to unearth some solid evidence. That couldn't be bad for us – at least now, he knew that our case had merit – but neither did it mean that we were going to win. Today was about the law, not the merits. If he was still in doubt I was sure he would tell us, but the overwhelming likelihood was that Judge Morrow had decided which way he was going to go, and if so, nothing we could say this morning was likely to change his mind. As an advocate, I have always found it hard to turn down any chance to press my case, but my instinct told me to have confidence in the arguments we had put forward. I'd decided that if Dave renewed his argument, I would reply, but otherwise I would leave it up to the judge.

Judge Morrow took the bench quickly, and seemed anxious to get on with it without wasting even a second. That was unusual for him, and even Maisie was looking bemused. I sensed that this was his way of keeping the judicial nerves under control. Dave and I followed his lead. We lost no time in standing and introducing ourselves, and we exchanged the morning pleasantries briskly.

'I've read the briefs again,' the judge said, 'I've reviewed the evidence, and I have my note of what you both said on the last occasion you were here. If either of you wishes to add anything, you may do so now, but there's no need to go back over ground you've already covered. Mr Petrosian?'

I saw Dave and Ellen exchange the briefest of glances and shakes of the head.

'Nothing, Your Honour, thank you,' Dave replied. 'The United States is content to rest on its brief and earlier argument.'

I leap to my feet at once.

'The plaintiffs are also happy to rest. Thank you, Your Honour.'

Judge Morrow nodded.

'Thank you both. Very well, then. I will proceed to rule on the government's motion.'

He carefully arranged his papers in front of him and put on his reading glasses.

'Today, the court must rule on the government's motion to dismiss this litigation based on the statute of limitations. The plaintiffs have sued to recover the principal and congressionally authorised interest due on loans alleged to have been made by their ancestor, Jacob van Eyck, in relief of the army under George Washington at Valley Forge during the winter of 1777–1778, which loans, it is said, the United States has failed to repay.

'The government responds by pleading the statute of limitations, arguing that the lawsuit was filed more than six years after the claim accrued, which removes the court's jurisdiction to entertain the case, and so bars the claim. There can be no doubt that more than six years elapsed before the claim was brought. The parties seem to differ as to whether the claim was out of time by more than 200 years, or as little as 130, but they also agree that it doesn't matter: a claim is either filed out of time or in time, and this one was clearly filed out of time.

'Ordinarily, that would conclude the discussion. But, as the plaintiffs point out, there are some unique features of this case. The plaintiffs' claim must have accrued, so it seems to me, not later than 1812, when Mr van Eyck died. At that time, there was no court in which a citizen could sue the government. The Claims Court was not established until 1855, and it may well be that some aspects of the claim could not have been pursued in this court until 1893, at which time the claims were barred any way you look at it. Essentially, the plaintiffs say, Mr van Eyck's descendants never had a chance to sue. The government argues that that makes no difference.

'In reply, the plaintiffs say that there is a much deeper issue at stake here. In her informative and at times scholarly brief, Miss Harmon points out that the first paragraph of Article Six of the United States Constitution guarantees the validity of any debt owed by the government dating from before the date of adoption of the Constitution. Furthermore, because the Constitution itself has no time limit, this article preserves the validity of all such claims without limitation of time. If that is true, and if the Constitution is the supreme law of the land – as it undoubtedly is – no later statute of limitations can invalidate such a claim, and the claim can be pursued at any time.

'The government agrees that Article Six does guarantee the validity of the debt without limitation of time, but argues that that doesn't mean that the plaintiffs can sue in this court when the claim is barred by the statute of limitations. In other words, the plaintiffs have a valid claim, but no longer have a court in which to enforce it, if indeed they ever did. Mr Petrosian agreed on the last occasion that this was a somewhat unattractive position to take, but he insists that the government is entitled to take it.

'And that really sums up the dilemma with which I find myself confronted. There is an elegance and simplicity about the government's position, and as a matter of strict logic, the argument they present is a compelling one. But it is a logic that is deeply unsatisfying. On the last occasion we were here, it seemed to me that the waters run deeper than that, and I wanted to take time to dive in and see what is really going on. The evidence discovered by the parties in the intervening period has helped to clarify the question for me to some extent. And the question, or rather questions, I have are: what did our Founding Fathers intend to happen in this situation, and what did Congress intend to happen?

'Let me start with Congress. No evidence has been placed before me about whether Congress ever considered the question of the war loans in the context of Article Six of the Constitution, and probably for good reason. Why would they? In well over 200 years since Valley Forge, this is the only such claim ever to have been presented. I'm quite sure that the question would never have occurred to them in the course of any routine debate about the rules of the United States Claims Court. It was almost certainly a question that never arose. On the other hand, the intention of the Founding Fathers could hardly be more clear.

'Miss Harmon has presented that intention as stated by Alexander Hamilton. As Secretary of the Treasury, Hamilton was responsible for managing the national debt, and there can be no doubt that he spoke with authority for the government on that subject. Hamilton was absolutely clear that the war debt must be repaid in full; he entertained no exceptions to that principle and he imposed no conditions on it. Indeed, he insisted that even speculators, who had shamelessly exploited the indigent after the war by buying up their loan certificates at huge discounts and then redeeming them at full value, must be repaid in full. When challenged in Congress about this unpopular stance, his reply was simple. The debts were guaranteed by the Constitution. Those who held loan certificates couldn't be refused.

'Hamilton was a hard-headed economist, and he was motivated partly by pragmatic considerations: he was concerned about what today we would call America's credit rating. If we failed to pay our debts, others would hesitate in future before lending us money, except perhaps at exorbitant rates of interest. But that wasn't the whole story. For Hamilton, there was a higher principle at stake. It was a moral issue for him. It was an issue that raised the question of the character and values of the new nation. The United States had repeatedly pledged its faith and credit for the war loans. The loans were the price of liberty.

'Now, some may think this strange, but in the days since the last hearing, in my mind, I've tried to imagine Alexander Hamilton sitting here in court with us. I've tried to imagine him listening to these proceedings, and I wonder what he would make of it all. I'm quite sure that he would find the arguments we've had in this case to be extraordinary. For one thing, the idea of suing the government in its own court would have been a long way outside the universe in which he lived. But I think he would have understood the argument about statutes of limitations, and

I think he would share the view that it was unattractive.

'In fact, I believe his feelings would be stronger than that. I believe that he would have been appalled. Of course, the idea of suing the government would have struck him as extraordinary, but the idea that a war loan creditor would be *reduced to having to sue the government* would be even more extraordinary. I believe that Hamilton would be horrified by the idea that the United States would renege on its promises; that it would fail to repay these debts that were the price of liberty. I truly believe that he would find that to be unacceptable, not just in terms of the Constitution, but morally. I truly believe that he would stand up in this court, and say, "What's going on here is wrong."

'Of course, I can't base my ruling solely on my ideas of what Alexander Hamilton might think. I have to decide what the law requires today. But at the same time, I can't ignore the implications of the law, either. If I dismiss the plaintiff's case, I'm closing the door on our country ever repaying the price of liberty, and in effect, I'm ruling that the first clause of Article Six of our Constitution has ceased to have any force. Now, I recognise that whatever decision I make today will be appealed by one side or the other, to the Court of Appeals for the Federal Circuit, and perhaps from there to the United States Supreme Court. That gives me some comfort, and some confidence simply to go ahead and do what I think is right.

'Simply stated, I'm not going to be the judge to say that the government need not repay the price of liberty, and I'm not going to be the judge to say that the first paragraph of Article Six of our Constitution has no more force. If the judges of a higher court wish to overrule me on those points at a later time, that's their prerogative. But I'm not going to decide in that way. This case will not end here today.

'The plaintiffs have presented evidence that may justify the inference that Jacob van Eyck made loans as described by at least nine loan certificates, and that he was never repaid. The evidence at trial may justify the conclusion that there were even more such loan certificates, perhaps as many as twenty-two, or more, in all. Calculating the value of those loans, and the amount of interest payable, will be a difficult matter, which will require expert assistance. But all of those matters must await trial. All I need say about the evidence today is that the plaintiffs have enough to go to trial and to require an answer from the United States.

'My ruling today is as follows. The government's motion to dismiss based on the statute of limitations is denied. The case will proceed to trial. The parties are ordered to confer, and to advise my clerk within fifteen days of the date when they expect to be ready for trial, and how long they expect the trial to take, after which the court will fix a date. Within thirty days, the parties will also exchange and file with the court provisional lists of witnesses.

'That's it. We are adjourned.'

Towards the end of the afternoon, Dave called.

'Congratulations,' he said, simply. He sounded ill at ease somehow, tense.

'Thanks, Dave. I really appreciate that. Are you OK?'

'Yeah. Sure. Great lunch at Benny's. I'm good.'

We laughed.

'When do you want to confer about trial dates?' I asked. 'I haven't given it too much thought yet, but I figure we could do this case in a week or a little more. What do you think?'

There was a silence.

'Dave?'

'Kiah, I'm calling because I have instructions to invite you to a meeting on Friday morning to discuss settlement.'

I remember holding the phone away from my ear for some time. Sam was sitting across the table from me, and gave me an inquiring look.

'What? Dave, did I just hear you correctly?'

'You did.'

'The government wants to talk settlement?'

That brought Sam out of her seat and around the table in a single bound. She knelt by my side to listen in.

'We'd like to explore some possibilities.'

I hesitated.

'OK. How does this work? Do you have an offer?'

'No. It's more complicated than that, Kiah. We're going to have to negotiate this from the ground up. With so many plaintiffs, and so many ways of doing the calculations, there are too many moving parts. You're going to have to tell us what you really want here, and give us some real numbers.'

'Wow,' I replied helplessly.

'Is that a problem?'

'No, not at all. I'm just taken by surprise. I thought you guys were pretty sure of getting Tomorrow reversed on appeal if he went with us.'

'We are…'

'Well then…?'

'Off the record?'

'Off the record: word of honour.'

'I feel good about our chances on appeal, as do Ellen and Harry. But it's been pointed out to us that if we're wrong, we're talking about serious money potentially coming out of the federal budget. There are people higher up the food chain who don't trust trial lawyers that much, and would prefer not to gamble for high stakes if they don't have to. Don't get me wrong, Kiah, we're not about to lie down. We'll take our chances if the numbers are too high.'

'I hear you,' I replied. 'OK. We'll start work on numbers for you. Time and place? I assume we'll meet at your offices? More space than mine.'

Again, some hesitation.

'Let me get back to you on that tomorrow or Wednesday.'

'Sure. No problem.'

He paused.

'Oh, and I'm sorry to break this to you, Kiah, but the President's not going for the Rhode Island thing. That's off the table.'

'Oh, no,' I replied. 'I was relying on that as a bargaining chip.'

We both laughed again, breaking the tension a little.

'That's fine, Dave,' I said. 'As long as the statue's still on the table. That's not negotiable.'

64

IT HAD STRUCK ME as odd at the time that Dave had to call me back to arrange a time and place for the meeting. Why couldn't we have worked those details out while we had each other on the phone? But it wasn't something I could stop to worry about then. A meeting to discuss settlement may seem a simple enough idea, and in many cases it is – indeed, Dave and I had been through this process together a number of times before – but not in this case. In this case, there was a huge amount of work to be done in the three days that remained to us, and that work would involve the whole team.

First, there was the question of the vote on whether to accept any offer the government might make. This was a class action, and it wasn't up to Sam alone. Every plaintiff had a vote. It was our job to set up a secure system to enable them to make their choice. Our victory on the summary judgment motion had brought in a late surge of new plaintiffs, who had probably been holding off committing their fifty dollars until they knew we were at least in with a chance. With the late surge, the total was now slightly more than 5500. That was not as many as I had expected when I first took the case. Statistically, the number of descendants from each of seven brothers over a period of more than 200 years should have been a lot bit bigger. Perhaps, despite all the publicity and all our efforts to reach out, there were people out there who had no idea that they were van Eyck descendants, and to whom it had never occurred that they might be.

There was nothing we could do about that now. In any case, 5500 was more than enough, administratively speaking, and I had a shrewd suspicion that, if we did reach an agreement, the government would ask us to close the door to new applicants within a tight time frame. Arlene had kept immaculate records, and she had set us up to contact all of the plaintiffs by email, or in the mercifully few cases of family members who hadn't quite caught up with the whole email thing, by phone or fax. With Powalski and Jenny, she was now working on our secure voting system. We would notify the plaintiffs of any offer made, and they would then have a limited time to vote whether to accept or reject it. I had taken an executive decision that a simple majority would be enough.

I guess I should be honest about it. Yes, it was the plaintiffs' decision, but it was one I was determined to make for them if I could. It was a decision that needed to be made by someone who knew what was going on. Don't get me wrong. I'm all for democracy in general; but there's a time and place for democracy, and this wasn't it. It wasn't just a question of what the government might offer. It was also a question of what came next if we turned it down. Yes, we had won so far in front of Judge Morrow. But the Court of Appeals was a very different animal from Judge Morrow. I suspected that with the Court of Appeals, the law would weigh more heavily than Alexander Hamilton, and there was a real prospect that they would go with the statute of limitations. On the other hand, it wasn't a foregone conclusion, and the government knew that. They were worried too; otherwise, they wouldn't be talking to us. How far would they go? It was a delicate balance, and it was vital to get it right.

So Arlene was also drafting letters for me to send out, recommending acceptance or rejection, as the case might be, and I had told her to make them strong letters. I'd also called Ed van Eyck and Jeff Carlsen, who agreed to back me up by sending out similar letters when the time came. Even leaving aside Mary Jane Perrins and three other residents of Boston, Massachusetts, this was a divided family. There would be waverers, and those who thought they should get more money, and those who just wanted publicity, and those who just wanted to be a nuisance and disagree for the sake of it. It was my job to build a majority to override all those people.

While all that was going on, Sam and I had to figure out what sum of money we thought the government might be prepared to budget to buy itself out of a high-stakes gamble. We didn't really know where to start. Dave and Ellen would be telling them that they had a great chance on appeal, and they shouldn't be too nervous about it. Those who actually held the nation's purse strings would be responding that so far the government had been on the losing side, and maybe it was time for some damage limitation. Sam was pondering how much it would cost the government to put up a respectable statue in Philadelphia. She had spent a considerable time online, and had even spoken to an old college friend who was a sculptor and had done some public work, but we still weren't confident we could put an accurate figure on it.

In the end, we decided not to try. The statue was the one non-negotiable plank of our demand. The government knew that, and the government had done this kind of thing before. They would be able to cost a project like this out, and they probably already had. If they agreed to the statue, two things would happen. First, I would recommend that we accept the offer, and I had every reason to think that the plaintiffs would react favourably. Recognition of Jacob was one of the few things they all seemed to agree on. But second, the government would deduct the likely cost of the statue from the financial offer, and that too might make a difference. It would be important for all the family members who had signed up to feel they were receiving some worthwhile tangible compensation. Late on the Wednesday night we decided on an absolute floor of $5000 per plaintiff, in addition to the statue, plus reasonable travel expenses to attend the unveiling. And attorney's fees; I wasn't about to forget that detail.

I was so focused on our preparations that I'd forgotten about the outstanding question of the logistics of the meeting, and it wasn't until Dave called late on Thursday afternoon that it registered with me that I had no idea where and when we were supposed to meet the next day. Remarkably, I would still be in the dark after we had spoken.

'Hi, Kiah, how's it going? I'm calling about the arrangements for tomorrow.'

'Right, Dave, good. What time do you guys want?'

'How would ten o'clock be?'

'That would be fine. Your offices at ten?'

He didn't reply immediately.

'Kiah, a car will pick you up in front of your building at nine,' he said hesitantly. It was Dave's indecisive voice; I'd heard it before. 'Just you and Sam.'

'A car?' I replied as soon as I could; it took a few seconds for what he had said to compute. 'What car? What are you talking about? We don't need a car. We can find our way to the Justice Department.'

'I know you can, Kiah. But tomorrow, we would like to offer you a car. Your driver's name will be Alfred, and it has to be nine sharp outside the front entrance of your building.'

I shook my head. It had been a long day, and I was getting irritated.

'You're kidding me, right?'

'No. I'm not kidding.'

'Look, Dave, I don't know whether this is a joke, or some feeble attempt to patronise us, or whether it's some screwed up way you guys think you have of messing with our minds, but Sam and I are both big girls, and we can get ourselves to the damn Justice Department without the government providing transportation.'

I heard him sigh into the phone.

'It's not a joke, Kiah, and this is not coming from me. In case you haven't noticed, I'm out of the picture at this point unless and until the case needs a lawyer again. I'm just the messenger now. Whatever is happening with the settlement is happening way up the food chain from me.'

'OK, but I still don't understand,' I replied. 'What are you saying? Are you saying there's no meeting unless we get picked up by, what's his name, Alfred?'

'That's the deal.' He paused. 'Hey, how bad can it be? It will be great car, I promise. I wish they'd take me to work that way. Alfred will probably have coffee and donuts –'

'Dave, knock it off, for goodness' sake –'

'Kiah, don't fight me on this, OK?' His mood had changed. His usual voice had returned. 'I can't tell you any more. If I could, I would, but I can't. Just be there, please. Nine o'clock outside your building.'

He hung up.

I called an impromptu team meeting and told everyone what Dave had said.

'They're just trying to butter us up,' Sam weighed in at once. 'They're going to treat us nice and hope we'll be nice to them. They think they can buy us off with coffee and donuts? They're pathetic.'

'If y'all ask me,' Arlene said, 'this ain't got a damn thing to do with being nice. These guys are about as nice as a copperhead with a headache and the bayou drying up. They're fixin' to kidnap y'all's asses and dump y'all in some field in West Virginia, where they ain't never gonna find y'all. Lord have mercy.'

Powalski laughed.

'I don't think so, Arlene. If that was the plan, they wouldn't call ahead of time to warn us about it.'

'So, what do you think?' I asked.

'I'd take it at face value,' he offered. 'It's coming from someone high up. For some reason, they want to give you the VIP treatment. That's the way they do things when you get up to a certain level in government. It's your tax dollars at work. It's got nothing to do with you guys specifically. It's just how things are done.'

'So we should go with it?'

'Yeah, go with it.'

I must still have been looking doubtful. He smiled.

'Look, just to be on the safe side, I'll be outside the building from eight thirty onwards. I'll be watching, and I'll have my car nearby. If anything seems off to me, I'll follow you. But I wouldn't worry about it. Focus on the meeting. That's what matters. And enjoy the coffee and donuts on the way.'

65

SAM AND I MET at the office, dressed in our most conservative business suits, at seven thirty. We had arrived early deliberately, just to see if there was anything suspicious going on. There was no sign of a limo, or of anyone looking like he might be Alfred. The area outside the building looked the same as it did at that hour every morning, the odd office worker coming in, the odd cleaner going home, the rush hour going on all around, nothing to mention in dispatches. Mistrusting Dave's promise of in-drive service we had brought some good coffee and bagels to fortify us for the work ahead. After we had done justice to them, for the most part in a nervous silence, I grabbed a collection of random documents from my desk, and stuffed them into my briefcase, enough to make an imposing pile if later emptied out on to a table. It's not something I would have done in any routine negotiation with Dave, or any other lawyer for that matter. They wouldn't serve any real purpose, and looking back, I probably clung to them in the hope that looking prepared would boost my self-confidence. The only indispensable items would be my pen, yellow pad and calculator, and my phone in case I needed Arlene to check information for me.

'I've never been to one of these things,' Sam said. 'I don't know what to expect. I won't say anything unless you want me to.'

'There's no way to know what to expect,' I replied. 'I'm not even sure who we will be dealing with. If they're really sending a limo for us, it may be Henry Shilling.'

'The Attorney General?'

'Yes, but don't let that worry you. Even if Shilling is present, he's going to rely on his trial lawyers to advise him, so it will be my job to deal with the legal issues. But there's nothing formal about a settlement meeting, and it's your case. If there's something you want to say, go ahead and say it.'

'But will you let me know if you want me to?'

'Sure. I'll nod at you.'

'OK.'

'But you don't have to wait for the nod. Say whatever you want.' I paused. 'However, there is one exception to that rule; only one, but it's a big one.'

'Whatever you say.'

'If they make an offer, try not to react to it, and don't give any indication of what you think about it. That applies whether the offer seems good or bad. Don't give anything away. You and I will step outside the room to talk before we give them an answer. Is that OK?'

'Sure. Got it.'

I nodded, and looked at my watch. Five minutes to nine.

'Good. Let's go do this.'

A sleek black limo was waiting outside the building. Standing quietly at the side of the car was a handsome African American man I judged to be in his fifties, with silver hair and a matching moustache, dressed in a pristine dark grey suit with a red tie and black peaked cap. He opened the rear door for us.

'Miss van Eyck, Miss Harmon? Good morning. I'm Alfred, and I'll be your driver this morning. Please make yourselves comfortable. You'll find some coffee and donuts in that little compartment between your seats. Feel free to help yourselves.'

I looked around. There was nothing unusual going on as far as I could see. I spotted Powalski to my right, leaning against the corner of the glass wall of the building. He was dressed in an open-necked shirt and blue jeans, and was wearing shades. He had the *Post*'s sports section under his arm, and he appeared to be in casual conversation with one of our security guards, who was on a smoking break. But he was facing our way, and I could see no sign of concern. We got in.

As we pulled away into the traffic, Sam opened the compartment and sure enough, as advertised, there was coffee and there were donuts – and from a decent coffee shop too, one I knew from my forays into Washington on business in times past.

'Want some?' Sam asked.

I shook my head. I wanted to concentrate on the journey.

'Are you sure? This could be all we ever get out of the government. Might as well grab it while we can.'

She was smiling, and I returned the smile.

'No, I'm fine. But you go ahead.'

The traffic seemed pretty moderate, and Alfred was soon pulling smoothly on to the Parkway and heading for downtown. I checked my watch.

'Were you expecting some congestion this morning?' I called out to the front of the car.

'No, ma'am,' Alfred replied. 'This is pretty average for this time of the morning. The worst of the rush hour is over. You never can tell, though. Sometimes the traffic downtown gets snarled up for no reason at all that anyone can see, and once in a while it can stretch all the way back here to the Parkway, but nothing like that today, fortunately.'

'I was just wondering why we needed to leave at nine for a ten o'clock meeting,' I said after a pause. 'Seems a bit like overkill.'

I saw Alfred smile back at me in his mirror.

'Just making sure,' he replied. 'And they always like to build in some time for security. You know how that goes.'

I opened my mouth, ready to tell him that I'd never known security at Justice to take more than a minute or two. They took it seriously, but they had their routine down, and they had a pretty brisk rhythm going on. But something told me to keep quiet. Dave's enigmatic comments from the previous afternoon came back to me. He was the just the messenger now. Settlement was being dealt with higher up the food chain. He was telling me, in his own way, that I didn't yet understand what I was dealing with. I sat back in my seat. We were driving to somewhere higher up the food chain. Less than fifteen minutes later, we were on Pennsylvania Avenue, and by then I wasn't even surprised when we drove straight past Justice without even slowing down. Sam was still enjoying her coffee, and I don't think she even noticed. We must be going to Treasury, I concluded. Well, that would make sense. Henry Shilling would want to play with home field advantage if he could. I couldn't blame him for that. I was ready to assume that security might be a bit more intense at Treasury. So that was why we'd had to leave at nine o'clock. It all started to make sense. Until we drove past the Treasury building.

So we weren't going to Treasury either, and then it slowly dawned on me that that could mean only one thing. There was only one more building on Pennsylvania Avenue: number 1600. We were moving up the food chain with a vengeance. In fact, we were going straight to the top. A minute or two later, Alfred was pulling up at a checkpoint and explaining to the guard who we were. The guard looked at us suspiciously before waving us through, but he did wave us through and Alfred dropped us off at an entrance just beyond the checkpoint. A young-looking man in a light grey suit was waiting for us.

'This is where I leave you, ladies,' Alfred said. 'It's been a pleasure. Enjoy your day.'

'Thank you, Alfred,' I replied.

Sam touched my arm. 'Kiah, am I imagining things, or is this…?'

The man in the light grey suit had reached us. He was smiling, and offered his hand.

'Good morning, ladies. I'm Ben Silber. I'm the President's

Deputy Chief of Staff, and I'll be looking after you this morning. Miss van Eyck?'

Sam took his hand.

'Yes, I'm Sam van Eyck. I'm sorry, Mr... Silber? Did you say the President?'

'Yes. I work for the President. And you would be Miss Harmon?'

'Kiah Harmon,' I replied, taking his hand in turn.

'Good. Follow me please. There'll be a bit more security up ahead. Hopefully it won't take too long. Do you have some ID with you, driver's license, whatever? They're supposed to ask everyone who visits to bring ID with them, but they don't always remember. It drives security nuts, but that's government for you.'

He turned away and beckoned us to follow. He led us at a good pace along two or three corridors. We came to a flight of stairs where we walked up one floor. We were led through double doors into a small hallway, where there was an airport-style security check. We put our coats and bags though the metal detector, and even took off our shoes out of habit, without being asked. On the other side, a uniformed officer carefully inspected our driver's licenses before allowing Ben to lead us deeper into the inner recesses of the White House.

During the walk, I glanced at Sam and saw that she was still looking thunderstruck. I felt the same way, and I was desperately trying to force my brain into gear, to work out what was going on. Home field advantage was one thing, but this was ridiculous. What did they hope to gain by bringing us here? Were they appealing to our sense of patriotism, our sense of being good Americans, relying on us to talk some sense into these van Eyck plaintiffs who were threatening to ruin the economy? Or had they simply chosen the most imposing venue available to them in which to warn us off? Was it possible that they had no sense of humor about the Rhode Island thing, and had concluded that we represented a threat to national security? These and other thoughts were roaming unchecked through my mind, and they were all disturbing. In the end, I forced myself to calm down and let all the thoughts pass unhindered and go on their way, and as I calmed down, it occurred to me that there was no reason why this had to be bad. It might even be good news. It didn't necessarily mean that they would make an offer we could accept, but if they had brought us to the White House they certainly weren't treating the case as a joke. If they'd thought it was a joke, I reasoned, they would have told Dave to take us for lunch at Benny's. I looked at my watch. It was almost ten o'clock.

We stopped at the door of a large conference room. Ben opened the door for us.

'I think you know everyone here,' he said as he ushered us inside, 'except perhaps for the Attorney General?'

Henry Shilling was standing near the door, arm outstretched, waiting to greet us. Beyond him I saw Dave, wearing an absurdly sheepish grin that made me want to slap him. He'd known all about this the afternoon before and he hadn't even dropped me a hint, hadn't even asked me to make sure we brought our driver's licenses with us. I thought briefly about ratting him out to Ben Silber for that gross dereliction of governmental duty. Beyond Dave I saw Ellen, Harry Welsh, and Maggie Watts, all standing in a line.

'So,' Shilling said, shaking hands with both us in turn, 'you're the two ladies who've been tilting at windmills on behalf of Jacob van Eyck?'

'That would be us,' Sam replied.

'Please take your seats,' Ben said. 'Kiah, we've put the government on this side of the table and you guys on the other side, if that's all right?'

'That's fine.'

I duly emptied my useless documents into a pile on to the table and looked around the room. The room was impressive, with a high ceiling and dark wooden panelling. It was a conference room from days gone by, and I couldn't help wondering what weighty conferences it had borne witness to in times past. But we had access to modern conference tools too, an overhead projector, and a white board with markers of several colours and an eraser. I almost wished I had some use for them. Perhaps when we got round to talking numbers, I could scribble a few calculations on the board, just for effect. Each place setting came with a White House pen and note pad. There was coffee and iced water for all. Henry Shilling sat at the top of his side of the table, with his staff in order of seniority arrayed at his side. He had no papers with him. He left that to the staff, in this case Dave and Ellen. They had brought papers with them too, and I wondered whether they were any more relevant than mine, or whether there were nerves on both sides. Had to be.

A smartly dressed young man came in briefly and whispered in Ben's ear. Ben nodded.

'Would you all stand, please?'

And then he made his entrance.

66

I DIDN'T VOTE FOR Greg Gascoine, and I don't care for him all that much. On the other hand, I don't especially dislike him either. I suppose I have no strong feelings about him either way, and maybe that explains why I didn't vote for him. But it's one thing not to vote for a president, and it's another thing to find yourself in a White House conference room with one when you never expected to be anywhere near the White House in the first place, and you realise you're there because he wants to talk to you. Gascoine greeted Henry Shilling like an old friend, and shook hands with his staff before coming over to our side of the room.

'Welcome to the White House,' he said, extending his hand to us in turn. 'First time?'

'For me, Mr President,' I replied.

'I took the tour once when I was in high school, Mr President,' Sam said, 'but nothing like this. This is... fantastic.'

Gascoine smiled.

'Well, we must arrange for you to take the real tour once we're finished here, if you'd like to. We can do that Ben, can't we?'

'We sure can, Mr President.'

'Good. Well I hope you'll stay and see the House from the inside. It's quite impressive, even to me, and I work here every day.'

'Thank you, Mr President.'

'Good. Well, have a seat, and let's make a start.'

He took a chair at the head of the table. Ben Silber sat down unobtrusively to his right, and back a few feet towards the wall, notebook in hand.

'Ben will keep an eye on the clock for me. I have to meet with the Jordanian ambassador at eleven.'

He poured himself a glass of water and took a drink.

'I don't suppose you expected to be meeting with me today, did you?'

We smiled. 'No, Mr President,' I replied. 'This is the last thing we expected.'

'That's because I don't generally get involved in settlement negotiations. I can't, wouldn't have time, even if I had the inclination. After all, the federal government gets sued, what, hundreds of times a year, Henry, isn't that right?'

'Thousands of times, Mr President.'

'Thousands of times. And Henry and his staff either settle those cases or they go to trial, and the White House doesn't get involved. But in this case...' He paused. 'I'm going to be honest with you. When I first heard about this lawsuit, I didn't take it seriously. Henry brought it to my attention, because it is kind of unusual. But my reaction to it was, I thought it was some kind of shakedown. I believed that the Justice Department would make it go away as quickly as it had come. I truly did, and in my defence, that was not just my own view; it was also the impression I was given by my legal team. I think it's fair for me to say that, Henry, isn't it?'

'Yes, Mr President,' Shilling replied, glancing darkly down the line towards Harry.

'But obviously, developments over the past few weeks have made all of us think again. Not only have you survived our challenge about the case being filed out of time... what's it called, Henry...?'

'The statute of limitations, Mr President.'

'Statute of limitations, right. Not only did the court go against us on that, but you've also uncovered some evidence that, as I understand it, seems to point to Jacob van Eyck having made some pretty sizeable loans to bail out George Washington's army when they were freezing to death at Valley Forge. Am I right about that?'

He was looking in our direction.

'Exactly right, Mr President,' I agreed.

'So now, what started out as nothing more than an old wives' tale has turned into a political hot potato, and it's something the White House can't ignore.'

'It's become a political issue, sir?' I asked. 'I'm not sure I understand.'

'Well, Jacob van Eyck is now, unofficially at least, an American hero. The public knows that he played a part, behind the scenes, in winning the War of Independence. Without him, we might never have beaten the Brits. We might still be paying taxes to the King, playing cricket or whatever they call it, and drinking tea and warm beer. In his own way, Jacob may be up there with Washington and Paul Revere and all the rest of them.'

'Forgive me, Mr President,' Sam said, 'I'm not sure I understand why you see that as a problem. Shouldn't it be something to celebrate?'

The President nodded. 'Yes, indeed, and we would like to celebrate it. In fact, I don't see that we have a lot of choice about that. The American people are now very much aware of Jacob van Eyck and they're looking to me, as their President, to do what's right.'

'That's all we've ever asked, Mr President,' Sam replied.

'I could tell you, "No deal, we'll take our chances in the Court of Appeals," and from what I understand, my legal team thinks we would have a pretty good shot there, right, Henry?'

'Right, Mr President. Very good, I would say.'

'Right. But even then I have a problem. If I refuse to honour Jacob van Eyck because of some technicality, just because his family filed their claim late, it's going to look like I'm a cheap son of a bitch who's playing lawyers' games with an American hero just to save a few bucks. The public are not going to like that, and when I run again in a couple of years' time, my opponent is going to beat me over the head for my lack of patriotism.'

'As I said, Mr President,' Sam persisted, 'all we've ever asked is for the government to do right by Jacob.'

'I understand that, Miss van Eyck, but the amount of money involved in your claim is astronomical. I can't pay out that kind of money, and –'

Oh, not again, I thought. Surely Henry Shilling has explained this to him?

'Mr President,' I replied, 'I sincerely hope your legal team has made this clear to you, but if they haven't, let me make it clear now. We've said from day one that we're not interested in recovering the compound interest calculation.'

'Yes, Henry told me that. I understand that you're not trying to take the whole farm, Miss Harmon, but you can slash a lot of money from your claim and still be left with enough to bankrupt the federal government several times over. I can't allow that to happen.'

'We're not asking you to bankrupt the government, Mr President,' Sam insisted.

'Well, what *are* you asking me to do?'

'We want the family to have some financial compensation, of course we do. But please understand, the van Eyck family are decent, patriotic people and they have no wish to bankrupt the government. We can negotiate the amount, and I don't think you'll find us unreasonable. The only thing that's not negotiable is the question of recognising Jacob for the national hero he is, and we want that to take a tangible form.'

'What kind of tangible form?' the President asked.

I'd been looking at Sam in admiration. Any nervousness, any reluctance to speak out, had evaporated completely. She was on stage now, in full flow, and she was putting her case. I saw every eye in the room turn to her. It reminded me unmistakably of the conference room at the New Orleans Intercontinental during the reunion. She was in charge, and every eye in the room had turned to her.

'The government will erect a statue to Jacob van Eyck in Philadelphia,' she replied with wonderful dignity, 'and the President of the United States will unveil it.'

67

No one reacted immediately. But after a few seconds of silence, the President turned his chair around slightly towards Ben Silber. Ben lifted himself halfway out of his chair and, grasping the arms, carried it forward in two or three jerky movements until he was almost alongside the President. They whispered for some time. The President turned back, and seemed poised to speak, but Sam had not finished.

'Mr President, we very much hope that you will be the President to unveil the Jacob van Eyck Memorial,' she said, 'and I hope you won't think this too presumptuous of me, but something occurred to me when you mentioned that you will be running again in two years' time.'

If the President thought she was being presumptuous, he didn't show it.

'Go ahead.'

'It's bound to take from now until then to get the memorial ready, and I was thinking how appropriate it would be for you to perform the unveiling during the campaign, perhaps at quite a late stage – especially if it turns out to be a close race. It would be a historic national occasion, and every TV station and newspaper in America would come to Philadelphia for the day.'

Greg Gascoine stared at Sam for some time, and suddenly burst out laughing. He turned to Ben Silber, who had now pulled his chair right up to the table.

'Ben,' he said, 'I want you to recruit this young woman for the campaign. She's a natural.'

'She is, sir,' Ben smiled politely. 'But if I may, Mr President, it seems to me that the first question is how much a project like that is likely to cost, and it's been my experience that they don't come cheap.'

'Excuse me, Mr Silber,' Sam continued, 'but am I not right in thinking that the main cost involved in this kind of project is the cost of identifying and securing the site? The memorial itself can cost as much or as little as you choose in commissioning an artist to design and create it, but the site can involve some difficult real estate issues – especially in Philadelphia, where they're not exactly short of memorials already, and sites are probably in limited supply.'

'That's exactly right, Miss van Eyck,' Ben agreed.

'What if I could make a suggestion about the site that would save the government a lot of money?' Sam asked.

I turned to look at her.

'What?' I intended it as a whisper, but I'm sure everyone in the room heard me.

'I'm sorry, Kiah,' she whispered back, 'I meant to tell you, but you were busy and with everything going on, it slipped my mind.'

'I'm sure we'd all be delighted to hear whatever ideas you may have, Miss van Eyck,' Ben said. His tone suggested that he wasn't expecting anything earth-shattering.

'Jacob van Eyck was a Freemason,' Sam explained, 'a member of the Pennsylvania Grand Lodge. That Lodge has many connections to the War of Independence, and they currently have a very active historical project going on to create a permanent exhibition of the period. They have recently come to realise what an important part of that history Jacob is. They are very interested in having Jacob recognised, and Mr President, if you were to ask someone to contact the Grand Master, I believe you would find him to be very helpful on the question of a site for the memorial.'

Ben was staring at her.

'Are you... are you saying that the Lodge might be prepared to host it?' he asked.

'Can I have a moment?' I intervened. I turned to Sam again. 'Sam, they didn't say anything to us about that,' I whispered furiously. 'They said they were interested in the case, but –'

'John Macey and I have spoken several times since our visit to the Lodge,' she replied. 'I'm sorry I didn't tell you, Kiah, but you had other things to worry about, and I wasn't sure how far it would go. But John had reported our visit to the Grand Master, and apparently he got very excited about it, and one thing led to another, and... look, I'll tell you all about it later, OK?'

She turned back to Ben.

'My understanding is that, if approached by the government, the Lodge would offer to host the site at the Grand Lodge itself. The details would have to be worked out, but no acquisition costs would be involved. There would be some cost in connection with developing the site, of course, but that would be far less than you would pay on the open market anywhere else in the city.'

'Who would I be talking to?' Ben asked.

'John Macey. He's the personal assistant to the Grand Master.'

Ben made a note, then leaned in towards the President, and they conferred in whispers for well over a minute.

'Is there anything else you'd like to tell me?' I whispered to Sam. I can't pretend I wasn't a little miffed about the way she'd kept me in the dark about this detail. Clients who come up with important new information for the first time at settlement conferences do their lawyers' nerves no good at all, and I'd had a few over the years.

'No,' she grinned. 'I think that's all.'

Eventually I had to return the grin. Yes, I was miffed, but how long could I stay mad at her when she might just have removed the only sensible objection the government could make to the memorial?

The President and Ben finally disengaged.

'Well,' Ben began, turning back towards us, 'Miss van Eyck, if the Lodge is prepared to act in such a generous way, that would take care of one major concern, and it might bring a project such as this within a reasonable budget. If that is the case – and I stress, if that is the case – then, Mr President, my understanding is that you would be happy to authorise us to proceed with the project as part of an overall settlement package.'

'With that understanding, yes,' the President confirmed. 'And also assuming that, as Miss van Eyck so perceptively observed, the memorial would be ready to unveil somewhere between a month and two weeks before polling day.'

'I see no reason why we couldn't do that, Mr President,' Ben replied. 'I think the way forward would be for me to put together a small committee consisting of Miss van Eyck, Mr Macey and myself, which I would chair with the assistance of White House staff. We can add to it if we need specific people for specific purposes. But keep it small, that's the key. We would make sure that you and the Attorney General are kept fully informed as we go along.'

'Whatever you think best, Ben,' the President replied.

He stood and consulted his watch.

'Well, I think we've made some progress this morning. Perhaps I should attend these things more often.'

He was looking at Henry Shilling, who smiled politely.

'Perhaps you should, Mr President.'

'On the other hand, maybe not. But in any case, you must excuse me – as I said, I have to meet with the Jordanian ambassador shortly, so I will leave you to continue your discussions. Just so that you know, Miss Harmon, I have instructed the Attorney General to offer you a reasonable monetary settlement for the family.

What "reasonable" means you may not be able to decide until we have a better handle on the cost of the memorial, but you may be able to come up with some ballpark numbers, don't you think, Henry?'

'I'm sure we can get fairly close, Mr President.'

'Good. I've also made it clear that the settlement must include a reasonable figure for attorney's fees. I understand how important that is,' he added, with a knowing grin in my direction.

I felt no embarrassment about returning that particular grin very directly, even if he was the President. Greg Gascoine's oldest son was a plaintiff's personal injury lawyer in Phoenix, whose dedication to recovering every last cent he could by way of fees in every case he took had earned him a national reputation, one which had not always been helpful to his father's political career.

'Thank you, Mr President,' I replied.

He began to turn away towards the door but stopped and turned back.

'Oh, and there's one more thing. Miss Harmon, Henry told me about what happened at your offices, and I want you to understand that no one in this room, and no one who works for anyone in this room, was in any way involved with that.'

'We accept that, of course, Mr President,' I replied immediately.

'It is something that should never have happened. The people who did it are misguided people who no longer work for the government. I have issued instructions to the department concerned, instructions that ought to ensure that nothing like that will happen in the future. But I also want to apologise to you. It should never have happened, and I'm embarrassed that it happened on my watch. I'm sure the losses were covered by insurance but it's not right that you should have to take a hit on your premium, so if you let Henry know how much we're talking about, the government will make sure you are fully reimbursed.'

'Thank you, Mr President,' I replied.

The President nodded.

'Then I will bid you all a good day.'

Ben waited a few seconds before sitting down in the chair the President had vacated.

'Well,' he said, 'if everyone's ready, let's talk about money.'

68

THE DAY OF THE unveiling was a glorious Thursday in late October, the kind of day that couldn't possibly occur in any other month of the year: a day with crisp blue skies and the first hint of a chill in the air; the kind of day that always makes me think of brightly coloured scarves and homecomings and college football and bonfires and roasted chestnuts and pumpkins.

When we arrived, just before eleven o'clock, the activity was frenetic. The section of North Broad Street in front of the Grand Lodge had been closed off to traffic since three o'clock that morning, long enough for the street to be filled with several hundred chairs and to allow for a dais to be erected in front of the building, just to the right of the Jacob van Eyck Memorial, which would remain veiled in purple until noon, when the President of the United States would open it up to the world's gaze. A section of the Marine Corps band was warming up in front of the main entrance to the Lodge. The caterers were carrying large folding tables and chairs, and vast coolers containing food and drinks, into the Lodge for the reception. Technicians were wiring a microphone and what I took to be a teleprompter in position by the side of the presidential lectern. The TV reporters were out in force, going through their pre-show routines, checking microphones and scripts, scouting out advantageous positions. Guests were arriving, and consulting the giant, hugely detailed seating plan drawn up by Ben's White House support staff, following which they were escorted to their seats by a legion of smart young ushers wearing armbands, recruited from local high schools.

Ben Silber's small committee had proved to be pure genius. The only person coopted as an additional member, for 'advisory purposes', was Aunt Meg. As Ben swiftly realised, Aunt Meg's participation removed any lingering doubts – not that there ever were any to speak of – about the van Eyck family's support for the agreement we had reached with the government. Jeff Carlsen, Ed van Eyck and I had cranked up the publicity as soon as we returned from Washington, and when we informed the plaintiffs about the terms of the deal, and added that it had been proposed to Sam and myself by the President personally at the White House, it was approved by an overwhelming majority. The limited size of the committee ensured that once approved, the project was carried out efficiently, so much so, in fact, that the memorial had been complete and ready to go since July, but there was no way it would be unveiled in July. Sam had won Greg Gascoine over completely: he wasn't about to schedule the unveiling before the latter half of October, shortly before polling day. Pennsylvania was shaping up to be a key state, and the President was determined to be seen to perform a ceremonial act redolent with history and patriotism, in front of hundreds of important guests and the assembled press of the world, in the heart of Philadelphia.

The two main decisions the committee had to make were: exactly where the memorial would be located; and which artist would be chosen from the several hundred who applied, to design and construct it. With so much enthusiasm within the Grand Lodge, the location was easily settled. With a little preparatory work, a space for the plinth was made in the right-hand corner immediately in front of the building itself, and so away from the street, removing any possible resistance from the city. Sam told me that the Lodge had shown no interest in accepting any money from the government for this not inconsiderable change to the appearance of its historic building. Some of the enthusiasm was due to Sam. Once the ink was dry on the settlement agreement, she collected up all the available loan certificates and Abe Best's correspondence, and presented them to the Grand Master as a gift from the van Eyck family. Within a few days, they were proudly displayed in a new historical exhibit, 'Freemasonry at the time of the War of Independence'.

The artist selected was a young French sculptor by the name of Henri Marot, who had already made a name for himself with some beautiful civic pieces he had executed on commission in his native Provence. What attracted him to the committee was his solution to the only serious problem encountered in designing a statue in the image of Jacob van Eyck, namely: there were no known images of Jacob van Eyck – no portraits done during his lifetime, or even verbal descriptions of his appearance, except for one suggestion that he was unusually tall for his day; and, of course, the nose. Apart from those details, no one had the faintest idea what Jacob had actually looked like. Most of the applicants proposed to overcome this obstacle by emphasising qualities they thought to be associated with patriotism, a high forehead, large hands and so on, none of which impressed the committee at all. Henri Marot proposed tackling the problem head-on. The height would be around six feet, certainly pretty tall for the time; the family nose would be prominent (he used Sam as a model); the rest of the face would be mostly hidden, with the eyes looking down, and the fold of his cape drawn up over the mouth. When Henri first introduced his idea it didn't sound promising, but his drawings were mesmerising. The subject was undoubtedly a van Eyck, but in many ways he remained an enigma – which, as Henri reminded us, he was. He won the commission immediately.

The whole work is executed in bronze. The life-size statue of the enigmatic Jacob van Eyck stands on a plinth bearing the following inscription.

SACRED TO THE MEMORY OF JACOB VAN EYCK
(1730–1812)

PATRIOT

HE GAVE HIS WHOLE FORTUNE IN THE CAUSE OF THE
INDEPENDENCE OF THE UNITED STATES.

*This debt was not contracted as the price of bread or wine or
arms. It was the price of liberty.* Alexander Hamilton

At noon, once the several hundred guests had taken their seats,
the chief dignitaries, those seated in the front row, made their
entrance. The President was flanked by Sam and Aunt Meg on one
side, and the Grand Master on the other. Beside them sat Henri
Marot, the Attorney General, the senators and several congressmen
and women from Pennsylvania, the Mayor of Philadelphia, two
Justices of the United States Supreme Court, and the British and
French ambassadors. I sat in the row behind with Arya, whom
I'd brought as my personal guest, Arlene, Powalski and Jenny. On
the same row sat Harry Welsh and his team, including Dave and
Ellen, Ben Silber, John Macey, and a lot of people I didn't know
at all. Behind us was a sea of guests and members of the public
who had applied for tickets. I'm told that more than 200 family
members attended.

To be honest, I didn't take in much of what the President said.
There's a written record, of course, which I've read a number of
times since, and I have to say, although much of it consists of weary
platitudes about patriotism, there was something heartfelt about
it, and cynical as I am, I don't think it was entirely electioneering.
I think the van Eyck story had touched the man. I'd had that
impression when we were with him in the White House and I had
it again at the unveiling.

The President didn't stay long at the reception. There were other key states to visit. Ohio was next on the list, and a presidential campaign doesn't allow for much down time. But he stayed long enough to talk with Sam, Aunt Meg and me and to wish us well. I'd introduced Aunt Meg to Arya, and they spent a long time together at the reception, sitting at a small table away from the throng. I would have loved to know what they were talking about, but I would never have interrupted.

When the reception died down, Powalski led us to the minibus he had rented for the occasion to accommodate us all. We had brought Aunt Meg with us and, of course, we had promised her a ride home. As if by some unspoken thought, we went to her house by way of the graveyard at the Old Swedes church. Dusk was falling on our beautiful October day by now, so we didn't stay long. But for a while, we stood together silently, looking out over the mass of gravestones.

'No gravestone for Jacob,' Sam said quietly. 'He's buried all alone.'

Arya took her hand and joined it to Aunt Meg's.

'Not for much longer, I think,' she replied.

Kiah's Postscript

MORE THAN TWO YEARS have gone by since the unveiling of the Jacob van Eyck Memorial, and I'm taking advantage of a rare quiet afternoon to take up my pen, as Isabel Hardwick might have said, to add a postscript, a note to record how those of us involved in the case have fared since that amazing day.

The President, as we all know, was elected to serve a second term. No one can prove, or disprove, that his unveiling of such a patriotic memorial not long before polling day played any decisive role in the campaign, but it was a close race and I can't see that it could have done him any harm. Henry Shilling continues to serve with great distinction as Attorney General. The Secretary of the Treasury, on the other hand, resigned shortly after the election to spend more time with his family.

Aunt Meg passed away about three months ago. She and Sam had become very close. Sam went to see her from time to time, and they exchanged letters regularly in between. Aunt Meg had told Sam that she felt she could die happy, now that Jacob had received the justice and recognition he deserved. I and the whole team went to Upper Merion Township for her funeral, which was attended by a huge throng of van Eycks, at least as many as had been present at the New Orleans reunion, and which turned into something of a spontaneous reunion itself, with an impromptu reception and dinner, which Aunt Meg would have loved. The family had been granted permission for her to be buried at the Old Swedes Church, where she joined many earlier generations of van Eycks.

While I'm on that general subject, a team of faculty and students from the archaeology faculty at Penn State approached us recently with a plan to locate and formally identify the remains of Jacob van Eyck, and to seek permission to have them reburied with military honours in Arlington cemetery. Sam and several other family members descended from each of Jacob's brothers have supplied DNA samples, and they plan to start work as soon as the King of Prussia Historical Society and the church elders, who have dominion over the church, sign off on the project. Whether they will succeed in finding and identifying Jacob's remains, and if so, whether they will be able to persuade the government to approve his reburial at Arlington, we can only wait and see, though I have a hunch that, if they can get it all done before this president leaves office, they have a good shot at it.

Sam goes from strength to strength. In the aftermath of the case, her agent was deluged with offers of work, everything from serious theatre to national commercials. Being Sam, she prefers to continue with the work she's always done, Arthur Miller, Tennessee Williams and the other American staples. The difference is that where before she was working with regional repertory companies in the South-East, she's now doing the same repertoire on Broadway and in the major regional theatres across the country. A spell in London's West End is pending, and she is under contract for two movies, neither of which will bear any resemblance to *Revenge of the Zombie Cheerleaders*. Consequently, I don't see as much of her as I used to, but whenever she's within striking distance, we get together. She is a friend for life, and that's a wonderful gift to have.

So, what about me? Well, I'm still practising law, but in rather different circumstances now. I'm the senior partner of the law firm of Harmon Petrosian Matthews & Associates. Once news of the settlement hit the streets, I was inundated with offers of work – and by work, I mean seriously good commercial work, as well as some far-fetched nonsense from fantasists with the federal government in their sights. I'm not sure what took up more of Arlene's time, taking on board the serious clients or discouraging the others. We succeeded in doing both, but it was obvious that we needed help, and needed it without delay.

Fortunately, I'd also been receiving unsolicited job applications from any number of young lawyers who'd been attracted by reports of the van Eyck case, and presumably thought it was the kind of stuff I did all the time, and that it would be great fun to work for me. Some of them I wouldn't have looked at twice, but quite a few really raised my eyebrows. These were bright young lawyers from top law schools with glowing résumés, lawyers who could have been applying to the big firms on Wall Street. I hired four of them immediately, and told another three that they would be next if the practice continued to grow. The three included Jenny, our faithful intern from Kate Banahan's Wills and Trusts class, who had actually dropped out of law school for the rest of the semester to stay with me when the van Eyck case was at its most desperate. She had asked for nothing in return, but I told her then that she had a job if she ever wanted it, and now that she's about to take her bar exams I hope she may join us soon. But having good associates wasn't enough.

I needed partners – experienced lawyers who could handle the pressure of big cases, work without my supervision, and supervise associates themselves. I approached Dave and Ellen almost immediately. I had no experience of having law partners, and the thought intimidated me, but I've always had a theory that lawyers go about choosing their partners in the wrong way. Almost always, partners come from one's circle of friends or colleagues, meaning that if you've worked together at all, it's been on the same side of the case. But partnership is an intimate relationship, one that has to be built on trust, and it's always seemed to me that you have a much better idea of how far you can trust another lawyer when you've been on the other side of a case. That was my experience of Dave and Ellen. I'd known them only as opponents, but I felt I could trust them with my life. To my surprise and delight, they didn't even think about it: they both jumped at the offer. I made a faint pass at Harry Welsh too, but he told me that he'd always been a government man, and always would be – not to mention that Maggie Watts was about to be promoted to Deputy Attorney General and he was about to be promoted to take over her job.

All these changes required new office space, still in Arlington but far bigger, and an office staff comprising legal secretaries and paralegals. Making that happen was a huge undertaking, and the credit for the smooth transition is due entirely to our Executive Practice Manager, Arlene, who rules the roost with her unique combination of extraordinary competence and homely Texas words of encouragement, the latter occasionally taking new associates and secretaries a bit by surprise.

At Dave's insistence, the firm has a policy that no one – partners, associates or office staff – works so hard that they can't spend enough time on their personal or family life. That was non-negotiable for Dave, and given my own tendency until that point to allow work to take over my life, it was a policy I was very glad to accept. I was ready for a change.

Arlene is a bit secretive about it – I'm getting this mostly from him rather than her – but I happen to know that she's been seeing quite a bit of Powalski. They've been for long weekends to New Orleans together once or twice, and Powalski's been taking Bubba to watch some NFL and college football games.

I still see Arya, of course. She's doing great, and her armchair, incense, foot rubs and occasional sumptuous dinners remain a big part of my life. Of course, my stress level is through the roof these days, but in a good way. It's not about the Week any more. It's about the stresses of handling a large, successful law practice, and I'm handling it just fine. All the same, Arya is still my rock, and I lean on her often.

And I guess that's about it.

Well… OK… I guess there's one more thing, although there's nothing definite yet, and I don't want to give the impression that there is. But… well, there's this guy. His name is Doug. He's a doctor, a cardiologist actually, and we met at a reception in Arlington a few months ago. He's a little older than me, but not enough that it matters. He was widowed by cancer about three years ago, and he has a beautiful little girl called Amy, who's almost seven. I met her at his place after our third date, and when I sat down on the sofa she immediately leapt into my lap and hugged me, and stayed there with me until she fell asleep, and it felt really good. I don't know. Neither of us knows. I don't know whether I'm ready to trust a man again, and he doesn't know whether he's completely over the death of his wife. But the thing is, even if we're not there yet, there's this feeling that we're getting there together, and that we've come most of the way. And there's something about it that feels incredibly good, incredibly right.

It feels like Kiah: a new beginning.

Author's Postscript

THE MAN WHOSE LOANS may have helped to save the War of Independence was Jacob de Haven (1730–1812) a citizen of Pennsylvania. The unbroken de Haven family tradition since Jacob's death is that he made loans of gold and supplies to Washington's army at Valley Forge during the fateful winter of 1777–1778, such loans totalling about $450,000 value at the time. With the passage of time evidence inevitably gets lost and whether, or to what extent, the family tradition is history or fiction may no longer be capable of proof. But more than one friend or patriot must have helped to rescue the army from the cold and starvation of that terrible winter. Jacob owned the land on the bank of the Schuylkill adjacent to Washington's encampment. Jacob and Washington were friends and both were Freemasons, and for whatever reason, during that winter Jacob suddenly fell from great wealth to a state of penury from which he never recovered.

In March 1989, Thelma Weasenforth Lunaas, a descendant of Jacob de Haven, sued the federal government in the United States Claims Court to recover the amount of the loan and the congressionally authorised interest on the sums loaned. She was represented by Jo Beth Kloecker of the Texas Bar, who enlisted me, her former law school professor, as her co-counsel. In January 1990, Judge James T. Turner held that the claim was barred by the six-year statute of limitation applicable to Claims Court cases, and dismissed the case. Judge Turner also refused to make an order for discovery, thereby preventing us from making the government search for and disclose such evidence as it might have relating to the de Haven loans.

Subsequently, the United States Court of Appeals for the Federal Circuit upheld Judge Turner's decision. The United States Supreme Court refused our application to hear the case. Consequently, the de Haven family no longer has any judicial remedy to recover a loan for which, according to Alexander Hamilton, the faith and credit of the United States had been repeatedly pledged, and which represented the price of liberty.

Jacob de Haven died in poverty in 1812. He lies buried in an unmarked grave in a remote churchyard in rural Pennsylvania.

There is no memorial in his honour.

Author's Note

THE STORY OF THE de Haven loans has inhabited my psyche since 1989, when Jo Beth approached me to work with her on Thelma's case. I had been one of Jo Beth's professors when she was in law school, but I hadn't seen her since her graduation. She had opened her own office, and she explained that Thelma had walked in off the street and asked whether she handled debt collection cases. Like any young lawyer anxious to build a practice, Jo Beth had said she did. It was only later that she, and I, appreciated the scale of the case she had accepted. It was the beginning of a fascinating legal journey in which 200-year-old events ran up against contemporary legal procedure.

During our time working on the case, we met a number of de Haven family members, and we were able to chronicle the consistent efforts the family had made since Jacob's death to draw attention to the loans. There had been political approaches to congressmen, in exercise of the right to demand the redress of grievances by political means, but none had borne fruit. Litigation was the last resort. No one in the family wanted to have to sue the United States, and there is one thing I want to make absolutely clear: in real life, as in my novel, no one in the de Haven family ever contemplated recovering the amount suggested by the compound interest calculations, or anything like it. They are a patriotic family, now just as much as in 1777, and what they wanted more than anything else was recognition of their ancestor: a statue for Jacob.

When Jo Beth came to me for help she told me that she felt out of her depth. Well, who wouldn't, with this case? But in fact, she had done an amazing amount of research, about the history of the War of Independence, the history of the de Haven family, and about the law. I was able to put that together and start writing the briefs, but it was her diligence that got the case off the ground. I was, and am still very proud of the legal arguments we made. I continue to believe that our argument – that the debt was recoverable, regardless of the lapse of time, because of the first paragraph of Article Six of the Constitution – has merit. I don't say that it's necessarily correct, but it is certainly very arguable and my only real criticism of any court involved in the litigation is of the United States Supreme Court, for ducking a case which turned on points of pure constitutional law. That's what the Supreme Court is there for, and their failure to intervene allowed part of an article of the Constitution to die without ever being judicially interpreted. On a lighter note, and this is really one for the lawyers, I'm proud too of having made parts of Alexander Hamilton's writings and speeches in 1790, while he was Secretary of the Treasury, admissible in evidence as admissions by a party opponent under the Federal Rules of Evidence.

The short, depressing history of the litigation is summarised in my postscript. For those interested in the detailed legal issues, the following technical citation may be of assistance. Lunaas v United States 936 F.2d 1277, 1991 U.S. App. Lexis 13116 (Fed. Cir.1991); rehearing denied 1991 U.S. App. Lexis 18175; Certiorari denied 502 U.S, 1072, 112 S. Ct. 967, 117 L. Ed. 132, 1992 U.S. Lexis 683, 60 U.S.L.W. 3520.

I'm not quite sure when the idea came to me of fictionalising the story. It must have been a year or more after the case had ended. Unless the government has the evidence that we were not allowed to pursue, it is very doubtful that the de Haven claim can now be proved or disproved definitively, but with such a persistent family tradition it remains a tantalising enigma. I thought that if I could write the story in a fictitious way, it might at least draw attention to this obscure man, who may well have been an important American hero, as well as hopefully writing an entertaining novel. But it has been by far the hardest writing project I have ever undertaken.

There are two parts to the story, and both offered major challenges. The contemporary part of the story, the litigation, was short and bleak. I didn't want the quest to end in failure in the novel, so I set out to imagine various ways in which it could have been successful. The characters and the story had to be very different from those in real life. I make clear now that this is a novel. The characters in the contemporary story are products of my imagination, and none of them bears any relationship or resemblance to the people involved in the real life events. Their personal details are entirely invented.

I am glad to make clear that at no time did the government play any dirty tricks on us, or behave in any of the reprehensible ways I attribute to them in the novel. The lawyers who opposed us from the Justice Department and the Bureau of Public Debt were highly competent and unfailingly courteous; and the only criticism I can make of them is a slight failure of sense of humour when we offered to take Rhode Island in settlement of the claim. I would like to reassure the inhabitants of that State that the offer was made in jest, in the hope – misplaced as it turned out – of lightening up the formal communications a bit.

I would like to record also my admiration for Judge James T. Turner, who heard the case in the Claims Court. Although he found against us, Judge Turner was courteous and helpful. He gave us the whole day for oral argument simply because he found the case so interesting, and he was generous with the compliments he paid us for our research and presentation of the case.

The historical story was even more difficult. The evidence surrounding the loans is circumstantial and incomplete, and the real Jacob de Haven has, more than somewhat, faded into the mists of time. I had the work we had done to prepare our legal briefs, which included: extensive research into Hamilton's Reports on the Public Credit and the contemporary congressional debates; the legislative history of the establishment and development of the Claims Court and its procedures; and the desperate situation of the army at Valley Forge in the winter of 1777–1778. But constructing a plausible view of what might have happened, and how it could be linked to the contemporary story was not easy, and in the end involved a slight detour into the esoteric.

Both stories underwent at least three manifestations over a period of years, until I finally settled on a version that I hope does some justice to both.

To the extent I have succeeded, I am indebted principally to Thelma and Jo Beth for the reasons I have already stated. I acknowledge also my debt to *The History of the De Haven Family*, by Howard De Haven Ross, Ph.B. First published on May 1, 1894, this short work continued as far as an illustrated fourth edition published in 1929, and was reprinted as recently as 1986. Alice Yocum Hill, a family member who had written a note for the third edition, honoured me with a personally signed copy of the reprint. Ross's book is informative and, in its own way, quite charming. It offers some interesting details, but is in the end frustrating to the extent that it fails to offer direct evidence of the material issues. In his preface to the first edition, Ross tells us:

> I have of late devoted both time and money at library work making a historical search of old records, documents and papers of family, church and state, and have been engaged in collecting and formulating the family evidence and tradition in connection with the De Haven Revolutionary Loan with all material and facts relative thereto.

But if this research yielded any direct evidence about the making or amount of the loans, Ross omitted to include it in his book. While his work provides a lively and interesting account of the family's genealogy and some insight into family activity in Jacob's time, and is not short of documentary references, Ross's claims about the loans consist essentially of speculation and innuendo. In evidentiary terms, the continuous family tradition is far stronger.

I must also add a word of thanks to my old and dear friend Professor Sherman L. Cohn. Sherman and I worked together for many years in connection with the American Inns of Court. We met first at the Supreme Court in 1983, when Chief Justice Warren Burger appointed us both to a committee charged with designing and putting in place a structure for the organisation, and we served together on its board for many years thereafter, becoming close friends in the process. Sherman, who before his retirement completed more than half a century on the faculty at Georgetown University Law School, is a veritable mine of information about Washington DC, everything from the city's buildings and infrastructure to its myriad political complexities. Over the years, he has illumined me about almost every aspect of the Capital, and this is not the first of my books to owe a good deal to the insights he has passed on to me.

Lastly, I must mention Alexander Hamilton. I knew very little about Hamilton when I first started work on the de Haven case, but as I read more about him, and studied his writings on the public debt, a clear impression emerged. He was that rare breed, a true statesman. He was a clear-sighted man put in charge of a very murky economic situation. His first concern was to right the ship, to keep the currency afloat and the economy ticking over, while keeping an eye on America's future credit-worthiness. This makes his attitude to the war loan debt all the more remarkable. He insisted that it must be paid in full. This was, of course, partly for pragmatic reasons to do with reassuring creditors abroad. But it ran much deeper than that. For Hamilton, the war loan debt was a debt for which the faith of the United States had been repeatedly pledged. It was the price of liberty. It was not to be evaded, reneged on, or diminished.

I have, for dramatic effect, conflated various of Hamilton's writings and statements about the question of whether speculators, who had bought up loan certificates at huge discounts from the indigent after the war, should recover the whole amount due under those certificates. My extract from the congressional debate on February 9, 1790 is similarly a combination of the actual record of the debate, statements made by Hamilton on other occasions, and my own imagination. I make no apology for this. I have every confidence that I have faithfully represented Hamilton's views about the case of the speculators, which he stubbornly maintained in the face of understandably intense congressional opposition. His position on that issue was crystal clear, and it became the basis for our argument based on Article Six of the Constitution.

Hamilton was a statesman for whom, where there was a conflict, considerations of principle, considerations of honour, must prevail over considerations of pragmatism and expediency. You don't hear that said about many contemporary politicians. But with every judicial remedy exhausted, the de Haven family's hopes may now rest on the chance that one such will one day step forward – not to pay the whole amount, which is beyond the ability of any modern government to pay – but to make some meaningful gesture, however modest, that will enable everyone to agree that the price of liberty has, at last, been fully paid.

As ever, I am grateful to Ion Mills and Claire Watts at No Exit Press, for their continued faith in my writing; to my indefatigable agent, Guy Rose; and to my wife Chris, who has lived the story and the writing of this book with me, for all her unfailing love and support.

●LDCASTLE BOOKS

POSSIBLY THE UK'S SMALLEST
INDEPENDENT PUBLISHING GROUP

Oldcastle Books is an independent publishing company formed in 1985 dedicated to providing an eclectic range of titles with a nod to the popular culture of the day.

Imprints vary from the award winning crime fiction list, NO EXIT PRESS, to lists about the film industry, KAMERA BOOKS & CREATIVE ESSENTIALS. We have dabbled in the classics, with PULP! THE CLASSICS, taken a punt on gambling books with HIGH STAKES, provided in-depth overviews with POCKET ESSENTIALS and covered a wide range in the eponymous OLDCASTLE BOOKS list. Most recently we have welcomed two new digital first sister imprints with THE CRIME & MYSTERY CLUB and VERVE, home to great, original, page-turning fiction.

oldcastlebooks.com

   kamera BOOKS creative ESSENTIALS Pulp! THE CLASSICS HIGH STAKES cmc V

	OLDCASTLE BOOKS		KAMERA BOOKS		HIGHSTAKES PUBLISHING
	POCKET ESSENTIALS		CREATIVE ESSENTIALS		THE CRIME & MYSTERY CLUB
	NO EXIT PRESS		PULP! THE CLASSICS		VERVE BOOKS